STRANGE FLOWERING

No place could have been more unlikely for the birth of a love such as theirs. It was in a degenerate French court, where every sin of the flesh was cultivated and no transgression was too shocking, that James and Joan first met and fell in love.

They vowed to keep themselves apart from the world around them, to keep their love pure before marriage, and sacred afterward.

But neither James of Scotland nor his young bride, Joan Beaufort, could keep themselves from becoming enmeshed in a game of power that was to lead them to a destiny they could not foresee or escape . . .

"A novel to be grateful for!"

—*Des Moines Register*

JAMES
AND
JOAN

BY ANNE FREMANTLE

CURTIS
BOOKS

NEW YORK, N.Y.

Dedication:

For

A.J.

who will never read it

CHIEF CHARACTERS

ANNABELLA, Queen of Scotland, wife of Robert III, and mother of:
    DAVID, DUKE OF ROTHESAY
    JAMES I, KING OF SCOTLAND (1406-1437)
ROBERT II, first Stewart King of Scotland (1371-1390) and father of:
    ROBERT III (John, Earl of Carrick before he was king), King of Scotland (1390-1406)
    DUKE OF ALBANY (Robert, Earl of Fife before he became duke), Governor and Regent of Scotland
    ALEXANDER, EARL OF BUCHAN, called WOLF OF BADENOCH
    DAVID, EARL OF STRATHEARN
    WALTER, EARL OF ATHOL
                              uncles of David and James

SIR JOHN DE RAMORGNY, Annabella's chamberlain; later in service of Robert III and James
WILLIAM GIFFARD, Annabella's page; later in service of James
EUPHEMIA LINDSAY, daughter of Sir William Lindsay of Rossie; betrothed of David, Duke of Rothesay
ELIZABETH DUNBAR, daughter of the Scottish EARL OF MARCH; betrothed of David, Duke of Rothesay

5

BLACK EARL OF DOUGLAS, father of:
> MARJORIE DOUGLAS, wife of David, Duke of Rothesay
> ARCHIBALD DOUGLAS, husband of James's sister; became EARL OF DOUGLAS when his father died; later became DUKE OF TOURAINE; father of:
>> ARCHIBALD DOUGLAS, EARL OF WIGTOWN; became EARL OF DOUGLAS when his father became Duke of Touraine

HENRY WARDLAW, Bishop of St. Andrews and James's tutor

MURDOCH, eldest son of Duke of Albany; became EARL OF FIFE; succeeded to Governorship of Scotland; father of:
> ALEXANDER STEWART
> WALTER STEWART

EARL OF LENNOX, Murdoch's father-in-law

JOHN, EARL OF BUCHAN, second son of Duke of Albany; Constable of Scotland and of France

ALEXANDER STEWART, bastard son of Wolf of Badenoch; became EARL OF MAR

SIR ROBERT GRAHAM }
SIR ROBERT STEWART } grandsons of Earl of Athol

HENRY PERCY, Harry Hotspur's son

GRIFFITH GLENDOWER, Owen Glendower's son

RICHARD II, King of England (1377-1399)

HENRY IV, King of England (1399-1413)

HENRY V, King of England (1413-1422); Prince Hal before he became king; brother of:
> THOMAS, DUKE OF CLARENCE, stepfather of Joan Beaufort
> JOHN, DUKE OF BEDFORD
> HUMPHREY, DUKE OF GLOUCESTER

HENRY VI, King of England (1422-1461)

LORD GREY OF CODENORE, Henry IV's chamberlain

LADY GREY, wife of Lord Grey of Codenore

JOHN BADBY, a Lollard

SIR JOHN OLDCASTLE, Lollard leader

THOMAS BEAUFORT, brother of Henry Beaufort and chancellor; became DUKE OF EXETER

HENRY BEAUFORT, Bishop of Winchester (later Cardinal); also Henry IV's half-brother and chancellor

JOAN BEAUFORT, niece of Thomas and Henry Beaufort, stepdaughter of Thomas, Duke of Clarence; became wife of James I of Scotland; she was the sister of EDMUND BEAUFORT, EARL OF MORTAIN, and JOHN BEAUFORT, EARL OF SOMERSET; mother of MARGARET (who became wife of Louis, dauphin of France), ELIZABETH, JAMIE (heir to the Scottish throne), ANNABELLA, JOANNA, and ISABELLA

SIR RICHARD WHITTINGTON, Lord Mayor of London

JOHN LYON, chaplain to James I and his representative at Council of Constance

THOMAS MYRTON, chaplain to James I

ABBOT JOHN FOGO, confessor of James I

CHARLES VI, (The Mad) King of France (1380-1422)

ISABEAU OF BAVARIA, Charles VI's queen

CATHERINE, daughter of Charles VI and wife of Henry V of England

CHARLES D'ORLEANS, French poet and Duke of Orléans; eldest son of Charles VI's brother Louis

CHARLES VII, King of France (1422-1461)

DAUPHIN OF FRANCE, afterwards Louis XI

ALAIN CHARTIER, poet and French ambassador to Scotland

EMPEROR SIGISMUND, King of Hungary and Bohemia and Roman Emperor

AENEAS SYLVIUS PICCOLOMINI, secretary to Cardinal Albergati; later Pope Pius II

PART ONE

1394-1417

UNCLE ALBANY

CHAPTER ONE

☐ James had not cried out once, the nurse said, neither for the water on his head, nor for the salt on his lips; he had looked about him the whole time with blue, bright eyes as though aware of the importance of the occasion. Annabella watched the old woman, who had been her nurse, as well as nurse to her elder son, David, take off the baby's fine wraps. Holding out her arms for him, Annabella put him quickly to her breast whilst the nurse stuffed the pillows comfortably behind to prop her.

"Did David make his responses rightly?" she asked, wondering what her handsome, arrogant twelve-year-old thought of his small brother, at whose christening he had just stood proxy godfather.

"David did grand," said the nurse. " 'Tis a shame his father wasn't there to see him." Annabella agreed aloud, though in her heart she was glad enough Robert was away in his splendid, sombre castle of Rothesay on his beloved island of Bute. For even though it was wild, cateran country; she felt him safer there.

In 1390 her husband had ascended the throne as Robert III, the one hundred and first king of Scotland, succeeding his father Robert II, the first Stewart to be king.

11

For six years before he became king, Robert III had been associated in the work of government. In 1384, the parliament summoned to Holyrood had given him the duty of enforcing the law, and had made him responsible in that to the king and the council. All officials had been ordered thenceforth to obey him.

Four years later he had been lamed from a horse's kick, and thereafter had been a chronic invalid, needing always his physician near him, requiring constant vinegar poultices, and totally unfitted by his nervous and increasingly depressed temperament for the daily tasks of administration. He was gentle and kindly, however, and very good to Annabella.

In the December which followed his laming, his younger brother, the Earl of Fife, had been entrusted by parliament with the business of government. Nevertheless, it was Annabella's husband who, despite his lameness, was crowned at Scone in 1390 on August 14th. He had taken the name of Robert III because his own name, John, was a terribly unlucky one whether the wearer be king of England, France, or Scotland. On August 16th he had received the sworn fealty of the whole barony of his kingdom. But the Earl of Fife was still called Governor of the Kingdom.

Ever since her husband's accident, Annabella had been disturbed by his increasingly unwarlike preferences. His father had been on the whole a wise and an able ruler, with enough vitality to keep his unruly nobles in check. He had been a splendid figure of a man, a tall bonhomme, surrounded by a multitude of children of both sexes, legitimate and illegitimate. But by the time of his son's marriage to Annabella, his bleary red eyes, swollen-veined from his excesses, seemed lined with cloth of scarlet, and his skin was the colour of sandalwood. Indeed, for all his regal looks, he was elderly and outworn, and sought to escape from the quarrellings of his eleven tall sons that loved arms, by withdrawing to his castle of Rothesay.

Robert III, on the other hand, for all he was witty and

debonair, and continued in all his father's policies, had not skill in the martial exercises that were necessary to secure the respect of the turbulent nobility, most of whom were his close kin—either in or out of wedlock. Indeed, when he was crowned, the proud earls regarded him, the second king of a new race, whose title was not hereditary but elective, as hardly better than themselves, and since the sickness of his person prevented him from restraining trespassers and evildoers, he might more fairly be said to reign than to rule. His life was very harmless, but, alas, his excellency lay in that he rather lacked vice, than that he was illustrious for any virtue. He had but two bastards to his father's two-score, and these—James Stewart of Kilbride and John Stewart of Ardgowan—had both been begotten before his marriage, and were douce enough boys, not meddlesome like his father's brats.

Annabella, watching the guzzling James nibbling softly at her breast, hoped she would not have to put him out to a wet nurse. It was long since she had nursed a child. She had put the girls out gladly; David she had nursed for nearly a year, but now he stood as tall as she and preferred men's company to hers, spending much of his time with her new chamberlain, Sir John de Ramorgny, to whom he had instantly taken a tremendous fancy, or with young William Giffard, her page, who was but a year or so David's junior.

The smell of hay came in through the opened windows, and above the steady rhythm of the child suckling, Annabella could hear the birds; mavis and merl were shouting merrily, and a late cuckoo had joined them, his tune throaty and cracked—it was said from the eggs he sucked. She heard, too, the creak of the monastery waggons, bringing in the hay, and kitchen talk and smells would float up to her. Dunfermline was a gracious, peaceful place and already showed few scars from its burning by the English less than ten years before. The royal lodging, attached to the Benedictine cloister, was a comfortable nest for her little red-head.

13

For David was no longer hers, she reflected sadly: heir to the throne, king that was to be, and already jealous of, and at odds with, his uncle, the Earl of Fife, for being governor. James would be all her own, she hoped, to raise quietly, civilly. Perhaps he would be a priest—she had named him for a vow she had made St. James of Compostella the day her little son Robert had died, just a year before. She had borne six children, four daughters and two sons, before her husband was harmed. She had not thought she would wish for more. Yet, some four months after the death of little Robert, she had gone into the king's room, one sad November evening, to talk with him as she always did, before withdrawing to her own room. When they had said prayers together, she had signed the maids and the men-at-arms out of the room, and had closed the door behind them. Then she had lain down beside her husband, and very sweetly, very gently had coaxed him into lying with her, taking every care that he shouldn't hurt his poor leg; she had puffed, as if with delight, as if in ecstasy, in the right places; though it was more from the stench, for most of Robert's remaining teeth were rotted. But it had pleased him that he still could ride her, and she had been glad enough that something which to her was such a trifle could still give him such pleasure; and she had cried for joy when she found she had conceived, for though no human being can replace another, and no child born, a child lost, yet now, praise God, there was a spare son, in case of what, she would not dare think, but only that now there was a son to spare. And she prayed James might inherit his father's gentleness—it could do *him* no harm.

The old nurse had come to take the baby and looked shrewdly down at her mistress. "Praise God now there's one more between the Earl of Fife and the crown," she said, and Annabella shuddered that the old crone could guess her thought so clearly. "You should not speak so of the king's brother; 'tis treasonable," she chided, but her voice carried doubt, not disapproval.

It seemed as though her father-in-law had made worse

each son he had begotten. Annabella's husband had real qualities; a love for and a real sense of truth and justice. The Earl of Fife, the next-born, was shrewd, energetic, domineering, with such a passion for popularity that he would be cock of the dunghill if he could not be cock on the steeple. The third son, Alexander, was the worst of the three. Dubbed Wolf of Badenoch by his contemporaries, he had burnt Elgin Cathedral the very year his father died and his brother had been crowned, just because the bishop had bade him return to the wife he had deserted, and had forbade him bring his mistress to Mass with him. A year later, Duncan, his natural son, had raided the Lowlands, killing and burning his way south.

But it was not only her brothers'-in-law wildness and wickedness that troubled Annabella. Both the Earl of Fife and Alexander had been born after their father's marriage to Elizabeth Mure of Rowallan, whereas her husband had been born before, out of wedlock. Robert II's marriage was unsavoury at best—Elizabeth was his cousin, within the prohibited degrees; she had been solemnly betrothed to Hugh Gifford when she was nine; and her cousin, Isabel Boutellier, had been Robert II's mistress at the same time as she, so Robert and Elizabeth's wedding needed much papal whitewashing to cover the smuts. And the two subsequent children might have dynastic claims over Annabella's children.

Even more of a menace were the children of the old king's second marriage. For when Elizabeth died, Robert II married Euphemia, daughter of Hugh, Earl of Ross, and had by her two sons: David, Earl of Strathearn, and Walter, Earl of Athol. These boys were both undoubtedly legitimate. Yet parliament had by statute prescribed the succession in an act—an act that was to make Scottish history for over two hundred years, and English history for nearly five hundred after that. The king's sons were to succeed in the order of their births, and only if one died without heirs could his brother succeed, and only after *his* death without heirs could the next brother, and then only the half-brother. The Stewart kingship was not hereditary but parliamentary; and Annabella, as she lay thinking, reflected that her husband was king, and her son would be king, by the will of parliament. And there might be some who would gainsay that will, would claim that the heir that was a bastard was no heir, whereas parliament had declared that the bastard who was an heir was no bastard. . . .

Too many grown men stood around her ailing husband's throne; Annabella wished her sons had fewer uncles, fewer cousins. Aloud, she said: "I doubt the Earl of Fife cares who is called king so long as his is the power over this kingdom."

The nurse nodded agreement. "Still I marvel," she said, "that he did not fash himself when your husband took his name at the crowning. I fancy he had rather been Robert III himself, than see his brother become it. Yet he never lets on what vexes his stomach or his mind, and I like it not: 'tis safer and healthier to cry out when you're hurt."

The nurse lifted James to take him away; he had fallen asleep without gurk or whimper. Stooping to lay him in the big carved oak cradle, she cried out, and Annabella, terrified she had slipped on the flowering, sweet-scented rushes with which the floor was strewn, and might fall, scrambled up out of bed, and stood beside her, her knees water-wembley, for James was barely twenty-four hours old. The nurse had him securely, but, standing beside her, Annabella could see, lying in the cradle, a crown or wreath of wee, yellow rosebuds, and a small sprig of bay leaves—laurel, as it was called. This was precious stuff, growing but rarely in a few sheltered gardens, and used for the crowning of bards at a pibroch festival, or for the flavouring of soups at coronation banquets.

"Whoever put those there?" the queen asked, snatching up the roses and the dark, shiny leaves.

"Not I, my lady," the nurse replied, "and not you. Nor has anyone but myself entered the room since you were brought to bed."

"Could David have placed them there for a greeting

for the bairn?" asked Annabella, but the nurse shook her head.

"He hasn't been allowed the room."

Annabella remembered there had been talk of some such offering in each royal Stewart cradle. She recalled her Aunt Margaret whispering to her how a crown of gillyflowers had been found in the cradle of Robert II, who became king in spite of all his uncle's efforts to prevent it.

"But there was nothing in David's cradle, nor yet in little Robert's," Annabella began, and realised then what this must mean: her baby Robert was dead, and if James were to be king, then David, too, must die. She spoke again to the nurse, to crowd out her thoughts with words, to banish and exorcise them. "They say it is one of the Breton Stewarts, the one that first came from Dol in Brittany to Wales, that clutters our cradles with such strange tokens," she whispered.

The nurse replied, very matter-of-factly, "I always heard it was Walter, him that came from Wales to Scotland in David I's reign, him that founded Paisley Abbey and owned the land over Renfrew-way, him that was sixth before your husband's father; 'tis him I heard say likes to play yon trick."

"Maybe so," Annabella answered. "I wish he wouldn't —whoever he is—or was."

"A crown for a king, flowers for a lover, laurel for a martyr," listed the nurse.

"Whoever laid them there, minded the bairn no good," replied Annabella.

But the nurse shook her head. "Nor good nor evil. Just knowledge of what is to come, and that were rather help than hindrance," she said.

Supported by the nurse, Annabella crawled back into her bed. The hangings were of rich green damask, embroidered with Annabella's initials intertwined with Robert's, and the baby's cradle was also draped in the same clear colour, for about a queen's lying-in all must by tradition be green.

17

Two girls came in to brush her hair, and change her linen, and brought warm water in a silver ewer, with sprigs of bog myrtle to sweeten it, and Annabella was glad to be clean, for she was bleeding like a stuck pig from her exertions, and was faint from them. She put on a green damask jacket embroidered in gold, and, weary but content, lay back on her pillows. "The prior may come now," she told the nurse, who sent the girls down to say Her Majesty was willing now to receive visits of congratulation. Annabella looked around the room, pleased with the comforts she had brought to it—small windows of real glass, rich tapestries to the walls. Downstairs, in the big hall, were even woven woollen carpets on the stone floors. Some said the queen was extravagant, with her taste for luxuries, but at her crowning, parliament had granted her an annuity of 2,500 marks, and she had never yet received it. The deputies of the chamberlain—the Earl of Fife, again, of course—kept it from her. Perhaps her own new chamberlain, Sir John de Ramorgny, might be of some use in getting her dowry for her. For she was ever short of money, she reflected sadly.

There was a gentle knock, and, preceded by two monks, the prior came in. He bowed low over the queen's hand, blessed little James in his cradle, and then sat down in the big high-backed chair that the nurse had put ready for him. He was a spare, short, dark man, obviously of Pictish, rather than Celtic, stock. He had dismally black teeth, and a stubble of greying beard. His dark face, passionate in its aversion to society, remote, finely chiselled, wore an expression of interested distaste as he looked at the soft, feminine face of the honourable and pleasant queen, as white and gold as he was black and grey.

"Would you allow Robert Logy, the granger, to pay you his humble duty?" he asked, and the queen said, "Yes, of course." One of the monks went to fetch him, and the prior smiling, said, "He is your most devoted servant." Annabella, too, smiled, remembering how, the morning of her own crowning, the day after her husband's, on the Feast of the Assumption, four years before, she and her Robert had been woken early by a serenade from the monks, accompanied by the singing of a crowd of workingmen and farmhands. Annabella had sent for them to thank them, and Robert Logy, the granger, had blurted out that it was they who were thanking her and her husband, for having saved them the trouble of harvesting. Enquiring further, she learnt how the day before, the king's retinue had so trampled the monks' ripe corn that there would be no crops. Robert Logy had complained to Robert's knights, but they had roughly told him to shut up, so he devised the serenade on his own, in order to reach the king. "Each year we sing Te Deum for our good harvest; this year we sing it for our holiday from harvesting," he had said, with a straight face, and, though the nobles murmured the fellow should get a hiding for his impudence, the king, ashamed and amused, had ordered that the monks be paid the full value of their ruined harvest, and had added a handsome gratuity to recompense Logy for his courage. Her husband was just and noble, Annabella reflected with a glow of pride, as now she gave Robert Logy her hand to kiss. But he was too shy to take it, bowing deeply from several paces away.

After Robert Logy had left, David came in unannounced, very handsome in his green leather jerkin. Tall, slender, and ash-blond, he kissed his mother's hand, and peered into the cradle politely, but without enthusiasm. Two of his sisters trailed behind him, and climbed on to Annabella's bed like kittens, to sit there babbling of what they were going to do that day. Sir John de Ramorgny came in too, somewhat mincingly dressed in the latest style, with slashed sleeves and very pointed slippers. He was rather a loud young gallant, perhaps all of twenty years old. He asked if he might take David hunting. "Isn't it rather hot?" Annabella asked, for the last day of

19

July felt sweltering to her, even in the dim high-ceilinged royal chamber, and she thought outside it must be very warm.

"We thought to try the Black Loch for wild duck," David said, "it's cool there, and we could strip maybe and swim too."

Annabella consented, only warning that neither they nor their horses should get into cold water when in a muck sweat or they'd get cramps. Then she asked Sir John if he'd fetch parchment and quill for her—she must write to the King of England, she explained, whose wife Anne had just died. "And we hoped she might sometime have borne him a girl you could wed," she smiled at David.

But he got scarlet, and said, "Wed an English girl, indeed, and England the hereditary enemy!" Why, hadn't Richard himself burnt this palace and this abbey but recently and sacked Edinburgh and reached Aberdeen?

"But there's a truce now, David," said his mother, "and maybe if you married an English girl, there'd be peace."

"Much good ever came of peace with England," said David angrily. "I can't think why you have even to write civilly to yon Richard."

Annabella explained that even when their countries were at war, there must be personal courtesy between sovereigns. And even between individual subjects, put in Sir John, asking David if he did not recall the usages of chivalry. Did David not remember how Sir David Lindsay of Glenusk, his own uncle, had sent his cartel to the Englishman, Lord Wells, even though their two countries were at war? And how Sir David had freighted a Dundee vessel to bring him a new suit of armour from London, and how when the suit was come, he had donned it, and, armed with a safe-conduct, had ridden down through England all the way to London, and how at the tournament before King Richard he had thrown Lord Wells out of the saddle at the first course? The cry had gone up that he was tied to his steed, so he vaulted to the ground fully armed and without touching the stirrups vaulted back and then stuck his dagger into the lower joints of Wells's armour, lifting him into the air, and giving him so heavy a fall that he could not rise again, but lay at Lindsay's mercy, and then, instead of putting him to death, Sir David courteously had raised him, and leading him to the ladies' gallery had delivered him as her prisoner to the queen?

"To that same Anne who now lies rotting," said the prior.

"Poor Anne," said Annabella, "she brought the most marvellous clothes with her from Bohemia. Our present headdresses all came in with her—the horned coifs and the steeples."

"It is the men rather should wear the horns, when their womenfolk think of nothing but prettifying themselves," said the prior sourly.

David tossed his golden head, and retorted, "I'm glad she's dead, for now she'll not bear any daughters that I must marry."

When the prior, David, and Ramorgny were gone, Annabella settled down to her letter writing. Privately, she rather agreed with David about Richard; he *was* the hereditary enemy after all, and it was faintly foolish to be apologising to him for the delay in answering his letter "because we lay in childbirth of a son, James." King Richard II of England was an hysterical, unbalanced fellow, who suffered from having become king at the age of eleven, with a horde of greedy uncles, and the memory of an heroic father and grandfather overlaying anything he might ever imagine doing on his own. The condition of England had been far from satisfactory, ever since the Peasants' Revolt, and Richard had already dealt none too successfully with several uprisings. Yet affairs in England were in a less parlous condition than in poor France. In Auvergne and in Poitou, not six years since, the peasants had killed all the gentlefolk and many of the bourgeois and they had even murdered a poor Scots gentleman by putting a basket of burning coals on his head so that he died in piteous agony. The French, Annabella concluded, her pen idle as she thought about Scotland's ancient and essential ally, were no better than they should have been. It is true that they rendered invaluable service to the cause of Scottish independence by keeping the English occupied elsewhere, but why, oh, why, must they unload on the Scottish market undrinkable wines they could not possibly sell to anyone else? Poor Robert had continual stomach-ache from their thin sour claret. That reminded her—she must send Robert his wine to Rothesay.

There was a knock on the door. It was the prior again. "I hate disturbing you," he said, "but there are some French knights below. They have been here over a twelvemonth, and are just off home, and would take their leave of Your Majesty."

"Give me a few minutes to prepare myself," Annabella said. "Send me my nurse." The prior smiled, a strangely warm smile, for so cold a face: it was as though someone lit a candle inside him. A holy man, thought Annabella, who lives in the flesh but already no longer according to the flesh. Even here on earth, his conversation is with the angels; no doubt but that he finds us boring after such society.

The three little French knights came in, their tight coats reinforced at the shoulders with light chain mail. They looked hardly more than boys, gawky and awkward, with down on their lips and spots on their faces and none too clean straight hair. Only the last, who seemed the eldest, had a gay mischievous face. They all bowed low, kissing Annabella's hand, then, stepping back from the great bed, they remained silent, standing. "You must be glad to be going home," she said. "Were you not homesick here?"

"One is always homesick for France, Madame," said the first, stiffly, "but we have nothing to complain of."

"Oh, yes, we have," said the third, boldly. "No one came to call on us. We had good lodgings in Edinburgh, when we were not fighting in forays on the Border, for we had joined up with the Earl of Douglas, and made raids with him. But the Scottish gentry do not love to make new acquaintances and we were sadly lonely."

"And Scotland is so poor," said the second, "that we could hardly find iron for our bridles nor leather for our harness outside Edinburgh."

The first spoke again, "In France a Scotsman may win gold and lands—I've met several such in my own father's house in Normandy, who have settled down in our locality and found themselves very snug there; but here it costs more than our pay to buy a little horse."

"Yes, yes, we were sadly cheated at our horse coping," agreed the second, mournfully.

"Boys, boys," the queen said, gently, "have you no good to tell me of my own country before you bid it and me adieu? Did you ask to see me only to chide me for the discourtesy of my subjects?"

The third young Frenchman blushed. "My lady, forgive us," he said. "Scotland is a most noble country, and the spirit of the Scots is good: they are both gay and gallant. When we pitied them because the English had burned their houses and stolen their cattle, they answered, even the poorest, 'What matter? Suppose the English do burn us out? A few beams and branches will rebuild all our houses within three days.' The Scots feel more like the French than any other nation, Madame; they are very easy to make civilised, for they have the greatest feeling for the French."

"All the same," the queen asked, smiling, "you would agree the thistle is a good emblem?" and the boys looked shyly at her to see if she were cross, and, finding she was not, they giggled, half amused, half embarrassed, and presently took their leave.

Soon it was time to feed James again; and after, drowsy but content, Annabella, murmuring the Compline hymn to herself in lieu of more complete prayers, went to sleep, whilst nurse sat sewing by rushlight, between the queen and her new son.

CHAPTER TWO

☐ Riding to the council meeting in Perth in January, 1399, David, recently created Duke of Rothesay, and Sir Malcolm Drummond, Queen Annabella's brother, were cold and tired, but also jubilant. The country through which they passed was desolate, bleak, mountainous, and barren, with few trees and fewer signs or traces of cultivation, but this they took for granted. For this was Scotland, this their own country: this was how it looked, and thus its climate. Their road was a dirt track, running mostly through heather, died down and dry now, but still good hiding for hare and rabbit, for grouse and ptarmigan. Their dogs were constantly putting up beasts or birds, and occasionally, too, if the flurry of wing or scamper of frightened feet were immediately under their noses, their horses shied or reared. But mostly, neither men nor mounts minded their hounds, pointing or coursing even to within a few feet of them. Sometimes they passed scattered crofters' stone huts, with a hole in the roof through which the smoke poured out and up; these occurred for the most part in the valleys set amongst birch saplings and scrub pine; around them sometimes a few orchard trees had been planted. Up on the hills there were no signs of human habitation: uncle and nephew, followed by some eight armed retainers on shaggy ponies, travelled for hours seeing no live thing but a kestrel hovering or a few hinds heavy with young. When their dogs gave chase to these, Sir Malcolm called them off. Neither took much note of their surroundings, except every so often to check their direction by David's instructions written on a scrap of parchment he carried, on which, too, was a rough map; or to grumble when their horses stumbled upon a fox hole or over a dead sheep. The going was far better than it had been on the Border—there three days of real desert, caused by the continual wars, separated Scotland from England. When the English invaded—which they habitually did once or twice a year, even in time of truce—they had now to bring their own supplies, for the country had been so thoroughly looted and despoiled that the inhabitants refused to till the ground any more, nor dared expose their few beasts outside, but kept them indoors in their poor huts, which were only made of logs with the gaps stuffed with heather, and the whole thatched with bracken; nor would man or woman venture out unless, and until, smoked out by marauders.

Uncle and nephew had plenty to discuss.

"Think you," David asked, "I can squeeze my burghs for more customs?"

"From which burghs have you collected?" asked Sir Malcolm.

"All of which I have the spending," replied David, "Edinburgh, Perth, Aberdeen, Linlithgow, and Dundee."

"For how long were the customs granted you?" Sir Malcolm asked.

"For seven years," David replied, lunging at a thistle with his sword, "and I've just had another 3,200 pounds, for my expenses during the negotiations with England."

"You deserved all that, since you made the truce of Hawdenstank," approved Sir Malcolm, "but why are you in such need of money, with all that received so recently?"

"I had to become a duke to match the English. John of

Gaunt, their man, was Duke of Lancaster, and the Scots would have me a duke too in their cursed pride. And it cost a pretty penny in accoutrements!" said David.

"You enjoyed the fifteen days of jousting and feasting that preceded your elevation, though, didn't you?" asked Sir Malcolm; a rhetorical question, for he knew David loved tournaments above all things earthly. The king's brother, Robert, Earl of Fife, Sir Malcolm recalled, had been made Duke of Albany on the same occasion. But when the king tried to make the Black Earl of Douglas, whose son had married his daughter, also a duke, and the heralds had called out to him "Sir Duke, Sir Duke," Archibald Douglas had quacked mockingly back at them "Sir Drake, Sir Drake."

"Yes," David said, "he muttered that 'Duke was a vain title of empty honour, a great increase to ambition and none at all to virtue, a nominal shadow of an empty honour.' My brother-in-law is savage and unmannered," David grumbled to Sir Malcolm, who was inclined to agree with the king's royal-looking son.

"The pipers made some pretty jingles about you," Sir Malcolm said and quoted:

> Sweet and virtuous, young and fair
> Honest, habil and avenand
> Our lord our prince in all pleasure
> Is cunning unto literature.

"Are you that?" he went on, and David, blushing, said:

"I'm afraid I'm more adjectival than bookish. That was a good party for my belting," he went on, "but our present errand will lead, I fear me, to no such junketings."

"You're after putting Albany from the governorship?" queried Sir Malcolm, and David replied:

"Just that. It's an impossible position, both for my father and for me, to take orders from my uncle. The trouble is, Uncle Albany is both rich and popular. He bribes and connives his way around in the most shameless fashion, and juggles with the various nobles

27

who should be resenting and resisting him, as though they were balls at a fairground."

"You could put his salary to good use, could you not?" Sir Malcolm asked his nephew, and David blushed again and replied:

"Forty thousand pounds for the governorship, and then from his earldoms, and from the crown lands over which he has jurisdiction another 60,000 pounds—I would be glad to have half such a yearly income."

"I advise you to challenge Albany in front of the whole council-general of the realm," said Sir Malcolm, "remain courteous and polite, thank your uncle for keeping such good care of your inheritance during your minority, but state quite firmly that now you are come to man's estate, your uncle must give over the leading reins. You shewed already last year at the Edinburgh tourney that you were of an age to rule. You did nobly upon that day."

David glowed with pride under his Uncle Malcolm's praise and encouragement. "Twelve knights against me, and I was better than any one of them—and I'm only a squire," he said.

Now, coming out of a small wood, they were in sight of Perth, and after about an hour's more hard riding, they were at the town gates. There were extra guards mounted at these, for with such a great number expected for the council meeting, it was just the moment for the wild caterans—the Highland men—to swoop down upon the city, and carry off a few nobles to hold them to ransom. And there were plenty of bad characters to lead them—the Wolf of Badenoch had three natural sons all worse than himself, and the Lord of the Isles was wilder and wickeder than they, for he did not even admit the king's writ ran in his lands, but maintained he was an independent sovereign.

Within the city walls, the horses' hoofs struck fire, and slipped on the cobbled stones. The narrow streets that were drains in summer, were ankle-deep torrents now in midwinter. It was not raining, for a wonder, nor was it cold enough for ice to have formed. But with each step, as the horses sank fetlock deep into the filth—human excrement, beasts' faeces, bones, blood, dish-leavings thrown from windows—the smell rose rich and mixed and fit to turn a queasy stomach. The riders' bodies were level with the jutting windows, and David amused himself looking in wherever he could. He wanted a girl for the night, and thought he might spy one that way as well as any other.

"There's Sir John come to seek us," said David, delightedly, as they turned a corner, "and he has my small brother on a pony beside him. Greetings, Jamie," he cried.

James Stewart, now aged five, was most beautifully fitted out in a short doublet, edged with marten. His scarlet hose reached almost to his waist, and he wore tall soft brown leather boots which came up to his knee, and a beaver hat, with a tiny circlet of gold, like a baby coronet, worn where the ribbon might have been. He was on a strawberry roan gelding, about fifteen hands high, which he managed very well indeed for a five-year-old; his gilt spurs made him look professional. He doffed his hat and bowed low to David and Sir Malcolm. "Welcome, brother; welcome, Uncle Malcolm," he said. He had a shock of red hair, naturally curly, and the fair, freckled skin that goes with it. His pale, grey-blue eyes were almost the colour of the winter sky under which he and his brother met. "Sir John said you'd be getting in about four," he said as he turned to his companion.

Sir John de Ramorgny was already deep in some gossip with David, stroking his horse's neck as he talked. "Did you get the 2,200 pounds you were owed for your trip to England?" David asked, and Sir John said, yes, the queen had paid him.

"But it's not for her to pay you," David said, angrily, "it's for the council. You weren't there on mother's business, you were there on a national errand."

"She'll get it out of the council, never fear," said Sir

29

John, "but I had to have something with which to pay my expenses coming here—the 800 pounds a year I get from you, David, isn't enough for such extras."

To James, watching them earnestly in the twilight, the two young men were the most wonderful creatures in the whole world, patterns of all that the canons of chivalry required. James worshipped David more than anyone alive, except only his mother, and David in return was charming to him. David had always understood what he was trying to say, even when James was a baby; David had let him feed his falcons; David had begged Annabella to give him a pony when he was only four, and had held him on the first few terrifying unsteady times, when James feared nothing would ever make the pony stop. James eagerly told David he was to go to the council meeting tomorrow as Annabella's page, dressed all in cloth of gold, with ermine trimmings and shoes sewn with tiny Scottish pearls, fished out of the Tay. He had seen his clothes, he chattered on, laid out on his mother's bed, and had watched her and nurse and the various maids getting out, and polishing her jewels. She, too, would wear cloth of gold: as stiff and heavy as a priest's cope on Easter; under it she would wear a long pleated skirt of white linen, and her belt was studded with big fat rubies and sapphires that made you hungry to see them; they looked good enough to bite or suck.

It was quite dark now, and they had reached the royal lodging. A couple of squires lifted Sir Malcolm and David off their horses, for in their heavy armour they were glad to be boosted off their tired beasts. James trotted in ahead to announce them, and, as he came into the great hall, saw his Uncle Albany standing with his back to the fireplace, talking to his father. The king looked considerably older than his younger brother, and the sad, lined face bore no resemblance to his brother's pert, conceited, lively one. Albany had his father's height. To James it seemed there was no end to him, tall like a giant, and broad, too. Grudgingly James had to admit him to be a kingly figure of a man. His son, Murdoch, even taller than he, but with a stupid, sullen face where his father's was crafty and spirited, stood beside him: it looked almost as if, deliberately, they were standing so to mark the contrast between their splendid flesh and the seated, crippled king. David, as he entered, directly after James, seemed slight and childish beside them; they filled his hearth, and little James thought angrily of the first David, him of Israel, going out to meet Goliath.

Next morning, January 27th, the king and his family, including Uncle Albany and Murdoch, heard the Bishop of Saint Andrew's Mass, and the Bishop, Walter Traill, breakfasted with them. James loved the bishop, for he could play all the tricks in which a small boy delights, make rabbit's ear shadows on the wall with his hands, fold a linen napkin into a pope's tiara or a dunce's cap. After a hearty meal of well-salted porridge with cream, followed by cold quail and heaps of griddle cakes and honey, washed down with mead or milk, the court proceeded solemnly through the raw rain to the meeting of the three estates at the courthouse. It was a stormy session; the misgovernance of the realm and defaults in the due administration of the laws were imputed by many to the king and to his ministers. Those who attacked the king urged that he defend himself; others, like the Earl of Ross, insisted that he might excuse his own misman-agement on grounds of ill health, but all declared he was bound to be answerable for his officers. These, it was de-cided, he must at his convenience summon and accuse before his council, whose decision was to be given after they had made their defence, "seeing that no man ought to be condemned before he is called and openly accused." David Rothesay got his way with an impas-sioned appeal, and was made governor instead of Albany "for the term of three years, throughout all the kingdom having the full power and commission of the king to gov-ern the land in everything as the king should do in his person if he were present." This amounted in fact to the gentle and polite deposition of both his father and uncle for which David Rothesay had been manoeuvring and

31

praying. But the brash young prince was still not to be free to run Scotland as he pleased. Far from it: Parliament placed a council of twenty wise men above him, by whose advice he should rule in the absence of the council-general. Albany, naturally, was chief instigator and senior member of this council, and thus was able to retain the substance of power, even after being forced to give up his title of governor.

All that winter, thereafter, James stayed with his mother at Perth. He hated the great hall, where his father either sat and worked at a table, in a tall, high chair near the fire, or at the thronelike dais at the end of the top table. For this great hall stank terribly from stale food and was overheated from the breaths of the many hundreds of people who constantly came in and out, and who practically lived in it. There was no ventilation, yet plenty of draughts; the great hall seemed always both stuffy and chilly. James loved, by contrast, his mother's gay room, with its bright blue hangings, and its view over the whole city, and he delighted in all the movement and coming and going of court life. Every day there were the falcons to be fed, and often whilst the stables were being cleaned he would saunter out to watch the grooms currycombing the sleek horses until they shone like peeled chestnuts. Or he would sneak down to the kitchens, and watch the cooks turning the great roasts on the spits, or broiling half a dozen fat capons on a huge gridiron, or beating up eggs for the sweet cakes he liked eating above all other food. The cook was irascible, however, and would chase James out. Sometimes he would go into the town to watch the jousting; every day that David was home, there would be practice at the lists, even if there was not always a full fight.

In February the wild snowdrops grew in massed clumps in the woods about the city, and James found aconite and primroses too in the sheltered parts of the royal gardens. Annabella preferred Perth to Edinburgh; it was a far milder climate and a more protected site.

David Rothesay was betrothed to Euphemia Lindsay of Rossie, a sweet girl whom he had met when she was attending upon his mother.

James thought it fun to go out riding with the lovers, and to wait until they thought themselves out of sight, in a coppice, perhaps. Then, when they were fondly kissing, he would gallop out from behind a tree, yelling the Stewart war cry, and laughing at their embarrassed discomfiture.

But soon the Earl of March came to court, and offered the king a huge sum of money, if he would make David marry his daughter, Elizabeth Dunbar. David was consulted: did he realise that the daughter of Sir William Lindsay of Rossie, a simple knight, was no match for the king's heir and lieutenant, the greatest man in the realm after the king?

David answered gallantly: "My revered and beloved mother, the queen, was the daughter of plain Sir John Drummond."

But money talks, and when he learned what dowry would come with Elizabeth, he yielded—the more readily that he had been sleeping with Euphemia for some time, and, since she was not pregnant, there was little reason left for which to marry her. But it was not of women he talked to his small brother.

"I've found another way to make money, Jamie," David told him that spring. And he emptied two bags of glittering coins before the small boy's eyes. There were even some English gold nobles amongst them.

"How did you come by so much?" James asked, running astonished fingers through the shining piles.

"They're my own—the customs of the cities I am owed," he said lightly. But he did not explain that he had uplifted the customs by overawing the collectors and extorting money from them, and even by kidnapping customs officials. He gave James a whole gold noble for himself, which James put into the leather pouch he carried on his belt.

"But what for shall I use it?" he asked David, and, indeed, there was no moment in his small life in which he ever needed money, nor could he think of any use for it. He would never have bought from the pedlars who came (though his mother did, as did all the court ladies) for the pedlars brought women's fripperies only. They bought farthingales and nets for the ladies' hair and stuffings for their high hennins, and needles, those wonderful, miniature steel blades, with a tiny hole through the head, which held a thread. There were no shops or stores, so James and David were both puzzled over how he should best lay out his coin. At the next fair, perhaps, or at market, if he sent some squire down, for the king's son could not go down into the market place. Or at one of the booths set up beside a tilting ground.

In May, James went with Annabella to stay at Melrose. This, the loveliest of all the Scottish abbeys, also had royal lodgings attached, and near by lived James's old nurse. Often he rode out to see her, and in her little croft he would forget he was the king's son, and would sweep the earthen floor with her good broom of long wire-stemmed moss from the marsh, and would milk the wee ewe into a cogue, a wood pail, and drink her milk from a birch bowl, and feed the calf from a luggie, a shallow stump, and stir the oatmeal porridge over the peats with a fine, thin carved horn spoon that was kept especially for his visits.

One morning, when he had ridden out on his pony through a glory of yellow broom, his nurse asked him if he would like to come with her to her son's shieling up the green grassy hill she called in her Gaelic the *airigh*. James accepted, and insisted she ride his pony; he could walk alongside, he said. The two squires, who had ridden down with him, had gone back, and would not fetch him until evening, so he knew he had a whole golden day for his very own.

A woodlouse crossed their path, and nurse gravely asked it, "What would the weather be?" and sung a song about how

34

On Beltane's yellow day
The mouse takes home a load of hay.

On their way up, they met young women coming down from the uplands carrying churns on their backs, "full of cream they are, that is butter when they reach their home in the valley," nurse told James, "then they salt the butter against the long winter."

The uplands were of green, mossy turf, with little huts banked up, bracken roofed, part covered with heather-tops. They stopped at nurse's son's shieling, and when he, a grown man, saw it was Prince James who had come, he went down on his knees and kissed the child's hand and then picked him up and carried him shoulder high to shew him the beasts grazing, with big bells on their necks, and the foxgloves growing white and red taller than the beasts, and they had a meal of whey porridge and wild strawberries and blaeberries, and to James nothing he had ever eaten was so good. The very milk he drank tasted of the smell of bog myrtle, "for the cows eat plenty on it," said the nurse. The food all seemed so different, eaten out-of-doors, on black bog oak stools, with the smoke of the peat fire creeping out of the hut and into the warm sunlight like a thin shivering blue snake. James, watching the light, wished he were a pig, for pigs can see the wind: he hardly hearkened to the grown-up talk around him.

"No lass is safe," nurse told her son, shaking her head sadly; "and to think that I should be having to admit that —I, who delivered him into this world."

James, now munching happily, was as yet unaware they were talking of his beloved brother. Nurse went on expatiating. "Poor young fellow," said her son's wife kindly, "mayhap he has a phallus in his head."

"He's a good governor," said nurse's son, defending David. Looking sideways at James, he went on: "Maybe we shouldn't talk so before him."

Nurse smiled, and fondled James's tousled head of bright hair. "Never fear," she said, "it would be well for all princes, ay, and kings, too, if they could hear just what their people think of them."

"Is't true that David Rothesay has jilted the Earl of March's girl?" asked her son.

"Indeed, it is, but 'tis in part his father's fault. March paid money that his daughter should marry the king's son; now Black Douglas has paid more."

"Douglas," gasped nurse's son.

"Ay, ay, Douglas' son is married to the king's daughter and now his daughter is wed to the king's son."

"Is wed? It has been done so soon?"

Nurse was silent, and it was James that spoke. "Is Marjorie Douglas my sister now?" he asked, and nurse smilingly replied: "As good as, Jamie."

"The Douglases are mighty nigh the throne the whiles, I'll be thinking," said nurse's son, thoughtfully. "With their son married to the king's daughter and now their daughter married to the king's son."

"They always were near enough," nurse replied, tartly. "Robert Bruce could not have freed Scotland from the English without the first Black Douglas. Nor could the king keep the Border today against the Percys, but for the Douglases."

The sun had begun to slant. James, rising to his feet with all the dignity his five years could muster, said they must be going. Nurse's son carried James down the green hill, to find anxious squires waiting for him at nurse's house.

James was silent all the way home, and William Giffard thought he must be sleepy.

CHAPTER THREE

☐ To Annabella, the deposition of Richard II of England, and the Lancastrian revolution, which culminated in the coronation of the usurping Henry IV on October 13th, 1399, seemed extraordinary. She had nothing against Henry Lancaster, whom she had met in Edinburgh when his father John of Gaunt was sheltering there from the consequences of his unpopularity with the London mob. And on the whole she had disapproved of Richard, for, quite apart from his invasion of Scotland, in which he reached Aberdeen, his inordinate affection for his favourite, Robert de Vere, had shocked visiting Scots, for whom girls were good enough. But she was sadly afraid king-changing might prove catching, and watched her brother-in-law Albany with ever-growing apprehension. She wrote to her married daughter, young Douglas' wife, to tell her the English news, and commented: "It is extraordinary to us to hear that a great and powerful king, who was neither pagan nor heretic, should yet be deposed like an old abbot who is superseded for the dilapidation of his benefice." Her husband, writing about the same time to Henry Lancaster on the subject of the truce, addressed him as Steward of England, not king, and got an upstart grumble in reply.

Meanwhile, David Rothesay's broken troths were boding him no good. Annabella frankly thought they were all her husband's fault; although he was a good man, she realised he was every bit as dependent on affection and popularity as his brother Albany. Robert III would never say boo to a goose, not from fear of the gander, but from a dislike of hurting the goose's feelings. On the other hand, he was poor and mercenary, as well as anxious to please all his nobles; so, as he could not cut David into pieces, to give each lass her share, he had promised him to each father that offered, so long as each had paid more money than the last. Nor would he do anything for the poor Earl of March, who was hurt and furious at his daughter's jilting. March had arrived at Bothwell where the church service was taking place, before young David's marriage to Marjorie had been consummated. He begged the king either to fulfil his contract with Elizabeth Dunbar, or to restore to him entirely the sum of ready money paid by him. Robert took refuge rather lamely in the fact that David's espousal with Elizabeth had not been celebrated with the consent of the three estates—"as though any king's son married by act of parliament," Annabella said. For she openly sided with the affronted March, who left the court in a huff, after warning Annabella that he was going to renounce his allegiance. March took his two eldest sons and his daughter to London to Henry IV and left them there as hostages, offering his fealty to the English king in return for a force to redress his daughter's wrong. Henry was glad of the excuse for action, being precariously perched as yet on his own throne. He came stravaging up into Scotland, with a large land force, assisted by a fleet co-operating at sea. But he did not do much damage, both out of respect to Queen Annabella, who was at Dunfermline, and because he wished to be recognised as lawful suzerain of Scotland and of Scottish blood.

King Henry did not stay long in Scotland, for Owen Glendower began his rebellion in Wales, and the English king had to return to fight him, leaving the Scots very much as he had found them.

James, meanwhile, stayed by his father and mother, following the latter's litter whilst the former marched out from Haddington to besiege Dunbar Castle, left by the Earl of March in charge of a feckless nephew.

James enjoyed the journey; he would canter awhile on his pony beside his father's litter, then trot up to his mother's palfrey, and shew off his new tricks to her—how he could do figure-of-eight, and make his pony change feet; how he could make him slow to a walk from a gallop without pulling on his reins, checking him only with his knees. In the morning, after stopping in a small village, a poor flesher ran after the king's litter, and pulled back the curtains, complaining loudly that the steward of the royal kitchen had failed to pay for the meat consumed by the royal party. Robert pulled out his own purse, of ring mail, and settled the account with a courteous apology.

"But if father is king," James asked Annabella, "is not all the meat in Scotland his own? Why must he pay for it?"

Annabella explained as best she could to her young son the difference between individual property, and sovereign rights.

Then, for many months, there was little James remembered save catafalques and black palls, horses muffled in stiff black harness and continual chanting. First the Black Earl of Douglas died. As James walked round the bier where the earl lay waxy in solemn state, tiptoeing so as to reach high enough to throw the holy water right on the dead face, he made his deasil three times clockwise round the departed, and thought life badly arranged. There should always be something nice to which one could look forward, James decided, even when one was grownup. When one was a child, years of tournaments and jousting, of marrying lovely princesses, and ruling fine kingdoms, stretched before one. But when one grew

39

old, it was terrible: there was nothing left to come—for his father, as for this dead earl—but this waiting for worms to eat one in a cold church, or in the colder ground.

After the Black Earl of Douglas, the Bishop of St. Andrews died, and the king and queen, with David and his sisters, and James, all attended a three-hour long Mass for him in the same church at Perth, where James remembered Walter Traill saying Mass before the opening of that parliament where David became governor.

After the bishop's death, it was Annabella's turn to sicken, and when autumn came, and it was the best time to gallop over the stubbled fields, she, too, died, and James felt he would never be safe or secure again. For, when the old Earl of Douglas died, then his sister's husband became earl, and, when the bishop died, there was much talk of the next bishop, but when his mother died, that was queen, there was no new mother, nor could ever be; nor, James thought, would there ever be another queen. James hid his grief, even from David: but with his nurse, though he was all of seven now, he would weep, sobbing into the comfortable manifold pleats of her long kirtle, and cuddling against her in the evening, at the time when his mother was wont to come sweeping in, her tall hair towered by her crown, to kiss him good night before she went down to eat beside the king.

On David Rothesay, his mother's death had no less severe, and an even more disastrous, effect. He gave himself completely up to evil courses; his wife Marjorie was now no more able to stay his wantonness than his council could prevent his looting customs houses, extorting sums from travellers, and generally behaving more like a bandit and a criminal than like the kingdom's governor and the king's deputy and heir.

At last his father, perceiving his son's youthful nature to rage after this fashion to the great reproach of them both, wrote to his brother the Duke of Albany, as head of the council, requiring him to take his son into his custody and see him chastised for his wanton behaviour, that he might amend the same.

James was with his father when he wrote that letter. He had a strange feeling that his father wasn't happy about sending it—he had read it aloud to Sir John de Ramorgny, who was standing beside him waiting to take it, and asked Sir John if he approved it.

"I, a humble knight, how could I not approve Your Majesty?" Sir John had answered, but still the king looked sadly uncomfortable. "There is too great an outcry in the kingdom. I needs must take steps so that he shall not continue to disturb the peace," he said, defensively, though no one had attacked him. "Maybe, though he will not mind me, the lad will mind his uncle," he concluded.

James followed Sir John out of the room. "What will Uncle Albany do to David?" he asked. "Will he shut him up in prison? Tell Uncle Albany I'll gladly go, too—I could play chess with David and keep him merry," he said, and he pulled out the gold coin that David had given him. "Give him this towards his ransom; he may need it."

"You wouldn't care for prison, James," said Sir John. "It's no place for a boy of your age—nor of David's either," he added.

Albany sent Sir John straight after David. "He's riding toward St. Andrews," Albany said; "he's after the bishopric. He means to seize it and keep the revenue until papal confirmation of the new bishop comes. Take Sir William Lindsay with you; he's anxious for a few words with David on his daughter's account."

The two men rode fast. When they were waiting together for a ferry, Sir John said: "I told Rothesay he should have his uncle arrested; I knew Albany was plotting against him. But he wouldn't heed me—of late I had no influence with him. I left his service for the queen's because there was nothing I could do. And since her death I've thought the best thing I could do was to try

41

and steady the king—try and remind him of her spirit that so long sustained him. But since I can do nothing for the king, there is indeed nothing left but to let Albany have his way."

"You know what that way will be?" asked Sir William, significantly, implying that he could guess well enough, himself.

"I fear I do," Sir John said sadly; "but the people won't stand for what's happening now. It's heads Albany wins, tails David loses. I'd like to keep Albany from the crown —just because his fingers itch for it too much—but he'll get it given him by the three estates on a platter if David goes on as he's doing. We'll have Albany persuading them to set aside the Act of Succession, on the grounds that the king's too sick, David's too evil, and James too young, to rule."

Sir William was silent. "David has done my daughter great wrong," he said; "but he's the king's elder son, and he's a bonnie fighter. The way he took Reras Castle with those new-fangled cannon was a nice piece of strategy, and well done. But I fear that if the shepherd turns wolf, then the sheep must turn watchdog."

"And if gold rust, then what shall iron do?" Sir John quoted under his breath.

It was raining now, a thin, cold determined drizzle that drove through their open vizors, and trickled down their necks. The men following them pulled their surcotes tightly round them; the horses slipped and stumbled on the loose wet stones. A green mist of linden trees in tiny leaf lay to their left; once past the wood, they could see a long way ahead, down a grassy valley to the roofs of the village of Strathgreen. Beyond it lay St. Andrews. If David Rothesay could reach it before they reached him, he could entrench himself there, and snap his fingers in their faces. Rounding a bend, they saw ahead of them a group of men. "Yon's David," said Sir William, pointing his gauntleted hand towards a tall figure, in full armour, about whom the others, dwarfed by his slender height and that of the tall grey mare he rode, seemed to cluster. Sir John put spurs to his horse. The leather reins squelched in his hands, and Sir William kept pace with him. As they caught up just beyond the village, on the road to Nydie beside the great cross, Rothesay halted, couched his spear, pulled his horse round. Nor he nor the two knights had pulled down their vizors.

"Stand, in the king's name," said Sir William.

"Only I can bid any man stand in the king's name," said Rothesay; "I that am Governor of Scotland by my father's grace."

"And by the good pleasure of the estates of the realm," said Sir William.

"Come quietly, David," said Sir John. "We have Albany's writ for your arrest here. It will be worse for you if you give an appearance of disaffection and revolt. Besides we are thirty men, and you but eleven."

"What does my uncle want with me?" said David, frowning as he tried to knock the warrant for his arrest out of Sir William's hand.

"Not so fast," said the latter, gripping it tightly. The parchment, not yet sodden, held, though some of the ink started to run.

"What is your will with me?" David asked, flushing. His men were fidgeting, mixed up now with the pursuer's men, and surrounded by them. The road was narrow, but the way ahead to Nydie and beyond to St. Andrews was still open. David clapped his spurs to his mare. "First catch your quarry before you skin it," he shouted over his shoulder.

Sir William caught at the prince's bridle, and missed. "After him," he yelled, but two of David's men grabbed his reins, and he had to cut himself free, jabbing at their hands with his dirk, so that their blood spurted stickily on to his pommel. Meanwhile, Sir John had caught up with David, and, parrying his blows, managed to catch hold of the cheek of his bridle. The two horses kept going, side by side, for another few hundred yards. Then Sir John stopped them both, and David drew his sword.

David had Sir John down, and had started off again, but Sir William and two soldiers had now drawn level, and he was surrounded. "The game's up," Sir William said.

"Then I'll die fighting," David said. "Would you kill the king's son?"

"Nonsense, no one is going to kill you. You're being put out of mischief under lock and key, that's all," Sir John said.

"Where'll you be taking me?" David asked.

And Sir John said: "To Falkland Castle, to Albany's place."

David did not struggle whilst three squires stripped his armour off. Sir John, when his own squire had bound his shoulder where David had thrust in, dressed him in a grey jerkin after the manner of a varlet, taking it from off one of David's own men. The man stood shivering, his teeth chattering in the icy rain. David stooped to pick up his own tunic woven of fine camel's hair that was worth a king's ransom. He tossed it to the red-faced lout. "Since I am to be dressed after your manner," he said, "do you be clad after mine." David was put on a small pack horse. Sir William then paid off David's men, and bade them to go to their homes and warned them they'd better not talk too much. He was afraid if he took them along they'd rouse for David the villages through which they passed, and help him give them the slip. Sir William dismissed all but ten of his own men, too, and chose three of these dressed as nearly as possible as David now was. Then they rode on through St. Andrews. They were afraid of recognition. David might easily win himself a following were he spotted. Sir William and Sir John rode on either side of him; as though he were a villein and they were riding him in to justice. "They say they tame elephants thus in India, riding a wild one between two tame," chaffed Sir John, but David glowered.

"Don't think to tame me," he said.

When they got to Falkland, the men who came to answer their ring did not seem oversurprised to see them. "You, Wright, and you, Selkirk, take this prisoner and keep him during the king's good pleasure," said Sir William.

But David turned to Ramorgny and said, "Ah, John, it was for this you left my service, and entered first my mother's and then my father's—that now the queen is dead the king might be seduced by your evil counsel to take steps against his own son."

Sir John replied: "Would *you* had heeded *my* counsel, and my warning, David."

Sir William looked nastily at David. "Wright and Selkirk both lost brothers when King Harry came to Scotland and besieged Edinburgh and his coming was for your fault that you jilted the Earl of March's daughter," he said.

"Give Marjorie my humble duty," David said; "I suppose my brother-in-law, the Earl of Douglas, is in on this, too."

"Certainly," said Sir John. Then they led the young man away across the portcullis and into the courtyard and Sir William said, "We must ride hard if we are to reach Albany tomorrow."

"The council is summoned to Culross to consider the disposition of the Duke of Rothesay," said Sir John; "and we shall have to be there to tell our story."

For three weeks James could get no news of David though he asked Sir John daily. It was Lent, and the diet of salt fish and porridge without milk, and of bannocks without butter, had made most of the court come out in boils and sores; everyone was irritable and petulant. James's father wore a hair shirt, and scratched perpetually. James went daily to Mass, and prayed that David might be home for Easter. On Easter Sunday, as they were riding in state to High Mass, a messenger pushed through the crowd and stopped the king's litter. When Robert III had read the brief message he had been brought, he ordered the company to proceed. When he reached the church and the officiating clergy came down

45

the steps to meet him, he stood painfully up and whispered to them.

The priests looked startled, then addressed the crowd surging around the king. "Sad news," they said, "His Grace the Duke of Rothesay is dead. He died of dysentery. Remember him in your prayers. When High Mass is over, we will begin Tenebrae for the departed."

James would not pray. He knelt between his father and his Uncle Albany, stubborn and silent. So this was God's answer—this was how David came home for Easter. He was sure Albany had murdered him—not with his own hands, for he was here at court, not at Falkland; and Sir John couldn't have done it either, as he'd been with the king. But there could be no doubt . . . one didn't die at nineteen. One died at forty-nine, or seventy, but at nineteen one was killed in battle, or . . . or sometimes, horribly one was murdered. And James vowed then, fighting back his tears, that someday he'd get even with Albany. "O God," he said, not in prayer, but as prince challenging prince, "you let my father's son be killed; let me kill Albany's son."

His father would not speak to James of what had happened, and James, sensing his father's guilt, avoided him, hated him, and spent all his time with nurse. Nurse had talked with the messenger who had brought the sad tidings and led him to James. "They put him in a small room and neither fed him nor cleaned him," the messenger told of David. "My sister was working at the castle there, and she heard a moaning when she was up in the loft getting corn for the chickens. She peeped through the chinks between the floor boards, and saw the young laird, and 'twas true enough he had dysentery, and the stench from him came up so she retched and was like to lose the child she was carrying. She spoke with him, and let meal fall through the chinks and he would scrabble and scratch for it amongst the filth of the floor. And each day thereafter for a week she came. But when Wright and Selkirk found the prince was getting stronger instead of weaker, and better instead of worse, they waited in his room with him, and he could not warn her, so when the meal dropped again, in the evening, one stayed with the prince, and one went up to the loft, and he knifed my sister there and then, and killed her. My brother-in-law came next morning seeking her, since she had not shewed up at home, and they gave him the body and told him they'd find ways to silence him if he talked."

"Did they kill David then, too?" James asked in a voice as steady as he could make it.

"No; they left him be. And my brother-in-law told another—a woman that had lately been brought to bed, and she worked with the fowls at the castle, too, but she knew the loft was watched now, so she never went there. She found a way to get to the window of the room where the prince was—right under it was a wall upon which she stood—and though the window was small she pushed her paps through and the prince sucked at them, and she had slipped raw egg yolks into her mouth, and spat them into his."

"God bless her, God bless her," moaned the nurse.

"She did that twice in each day for five days," the messenger went on, "and then one day, her foot slipped, and she came tumbling down upon the sentries, and they wouldn't have told on her, but Selkirk was there playing at cards with them, and he looked up to see where she'd come from, and she had clutched at the ivy outside the window to break her fall and that left a trail. So he put her to the torture, and when she was on the rack, and they'd started to pull out her fingernails, and to put the red-hot irons on her breasts, she told all, and they went on until she, too, was dead."

"And David died then?" asked James, in a high, cracked voice, squeaky from excitement.

"About five days after, when they went for his body, them that was to take him to his burying found he had eaten his own offal, and his own hands, four fingers off one, and down to the wrist of the other, but for the thumb."

47

There was a silence and then the nurse asked: "What manner was his burying?"

"He was interred at Lindores Abbey, near by. It was a mean funeral, that cost but two pounds," said the messenger. "Kings should take a lesson not to trifle with men of fierce temper, nor yet with their daughters," he concluded with a sigh.

"If David had wed that sweet lass Euphemia Lindsay of Rossie, none of this would have happened," said nurse.

But James said: "Sir William Lindsay was with Sir John when David was taken."

"They do say," the messenger began, "how the night after he was buried little Nance MacDonald, she that was born crippled, was ailing terribly and her mother prayed that the Duke of Rothesay might heal her, and, next day, she took Nance to the grave—right in the chancel it is—and knelt beside it, and held the child close to the stone, and she straightened up, and trotted out of the church on her own two pins, though she had never walked before in her life, but had to be carried every place, and she all of seven."

James's nurse turned to him. "You mind now what I say, Jamie. You are not to eat anything except I taste it first. You are always to sleep in beside me, and I'll have your father post us extra guards, and they men we can trust. Will you bide with us here and take care of Prince James with me?" she asked the messenger, and he gladly agreed.

"I know too much, I'll not go back," he said.

Robert III shrank into a terrified piety. He endowed for Rothesay a daily Mass at the abbey of Deer, and gave an annuity to be paid to the bishop and the Cathedral of Aberdeen from the customs of the city, for a chaplain to celebrate the Holy Sacrifice daily for the souls of Robert III, his ancestors and his successors, until the Universal Church shall regain her unity; he paid for daily Mass in the parish church of Dundee and for daily Mass at Culross for the souls of Annabella and Rothesay; but still nothing could ease his sore distracted soul. His

48

irresolution and timidity, and his anxious desire to concil-
iate the affection of all parties, had led him to acquiesce
in the loss of his eldest son: now he practically would
not let James out of his sight, yet James hated him—despised and mistrusted him. And James's nurse also
loathed the king. "He gave David to your Uncle Albany
because he wanted him killed—he was afraid of those
earls, of both March and Douglas, and if Rothesay were
dead, they would have no more a grievance against him.
He spared not his own son," she snorted angrily, "he's no
true father to you. It is an orphan you are, poor bairn."

By May everyone was talking of the murder. The king,
in Edinburgh for the meeting of the estates, left James at
Perth with his nurse, William Giffard, now his favourite
squire, and a strong bodyguard. When he came back he
broke the silence he had kept about Rothesay. "Your
Uncle Albany and your brother-in-law, Douglas," he told
the boy over supper, "made the compliant estates affirm
that your brother 'ab hac luce divina providentia et non
aliter migrasse dinoscitur.' Can you undo me that Latin,
Jamie?"

James looked straight at his father. "Better than you
can undo your letter to Uncle Albany," he said, steadily,
and very slowly. Then he translated, gasping and
clumsy, each word coming out separate and slow: "He
departed from this life through Divine Providence and
by no other means."

"And they added that Albany and Douglas were in no
way guilty of his death, and that to say they were was
slander and would be punished," Robert III looked back
steadily at James.

"Would it not be an offence for you and me to say otherwise?" asked James.

"We might be punished," James's father half smiled,
ironically.

"You still are king," James answered. " 'Tis for you to
make men suffer who tell lies; 'tis not for them to make
you suffer for telling truth."

49

CHAPTER FOUR

☐ Since Albany was governor again, the nobles did pretty well what they pleased. Having grumbled in seeming solidarity at David's conduct, their own behaviour now brought Scotland lower than any loose living of his had done. Douglas and some lesser Lothian lords made delighted forays into England, playing grandmother's steps, invading daily until the English looked around and then scuttling back, unharmed, until the renegade March's sons led two hundred Englishmen out of Berwick and defeated twice that number of Scots at Kimmerghame on June 22nd.

Twelve thousand Scots then marched down upon Carlisle, amongst whom were Douglas, Albany's eldest son Murdoch, and three other earls. On September 14th, on Homildon Hill, the Scots suffered one of the major defeats of the century. The Scottish force, almost entirely mounted, drew the fire of the English archers, which was so deadly accurate that Harry Hotspur and March lost only five men, whereas seven Scots nobles were killed and twenty-eight more were taken prisoner. Whilst the ranks of Scots horsemen waited on the hill, receiving in serried, suffering ranks the deadly rain of arrows, they were rallied by one Sir John Swinton who cried out: "My friends, why stand we here to be slain like deer, and marked down by the enemy? Are we to be still, and have our hands nailed to our lances?" The subsequent sally sealed the Scots defeat, for this senseless abandonment of their position threw all ranks into confusion. Murdoch and Douglas were amongst the captives taken by the English, and when the news was brought to Perth, where James was with his father, he rejoiced, clapping his hands together. But Robert chid the child, saying: "No, my son: Scotland always comes first. It's always a disaster when England wins, however many of our own personal enemies we lose, temporarily or permanently, through her victory."

That same fall, James's uncle, Sir Malcolm Drummond, Annabella's brother, who was married to the Countess of Mar, and earl in his wife's right, was murdered in his own castle of Kildrummie, by Alexander Stewart, one of the king's illegitimate nephews—a bastard of the Wolf of Badenoch. Alexander Stewart also forced Sir Malcolm's widow to marry him, and hand over the earldom of Mar. Even Albany was shocked—or pretended to be—but he did nothing.

Nor would Albany's council send help to young John Gladstone, the lord of Cocklaws Castle, when it was besieged by the English. But this time Albany huffed and puffed, and swore.

"By God and St. Fillan," he said, "I shall be there on the appointed day, if God lends life, though no one go with me but my boy Patrick." But he took so long getting there that the siege had been raised; it had been no more than an excuse for the Percys to gather their forces together for a rebellion against the English king, Henry IV. This time Robert III praised his brother Albany to James, who objected that his uncle was a bloody murderer and could do no good. "You must always be glad of any good, whoever does it," said the king. "A good is a good, even if it is to your disadvantage, even if it is your enemy, or Judas Iscariot, who does it. It is a poor heart that never rejoices. And you must always be angry at evil, even if your best friend committed it to help you, and even if his sin should profit you greatly."

"But, Father," James objected, "if Albany or Murdoch did any good, even a little good, God is so dreadfully merciful that perhaps they might repent of their sins and mayhap He would forgive them."

"Let us hope so," said Robert.

"I won't hope so," James burst out; "I hope they'll die in sin and burn and burn and burn. They must burn, they *must*."

"I'm glad we're alone here, James." Robert said; "let no man ever hear you speak thus, nor any man know you feel so. For, Jamie, don't you see there'll be no end on it; that if you feel that way, then Murdoch's sons will, too; should you kill Albany, then till world's end there'll be no peace nor quiet?"

"I don't care for peace or quiet," said James. "Unless man or God punishes Uncle Albany, there'll be no justice; and if there's no justice, there might as well not be a God."

"And mercy, James?"

The boy was standing, straight and stiff, staring out at the cloister garden, cluttered with autumn leaves. He was very white—his anger drained his pale skin instead of flooding it, and he ran his fingers through his wavy red hair, and almost spat out at his father: "Mercy—that's for women and priests—not for men and kings."

The boy's outburst decided his father that it was time his character received more formative influences than the chatter of a bitter old woman, and the babbling of a melancholy old man. Physically, James was good enough—as hardy and tough a youngster as ever climbed after sea gulls' eggs. And he had great personal dignity, too, in spite of being small for his age; when he walked up to a sentry the man saluted; when he rode in the streets men doffed their hats. But he hadn't enough discipline, roaming about the royal lodgings, escorted only by a squire, or traipsing off to fish, to swim, or to ride, with half a dozen of the pages. Now that he was sole heir to the throne he needed better care, more guidance. Luckily, the vacant see of St. Andrews had just been filled. Pope Benedict XIII had nominated Henry Wardlaw, lecturer in philosophy at the University of Paris. Wardlaw was one of the outstanding scholars of his day, and a likeable and able, as well as a brilliant person. He was a young man for the job, too, and Robert sent for him immediately on his arrival, and confided James to him. He told him privately all that had gone before, and warned him of Albany's ambitions. Should he himself die, Robert said, he wished Henry Wardlaw to retain management of the young king.

James left his father, travelling with his new mentor over the same roads David had ridden before he had been taken, but James hardly thought of that now, being fully occupied with the journey. He had never ridden so fast before; either he had travelled with his father, whose litter slowed the pace of the company, or with his mother, who rode sidesaddle, the new-fangled way (most women still rode the traditional way, astride, with their clothes tucked into a bag), and she, too, never hurried, for usually when she travelled they were a great company. But James and the bishop had only half a dozen men, and rode as fast as their horses would carry them, for the new bishop was in a hurry to get back to his see, and he also was decidedly afraid that something might happen to his precious charge. It would be so easy for wild Highlanders, bribed by Albany, to fall upon the party, and no one would be able to prove anything should James disappear.

But they reached St. Andrews in safety, and James was delighted with the grey city, and with the sea. He had never been on a seashore before, and the rocks with tiny crab-filled pools, the red dulse seaweed that tasted so good fried in butter, the endless variety of shells and sea-anemone and starfish and sea-urchins, and the strange tales of the fishermen, were wonderfully of his age after the wearisome hours at court, and the constant pretending to be grownup, and having to do adult things for civility's sake, and seem to enjoy them. Bishop Wardlaw was a gifted teacher, and he saw that what James needed most was monotony, security, a sense of safety, and space and air and light in which to grow.

One morning, after Mass, James was buttering his oat-cake and had just reached for the honeycomb, when the bishop, who always spoke to him with great formality and either in Latin or in English, said: "My Lord Prince, I have news for you. I am to have another pupil, and you will have a companion to share your studies."

"Who is he, my lord Bishop?" James answered.

And the bishop replied: "An English lad, just your age, my lord of Northumberland's grandson, Harry Hotspur's son, Henry Percy. He is seeking sanctuary here. His father died fighting against his king in open rebellion at Shrewsbury, where your brother-in-law, the Earl of Douglas, fought with Hotspur against the Earl of March, who was on the English side."

James repeated in astonishment: "A Douglas and a Percy fought together; that's hard to take even from your Lordship! Why, they've fought on opposite sides all through Scots history."

The bishop smiled. "You must believe that they really did fight together," said the bishop; "and with singular lack of success, for the Earl of Douglas is now in an English prison, and the old Earl of Northumberland has brought his grandson to your father. They were received by Sir David Fleming, and Henry Percy arrives here tomorrow."

"He won't sleep with me, will he?" James asked. "I so love having a room of my own."

The bishop said no, there were rooms aplenty in the palace. Next day the old man and the boy arrived. James had never seen any Englishman close to and a Percy, famed for killing Scots, was to him like some strange carnivorous animal or cannibal. Indeed, he felt as though he were seeing a unicorn or a dodo. James felt he ought to hate Northumberland for all his raids on Scotland, and the breaches of the truce made by him and his family.

For he'd helped the Earl of March against David Rothesay, and—and—. But here he was, a stranger and a guest, and every courtesy must be shewn him.

"I hope you're not too tired by your long journey," he said politely to Henry Percy when the latter had been shewn his room. James, himself, had poured water for old Northumberland, and another squire held the silver ewer whilst he washed his hands, and William Giffard held the towel.

"Tired? What of? Scotland? Yes, I am; and of exile and of running around without any of my things. Do you know I have six daggers of my own, and two have Damascus blades."

"If you're tired of Scotland why don't you go home?" said James quickly. "We don't need traitors here, or rebels."

"Traitors . . . rebels. We're here because we were loyal to our anointed king, Richard, and he's your overlord, too, in Scotland. Take that—" and he lunged out at James—"and that."

Henry was older and taller, but James was chunky, and soon both boys were rolling over and over on the big bearskin in front of the chimney piece, but mostly James was on top. He had pulled his skean dhu—the tiny, jewelled knife Scots carried tucked in their sock or boot—out of its sheath, and Henry had a pretty murderous looking dagger in his hand when Bishop Wardlaw crossed the great hall and dragged them apart.

"He said—" began James.

"He said—" simultaneously began Henry.

But the bishop interrupted them both, and put one of his hands over each of their mouths. "Shush to you both, and you should be ashamed," he said. "You're behaving like heathens. You, James, will learn by heart the corporal works of mercy, and read, and recite to me what St. Thomas says are our duties to our enemies."

"You, sir," he addressed Henry Percy, "had better learn to cut your coat according to your cloth. You are a suppliant here, seeking sanctuary: if you disturb again the peace of this holy place, I'll have no more of you; you can take yourself elsewhere."

After which turbulent beginning, the boys settled down together and became good enough friends. Both were keen on jousting and sword-work; both good riders and poor archers. James was bookish and good at languages: he enjoyed learning. Henry Percy found even reading a dreary chore and cared for nothing beyond his nose. To talk all evening of which dog went best during the day's hunting, to think what fly he'd take to the salmon next morning—these were the highest exercises of his mind.

James, under Wardlaw's care, began to understand a little of the enormous role of the Church. Bishop Wardlaw was not only a feudal overlord, and a judge with powers of life and death—after all, *any* baron was that—he also administered all the schools in his diocese. There were no secular schools, but by canon law every cathedral was obliged to have at least one grammar school attached. Also the bishop negotiated the truces between Scotland and other countries, notably, of course, with England. The bishop was a member, too, of the king's council, ex officio, and had moreover to manage all the charities, hospitals, almshouses for the aged poor, soup kitchens, leper houses, all the paraphernalia of organized relief now distributed between perhaps a dozen various societies, but then the responsibility of the Church alone.

Bishop Wardlaw took the boys with him as pages and acolytes on his visitations, riding over every inch of his diocese with them. They would enter a poor croft, stooping into a dark hole that was all the living and sleeping place of a whole family. The smoke escaped through a hole in the roof; everyone was rolled in woollen rugs sleeping around the hearth. If anyone were ill, either they were just let die, or they were carried to the nearest monastary, or, if the fear of contagion were too great, they were put into a hastily built hut outside, away from the others, and food and drink left for them outside the door, and it was just the will of God if they were too ill to

57

crawl out and get it. James, seeing the pitiful results of a local feud, ruined crops, starving children, straying cattle, vowed that when he became king, he would insist on justice, justice . . . justice: for in spite of his beloved bishop he still did not feel mercy mattered half so much. Looting Highlanders would take a poor man's only cow; looting English would drive off his flock of sheep, or would seize a castle and imprison its laird, even if he had avoided being killed in the skirmish. And always it was the poor who paid.

James and Henry, in their different ways, learnt much statecraft from Bishop Wardlaw, who was well aware of the importance of his charges. The bishop was all James's father could never be: for James could not forgive David's death, nor trust his father not to betray him also. Love was interred in David's grave, and Annabella's; all his life, James was to sorrow that the springs of his affection had been so early sealed. Men, later, were to call him a cold fish; it was not until he married that the ice in his heart would melt; but he was devoted to the good bishop in a dutiful way, and fond of Henry Percy in the exasperated, competitive fashion small boys hate and delight and vie with each other.

Except for the great feasts, James stayed with the bishop; St. Andrews was his home, where his treasures were, his hunting knives, his collection of gulls' eggs, his little garden, where he grew lettuces and parsley and onions. When his father sent for him, generally to Dunfermline for Easter, James would ride to him with a heavily armed escort. He would ride delightedly across the broad plain and through the great wood which surrounded the city as with a girdle. In the very midst, it seemed, of the forest appeared the castle hill, crowded with flowers of every different colour, gracious and verdoyant and wholly attractive to James after the bare seascapes of bleak St. Andrews. Or sometimes James would join the king at Perth for Christmas.

The year he was ten, after High Mass on Christmas Day, James's father bestowed on him, in free regality, the Earldom of Carrick, the baronies of Renfrew, Cunningham, and Kyle-Stewart, of Ratho and Innerwick; the islands of Bute, Arran, and the Cumbrays; the lands of Cowall and Knapdale. Of the Dukedom of Rothesay no word had been spoken either by father or son.

On that Christmas morning James dressed himself in a doublet of white satin laced with gold; his white morey hose reached up to his waist; his houppelande of cloth of gold had huge bagpipe sleeves trimmed, in the very latest fashion, at the wrists and the collar with ermine. His belt, which cost forty gold pounds, was of tooled hide, set with huge garnets, blood-red, from the Scottish hills, and the hasp was of beaten gold.

All the great nobles were present to do honour to the king's son: Albany, of course, and all his sons except Murdoch, still detained in his English jail. Douglas' wife, and his widowed sister Marjorie, and even the new, graceless, murdering Earl of Mar. King Robert's present to his son was a missal, handsomely written and illuminated, bound in crimson velvet, with two clasps of silver-gilt, the velvet richly wrought with roses worked in gold thread in the centre.

As he swore fealty at the altar steps to his own father, promising to be his man before and against all other men, James felt a new, impersonal loyalty to the sick man on whose tired knees he had placed his upturned hands. For it seemed to him that now he, James, was the protector; it was he who must take care of this ill, old man. He rose from his knees for the Te Deum feeling tenderly toward his father for the first time since David's death. Perhaps, he thought, all relationships are quite other from what we suppose them to be. Fatherhood is not created by the accident of begetting: it is a guarding and a guiding that must be assumed and lived by a grown man. Just as motherhood is a caring and a cherishing, a love that grows to be even more than the pain endured by the sheltering flesh. And he wondered about the Fatherhood of God: what had that to do with this poor fumbling earthly father of his? What connection was there between Robert III of Scotland and the "pa-trem immensae majestatis"—the Father of an infinite majesty—whom the choir were glorifying at that very moment? How *could* human beings share in that tremendous and terrifying Divine Paternity?

Waiting at the altar rail later to receive his first com-munion, James knew he must be as truly dedicated to his coming kingship as any priest to his altar. Indeed, to be king was even more of a vocation than to be priest, be-cause there simply was no way out. His kingship was compulsory. So, very solemnly, the stiff, red-headed small boy, who now was Earl of Carrick, wriggling in his hot, tight, uncomfortable grand clothes, promised his dead mother and his living father, and the white God on his tongue, that he would be the best king he could be—and, if God granted it, the best king Scotland ever had.

CHAPTER FIVE

□ James was sitting at his desk one February morning translating Cornelius Nepos' *Of Famous Men*, when Bishop Wardlaw came into the room. James and Henry —who was reading the Latin aloud whilst James Englished it—jumped up and bowed and the bishop told James his father wanted him. Following Henry Wardlaw outside, James saw a big troop of men—knights in full armour, about forty or more, the whole courtyard full of them, the sun shining on the silver steel, on plumed helmets and burnished shields. James's eyes danced. "What is up?" he asked, "is it a tourney? a raid?"

The bishop said, "No. You are leaving me, and I'm very sad of it. I did not tell you anything of these plans before, because you mightn't have been able to resist telling young Henry and we wanted absolute secrecy. But here now is Sir David Fleming who will take you to your father. I have had all your belongings packed, and William Giffard who will go with you is in charge of carrying everything that can be carried."

"But my collection of gulls' eggs?" James asked anxiously; "they'll never be safe bumping about on horseback."

"I think you had, maybe, best leave them here till you

come back, and I'll mind them for you," said the bishop.

"But how long will I be gone?" said James. "And there are those moleskins I was drying to make a quiver; they have to have grease rubbed in every day, or they'll go hard and stiff."

"You shall come home when you are grownup, and able to take care of yourself and your moleskins," said the bishop smiling kindly. "The king has just learnt that your Uncle Albany was about to hand Northumberland and young Henry over to Henry IV in exchange for Douglas' hostages and for Murdoch; Northumberland has fled to Wales, to the magician rebel prince, Owen Glendower, the Prince of Powis."

"What has this to do with me?" asked James, and Bishop Wardlaw hesitated before he replied:

"Your father is fearful of your uncle."

James nodded. After a silence, he said: "Does my lord Duke of Albany plan treason? It is then he whom the king should banish from his presence, not his loyal and loving son."

But the bishop shook his head. "Your father is right, James; we cannot keep so precious a treasure here in such fragile safety. The conditions of this country are too unsettled. There is truce with England until Easter; you must leave whilst it is still in force; there is not overmuch time. God bless you, and give my love to Paris; it's the fairest city in the world. You'll be happy enough in France."

"But I don't belong there—I'm Scottish," James said.

And the bishop replied: "The French are our hereditary allies. Were you a little older, you would most certainly go there to fight the English, or for jousting and tournaments and to learn courtly etiquette. It will do you no harm to go now, to learn the language and some manners." The bishop stroked James's head affectionately to take the sting out of his words. "And, remember, it's not where you are, but what you are, that matters. As St. Augustine says: 'The Lord did not say, go East, and learn wisdom, travel to the West, that you may acquire understanding. Where you seek, there you shall find, for to Him Who is everywhere present, one comes by love and not by sail.'"

The boy knelt and kissed the bishop's ring. He was in tears, and when he looked up, it was to smile damply without speaking. He saluted his escort, mounted his horse, and the company started.

There was snow lying when James, numbed by cold and sorrow and the ache of many farewells, left Linlithgow, in full moonlight. The palace looked unbelievably lovely, and friendly, and the sleepy boy, who would much rather have been mounting the shadowy staircase with his candle in his hand, wondered whether anyone would notice or pick him up if he should fall off his horse. Sir David Fleming, with his strong contingent of local nobles, insisted on their riding through the night, while the moon was favourable. They slept by day. They arrived at North Berwick early on a grey spring morning, and Sir David bespoke a rowing boat and took James and William Giffard together with James's retinue of two personal servants, and one groom, over to the abrupt Bass Rock. From the boat, James looked shorewards at the tilled fields stretching up to the crest of the high cliffs on which stood Tantallon. He turned towards the lowering Bass, then looked at Sir David. "My brother must have looked at what I see now?" he asked.

Sir David nodded. "And you may thank God your view of it is yet so different from his. He saw as a prisoner what you see as a free prince."

"Yes, I imagine this same view must have looked very differently to my brother," James said, and suddenly was choking, silted up by self-pity, for if only their mother hadn't died, he thought, none of this would have happened. David wouldn't be dead, and he'd be at home; and bitterness filled him. Then, luckily, nothing, nothing at all, nor his mother's death, nor his exile, nor David's murder, nor leaving nurse, mattered any more, for from the boat's rocking he was horribly seasick.

Climbing the slippery ladder to land, James wondered where there could be any shelter for them on the steep rock, but after a precipitous climb, they found a fisherman's cottage, simply enough, but with a certain snugness. There was even the semblance of a chimney, and the inside was clean, though the floor was matted with seaweed.

James waited here for a month whilst his escort gathered. One day came a silly, terrified, giggling Welsh bishop, Griffin Yonge, his episcopal robes spattered and draggled in foam and rain; the next day came Henry, Earl of Orkney, a genial, bluff, handsome islander, blond as a Dane, who climbed with James over every inch of the rock, sought tern's eggs in impossible places, had an inexhaustible physical energy and good humour, and comforted many of the defects of James's loneliness. Last came Sir Archibald Edmonstone, with bad news; as Sir David Fleming rode back through East Lothian on his return journey to the king, he had been waylaid by a trio of the Douglas' men. Sir David had been killed after fiercely defending his life for nearly an hour, single-handed, having wounded all three of his murderers. James Douglas of Balvany gave the death thrust. James asked the bishop to say the morrow's Mass for Sir David, and with James for acolyte, and a handmade catafalque and pall, they mourned him in the tiny, icy stone chapel over whose low roof fishing nets were spread to dry.

At last, on Passion Sunday, a merchant ship, from Danzig, the *Maryenknyght*, whose master, Henry Bereholt, was a Lithuanian, sailed from Leith down the Firth of Forth, and anchored off the Bass. James and his retinue rowed out and boarded the little vessel with her stinking cargo of wool, hides and woolfells, on March 12th. Aries was four degrees past midday. The men stowed their bundles amidships, and sat up on deck, very cramped for space, and after a few hours, very bored. The Earl of Orkney had brought dice, and for a while they gambled; James bet he could stand on his head in spite of the ship's motion, and was knocked flat, as they tacked at that very moment. The bishop's knight, a wiry little Welshman with almost no English, had his eyes bound, and for a while they played blindman's buff. Then the knight wagered he could climb to the top of the mast in full armour, but as he neared the top, a great gust of wind laid the vessel on her beam ends. As she shook herself clear of the water, the knight's gauntleted hands, clumsy on the wet rigging, lost their hold and he fell directly into the sea. They instantly put the ship about, but though she came around exactly to where he fell, there was never any more sign of him. Soon it grew dark, and with no lantern at the masthead, and with only one below to light the mariner's compass, and one other for the use of him who held the wheel, the ship was almost in total darkness. The gust that had blown the knight to his death was the beginning of a squally night, and James and his escort lay huddled with hardly room to stretch or lie flat, let alone to turn or toss, in the stern cabin and the hold. Everywhere was cold spray blowing and the outer dark.

Next morning, the wind had dropped, and instead, the ship had run into a mist, "a haar" the captain called it, and was practically becalmed. James, so sick he could not stand, was carried on deck by Orkney who was afraid the boy was going to die, for still he retched and retched, though nothing came from his lips but a little foam. Orkney laid James on a coil of rope and conferred with the captain. The ship was pitching even more, if possible, from the ground swell than she had been rolling in the wind; the gentry had to clutch the roofing of the low deck house as their leather soles slipped and skidded on the sodden surface. Just as they had decided to try and reach land—the captain reckoned they must be about off Flamborough Head—they heard voices shouting at them and a stubby-looking boat rowed alongside. Another appeared on their starboard. Henry Bereholt ordered all hands to launch the boat, but the two craft now had the *Maryenknyght* pinched and sandwiched between them and a burly, bearded man threw grappling irons across from the aft boat and in an instant the starboard boat had done the same, and men began scrambling over the rail on to the *Maryenknyght* from either side. Sir Archibald lunged forward and pushed the bearded man overboard; he managed to clutch the rail with one hand, but Sir Archibald cut at his fingers with his sword and he plopped into the water. Meanwhile several men had boarded the deck. Lord Orkney had stuffed James back under cover, but in a few moments the *Maryenknyght* was swarming with the pirates. Henry Bereholt had been quickly killed. Most of the *Maryenknyght*'s crew were defenceless and were briskly herded to the end of the deck. Of James's escort Sir Archibald was wounded and disarmed, the others surrendered quickly, being overpowered before they could reach their weapons left in the hold.

Anxious to save James, Orkney whispered to his captor who the boy was, at which the man roared with laughter and said: "Bless you, Sir, we knew that. Him's whom we've come for; worth a king's ransom, he is."

"Who are you?" Orkney asked, and the man replied:

"I'm Hugh atte Fen, one of the chief merchants of Great Yarmouth. We're no pirates; this here is William Oxeney the elder, this John Hacon. They be burgesses. Yon's Nicholas Steward of Cley. In Norfolk I'm mayor of the wool staple, and personally I'm more interested in your cargo than your passengers. But there's someone else where we're going who's mighty keen to get a sight of your princeling."

"Were you the fellow who took Thomas Ra's ship last December, that had to restore the goods to the Scots but lately?" asked Orkney.

"No, no, they were Newcastle folk; they robbed the crew even of their clothing, and sold the cargo on Holy Island. We're taking you down to Westminster, and you'll not be robbed of any of your personal belongings; no petty thieving for me."

"To Westminster? You're taking us to the English king?"

"To whom else? Since 'twas he bade us look out for you, and bring you all to him as quickly as we might."

"But how did the king know of our ship's sailing?" enquired Orkney, and Hugh atte Fen shrugged his shoulders. "You might congratulate me on my sleuthing," he said; "your little cockleshell was about as easy to find in the fog as a bodkin in a truss of hay."

James looked so ghastly that the pirates were concerned. "It will never do if he dies on us," Hugh atte Fen said crossly, and poured some strong spirits from a flask at his belt down the boy's throat. James coughed and choked and spluttered, but the alcohol revived him enough to spit out what he could and to say, angrily: "You know you are breaking the truce? It's mortal sin so to do." Then, abandoning anger and dignity: "Christ, I feel so sick," he said and returned miserably to his retching.

But when they sailed up the Thames three mornings later, James had recovered enough to hang over the ship's rail in great excitement and to enjoy the sights. The river banks were greener than any he had ever seen, and were thick with flowers—primroses, cuckoo-pint, celandines, cowslips, orchis, wild blue forget-me-nots—whilst foaming orchards of frothing cherry and pear and early plum made England, at this first view, seem a garden from out of an illuminated initial in his missal. London was the whitest city he had ever seen; all the houses were whitewashed and dazzling like fine laundry, and even the Tower stood out white like some proud swan, foursquare and shining, in the light of that Maundy Thursday as the *Maryenknyght* came gallantly up the stream on a full tide.

As they came to London Bridge they were stopped for toll. "What pays toll here?" James asked, and Hugh atte Fen, who had grown to like the lad, told him: "Toll's paid on wax and lead, sugar, liquorice, ginger, red and grey squirrel skins, woad and wine, scarlet cloth, fustian, linen and cloth of gold."

"Anything else?" asked James, laughing, as Hugh

paused for breath. And he went on: "Oh, yes, lampreys, salted haddocks, eels, arrowheads and staves; and pigs, sheep and cows, of course."

"And kings' sons?" James asked. Hugh grinned and said, of course, they were extra heavily taxed.

A Lynn boat lay alongside them whilst the customs men were searching the *Maryenknyght* and adding up the bales of wood on their tallies—long sticks with notches. William Oxeney knew the skipper, John Brandon, who shouted to him that William Gideney, Thomas Trussebut, and Robert Bremham had been permitted to employ their vessels the *Trinity*, the *Gabriel*, and the *Holy Ghost* in acts of war against the Scots and Frisians. They had sailed north and had just captured a Scots vessel near Berwick with Sir Robert Logan the Scots Admiral and David Seton the Archdeacon of Ross on board and the king had rewarded them with 500 marks. "We should get at least a thousand for this fledgeling then," Oxeney said, pointing to James who smiled ruefully.

The *Maryenknyght* was moored right opposite the Palace of Westminster, and prisoners and captors rowed up to the water steps. James felt very dishevelled after his sickness and his travels, and feared he did not look his part. He had tried to clean off his scarlet hose, but they were horridly spotted and blotched and he had been sick over the wide sleeves of his blue gown, and everything he wore, even his beaver hat, seemed to smell of salt air and seasickness. He'd never go to sea again, if he could possibly help it, he vowed. Living on an island was a mistake, he felt certain, and he was half relieved he hadn't to go on to France, but on second thoughts considered nothing could be worse than to have arrived so young, and a prisoner, at his journey's end.

The king, Henry IV, was a heavy man, with a square, thick-set jaw, in early middle age, with already greying hair. James was brought straight into a fine room where he was sitting surrounded by a number of courtiers, and the first thing James noticed was how many more chairs there were in England than in Scotland, and then, how many more people. The big room was crowded, but by a continual flowing and movement, a coming and a going of men and women, all dressed in the latest fashion, the women with their hair stuffed back under coifs or horns or steeples or hearts, all with little veils, and most of them seemed to have shaved off their eyebrows, which gave them an eggy look. The men were magnificent; no one in armour, all in peaceful and expensive costumes, so much vair and ermine, gold and marten, so much taffeta and velvet, such figured satins, such an abundance of embroidery, as James had never seen. He bowed profoundly to the king, and stood silent while Hugh atte Fen described his capture. Next the Earl of Orkney, Sir Archibald Edmonstone and William Giffard made their obeisance (Bishop Yonge was somehow missing; James, wondering where he had seen him last, then remembered he had not noticed him in the rowboat). Henry IV laughed loudly as he listened to Hugh's tale, and slapped his calf, roaring out: "If the Scots were grateful, they would have sent this youth to be taught by me, for I, too, know French!" At which the assembled courtiers tittered and guffawed. Henry told Hugh he could keep the boat and its contents for his pains, a recompense greater than even Hugh had hoped, and the man's eyes shone as he kissed the king's hand.

"But have both vessel and cargo valued, in case I have to make retribution to the Scots," said Henry.

James then knelt on one knee and proffered a letter his father had given him for Henry, should misfortune put him into the King of England's power. King Henry handed it to a bishop who stood by his side, and said: "Bishop Beaufort, you're a learned man, English me this."

The bishop bowed, unfolded the parchment and read aloud from it: "Robert, King of Scots, to King Harry, greeting. The world is so full of perverse malice that no cruelty nor offence can be devised that may not be wrought in motions of gold and silver; therefore, because we know Your Highness full of many and noble virtues and with such power and riches that no prince of our day can be compared thereto, we desire thy humanity and support at this time. We trust it is not unknown to you that our elder son, David, is slain miserably in prison by our brother the Duke of Albany, whom we chose to be our governor when we were falling into decrepit age; be so kind, therefor, as to be favourable that the bearer James, our only surviving son, may have permission to live under thy faith and justice."

There was a long moment of silence as he ended, and the king looked with real kindness at the boy, as a low murmur of horror and pity went up from the women. "He's right coloured for a lion cub," the king said to the bishop.

Then James asked: "Your Majesty, please may you tell me who advised you of my journey?"

The king hesitated a moment, and then said, quite loudly: "Your Uncle Albany." And James said: "I suspected as much."

After, the king said: "Take these prisoners forthwith to the Tower. They shall be lodged there with other of their countrymen. Will not the Earl of Fife greet his princely cousin?" And as James rose from his knee, he saw Murdoch shamble forward out of the crowd, as beef-faced, loutish, obese, and odious as ever. They greeted each other coolly whilst the king, watching them, smiled and said: "Your cousin will tell you I am no brutal keeper; he does not complain of his treatment." Whereupon Murdoch bowed low, a sultry smile on his thick lips, and replied that, indeed, no, he had been most civilly used; indeed His Majesty was most generous.

"We will meet for High Mass in an hour," said King Henry and bade two of his captains show James to his prison. These dandified young men, in splendid clothes, brought horses, and James and his suite mounted and rode through cobbled streets, far cleaner than those of Edinburgh or Perth, to the Tower, where gaily-dressed beefeaters took James and his escort in tow. They were lodged in small rooms looking onto the water; pleasant enough, and near the chapel, a round pillared gem of Romanesque architecture, and to James, the loveliest thing he had ever seen. He went there as soon as he had washed, and gave thanks for his safety, and prayed for his father, and Annabella and David and Bishop Traill and David Fleming. How far all seemed now, the living as remote as the dead. But he didn't doubt then but that his ransom would be arranged and he would be home in a few weeks—or perhaps he would have to go straight on to France? Maybe he could go in the company of some of Henry's lords—with an embassy, perhaps, or a bishop? His spirits rose, and dressed in his best-laced doublet—the one he had worn for his belting, a bit on the tight side now, but brought up to date with bunched shoulders and a dagged gorget—his jewelled belt and a houppelande of green broadcloth, high-necked to his ear and fringed with beaver, he felt the equal of any prince in Christendom. Orkney came to fetch him, and guarded by the two captains and attended by six English archers, with short daggers on, to make sure they would not attempt escape, the Scots rode back to Westminster, and dismounted at the Abbey. Within, for all the bustle of the day, with the king and the court arriving, there was immense emptiness and calm. The court itself, on their prie-dieus far up in front, the monks in their stalls, the officiating clergy, seemed tiny, insignificant insects crawling about a giant stone. Hitherto, the great Norman nave at Dunfermline had been James's favourite place in the world; now he knew he preferred Westminster. He learned, later, that the monks were very jealous of the quiet and space, and had built St. Margaret's, just outside, for the common people. The Abbey was open only on great feast days, and then only to the king and his friends; ordinary folk used St. Margaret's or St. Paul's. High Mass went interminably on, and at the place where usually the officiating clergy wash the feet of the poor, King Henry, in crown and full regalia, stepped down from his dais, girded in a towel, and washed the feet of twelve beggars seated ready in the chancel waiting on

71

their stools. A priest held a golden basin, and another poured water from a gilded jug. James was tremendously impressed, though a young lady sitting next him whispered it was a sad pity that the poor didn't enjoy it, and could only be persuaded to come by being well paid. After the service, James stood by whilst King Henry distributed the Maundy pennies outside to the beggars and to all who came. James himself collected a coin to send his nurse as souvenir.

The prisoners that noon ate at the king's high table, seated according to rank. As it was a great feast day, there were roast peacocks served in all their feathers, tame enough meat, and tough, but a delight to the eye on the polished tables. They had trenchers of bread, just as in Scotland, but James observed that instead of dipping them in the gravy and eating them, they were left till the end of the meal and then given to the poor who swarmed into the room when the king and his nobility had done their eating. Several of Henry Percy's relatives came and asked James how he was, and he was introduced to young Griffith Glendower, Owen Glendower's youngest son, who was sixteen, and had already been ten months in the Tower, having been taken after the battle on the Usk in May, 1405. Griffith was a gawky hobbledehoy, with a pointed, ferrety face and freckled skin and sharp cheekbones that armoured weak blue eyes; the whole face was thatched with straight lank hair of a pale mouse colour. James looked him over coolly, with that schoolboy cruelty that sees only too clearly, and decided he was second rate but unobjectionable. "He'd do beautifully as my squire—only in view of our ages being the wrong way round, I imagine I shall have to be his," thought James.

The first night in the Tower was terrifying; so many soldiers, the midnight changing of the guard, and constant noise of clanking through the night. James wondered if it were true that Owen Glendower were really a wizard, and if so, whether Griffith could read in the dark in James's mind all the not-very-polite things he'd been thinking about him. James was cold too, and could hear the rats scampering about his room, one jumped on his bed, but James squealed so the beast was more scared than he. Yet Griffith did not wake.

Next morning, being Good Friday, the two boys, James and Griffith, with William Giffard and the Earl of Orkney and Sir Archibald Edmonstone, rode to St. Paul's, which was hard by, for the Mass of the Pre-Sanctified. First there was Tenebrae, and the children, and many of the grownups too, had brought clappers, and waited tensely for the moment when all the candles are put out, and they could make what noise they would to signify the rolling to of the sepulchre stone. After Mass, followed the Adoration of the Cross, when first the priests, and then all the people, crawled on their hands and knees to kiss the uncovered feet of the veiled crucifix, and the rich brought money and the poor brought eggs for offerings. Then crucifix and empty pyx were placed together in a violet-strewn grotto, and covered with a purple pall. James was shocked, after the greater decorum of Scotland, to find how here the churches seemed to be the real home of the people; in them the beggars begged, women whispered gossip, merchants came to discuss the rate of exchange, pickpockets plied their trade, and prostitutes solicited. The markets were open—or, rather, though roofed, they were in no wise weatherproof, and it was the churches which served the common people for all indoor purposes, even eating and sleeping. James saw several workmen pulling out their hunk of bread and bottles of ale or sack and munching contentedly and unconcernedly in the very presence of their Maker, whilst on a hard bench two aged women snored.

On Easter Sunday morning, the boys went again to St. Paul's and during Mass, there was a procession to the grotto, where now three figures, dressed as the three Marys, asked the traditional questions of another clad as an angel, and the choir apostrophised: "Dic nobis, Maria, quid vidisti in via?" "Tell us, Mary, what did you see on

73

your way?" and the answer came back, "Sepulchrum Christi viventis, et gloriam eius resurgentis." "The tomb of the living Christ and His Risen Glory." It was the first Easter James had ever been away from home, and he felt very far away, though kind Lord Orkney did his best to cheer him, and Henry asked James to the palace for supper, which was a splendid feast, lit by many torches, at which the girls and women ate at the same tables as the men. James was surprised at the freedom women had at the English court, for it seemed they shared in the whole life, and, indeed, shared in almost everything the men did. On the morrow, Easter Monday, for instance, most of the ladies were going hawking with the men, and those to whom James talked seemed to know as much about hoods and jesses and hawk-handling generally as any boy.

In a very few days James had already had enough of the Tower, and indeed, of England, and was aching to go home, or to get out and to get on with life. He was fretting, too, to know what Henry intended to do with him, how much ransom he would ask, and was finding his captivity most wearisome. For he was no longer allowed outside the keep, and when he asked the men-at-arms or the varlets who brought his meals, what had occasioned this change in his treatment, he could get no reply. Henry IV seemed to have forgotten him, and the excursions, to church and court, that had amused him so well over Easter, and had been freely permitted and even encouraged then, seemed already in a far past. James felt himself for the first time now verily a prisoner.

One morning, James had not counted how many mornings after, the constable of the Tower sent for him. "What can I have done now?" James asked Griffith, for Griffith had told James that he had never been sent for except to get a scolding—after he had been caught drinking with the guard, or dicing with them, or trying to climb down the walls and escape by swimming across the moat; and though James had done none of these things, all the same he felt anxious.

The constable had a letter in his hand, and bade James be seated. "I have sad news for you," he began; "your father, King Robert III of Scotland, is no more. He departed this life on St. Ambrose's day." James had started at the news, but now was suddenly wary. He feared some trap. Aloud, he said:

"He was in good health when I left. Can you tell me what was the manner of his death?"

The constable paused, and James blurted out, "Was he murdered?"

"No," replied the constable. "He was at his castle of Rothesay. The bishop that was with you—Griffin Yonge —escaped, by night, from the *Maryenknyght* before you reached London. Yonge swam to shore in Kent, and found men willing to set him on his way back to Scotland. I imagine the local priest or abbot helped him. Anyway, he got to Scotland in seven days, and on Easter Sunday evening your father was informed of your capture as he sat at supper. He left his meat, and, thereafter, refused either food or comfort."

"And then?" James asked.

The constable referred to a letter in his hand. "The most excellent prince lingered for some time in failing strength, but after a few days departed this life, giving his body into the keeping of the mother of all, and sending back his soaring spirit to his Maker with all devoutness."

"Left he any messages for me? Did he not speak of me?" James asked, but the constable shook his head.

"This letter says only that he asked that he should be interred at Paisley, before the same altar in the abbey church where Walter Stewart, your ancestor, is buried, and that on his tomb should be inscribed these words: 'Here lies the worst of kings and the saddest of men.'"

James was silent, staring out of the window at the busy Thames, crowded as a market place with barges and skiffs and rowing boats. He seemed far away, and the constable was embarrassed. He had expected the boy to weep; then he could have essayed consolation. He was confused by this rapt, distant silence. After several minutes he spoke: "Have you nothing to say? No further questions to ask?"

James looked at him as though seeing him for the first time. His clear eyes were cold, hard, unmoistened by tears. "Nothing," he replied. "Have I your leave to go?"

"To be sure," said the constable as graciously as he knew how, and was opening his mouth again to say some little phrase of condolence, some trite banality of current courtesy, when James, his hand on the door, turned to him unsmiling.

"My first act as king is to ask a permission of my jailer," he said. "That, I shall never forget."

CHAPTER SIX

☐ It seemed that from whatever direction the wind would blow, the boys could yet smell the sweet, putrid stench of the corpses. The plague was abroad in May, 1407, in London, and in the first twelve days of June, fifteen thousand died from out of that city then numbering forty thousand souls. At the same summer, in England, over thirty thousand perished. No man stirred abroad without rue or wormwood in his hand, and myrrh and redoag in his mouth; no man spoke to another in the street lest they come from a plagued house or carried the infection. The country flowers withered unpurchased in the markets, lest any smelling them inhale infection, and in every house people burnt odoriferous woods, juniper and ash, rosemary and pine, cypress and laurel.

James had already grown accustomed to the continual tintinnabulation of the bells, for England then was indeed "the ringing isle" and from dawn to dusk there was forever a sound of bells from the one hundred and fifty churches of London. But now it was mostly the soul-bell or the forth-farre bell that kept ringing, for thousands were dying daily, and the priests as fast as their penitents, so one might go in to shrive a man, and die himself beside him, so swiftly the disease ran its course. At first it was possible to distinguish between three-day and five-day plague. The first came with a fever and a spitting of blood; the second began with pallor, a bitter taste in the mouth, some sneezing and swellings in the groin and the armpits. People caught it by looking at each other, even without speech: cattle and sheep caught it from men, until the very wolves would not approach a village where the plague was, but let the healthy bide safely with the sick, nor molested any.

"You must shut all southern windows, and avoid the sun, warm winds, and everything which generates heat," the constable of the Tower told James and Griffith, and he would not let them leave the Tower grounds. But as they walked on the walls they could hear the dying groans from the miserable hovels propped against them, or the ravings of delirium. They heard a woman first shrieking in childbirth, then suddenly silenced by death, whilst her infant gave but one cry between womb and tomb. Some of the Tower varlets were so scared that at the sight of a coffin they would fall into a shivering, and die as much of fright as of the ill. Once the boys saw some pigs a long way down below them in the mud, tossing and tumbling with their snouts some clothes that had been thrown down into the street: they turned but once or twice about, and then fell dead.

James reacted by eating sparingly, hearing Mass daily, and trying to live so that if suddenly he were to die, he would not be surprised. He played musical instruments all day long, or had them played to him: he hardly looked out of the windows any more. Griffith, on the other hand, became a very heavy drinker, and collected gruesome stories and anecdotes. Some of the poor squatters, in the hovels close to the Tower walls, to exclude the white spirit of the plague, had spun threads and webbed them over the openings of the doors and windows. With the dew on them they shone like giant spiderings.

"Dost know, James," Griffith asked him, "that the buboes are of all sizes; some are small as a lentil, others big as a pea or an egg, and some grow hard and will not burst, causing such pain that men wax mad and throw themselves from windows or wrapped only in a sheet run into the churchyards and lie down in any open grave they can find?"

James regretfully let Griffith lead him to the shuttered window, through whose slats the boys saw a man climb high on to a roof and hurl tiles into the street, aiming them at the passers-by. "He's mad with pain," said Griffith, gloating.

The constable did all he could to protect his young prisoners. He made them eat a fig and several filberts every morning before breakfast, and take rue on a fasting stomach. He urged them to avoid wrath and sadness, and warned James that intellectuals took the plague most easily; idiots, he declared, with a sideways glance at Griffith, survived best.

Corpses were buried as quickly as the Cellites, or burying friars, could carry them to the plague pits and shovel earth and quicklime over them. They would throw sand or peas against the windows of each house as they passed in melancholy procession. If no one answered, the corpse bearers went in and brought out the bodies. The dogs were more faithful than their masters, for, whereas a mother would desert her child, or a husband his wife, if he thought them stricken or himself, the dogs stayed even by the decomposing bodies. Men died so fast and their relatives, when left alive, were so anxious to get them out of the house, that often the bodies would be bundled into the street and left, sitting or standing, or propped into some angle or wall or cornice, to rot before they stiffened.

Henry IV, before himself leaving for Windsor, gave James and Griffith into the care of Lord Grey of Codenore, the king's chamberlain, and keeper of Nottingham Castle.

It was already fifteen months since James had been taken prisoner, and he had not yet lost hope that he would be redeemed or ransomed. The Scottish council-general that had met in June, 1406, had recognised James as king, but had confirmed his Uncle Albany as governor. From then on, Albany dated acts of state by the year of his governorship, and used his own great seal. An embassy had been sent from Scotland in July to demand James's release; four knights had been well paid to act as commissioners "sent to England for the liberation of the son of the late king." But they had failed, and James wondered if indeed they had tried very hard; for though another embassy had been appointed, this one had not even set out. Meanwhile Henry IV conferred often by letter with Albany, about the truce between England and Scotland, but there was no mention of James in all their letters. Young, sanguine, and hopeful as he was, James began to grow bitter.

"I count here as much as that poor fool mammet counts at my uncle's court," James told Griffith. "Thomas Warde, the beggar from Trumpington, near Cambridge, that was discovered in Skye by the Lord of the Isles, and was thought by him to be King Richard, is as truly King of England as I am King James I of Scotland." And he went on sadly to quote the jingle:

> It is of English nation
> The common kind condition
> Of truce the virtue to forget
> When they will them for winning set.

A soldier would bring the two boys their breakfast: half a loaf each of household bread, two pints of beer, and three mutton bones broiled. Sometimes instead they had a chicken, or a piece of broiled beef. This morning there were some new-pulled radishes, and a taste of precious salt, for the constable believed in vegetables and exercise as specifics against the plague.

"You are to be ready at eight, my lords," the man said. "Lord Grey will be calling for you at that hour."

James looked out at the Tower gardens, heavy with roses: it was a perfect summer day. "One accustoms oneself to everything," he said, thoughtfully. "I never imagined I'd be sorry to leave this place, and yet I am: at least we had the ten lions and leopards to watch, and their melancholy roaring was companionable: king of beasts, King of Scots, both mewed up and fed by hand. . . ."

Griffith interrupted: "I bet your food costs more than sixpence a day—that's all the beasts' costs each daily."

"William," James called, struggling into his skin-tight waist-high pants; "William," and William Giffard appeared.

"Your Majesty?" he asked.

James grinned. "What have we got to wear?" he asked.

"Our wardrobe is pretty thin," William Giffard replied. "Your Majesty has grown out of most of your clothes since last you went travelling."

Murdoch now appeared, and James groaned. "About as much privacy as on the *Maryenknyght*," he said, loudly. "I always imagined prisons had the advantage of being solitary places."

Murdoch took no notice of his cousin's rudeness, but asked, "D'you ken this Lord Grey?"

James said he'd seen him around the court. "He's pillaged Scotland right up to the Firth of Forth. I've been out against him myself," said Murdoch. "He held Roxburgh Castle for three years."

"How tactful to give me into his charge," James said.

"He fought against my father, too. He held Brecon Castle against him," said Griffith.

"He's a learned sort of fellow," said Murdoch, "and his wife was a cousin of that poet you rate so high, James; of Geoffery Chaucer."

"That's news," said James. "He can be my jailer if he's a poet, and welcome."

"King Henry means you to be well schooled," said Griffith; "he means you to grow into a nice intelligent vassal king, full of good will towards England, with a first-rate English education at the back of you."

But before he'd finished speaking, James had thrown

himself on him. "Say that again, even suggest that Scotland's king could be England's vassal, and I'll murder you, I'll throttle you, I'll . . ."

Griffith was twice James's height, but the suddenness of the attack had thrown him down. Now he got up, shook James off as though he were a setting dog, and Griffith himself a baited bull.

"You needn't take on so," said Murdoch; "your brother-in-law, the Earl of Douglas, became King Henry's man, and his four sons with him, for his whole life, before he and Orkney set off for Scotland, and they left hostages aplenty, too."

"They've been home over a year," said James, longingly.

"Douglas is back here now," said Murdoch, "that's what I came over early to tell you: he's been back in captivity over a month, now he's after going to Scotland again, and he's coming to pay his duty to you here before he goes."

"His duty to me, when he's Henry's man. Whom does he think he deceives?" growled James. "But I'll be glad if he takes some messages from me to your father, who doesn't seem in any hurry to get us home."

Murdoch reddened. King Henry had shown him, only yesterday, Albany's letter, thanking the English king for the favours shown his son, Murdoch, his cousin, the Earl of Douglas, and his dearest nephew, the Earl of Mar." Of his other nephew, that was his king, Albany had made no mention. Murdoch knew his father was doing everything he could to obtain *his* release, whilst leaving James exactly where he was. He knew, too, that his own duty was to James, his king, above even his father. But his thick mind, hardly less clumsy than his lumbering, huge body, was thinly penetrated by conscience or soul; both illumined it in brief flashes only. After all, he reflected, there was nothing he, a prisoner, could now do. And maybe James was safer and better off where he was. So he comforted himself and stilled whatever qualms he may occasionally have had.

William Giffard came in again, carrying James's tall boots. "The Earl of Douglas is come, and Lord Grey is at the gate, and has sent up for you."

Douglas followed him in, in full armour, but bareheaded. He began to bow low over James's hand, but James hugged and kissed him, eagerly asking after his sister, and his widowed sister-in-law, and the others at home. Douglas looked superbly fit; he had ridden hard, and the long outdoor days had tanned him; his hair was tawny with sunlight. "I must have word with you in private," he whispered, and James led him to the round chapel, and knelt beside him, well away from the walls.

"Now speak," he whispered, and Douglas told James, what he already knew, that Albany was trying to prevent his return, not to hasten it, and added that, as far as he could gather, Henry IV wished James well, and that he, Douglas, thought the best thing would be if he could gather a king's party, whilst in Scotland, and bring pressure indirectly, through such a party, on Albany. "The trouble is he cares for nothing except to be popular," Douglas said. "He doesn't care what happens to the country; his liberality costs him nothing. For example, he has refused to impose the general tax on every hearth, which had been proposed by the parliament at Perth, lest the poor curse him who introduced such a measure. He seeks the blessings of the common people beyond measure!" Douglas snorted. "You'll never get him to raise your ransom. He's making it hard, too, for you to govern when you do get back, with his happy-go-lucky softness."

"Why cannot I run away?" James asked. "After all, my kingly word was given under duress. I was captured in a time of truce and am held here against my will and the will of my people. I have absolutely no obligation to stay."

Douglas shook his head. "You gave your word to your people that you would do what was best for them. It's not a question of your duty to King Henry, even if you had given your word. The fact that he jails you for no fault, and sets guards over you, would absolve you: for a man cannot be jailed and paroled at the same time, and the king breaks his side of whatever covenant you have made by not trusting you, by putting soldiers and spies about you. But I'm not sure this is the moment to go back to Scotland. Woe to the land whose ruler is a child! I think Albany will do less harm than a council of regency might, with me to run it and you as king."

James looked miserably sad. "But I belong there—in Scotland. And I've only one life, and I'm wasting it here."

"You've got to study awhile yet," said Douglas. "There's small harm that I know not enough Latin to follow the Mass, but you have many things to learn."

"But I'll be a stranger when I get back. I'm fast forgetting my Scots already, speaking only French and English here, and my people will not love a fancy foreign king."

Douglas wondered whether he should try and explain to the boy that his best, possibly his only, chance of survival lay in remaining where he was. The anarchy in Scotland was worse than during his father's lifetime, and Albany no longer made any serious attempt to rule. Over the great western nobles he had little control: the Earl of Sutherland ruled more than a million acres; the Earl of Argyll almost as many. The western nobles dwelt as kings in their castles, with many pipers, harpers, bards, and fools; with absolute sovereignty over their subjects, who were bound to them not only by feudal ties, but also by blood. Aloud he said: "You shall come, I promise, when you are needed and wanted. But not yet. No one has yet asked for you. You must wait. I promise I'll do everything I can, and I can keep you fully informed. Get out of London now; it would never do for you to perish of the plague. And mind your books; you'll need all your learning when you come home, and you won't have much time for reading when you're king, in fact, as well as in name."

William Giffard, who had been waiting in a back pew, came up, and reminded James that Lord Grey was waiting below, and they all clattered down the stone stairs.

James held his brother-in-law's stirrup whilst he mounted.

"I'm buying a whole lot of flour and barley to take back with me," Douglas said; "we've had woeful harvests these two years, and our stocks are low for seeding this autumn."

"God speed you," James said, and the tears blinded him, so that he hardly saw Lord Grey who had reined back his horse and was waiting till Douglas had started.

"James, could one of your men see about the keeping of my London hotel?" Douglas called out, reining back his horse.

But James shook his head. "I've no one left in the city now, I'm taking the few I have with me to Nottingham. You'll have to send someone down," he called back. Then mounted. "I'm sorry to have detained your lordship," he said, politely, and Lord Grey laughed. "No hurry, except to get out of this charnel house. I've seen and smelt more corpses today than in all my life heretofore."

"One gets accustomed to the stink," said James; "though it cuts the edge of my appetite still."

All that day Lord Grey and his charges were sizing each other up. Grey admired the truculent dignity of James, who, though he was rather short and slight for his age, was beautifully proportioned, and stood the long hours—they rode nearly fifty miles, and it was pretty warm—without a murmur, whilst Griffith, on the contrary, was a scatter-brained chatterbox who burbled ceaselessly on, now grumbling at his stirrup leather that chafed his leg through his red hose, now at the horseflies that maddened horse and rider indiscriminately. James, who had not stirred out of London since his capture, was enchanted to be again in the country. The green fields made him almost cry out with excitement, and he kept asking about every bird and flower and tree they met, though it was Griffith he asked, nor spoke to Lord Grey unless spoken to: then he always answered politely, and to the point, but made no bid to continue the conversation. His face was wonderfully mobile; once, when a kingfisher darted across a small stream they were fording, it was suddenly so lit up that Lord Grey caught his breath sharply; to care so much, to be so vulnerable, must mean the boy's orphaned, prisoner's life was unbearable. And the loneliness! And yet, he reflected, to live so completely in the present, in the moment of a bird's flight, must be reward no less than punishment. For James seemed a normal enough lad, not introspective nor unduly quiet. He and Griffith sang songs together as they rode, and William Giffard, too. In fact, they all enjoyed themselves and each other, and James had decided by nightfall that he was not sorry, after all, to have left the Tower, and be once more free to ride, even though he was not free to choose whither he rode. What freedom had anyone, anyway? Boy, one was held by pastors and masters; man, by professional duties and service; and a king had less of liberty than any of his subjects, so fiercely light-encircled was he from dawn to dusk. Free to abdicate, he supposed; free to commit suicide; those were a king's two freedoms, for freedom, like everything else including the Godhead Itself, could only be negatively defined. A king is not free to choose his country or his consort; but perhaps his court and his councillors? Yet, even there, only to a certain limited extent.

Nottingham was far the most comfortable castle James had ever known. Lady Grey was not only very beautiful, and still young, in her late twenties, she also was intelligent, well educated, and a good musician. Her friends were civilised, and she expected a very high standard of manners. She was a feminine, dainty, imperious woman, whose small nose went up if anyone spat or belched in her presence. She was frankly bored with children, her own or anyone else's, and treated the boys, James and Griffith, from the first, as though they were young men. She expected them to remain standing so long as she was in the room, to carry her embroidery, to hold her stirrup when she mounted her horse, to carve her meat, to carry her messages to kitchen or pantry. In short, these pensioners, for whose keep and care her husband was well paid, were treated as esquires, though one was a king, and the other the son of an independent prince. Both boys grumbled, to each other, though not to her, and both tumbled over each other to do her bidding, and boasted of her favours. They had no time to find life in the castle dull, for they had a heavy programme of work: tutors, lay and clerical, came at almost every hour of the day: James learnt to speak French fluently, and learnt Latin and Spanish well enough to write and read both. He had already completed the *trivium*—grammar, rhetoric, and logic. Now he began on arithmetic, geometry, astronomy, and music—the *quadrivium*. Besides he learnt fencing, and tilting, and shooting with the bow, which he inwardly despised as a peasant's pursuit. Yet he took great pains to learn to shoot exceedingly well, for he knew the English victories of Crécy and Poitiers, as well as the recent Scots tragedy of Otterburn, had been due to the archers alone. James learnt history from English teachers, and spat it out as he learnt, yet still it left a mark on him, if only in that he realised there was another point of view; that the English had an argument, and that all and each of the awful things they had done to Scotland they similarly accused the Scots of doing. Constantly on the defensive though he was, James had no feeling of being in a minority nor of inferiority: he was king, and thus knew exactly what his people felt; he belonged to every Scot anywhere, from the great Bruce his ancestor, to the poorest hireling fighting the English on the muddy fields of northern France, and they to him. By especial grace of God given him to fulfil the duties of his estate, he shared in all their feelings. This, to James, was no strange esoteric doctrine, but a simple fact, that was part both of the communion of saints, in which he believed by faith, and of the structure of society, into which he was born and to which he adhered.

The boys each had a room of their own, and to James his was a sanctuary. He would lean out of the window for hours on end happily looking at the flat fields, osier-edged, or staring at a heron fishing in the moat, or a kestrel circling over the lawn above some unseen shrew or vole. He would see all of each sunrise and sunset, and came to hate missing either, for his two windows faced south and east, and he felt cheated if dawn or dusk happened and he were not there to watch.

One day, as he was leaning out, he was suddenly aware that Lady Grey stood by him. He had not heard her come, but now she was so close he could feel her breathing. As she turned to speak, he smelt her breath, and it smelt sweet and most pleasant, and he could see the down on her cheeks against the late afternoon light. It was mid-August, and James was fifteen; he was a little taller than his hostess, and, quickly, he put his arms round her, and kissed what he could reach—her cheek, her ear, and, because she turned her face away, her tall forehead. They stood so a few moments, then she looked up, half laughing. "Did you enjoy that, my squire?" she asked, and James didn't answer except now to kiss her more—her eyes, her nose, but she still kept her mouth away. Presently she stirred, and pulled herself neatly from him. "Is it the first time you've kissed anyone?" she asked, and James blushed, and said: "Yes, do I do it so badly? Or did you really not know, and ask to find out? Let me do it again . . . now, please."

But she shook her head, holding him at arm's length (which wasn't so far, for he still could feel her two breasts against his two hands, and her heart beating), and she sighed, and said: "No, you do it very well. Indeed. I asked, because I thought you had done it before, but I'm glad you haven't." Then, looking away from him, she said: "I wish I hadn't."

And James, puzzled, said: "What do you mean? Wish you hadn't let me—or wish you hadn't ever let anyone?"

And she said: "I wish I hadn't ever before, and that this were the first time."

"Isn't it always the first time, if it's someone else, someone new?" James asked.

88

And she sighed and said: "I suppose so. But it would be lovely to be fifteen once more, and all to do again."

James began kissing her hands, and her tiny wrists, and fumbling with her sleeves, trying to get his hands inside her dress, to reach her bare breasts. But he half stopped to look at her, and say: "You're so lovely. I wish you were me, so you could have the fun of seeing you, of touching you, of enjoying yourself, and knowing just how wonderful you are." Then his desire came over him like a fever, and he felt he must go on, and on, kissing her, must not stop to speak or to think, hardly to breathe, for there was so little time. Someone was sure to come, and he must get her down somehow, must crush her, choke her, get onto her, into her. Yet all the while he was actually only standing shyly beside her, pawing her veil, and awkwardly kissing her chin, and stroking her hair where her coif had fallen back. He was trembling so violently that he could not steady his cold, damp hands. It was she who now drew closer to him and laid his hands inside her dress at the neck, so they could feel her warm flesh directly.

Even whilst he wanted her so that it hurt, so that he felt swollen and urgent, James thought: "This is my goddess—this is all, this woman I want," and now the more she pushed him away the more immediate became his need of her, so that his discomfort was part of his desire, and he felt he must rape her or burst. Meanwhile she wriggled and squirmed in his arms, half scared of what she had provoked, and he squeezed her tighter and tighter kissing her violently now, biting her cheeks and still trying to reach her lips. Suddenly Griffith's voice outside calling James froze them both, and James settled her headdress, and patted and pulled her sleeves silently into place. She drew away from him, and said crossly, aloud: "Well, don't forget next time," as though she had been scolding him, and walked away from him to meet Griffith in the doorway. James stayed where he was, half hidden by the arras.

Griffith took a step toward her. "My lady! You here! Forgive my shouting—I'd no idea."

And she smiled conspiratorially up at Griffith in the almost dark and said: "Like you, I couldn't find the king and so sought him. He was watching the dogs."

James felt sick with shame, and dared not look at her, knowing her mischievous eyes burning him. How had she known that when she came in he had been watching three hounds trailing a bitch over across on the far side of the moat?

He hardly heard Griffith, now standing beside him, apologising: "I came only to tell you King Henry is on his way to stay here, and is bringing the Prince of Wales with him." Then Griffith looked down and saw, in the half-light, James's clenched hands trembling, and with rare reticence looked quickly up, all the way up, to James's scarlet face, and then out at the solid, velvety sky, and added: "But my news is stale; I expect her ladyship has told you herself."

And James lied squarely, and said: "Yes, she did; it should be fun, and I expect we'll get some good hunting, and at least one day's holiday."

The boys went down to supper together, and Lady Grey treated them no differently, though she could feel James's eyes glued to her. She kept her own modestly down, her long lashes curling unfashionably along her cheek, for though most women cut theirs off and hid their hair and shaved their eyebrows, she had not touched her lashes nor her thin black eyebrows that grew like featherstitching, above which her forehead rose tall and white and astonished. She was purring inside at James's homage, blushing and clumsy though it was, for she liked more than anything in the world for a man to be in love with her; any man, even a half-fledged one, like James. She did not enjoy the act of love itself, that was the end of the game, checkmate, touché, half as much as every move of the approaches. These to her were more than anything else in the world, and she played her lovers as she sucked her sweetmeats, slowly, to make them last longer—each time, each one more slowly, hoping each would last still longer than the previous one. She was looking forward excitedly to King Henry and his son's visits, for she had heard the prince was a lusty young man, in constant disgrace for wenching. Two kings and two princes, all at once! She had never felt so nourished nor so happy in all her life, and looked quite kindly at Lord Grey down the length of the high table, whilst James, catching her glance, wondered how she could stand her husband. She looked so young and he so old; he was certainly all of forty, and it must be horrid for her. James blushed at his own thoughts, that had run forward to her undressing, and he bit his lips and blushed again; how unseemly that he, a Christian, that he, a king and a king's son, should be drooling after his keeper's wife, for all the world like the dogs he had watched after the bitch in heat. Luckily, his constrained, feverish air passed unnoticed in the general chatter about the king's visit, or was put down to James's excitement at the news.

That night James dreamed he was riding a splendid charger, that stood all of seventeen hands. He turned the horses head towards Scotland, laid his hand on its mane, and together they covered the ground at a steady gallop. Gradually, horridly, the horse shrank, grew smaller and smaller, until James's legs touched the ground on either side: the beast slowed up, too, until it was but a hobby horse that James pushed along with his feet. Suddenly, instead, he found himself swimming in a warm lake or sea—the blue deep around him was so clear he could see his feet as he trod water. But inevitably, the water began to grow shallower: his feet touched land, he lay down to swim trying to stay covered, but the water receded, until he woke, scared, in a sticky mess. Again he dreamed, of a girl's face that was Lady Grey's, yet not hers, more mocking, sadder too, and, as he kissed her, he found himself looking into the calyx of a white water lily, that closed and sank into the cold deeps. He half woke again, and this time before losing consciousness willed his

dream, that he might enjoy her—or at least himself. And
then thought, that is a sin, to will an evil dream, and to
fall asleep willing it so he made an act of contrition, but
was afraid to go to sleep again lest he die in his sleep
and in his sin. Then the lines of the hymn for Compline
that in Dante the souls in Purgatory sing so sweetly,
came into his mind: he had never before known what
they meant; now he said them over aloud:

> Procul recedant somnia
> Et noctium phantasmata
> Hostemque nostrum comprime
> Ne polluantur corpora.

His body was polluted now, he supposed, for to desire to
dream was no less sinful than to do: perhaps more sinful,
for to do implied some love, some charity, it could not be
pure lust, mere self-gratification, at least there must always be the hope that the beloved was enjoying herself
also. But he must stop such thoughts, must—but could
not, for the cocks had begun crowing, and her face as it
had been under his kisses came into his mind; she is
looking so now, asleep beside her lord, he thought, and
then got out of his bed and knelt on the cold stone flags
beside it, and looked out of his window that faced east,
and read Prime. But his teeth chattered, and his skin was
goose-fleshed, and the shadow of her image came between him and the stiff vellum page he held and her
warm ghost mocked his chilled thought and prayer. So
he got back into bed, and as the warmth thawed him he
came again, and the orgasm made him feel as if hot and
cold water were flowing into him, and out from him; his
head felt so heavy he could hardly lift it from the pillow.
Then knowing himself to be empty and utterly lonely, he
cried, and, stuffing the pillow into his mouth to make less
noise, he fell into a dreamless sleep.

CHAPTER SEVEN

☐ King Henry did not look well, James thought, and it was obvious he and Prince Hal were getting on badly. The prince brought his own retinue, and whenever he and his father were together, they snapped and yapped at each other in such a way that, had they been curs, they would have been separated; as they were king and king's son, their loyal and less loyal subjects sat uncomfortably listening. Henry IV was unreceptive to the flirtatious Lady Grey: he seemed to prefer hunting hare with her husband: Prince Hal, on the other hand, cut James right out, and no wonder: he was most beautiful of visage, his neck long, his body slender and lean, his bones small. And he was so swift and strong that he would take James and Griffith with him into the park, and, on foot, without hounds or bow, he would catch a wild buck or a doe with his bare hands. James and Griffith hero-worshipped him and were madly jealous at the same time. Prince Hal evidently liked King James, though he poked fun at him for being so serious and obedient and studious. He reminded James of David, his dead brother: there was the same nervous anxiety to have his cake and eat it; to have the honour and respect due him as king's son, and the fun and frolic that were of his age

—or, more correctly, that became his youth. There was also the same fundamental seriousness of outlook, and a powerful ambition; both David and now Prince Hal behaved as though they knew their time was short.

"There must be a tournament, there has to be a tournament," Prince Hal had said as soon as he arrived, and after many consultations, the lawyers in the royal suite produced two Bordeaux squires—at least one was a squire, and the other was a franklin, a burgess, who had a grievance. The burgess accused the squire of trying to persuade him to go over to the King of France—incitement to treason, in fact. "So they must fight it out," Prince Hal told James, and the three young men went off to ask Lord Grey about carpenters and joiners, for the stands and seats and the date.

"They'll need a lot of stripped and sawn wood," said James, and the harassed Lord Grey wondered where it could be found, but a fine arena was finally made, and the boys tilted so much in it before the tournament began, that the ground was horridly cut up and muddy and the horses slipped and squelched and skidded. But it was a great success. Lady Grey looked her loveliest, and gave red roses to the victors; a vast crowd came out from the town, and gaped at the king and the nobility, and huzzaed for King Henry. In the evening, there was much music, and dancing, too: basses dances, that were a gliding to the music of viols, harps, cor, and flageolets, and hauts dances, which were country dances, boisterous and bouncing. Lady Grey danced with both kings, and with Prince Hal and with Griffith, who she insisted was a prince, too, though it made King Henry frown to hear her say it. But James made it quite clear that he preferred dancing with girls of fifteen, and, he thought, behaved with great dignity and kept her ladyship in her place; though to her he seemed but a sulky boy with whom she need not bother, now she had grown men and great warriors with whom to wanton.

Prince Hal told James the Scottish news: Jedburgh had been retaken by the Scots, and Douglas was still at liberty. The Earl of Mar had seized a ship of Dick Whittington's, and a Flemish ship carrying Scottish goods had been taken in exchange. Yet in spite of these skirmishes, the truce between the two countries had been renewed for another year.

Prince Hal was very frank with James, treating the boy, for all he was seven years his junior and so differently circumstanced, as his equal. He told him of the current labour and Lollard troubles that Henry IV, his father, had inherited from the last region.

The day before the king left he sent for James. The boy found him alone, in a sunny parlour that looked west over the park. As James came in, Henry said to him: "Are you happy here?"

James said: "Happy, Sire? When I'm a prisoner, in exile and unable to do the job I was born to do?"

"That's politics, ethics, not an answer. Are they good to you here? Are you enjoying just everyday life—your food, your lessons?"

James froze. "Lord Grey is just and considerate," he began stiffly.

But Henry impatiently shook his head. "Forget I'm King of England, and you are King of Scots. I asked because I'd like to have you with me at court, now you're grown up. I'd like you to learn some law, have some idea how a kingdom works, how things get paid for. But if you are very happy here, I'll not move you again. It doesn't always pay to pull things, or people, up by the roots to see how they are growing. But if you would like to come, James? To be raised with my own sons, as one of them?"

James considered. "My uncle delays overmuch in the matter of my ransom," he began. Then noticed how old and ill King Henry looked, unhealthily stout, pasty-faced and puffy, and thought: "I'd much better be at the centre of things, watching the play at the top table, even if I can't join in the game yet." So aloud he said: "I'd love to come, Sire; Your Majesty is most kind."

King Henry's pug's eyes, like lollipops on sticks, twinkled. "I think Your Majesty is well advised to accept my offer," he said.

James thought, with a sudden rush of emotion, of Lady Grey. Could he live without her, he wondered, and knew, with a child-like acceptance of this truth, that no person mattered or would matter enough, ever, to change the pattern of his life. "I must dree my own weird," he told himself, and bowing himself out of King Henry's presence, went to join Prince Hal on the tennis court.

That evening, James sat at the high table next Prince Hal, and the talk was all of Lollardry, for there had that day been trial made of a Lollard, one John Badby of Evesham, who had been sent to be examined by Thomas Arundel, Archbishop of Canterbury.

As Langland wrote, James thought:

At meat in their mirth when the minstrels are still
Then tell they of the Trinity a tale or two
Thus they drivel at their dais the deity to guard
And gnaw God with the gorge when their gut is full.

"What did your man, Badby, pretend?" asked the king.

"He was very blasphemous," said the archbishop sadly. "I only arrived today for the trial, so had no chance of conferring with him before it. It is as Lord Grey has said, that as reformers we cannot quarrel with the Lollards; they are right, every time, and we are wrong."

"Yet the Lollards do not accuse the clergy or the bishops of atrocious crime or of sinful life," said the king's younger son, John, Duke of Bedford.

"No one would hearken to them if they did," said Lord Grey; "it would be merely ludicrous. Respectability compasses the clergy about. The trouble is that their high secular offices absorb them; the dye of their many worldly contacts comes off on them, so that they are rainbow-hued, instead of dressed in the single white shift of unworldliness."

"Some are even leaders of very earthly armies," said the archbishop. "My lord of Norwich glories in his crowds of slain."

"Since the Franciscans no longer keep to their primitive poverty, the poor priests, as these Lollards call themselves, are certainly the most spectacular group of people in England, publicly practising Apostolic poverty," said Prince Hal.

"To the people," agreed John Bedford, "it is the russet-robed Lollards who represent true reform. Their heretical views are over most people's heads. Most people's theology doesn't go beyond their first catechism. It's the social revolution of 1381 for which they're grateful. Do you remember that Wycliffe said that Archbishop Sudbury and Chancellor Hailes both died in a state of sin?"

"I wonder how he knew," mused the archbishop; "the Church doesn't; she doesn't know that even Judas is in hell; she only knows some of the names of those who are in heaven."

James asked: "From what does the name Lollard come? I am sure we don't have them in Scotland."

"Alas, my lord, since you left your kingdom we, too, have been afflicted with them," said John Badby; "but so far only one has remained obdurate. Lollards are the followers of John Wycliffe. The name comes from Lollen, or lullen, to sing softly," he added.

James asked again, "Richard II was a Lollard, was he not?"

King Henry looked annoyed at the mention of his predecessor's name, but Prince Hal replied instantly: "Oh, no, King Richard was most orthodox in his faith. But Anne of Bohemia, his first wife, whom he greatly loved, had been imbued with heretical doctrines from the teaching of one John Huss, in her own country before coming here."

Archbishop Arundel interposed: "The Lollards go back to last century—to the spiritual Franciscans and other heretics."

"Do you not think it is the present deplorable schism which accounts for such unnatural symptoms in the Church?" asked Prince Hal.

"I don't know why it should," said the archbishop. "The schism is most regrettable, but it does not affect the deposit of faith: a treasure is bequeathed to me: I do not know in which of two caskets it is, but I am none the less the legal possessor of the treasure."

Although the papacy had lost much prestige from the seventy years of its captivity in Avignon, no one had thought that its return to Rome would be the occasion for a break in the unity of the Church. However, on the death of Gregory XI in 1378, the sixteen cardinals present in Rome had elected Bartolommeo Prignano, the Archbishop of Bari, as Urban VI. As the noisy crowd was obstreperous, thirteen of the cardinals re-elected Urban VI in the same evening of April 8th. The very next day the six French cardinals were notified, and they recognised and approved their colleagues' choice. Urban was crowned in St. Peter's on April 18th, but, in September of the same year, thirteen of the cardinals slunk out of Rome on the pretext of the heat, and proceeded to elect Robert of Geneva as Clement VII. Driven out of Naples he fled to Avignon, and countries and saints were divided in their allegiance. Saints Catherine of Siena and Catherine of Sweden were for Urban; Saints Vincent Ferrer and Colette were for Clement. England, Germany, Italy, and Flanders were for Urban; France, Spain, and Scotland for Clement. Jean Gerson, the great canon lawyer, was for Clement. The Council of Pisa, called to end this sad state of affairs, further complicated it by electing a third claimant, John XXIII. "Alas, there are two masters in the vessel who are fencing with and contradicting each other," sighed a great humanist, and indeed, the schism of the west was a gloomy precursor of the Reformation.

The rival popes excommunicated each other, and each other's followers, and both created cardinals, who, after a papal demise, elected further schismatic popes. Yet, though the discipline of the Church was gravely inconvenienced by the Great Schism, it had little or no effect on the faith of the people. To this faith Lollardry was a far graver menace, and the commons had given great scandal, first in King Richard's reign by refusing to pass anti-Lollard legislation, and now, in King Henry's, six years after the statute "De heretico comburendo"—of the burning of heretics—which had ensured the co-operation of the lay arm in the punishment of persons convicted of heresy, by a Lollard-sponsored petition which proposed to solve the country's financial difficulties by confiscating the estates of the Church. The king had refused even to consider it. In fact, King Henry had already shewn himself stern towards heresy, which was why John Badby, the Evesham tailor, had that day faced trial for his life.

"It's you secular folk that are so keen to burn," said the archbishop with a sigh, to King Henry. "We're anxious above all to avoid scandal, and to prevent this malignancy spreading. Burning a man is apt to make a martyr of him, and I'm all against it: you can't hide light, even if it be only rubbish that is feeding the flame."

The king replied: "Unfortunately, as you know better than I, what a man believes, determines what he will do. If he calls confession an earwigging, and refuses to take off his cap as the Host goes by, the chances are he will refuse to obey the king or to pay taxes. For if the individual can pick and choose what dogmas he likes and spit out ones he can't take, he'll only obey those rulers who behave as he thinks right. The king's right to rule is confirmed by the people, it is true, but it derives from God."

"That's a long speech from Your Majesty," said the archbishop; "and I hope you do not think I have dealt too leniently with our friend Badby. I gave him a year to reconsider his ideas. He's woefully illiterate. We must have a very bad grammar school down at Evesham, for he seems to know no Latin at all, and to have a somewhat simple approach to the scriptures. I did my best, translating for him, to try to explain what the doctrine of the

Church really was. But he was completely contemptuous of all learning but his own."

"Yes, Father," said Prince Hal; "he said if priests could make the bread to be the body of Christ, then there were 20,000 Gods in England every morning, and he believed only in one."

"When I read him our Lord's words of institution, he replied: 'If he had heard our Lord say *This is my body,* he would have said our Lord spoke amiss,'" said the archbishop.

James felt cold as he heard this blasphemy, and blushed as though he had heard filthy, lecherous talk.

"I don't see much point in giving such a creature a year to spread his poison," said Prince Hal.

The archbishop replied: "It might work itself out. Or he might die naturally. I believe one must give a human creature every possible chance."

"I think a good war is what this country needs to purge it of such poisons," said Prince Hal.

"A crusade," said his father; "I always promised myself I should lead a crusade."

"No," said Prince Hal; "crusades are discredited. Latterly they've been nothing but mercantile expeditions backed by force. The spirit of this age is against them. They were all very well in past centuries, but nowadays too many people have outgrown, or worn out, the simple faith of their forefathers. Now, war must be with France," he said; "or with Scotland." And he stared arrogantly at James.

"My son," said the archbishop, gravely, "you speak altogether too frivolously of serious matters. War is not to be entered upon lightly, unadvisedly, to satisfy your youthful vanity, or because you wish to check Lollardry or domestic disaffections at home. War should never be an alternative to peaceful avocations, or if it is, you are yielding to Satan himself who finds such mischief for idle hands."

Prince Hal looked furiously at the archbishop, but he made no reply. There was one of those silences like a hole in the road; one must pause and jump before conversation can go on. The candles guttered, and after a few uncomfortable moments, James asked leave to be excused. On his way upstairs, as he passed Lady Grey's door, he paused, listened, then knocked, and went in. She was lying in her big crimson-hung bed, her dark hair free and loose around her face. She looked very young; with her white nightshirt high about her neck, and fastened at her wrists, her whole air was almost girlish.

"My lord," she exclaimed. Then, half out of bed, tiny white feet on the grey stone: "What are you doing here?"

"Have you . . . have you forgotten I'm leaving tomorrow with King Henry?" James said. "I just came to say thank you and good-bye. And please, please, let me kiss you again. You must, please."

She put up her face, and then her hands stroked James's hair and his face softly as he kissed her. This time she let him have her mouth. Again he was shivering all over, and she said gently, "Go, now, James, and think of me sometimes. I've been pleased to have you here. You'll make some girl very, very happy. God keep you."

James kissed her hand, and went to his own room, feeling somehow inadequate, and with an ache inside. "I suppose one breaks one's heart first when one's weaned," he thought, "and goes on breaking it again and again with every girl one cares for; or, if one's a girl, with every man. I've got a long list of breakages to go through, no doubt, but just now I want one woman only and someone else has got her."

CHAPTER EIGHT

☐ James sat playing the clarsach, his favourite instrument, in the deep embrasure of one of the windows of Thomas Beaufort's palace. He played expertly upon all extant instruments, and could make up a tune, too, for any occasion, and write the words also; so he was much in demand about the court. In the past year he had matured greatly—civilised society, Henry IV told him jestingly, could refine even a dour Scot. Though James winced at this, as at many of Henry's sallies, he had learnt to conceal his temper, and to temper his natural hauteur; he had learnt, too, that it paid to be charming, agreeable, affable, and to appear entirely unambitious. And, after all, what axes had he to grind? Alone of all the courtiers there was no position he sought; among all the clamorous, vociferous requests made of the king by everyone who scraped or wormed or fought or bribed their way into his presence, only this sixteen-year-old king wanted nothing—except leave to go. So Henry IV grew always fonder of him and James concealed his dislike of Henry in courteous fashion, never blenching when the none-too-clean, foul-smelling king flung an affectionate arm round James's shoulder, nor did the young king retch when the old one breathed friendlily but sourly into his face. For Henry was already at the lag-end of his life; his face cancerous and horrible, his body wasted, so that muscle and nerve could be seen stretched over the visible bones.

James, sitting strumming, looked now out on to the Thames, as always crowded with barges, ferries, sailboats and every sort of craft (for the river was the greatest of London's thoroughfares, and the quickest way to get from one place to another was to take a boat), now into the great room, at one end of which Thomas Beaufort, the chancellor, was working at a massive table, surrounded by clerks of various sorts, some taking dictation, some tying up vellum briefs; there was a constant coming and going and a general air of importance about that end of the room. At the other, the king's two younger sons, John and Humphrey, were playing chess; their dogs lay or fidgeted around them—greyhounds, mastiffs, setting dogs, bull dogs, quite a variety of dogs, some squabbling over a bone or a ball, all handsomely collared, and all disregarded. Suddenly Humphrey, bored with waiting for John's move, came over to James, a cushion in his hand.

"Sit on this, you young idiot, or you'll get piles," he said; "cold stone under the buttocks is fatal."

James accepted the cushion, and asked, "Did you get the book?"

"Yes," Humphrey said; "the Petrarch, you mean? I did. And did I tell you John Somerset is selling me most of his uncle's library?"

"Geoffrey Chaucer's books? You don't mean he's willing to part with them? Oh, Humphrey, let me buy some, please; just the ones you don't want."

Humphrey looked down at the seated James. "What with?" he asked, with amiable contempt. "You know you haven't enough money for clothes, or to pay your chaplain, or to give your squire pocket money. You can't start buying books; they're about the most expensive things you could buy. Wait till you get back to your kingdom; then, maybe, we can do business."

104

James reddened, and was about to explode in anger, to explain he had plenty of money at home, if only he were allowed to go there, but suddenly he shrugged his shoulders instead: what was the use? After all, it was quite true that books were a tremendous luxury, and that Humphrey, himself, was only able to buy them by stinting himself in every other way; he had sold all but a few of his horses, he wore the plainest armour and certainly was single-minded about his collecting. John had made his move now, and called Humphrey back, his good, earnest, stupid face a contrast to his brother's dark, sensitive, almost anguished features. The big doors opened, and two pages announced the Bishop of Winchester, and Henry Beaufort swept in, the chancellor's brother, the king's half-brother. He barely acknowledged the salutations of the king's two sons, who stood up as he passed, or of James, who did the same. He walked right on up to his brother, and sat down by him. Then Prince Hal came in, with his big nose, close-eyed, and calm-lipped, his whole face as shuttered and unrevealing as his quiet mouth. His brothers stood up again on his entry, but did not smile: he passed them to go up to James, who was still standing.

"The burning's for tomorrow, at Smithfield," he said. "Will you come with me?"

James bowed slightly. "Of course. At what time?"

"Directly after Mass, at ten," he said.

James waited a second, in case Prince Hal had more to add, then asked: "He would not recant?"

"On the contrary; he declared yesterday that a spider and a toad were superior to the consecrated Host and more worthy of reverence because they were alive. So the archbishop had no option but to hand him over to the secular power, which quickly ordered him burnt. The archbishop earnestly petitioned that his life might be spared; he thought the man too ignorant to know what he said, or else insane, but I'm glad he wasn't able to prevent the sentence: there are altogether too many of those sort of people around, and they're all rebels at heart. If you're against the Church's order, you'll be against any order—civil order, family order."

James said, quoting St. Austin: "A brief and true definition of virtue is that it is the order of love."

Prince Hal thought for a moment, then said: "You think John Badby has his place too, in the order he disturbs?"

"Of course," said Humphrey, joining in. "He can't see it—and maybe we are too near ourselves to see it either, but of course he is integrally part of the order he disturbs."

"Doesn't he sin, then, in disturbing it?" asked Prince Hal, and there was a tense moment, for if James's answer was heresy, he might find himself in the same plight as the Evesham tailor.

"Of course, he's committing sin," James said confidently. "But the sin he commits cannot destroy God's order, nor even interrupt it. God uses our sin as He uses our virtue, for His own pattern. How could we make any difference to Him? Or to His ordering of His universe?"

"We caused the Incarnation all the same," said Humphrey. But just then the Bishop of Winchester, who had come toward the group of young men and had been listening, interrupted with a loud: "Humphrey, what a thing to say! God's love caused the Incarnation—not our sin. Don't you know that passage of St. Bernard's on love, where he says love is so powerful that it constrained God Himself to die of love?"

"But how can you separate God and love?" asked James. And Henry Winchester roared with stout, contented clerical laughter and said:

"That's just the point—you can't. It was the nearest St. Bernard ever got to a joke or a riddle."

"Then if John Badby loved enough, what he said wouldn't be a sin?"

"Of course not. That's all sin is, a lack of love, a misdirection of love."

"So if John Badby really believes what he is saying,

106

and loves God with all his heart, he will go to Heaven in spite of our condemnations?" asked Prince Hal.

"Of course," said the bishop. "And if Archbishop Arundel, or I, who handed him over to the secular court, love God less—not less than John Badby, but less than He created us to love Him—we shall go to Hell and John Badby can laugh at us all he pleases from the other place."

At Smithfield the next morning the straw was damp, and it took a little while to get the fire going. John Badby was tied to a big stake and was almost entirely hidden by the piled faggots. Prince Hal had been with him since dawn, pleading with him to recant. Now he stood beside the pyre, with James; no one else was so close, except for a few guards and the soldiery in charge of the execution. As the flames first flickered and then began to blaze, Archbishop Arundel appeared, with a chaplain, and stood next the prince and James. Badby was unshaven, and looked wild and unkempt; he did not speak at all. As the flames reached him, he began to writhe, and then to moan and scream. Prince Hal, shouting, "He recants, he recants," ordered the execution stopped, the flames extinguished. When he reached Badby, across the still glowing wood, he offered him a pension of threepence a day for life, if he would recant. But Badby shook his head. "No," he muttered in answer to the prince; "bread—that's all it is, bread, just bread." And then he screamed and screamed, as Prince Hal told the soldiers to get the fire going again, and made James stand there and watch the terrible twistings and contortions, until, mercifully, Badby fainted from his pain and his body fell into the flames and could be distinguished no longer from the glowing embers, white-hot now, into which he had fallen.

CHAPTER NINE

☐ The next summer the coronach was cried on Bena-
chie, and down the Don. James learnt from John Lyon,
the chaplain of Donald of the Isles, who had been sent
by him to King Henry to negotiate Donald's claim to the
earldom of Ross, of the Battle of Harlow. Donald insisted King Henry was his overlord, and not King James,
nor yet the Regent Albany. John Lyon was a smooth and
shrewd young cleric, very ambitious. As soon as he had
met James, he decided to throw in his lot with him, and
refused to return to Donald. But his brother had been
called out by Donald together with many hundred other
Highlanders and islanders, to march on Inverness, which
was quickly taken and burnt. The motley rabble then
marched on Aberdeen, but was met and crushed by the
Earl of Moar at Harlow. Listening to John Lyon's account of the battle, James was delighted. Donald, he
knew, had ideas about an independent northern kingdom
of the Highlands and the western isles. His defeat would
help preserve the unity of Scotland.

Also, James was glad to be beholden to the Earl of
Mar, ruffian though he was, since he had shared his captivity. Albany had been skulking as usual; for a man of
his size and build, he was singularly timorous, and had

succeeded in staying snugly ensconced in his castle of Falkland ("I hope David Rothesay's ghost plagued him sorely," said James) until all danger of a raid from the wild Highlanders was over, and then had proceeded north to Lochgilphead, where he had received Donald's submission.

John Lyon was most hopeful of the outcome of the Battle of Harlow. "With Douglas in the south, and Mar in the north, Albany cannot do much mischief," he told James. But James groaned, and said: "If they run my kingdom for me as a triumvirate, I shall have as hard a time reducing it again to a unity as you would the Trinity." James soon sent John Lyon north again, with dispatches urging the Scottish Government to negotiate his liberation.

Albany's only answer was to send ambassadors to treat with Henry IV for the freeing only of Murdoch; the most deliberate insult Albany had ever dared personally make James, and one James found it hard to swallow, being now rising eighteen, and a grown man in all men's estimation. What made it infinitely worse was that Murdoch was right there with them at the court, and, though the king was apparently more inclined to James, and there was never any question in anyone's mind who was King of Scotland, yet Prince Hal was rather fond of old Murdoch, and had him around a good deal, treating him as a sort of country cousin *cum* boon companion: he was not quite reduced to Sir John Oldcastle's level who was Prince Hal's pet crony, but was alternately his butt and confederate. And the very fact of his being there, on practically the same footing as James, made the latter furious and miserable: he felt made cheap, humiliated, and continually shamed. It was so undignified to see this son of the uncle who had killed his brother, and was even now robbing him of the kingdom, enjoying practically the same—and indeed in some ways rather more— consideration than he, James, did. He tried to reason himself out of his hatred for Murdoch. After all, there they both were, prisoners, exiles, first cousins; if they

110

could not pull together at this alien court, surely there was no fraternity in this world. But it was no good. As soon as he saw Murdoch, heard his unctuous, pseudo-humorous toadying to Prince Hal, his semi-facetious humble-pie attitude to King Henry, his patronisingly hail-fellow-me-lad chattiness to himself, James, the nausea almost overcame him, and he felt such hatred that he would only mutter between his teeth: "My lord of Fife, when my kingdom comes, I shall certainly remember you."

"How can I be sure that Albany will even open my letters?" James asked John Lyon. They were at Stratford Abbey, in Essex, with the court, and James looked out over the osiered flats, frozen with a patina of grey-green ice on the sluggish, muddy pools, and gloomed because John Lyon, just back from his mission to Scotland, reported that the regent had barely glanced at James's letters, tossing them aside whilst he eagerly tore open Murdoch's.

"Alas," John Lyon said; "could you but borrow Murdoch's seal!"

"I'll get it for you, Sire," said William Giffard.

James smiled at his most devoted follower. "Will you steal it?" he asked.

"Borrow, was what you said, Sire," laughed William Giffard.

James said: "Please do—and that quickly, for I think this is a most favourable moment to open negotiations about my ransom. The king is largely recovered from his recent heavy sickness, and Prince Hal is out of favour, for having sent off a military expedition on his own authority to help the Burgundians in France: for this the king has discharged him from the council, and has publicly disgraced him."

"How can that help you?" asked John Lyon.

"The king is kindly inclined to me, and would rather have me well-disposed to him ruling in Scotland, than Albany. If I promised to keep peace with England, I am sure King Henry would let me go. Not so Prince Hal. He

111

plans a French war; he intends to pretext coming in on the Burgundian side, or on the other; he's not particular, so long as there's fighting, and he is in it. And he wants to keep Scotland quiet during his absence abroad by threatening Albany with me."

"To get back to Murdoch's seal—how are you proposing to get it?" asked John Lyon.

William Giffard smiled. "I shall not tell you," he replied.

"It won't be easy," said James; "he always wears it on a gold chain around his neck."

William Giffard opened the door for James, and when he was gone, turned to John Lyon. "I would not tell His Majesty my plan, for fear he should forbid it, but I propose to bribe Murdoch's mistress to borrow the seal for a day."

"He hasn't one," John Lyon said, "unluckily for you— he just takes any girl whom he can bribe or bully into his bed."

"Well then, what about the jailer's daughter? There's classic precedent for using her."

"If you're referring to Jael and Sisera, I think you talk irreverently of Holy Writ," said the chaplain.

William Giffard went off to search for Mary Cheney, who minded the abbey laundry, and whose husband was the night watchman. "Can I have speech with your daughter?" he asked her, finding her ironing James's nightshirts, which she always did with loving care. She dropped a profound curtsey and went off to find her girl, returning in a few minutes, pushing a shy sixteen-year-old, buxom and still heavy with puppy fat, but a handsome wench, with rich glossy brown hair and good honest hazel eyes. William looked at her doubtfully, and shook his head; he was afraid he'd come on a fruitless chase; Blanche looked too young for the job he had in mind. He told Mary his doubts, but she, smelling a bribe, asked what was his desire. William explained, as much as he dared; he didn't want to incriminate James, and made it clear it was his own idea for helping his beloved sovereign. Mary came straight to the point at once, and was more straightforward and efficient.

"Lord bless my soul," she said, "that's no job for Blanche. She'd drop the signet right on my lord of Fife's sleeping face. Let me do it, and you're most welcome to my services," said Mary Cheney.

"Aren't you a trifle . . . past that sort of thing?" William had said, colouring; he didn't want to say, old, for Mary looked young enough with her red cheeks, and her tawny hair, that wasn't all hidden by a coif like a lady's, but curled around her kerchief, and her blue eyes were very merry at the Scotsman's embarrassment. She said nothing to this, so he added: "Well, there's good money for you if you bring me the signet, whatever way you come by it, and I'll ask no questions." And he left the mother and daughter looking at each other knowingly.

Next morning, when his breakfast came, it was Blanche who brought it him blushing prettily, and she had the signet on its gold chain around her neck. "Mother says if you can have done with it by this evening," she said, "she'll put it right back where she found it, and no one will be any the wiser." Giffard rushed in to his king in triumph, and James was so delighted that he readily agreed to ask no questions. He shut himself up and wrote hard all day, and by evening five letters were ready and securely sealed with Murdoch's seal. The first was of course to Albany, beginning: "Most dear and well-beloved" but saying boldly enough that as his uncle had not even answered, nor opened, his letters, and had taken no steps for his release, James would seek "remedy of our deliverance otherwhere in time to come." It was signed "With our proper sign manual and signet and with the signet of our well-beloved cousin of Fife." Then James wrote to both the Earls of Douglas and of Mar, and told them of his special trust in them, and that the delay in his homecoming was the fault only of him who should most vigorously have pursued it. The English king was ready and willing enough, James declared, and had treated him courteously and conscientiously: there was really nothing he would amend in his conduct. James concluded by asking the earls if his suspicions as to the cause of the delay were well founded.

John Lyon set off once more with the letters, on his eight-day journey, and James's hopes rose high. The news looked better too: a general truce by sea was signed between England and Scotland for six years, and a particular truce by land, from the River Spey to St. Michael's Mount. James went with Humphrey, the English king's son, down to Southampton where the fleet was mustering, and Humphrey wrote to his father how happy James was, as glad as any man can be, "for he was thanking God that the king's sufferance was about to work his own good will."

But fate was to foul James's hopes once more. Prince Hal and the Bishop of Winchester after their year's rule of England—for during King Henry's illness they had practically run the country—were out of favour, and the king did not allow his son's men into the body of Westminster Hall.

In France, Isabeau, the Bavarian queen, had married off her daughter, Isabella, the child widow of King Richard II of England, to Charles, Duke of Orléans. Young Isabella's dowry had never been returned, and there was a good deal of anti-English feeling. When, in 1407, the old Duke of Orléans had been murdered by the partisans of the Duke of Burgundy, civil war flared up, and the poor insane king of France, Charles VI, was quite unable to compose the rival factions. In 1411 the Armagnacs—as the Orléans party were called—besieged Paris, and young Prince Hal sent 2,000 men to help the king, and made a suggestion about marrying his daughter, Catherine. James threw his cap in the air and caught it when the French answer came: thank you so much for the help, but we think Catherine is a trifle young. It was then that Henry IV, recovering unexpectedly, had turned Prince Hal out of the council, and sacked Thomas Beaufort, giving his job of chancellor to Archbishop Arundel.

114

James began packing: he felt the time for his release had really come, and in May a fifty-man embassy, led by Sir William Douglas of Drumlanrig, arrived from Scotland to negotiate terms. On November 30th, 1412, James granted William Douglas and his brother Archibald each a charter, confirming their lands. These charters were "writ in our own proper hand under the signet used in sealing of our letters: and are to be sealed with our great seal in time to come." James wrote a lovely script, but looked sadly down at his beautiful penmanship before handing the charters to the grateful Douglases: "A pity that this is how I exercise my sovereignty," he said; "a scribe would do it better; a Pharisee is doing it just now in my country so much worse."

It was mid-Lent and James's release was still delayed, when one early spring day, while King Henry IV was making an offering at the shrine of Edward the Confessor behind the high altar, he was seized with dizziness and fell down unconscious. He was carried out of the abbey, and laid on a straw pallet in a side chamber, called the Jerusalem room. The crown, which latterly he had always had borne after him wherever he went, was laid on a cushion of gold cloth at his side. Some said the king was fearful of his own son, some of the English Earl of March, Edmund Mortimer, who had been Richard II's heir, and was far nearer to the English crown than was Henry. The king's face was covered with a silk scarf, and Friar Tille, his confessor, was hurriedly sent for to stand by for the end. After he had received the holy oils, he seemed to cease breathing; after again a long waiting, his body grew cold, and when Prince Hal arrived—he and James had been practising archery in the Tower gardens—the king appeared to be lifeless. James stood near the door, at the back of the little chamber, whilst Prince Hal kneeled down, and gently took up the crown. He carried it tenderly in his two hands out of the room. "To think," he whispered to James, "that a few days ago a justice of the peace boxed my ears for striking him, and threatened to jail me. And now I am king. But the man

115

did right, for the law is above the king, and the king cannot be above the law—is it not so, Jamie?"

James, bowing slightly, his eyes riveted to the crown, replied: "I have had occasion to believe that this may be true also in England, Sire."

Prince Hal, seemingly impervious to James's sarcasm, jumped at being addressed as sire. Just then the friar ran out, and came breathlessly up to the two young men: "Your father has regained consciousness," he said, "and asks that you return him the crown."

Prince Hal blushed, and ran back, replacing the crown on its cushion. The dying king's hand was raised, and his eyes were open. He had thrown the silk handkerchief from off his face, and it lay beside him, all soiled with pus from his sores.

Without lifting his head, he said to his son, now kneeling: "What right have you to the crown, my son, seeing that I had none?"

"Sire," replied the prince, "as you held and kept it by the sword, so will I hold and keep it while my life shall last."

"Do as you will," said the king. Then, after a pause, he added: "As for me, I commend my soul to God."

There was another pause. James could hear the flies buzzing in the leaded panes.

King Henry said, speaking now with difficulty:

"A soothsayer told me that I should die in Jerusalem. I was there once, as Earl of Derby, before ever I thought of the throne. And I hoped it might be a true prophecy, and that I should return leading an army to free the Holy Places. That is how a soldier and a king would wish to die, in battle for the right. But when the friar told me that they call this the Jerusalem chamber, I knew my end was come." Then he paused, and said even more slowly: "God bless my boys, all four."

He did not speak again, and James, standing in the shadow, watched the soul pass up from the king's feet, flit like a little shadow across his stomach, and finally flicker out at his lips and vanish clean away. "Sic transit

116

gloria mundi," said Friar Tille, and James thought how strange that this stinking carrion, with the red square beard stiff over the dropped jaw, and the wide, sore nose, this already decomposing corpse, had been the wisest and wittiest man of his age; so charming that in far Italy a Visconti girl had wept six years for him, refusing all other suitors; so lusty that at sixteen he already had a child by his twelve-year-old wife. I have seen the patron of Chaucer, and Gower, and Hoccleve die, James thought, who to me was more than the murderer of Richard II, the enemy of Scotland and of Wales. Because he tried to coax Christine de Pisan to come to England, I forgive him the feats of glory that spread England's renown to Norway and Austria, Palestine, and Sicily. He was kind to me, James mused, as Prince Hal stooped and closed the staring eyes, in his clumsy, bluff way. I shall aways be grateful that he taught me music, and praised my verses. And so, forgiving Henry from his heart for his own capture, he walked quietly out of the room where King Henry V prayed-beside King Henry IV, on the day that the latter was alive and was dead, March 20th, 1413, in the forty-sixth year of his age.

CHAPTER TEN

☐ The very next day after his father's death Henry V sent James and Murdoch back to the Tower. The faithful William Giffard went, too, and William Douglas of Dalkeith, who had come down from Scotland as a hostage for his powerful cousin the earl. The following day they were joined by twenty-four more Scots, all members of James's suite, including John Wells, his valet. These were released on April 12th, but James and Murdoch stayed on. James felt utter despair on seeing the dreaded, familiar portcullis shut down on him once more. He was rising nineteen, it was spring, and a few days before he had been so nearly home. Now, there was no future in life. Here his own reign had begun; here Henry V's was beginning for him, and Henry was but twenty-six, and "He'll last forever; he'll certainly outlast me," sighed James.

William Giffard tried to console him. "It's only a precautionary measure," he reassured the despondent young king, "King Henry believes that Your Majesty and my Lord of Fife might avail yourselves of a notion that between the death of one king and the accession of another, there is a sort of interregnum, and you are not

119

bound by your parole: you could consider yourselves free to escape, he thinks."

"And there are all those Lollard intriguers, still calling out for King Richard," James groaned.

"Yes, indeed, and they might kidnap you. Maybe you are safer here than outside," said William Giffard. "The king might think you tangled in some plot you knew nothing whatsoever about, and you would come to a sticky end all to no purpose."

Henry IV's body was washed, brained, bowelled, and embalmed. Then it was wrapped in a cerecloth that left only the face and hands exposed. After, it was taken down the Thames to Gravesend on a barge, hung with black, and blazing with lighted tapers and flares. From his window James watched the slow progress of the cat-afalque-convoy; as he later watched the snowstorm that raged and flurried and howled round the Tower and round the abbey on April 9th, the day King Henry V was crowned.

"You're no better than a peregrine in moult," Murdoch told his cousin, coming in with a letter in his hands to find James sitting all bunched up, huddled in his misery. "Here's our invitation to the coronation banquet. We'll not bide here long."

"*You* won't," said James gloomily. "At least one human being wholeheartedly wants you home." And then he retired to his own cell-like room and dismissed everyone, including Murdoch. There he wrote, to ease his heartache:

> O, busy ghost, aye flickering to and fro
> That never art in quiet nor in rest
> Till thou camest to the place thou camest fro
> Which is thine own and very proper nest.
> From day to day so sorely are thou prest
> That with thy flesh aye walking art in trouble
> And sleeping art in pain, so hast thou double

but he couldn't bear to go on, for the hot tears spotted his page, so he lay down and sobbed into the coverlet.

The coronation banquet, in Westminster Hall, was an affair of great pomp. The mounted servers rode from the kitchens to the tables, bearing the huge dishes of fishes and meats, and the fantastic pastries, mottoed and prettified with sugar spun into strange shapes. There were two panniers of Brittany lampreys contributed by Queen Joan, King Henry's mother, and two Sussex does sent by Sir John Pelham from Pevensey. James, in a robe of sanguin furred with miniver, was sitting at the top table and found the noise of the loud supping and the fidgeting unbearable. Some men played with their knives, almost everyone scrambled for the best portions in the dip charger, others made sops of bitten bread, many licked their plates with their tongues, blew into their cups, spread their butter and cheese with their thumbs, sucking them after, and wiped their knives, their hands, and even their teeth on the table covers. Coughing, spitting and farting were general: even the ladies did not scruple to break wind, though mostly only the older ones, and many picked good morsels for husband or lover and leant across to put it into their mouths with a caress, as though they were in the nursery giving their puling babes the pap. James was not sorry to get back to the Tower; he was in no mood for making merry at someone else's coronation, and he found English manners wanton after the more decorous Scottish.

As a crowning gift, he had sent Henry three palfreys, named Bayard Kyng, Lyard Kyng, and Blanche Kyng. Henry, on the other hand, to James's fury, gave two palfreys to the Earl of Fife and none to him. One, called Dun Wodegyle, was a real beauty. Luckily Murdoch was too heavy for her, so James borrowed her frequently.

The new king reversed completely the policies of the old. He took the great seal from Archbishop Arundel, and gave it to the Bishop of Winchester, Henry Beaufort. New ambassadors came from Scotland for the release of

King James, but though a truce was concluded with Albany, to last from the Assumption until the following June, nothing was said or done about the young king's liberation.

But Bishop Henry Beaufort found time to come and see the fretting James and was very practical in his consolations. "King Henry is a sincere and a devout Christian," he told James, "but he firmly believes that there is no evil he may not commit, no injustice he may not perform, in order to remain on the throne, in order to reign. He really believes Almighty God has especially created him to be king, and that it is his mission in life: whatever helps him fulfil God's intentions and Holy Will in this respect is right; whatever hinders him is wrong. He values no human life above a beetle's, should it cross his sacred and anointed path. You must remember, too, that he is not as strong as he appears; nor was his father before him—he was always consulting physicians, and taking pills and medicines even before he fell ill. But when King Henry is not frightened any more, he will come round to letting you go; at present you are a great help to our young King Harry: he can make Albany do whatever he wants by threatening to release you, and send troops up with you to help you regain your rightful throne. Let loose, you might be snapped up by the Lollards, who would use you for blackmail. They might threaten your uncle, and if it embarrassed King Henry enough and perhaps caused a civil war here, Albany might do it. So on all counts, our new sovereign thinks you are better off here, and I'm inclined to agree with him. And for another reason. You are King of Scots, and when you go home, I want you to have the whole will and love of your people calling you back. Scotland is in a very disturbed state. Your uncle cares for nothing except to remain in power. He does not reck what will happen after him. Let the deluge come, he thinks, so long as he doesn't have to weather the storm. So your whole country is in a fearsome state of insecurity. Did you know that the Earl of Strathearn was murdered by his brother-in-law just after they had sworn perpetual friendship on the Blessed Sacrament? That is the way things are, and perhaps you are more fortunate than you realise, young man," concluded the chancellor, and departed in high good humour with himself, for was not visiting prisoners one of the corporal works of mercy? And he genuinely liked the young Scots king, and thought he should shortly be sent home, "with proper safeguards" of course.

When he had gone, James tried to settle down to writing verse again, but he found concentration hard. First he felt he must walk out, since the day was sunny, and then he called for William Giffard to bring him some ale, and then he cut his nails with a penknife, and still he could not feel settled, nor did it seem to him that anything he wrote would ever matter again to anyone, even to himself. Fidget, fret, fume: it was all very well for smug Henry Beaufort to preach patience, but he was not nineteen. James felt he would boil, or blow up. He longed for knives with which to cut himself, for a flail with which to beat himself, or hooks to tear himself with: for anything, in fact, that would check the restless itch in his body and his blood.

William Giffard called in Mary Cheney, for now she and young Blanche were installed at the Tower. Mary had been promoted from laundry work to the kitchen, and when Blanche brought up James's ale, William Giffard greeted her pleasantly. "This girl will see to your comfort finely, my lord," he told James. "She's a bonny lass and a kindly." He was careful to warn both her and her mother, however, on no account ever to breathe to a soul how Murdoch's seal had been obtained. William Giffard knew James would be horrified to think he owed anything to a woman's sin. "Though he owes the Incarnation to Eve's," William thought, gaily.

James was quite ready to flirt with Blanche when she brought him his meals or did his room. Life was much more fun for a girl of the people, James reflected, for her pastures were limitless. "Think of it, William, everything

123

is grist that comes to her mill; from king's son to scullion, every male is her natural prey."

"Yes, I imagine that between the ages of sixteen and sixty, from the moment she wakes in the morning until she goes to sleep at night, she can flirt all she wants," replied William Giffard.

In his present mood, James thought flirting might enliven his tedium, and he began to pay Blanche trifling attentions, from sheer lack of anything better to do. He even began to write verses to her. And from make-believe, he was in such low spirits that soon he almost fancied himself genuinely in love with the girl, who was civil spoken, and gentle in her manners and movements; a tender, simple soul, who looked at James with cowlike devotion, and was grateful for every word that fell from his lips. She was truly humble, too, and one day James came upon her cleaning his room: she had not heard him come in, and was on her knees, stroking one of his fur-lined slippers, and kissing it. James, touched though he was, wondered if perhaps she were not a trifle wanting, and was caressing them only for the sweet feel of the soft fur? He would never know, he reflected, as he crept out of the room unobserved.

One day Blanche's mother, smearing both hands shyly on her apron, asked if she could speak to James alone, privately, on an urgent matter. "If you will let Blanche guide you," she said, "she will bring you to your kingdom. Horses will be found, and posted along your route; you shall travel along byways so no man will suspect your errand, and you will be over the border before the hue and cry can be raised for you; your country will have no ransom to pay, and you will be safely home."

"What shall I owe, and to whom for these advantages?" asked James.

Mary Cheney hesitated before replying and then said: "You shall marry my daughter."

"Marry her!" cried James. "That's not possible. My marriage has to be ratified by the Scottish parliament, and they would never, never consent to it. Your scheme is

124

unthinkable. Marry a washerwoman's daughter! How could I?"

"You would not need to produce her as your queen," said Mary Cheney. "Simply have a priest marry you, so it wasn't sin for either of you to enjoy the other—for you would, you know—you're a well-built pair, and would lie comfortably together. And as for washerwoman, remember William the Conqueror's mother was just that and nothing else."

"No doubt," said James, and, fearful, if he refused outright, she might, for vengeance or in pique, take some tale to King Henry about his having tried to seduce the girl and carry her off with him, he determined to restrain his feelings, and to avoid any outburst. So he gently asked, had Blanche been consulted? And her mother said she could be counted upon to make no objection to the scheme, which made James laugh bitterly. Stood his score so low that a washerwoman's daughter might be expected to make objections to becoming his wife? Or even his mistress?

When evening came, and Blanche brought his supper, he was playing the tune he had made for his new ballad on *Trust in God* and was humming to himself in melancholy fashion. He began to chaff Blanche a little and to ask her what kind of heroine she might be, that would ride through England with a strange man, and find horses for him, and protect him from all dangers. Did she not think it was the man's place to shield the girl? It did not sound a chivalrous plan to him. But with tears in her eyes Blanche begged him to accept her mother's offer, and added, her eyes downcast, her cheeks scarlet: "My lord king, you do not need to marry me, nor even to sleep with me, an' you like it not; I shall be contented only to have brought you to your kingdom and to have helped you to your rightful inheritance. 'Tis my mother only that has such great ideas. I do not look so high."

At that James, much moved, hugged her close and kissed her fondly, and she, taken aback, responded warmly enough, and they might have gone further, but

125

for Murdoch, who came in then, and, as James was ravenously hungry and the supper that Blanche had set down was getting cold, he did not mind the interruption as much as he might have done at another time, though he added it to the invisible score he was keeping against Murdoch.

It was a hot summer, unusually hot, and James sweated it out in London. Many towns burnt, owing to the prolonged drought: Tewksbury and Mayfield were both gutted. Severe hailstorms damaged the crops, and the news from Scotland mentioned famine conditions in several of the Lowland areas.

Before the situation could become embarrassing, or James make up his mind whether to accept or to refuse Mary Cheney's offer (which he learned later was backed by the Lollards, who had worked out all the details), another outbreak of the plague occurred, and poor Mary and Blanche both fell victims to the disease, and died within two days of each other. James was ungallantly scared of having been subjected to the contagion by these ladies, and Henry had him and Murdoch quickly transferred to Windsor on August 3rd, whither he followed them a few days later.

James found King Henry V, personally, charming. They rode together in Windsor Great Park, and Henry insisted that James accompany him everywhere, whether he went hunting, or attended to state papers. James was treated rather as a beloved vassal, than as a prisoner. But he resented the king's charity no less than he hated his own captivity. Watching Henry summon the parents of poor folle Kate, the king's dwarf, and condescendingly give them a goodly sum of money, James saw also how the king had at the same time summoned his locksmith, and had bidden him make two collars of fine steel, with long, linked chains. When they were ready, one was fastened around the neck of the king's pet monkey, and the other around the tiny neck of folle Kate. From this tiny incident James drew his own conclusions as to the true kindness of kings, and he thought himself lucky to have avoided a like fate. Yet have I? he mused; my chain is invisible; that is the only difference.

And he soon tired of court life, even though Windsor was infinitely preferable as a lodging to the Tower. It was vastly more comfortable too, and warmer. The sheltered Thames valley was very gracious, though the constant mists and fogs were depressing. But Henry V was a moody young man. He could be the most delightful of companions; he could also, for no known reason, settle into a black sulk that might last days. Constantly having to adjust himself to the young king's temper wore James down, and he became thin and nervous. Then one day, late in September, James and Humphrey, Duke of Gloucester, the king's brother, came in early. They had gone out at crack of dawn after woodcock, and came in carrying a nice bag of game, to find the king in a darker mood than either of them had ever before seen him. Neither spoke, to each other or to him, but slunk away, to ask the seneschal what was the trouble. There was an air of expectancy about the castle; self-important minor officials and puffed-up wardens knocked impatiently at the great gates.

"It is Sir John Oldcastle, the Lollard knight," said the seneschal, "who is the present cause of the king's displeasure. He was safely in jail, but his followers broke in and rescued him."

"He was lodged in the Tower, was he not?" James asked. And the seneschal said:

"Yes, Your Majesty. And it is to be feared that there were Lollards amongst the servants there, who connived at his escape."

"This won't do you any good, James," whispered Humphrey sympathetically. And the two young men looked down at the lovely gardens, ablaze with Michaelmas daisies and many sorts of aster, and out at the yellowing trees, the sunlight spilling off them on to the gay green grass.

Sir John had been Prince Hal's boon companion until his father's death, and had served with him on the Welsh march. He had been summoned to appear before the archbishop to answer charges of heresy on September 11th, but had stayed quietly at home at Cooling Castle. On September 23rd he had been taken to the Tower, and given a fair trial; his contumacy for refusing to answer his summons, was held up against him, but the archbishop offered to absolve him from the excommunication that had followed. Oldcastle refused his offer, and proffered instead a statement of his faith, harmless enough, but exclusive of all the Lollard-debated points. When the archbishop asked him what happened to the bread and wine at the sacring of the Mass, he was evasive, refused to commit himself, and was sent back to the Tower. He was examined again on the 25th, was judged guilty of heresy, but recommended to mercy. It was after this, almost immediately, that he had escaped.

"Let's hope he slips overseas quietly and joins some of his fellow doubters," said Humphrey. "I hope he lands up in Bohemia and troubles us no more."

"I am so entirely dependent on other people," James sighed. "Nothing that has ever happened to me, of evil or of good, has been by my own fault, or by my own virtue. I'm tired of being the butt of someone else's jokes, of another's experiments." And he went on, sadly, and as though speaking to himself: "And I wish, too, that I had not such self-control. If only I could drown my sorrows in drink, or console myself by a life of dissipation! If I were like my brother David and could lead a life of dissipation until the last possible moment, and then become edifying! If I could plot treason, lose my temper, get drunk, fornicate—anything, anything, to get away, to escape this place, and above all, to escape from myself! I'd barter my immortal soul for a chance to lay down the burden of my own individual consciousness." Humphrey took James's arm and squeezed it. "You know you wouldn't," he said. "You know the Passion is now, and your discomforts are but your share in it—that part of it you are allowed to feel."

The Lollards had brought off a coup. Sir John disappeared into hiding in Wales just as Owen Glendower had. James envied them both yet made no move to copy them. He continued to behave with the greatest possible decency and dignity. It would seem that his wishes were not even beggars, horses, on which to ride home, for he even took it meekly and quietly enough, when, in October, King Henry, who was leaving Windsor for a tour of the more disaffected areas (Sir John Oldcastle had quite an underground behind him), had both James and Murdoch sent back to the Tower. James was sorry only to leave Humphrey. For Humphrey had become a true friend. James and he had much in common. Bookworms both, both were also good at sports and games. It was Humphrey who, as chamberlain, asked Henry V for a new mattress and blanket for James's bed, those in use being all rotten and filthy, and for two pairs of sheets, since the sheets had not been changed nor renewed for two years past and were crawling with vermin. James would spend half his nights writing poetry, sitting up on his big oak chair, as much from dislike of being bitten as from inspiration.

Christmas was spent by both James and Murdoch in the Tower, and they heard the stirring news rather late. King Henry had been spending the feast at Eltham, when some Lollards conspired to kidnap him there. But one of the conspirators lost heart, and warned Henry of the plot. So the king returned quickly and quietly to London, where he was popular with the people, and felt safe surrounded by them.

But on the night of January 12th, Sir John Oldcastle himself was rumoured to have been seen in a field outside St. Giles's hospital and many people found their way there—one hundred thousand of them, some said. The king ordered the gates of London to be strictly guarded, so that no man might slip out to join the men camped at St. Giles, and, with a handful of armed men, he marched out to meet the rebels, but they had been warned, and most fled, though the king was able to apprehend and to execute a few. But none, even under torture, would give away Sir John Oldcastle's whereabouts. The king could not even be certain whether or no he had really been at St. Giles that night. All over England royal officers reported many people travelling as if to London; when questioned whither they were bound, they all replied: "To my Lord of Cobham" (Sir John being Lord Cobham in his wife's right). They were all detained, in the hopes that Sir John would try and communicate with them, but as they received no suspicious messages, after a while they were all again set free.

James suffered for these disturbances, in worse food, fewer privileges, increased guards, and, most galling of all, in less pocket money. For Albany was constantly pleading his poverty, and his own inability and Scotland's to raise the required ransom, as among the most cogent reasons for James's continued captivity. And would often even prevent the young king getting his rents.

King Henry was already deep in his preparations for the French war. He was a man of limited vocabulary. "It must be done" or "It can't be done" were his two favourite forms of reply. To Maxwell and Lanyn, the new ambassadors from Scotland sent to ask James's release, he made the latter answer, declining to give them any reasons for so answering. For over a year he had all the housewives in England baking, smoking hams, and putting up preserves for the victualling of his army, and he had pre-empted the whole surplus on the harvest in southern England and was storing it aboard his great ships.

At first he had supplied both the Armagnac and the Burgundian factions impartially with money and men; he did not think the time had yet come to take sides. He renewed his offer of a French marriage, but Queen Isabeau still refused. At the same time he proposed to the Duke of Burgundy a joint attack on France.

CHAPTER ELEVEN

☐ On a cold drizzling February day, James was woken early by William Giffard. "We are travelling again today, Sire," he said, "here are King Henry's latest orders."

James read them, and learned he was to be delivered that day into the care of Sir John Pelham, at Pevensey Castle, on the south coast, in Sussex. "Your own horses will carry you; you can take what baggage you will—there is ample space where you are going."

"Why am I going?" James asked. "Am I not safe enough here?"

"Since John Oldcastle escaped from here," said William Giffard, "King Henry has no longer the same confidence he had of old in the Tower. And there was suspicion then of Lollard intrigues within the Tower itself. There are no such rumours about Pevensey!"

"Will Murdoch be coming too, and Griffith Glendower?" asked James. The young Welshman had remained solidly in the Tower all through the happier days when James was with King Henry V at court, and James had found him, on his return, sadly etiolated by continuous imprisonment.

"Griffith is being released—the king fears for his life, as he has developed a wasting sickness," said William

Giffard, "and he has offered old Owen Glendower, his father, a free pardon."

"And Murdoch?" asked James.

William Giffard hesitated. Then said, "Murdoch is returning home to Scotland. He is being exchanged for Henry Percy."

James caught at Giffard's arms and shook him. "William, it's not true—say it's not true. It can't be true," he almost screamed. "Say you made it up to anger me. To shock me. For fun. Say anything except that it's true. Please, please, say it's not true."

But William merely nodded his head. "It's perfectly true. And, Sire, you must also face the fact that both you and I have had an inkling that this might happen, for quite some time now."

James, looking out at the Thames, dropped his hands, and sighed. "Yes," he agreed, "ever since parliament asked for the return of Percy."

Suddenly he felt he didn't care any more. What did Scotland matter? If his own people could not care for him enough to ransom him, if they preferred Murdoch to him, let them have Murdoch. Then the awful feeling of emptiness, almost of annihilation, passed. "It isn't what Scotland wants, it's what Albany has imposed on her: the more successful Albany is, the more clearly my duty is to save Scotland from him, to rescue my people from this usurper," James thought as he came up out of the blackness of his despair. He turned his mind from his own personal feeling of disappointed resentment, and, refusing to look back at the baying, snarling dogs of despair at his heart's heels, he asked William Giffard for further details.

"It's what Albany has always wanted—I knew that," he commented when Giffard had done with speaking. "But I don't see what good it does King Henry. Why should the establishment of Albany's dynasty in Scotland be better than my being there? I have been taught English ways, shewn how English law and order works,

132

watched English archers shoot and learnt why they conquer Scots gentlemen every time. I'm practically a retainer of the House of Lancaster—why wouldn't I suit King Henry's book every bit as well as Murdoch?"

Griffith had come into the room now, and put an arm half round Giffard's shoulder. "Shall we tell him, William?" he asked, then said to James, "Because King Henry's going overseas, and your Uncle Albany keeps making silly little frontier forays that take men and matériel. Albany does it to keep your friends busy, so they may not occupy themselves instead with intrigues for your restoration and for his own deposition. Peace encourages your friends, so Albany's for war. From King Henry's point of view, if he keeps you safe under lock and key, he can threaten to let you out and send you home whenever the Scots or Albany get a bit obstreperous. Whereas Murdoch and young Percy cancel each other out beautifully."

"But why should Henry want Percy home? The boy's father died a rebel, and there are conspiracies enough for him to join as soon as he gets here," said James.

"He is to take charge of the north-east march, whilst the Duke of York is sent to the French wars," said William Giffard.

"So a rebel and the son of a rebel are brought home to honour and glory, whilst the noose is tightened around me," said James.

Just then Murdoch shambled in, and said, "I'm off away home, James," and looked so good-humoured, so red-faced and so pleased, that James, pausing an instant at the effrontery of his remark, wondered if, after all, he might be innocent of conniving at a result so favourable to him, that had hitherto been beyond his wildest dreams. So all James said was, "Whilst I stay here."

Murdoch looked honestly taken aback at his cousin's icy tone and manner. "But we'll have you out soon, James. Don't fret yourself now, my lad," he said, "I'll do the very best I can for you as soon as I get home."

133

"Thank you, indeed," said James, without letting his sarcasm shew in his voice. "I certainly need all the help you or anyone else can give me."

"Think of it, though, James, I've not been home for over ten years—I've not seen my boys—they're grown men now, who don't even remember me."

James looked down at the point of his sword. "There's no one except Bishop Wardlaw that remembers me, it would seem," he said, in a voice near tears.

"We must be going," said William Giffard, who felt that the situation was becoming difficult, "we must to horse, Your Majesty."

James kissed Murdoch coldly, Griffith warmly, and left, William Giffard following with his helmet and a couple of warm cloaks.

Pevensey was bleak enough, set in dreary flats: one would hardly want to escape, thought James, for what would one escape to? To be lonely as a bittern, mournful as a peewit, solitary as a heron? He still was interested in birds and in birdwatching. Better remain so and cultivate only his mind. But he wished Sir John Pelham lived there. Instead most of the time he and his family were at Hurstmonceaux—they only came occasionally to disturb the King of Scots on the edge of the narrow sea. Yet it was nice to have the place to himself, James reflected, and here, at least, he could keep proper style—he had linen sheets and plenty of blankets, and hangings for his rooms, and enough furnishings, and his own chaplain, so he could hear daily Mass. And because of the danger from the plague daily communion was allowed. James kept quite a court here, and even entertained, to a small extent—Sir John knew his literary tastes, and brought over any visiting writing folk—and sometimes there was dancing in the evening, for Sir John's daughters loved music and dancing, and James made merry with them when they came.

On April 16th, Henry V summoned the Council of the Realm—thirty lay peers and fifteen spiritual. John, Duke of Bedford, was named Regent, the army was contracted

134

for a whole year, and was regularly paid, every archer earning three times the wages of an artisan. Parliament gave a tax of three shillings, which was very ample, indeed, an almost unheard-of amount. King Henry went on board at Southampton on August 10th. He had a fleet of 1,000 vessels, that carried 30,000 men. And he took with him the results of two years' baking and brewing.

James heard the news from his squires, his chaplains, from everyone who came and went; he had cried himself to sleep when he heard he wasn't going, too. It didn't matter which side to be on, just to be going to the wars was all that mattered. He felt more desolate than ever before: not to be allowed to be king was one thing; to be prevented from being a man was infinitely worse: and what was a man for but to fight and to make love?

"And to pray," said John Lyon, "never two without three, and man exists first to pray. A beast fights and makes love, even a king of beasts; but a King of Scots must pray; and then, after, he may fight, and then, after, he may make love."

"Oh, may he," sneered James, "how good of God—if I pray first, then I can go to the party," and, for all his twenty-one years, he put his head down onto his pillow and sobbed aloud.

October 24th was cloudy, with no moon; on the 25th, it was cold, and it rained. For James, staring across the straits toward the France he could not see, it was a day like any other: he went otter-hunting in the forenoon; in the evening, some boys brought the first sweet chestnuts to the door, for which James bade his seneschal give them a penny. Not for nearly a week did he learn of Agincourt: how, on clay soil, that slipped and slithered under their feet, three thousand Englishmen on a dank drizzling day met ten thousand French, and left four thousand dead. They also took fifteen hundred prisoners, at a cost of but thirteen English gentlemen dead.

James rode to London on November 22nd to witness Henry's triumph of the 23rd. Sir John Pelham rode with him, and her ladyship, too, and their daughters; it was a hard day's riding, from dawn to dusk, but they managed it agreeably enough. Watching the procession from Henry Winchester's room in the palace of the Savoy, James was thankful he did not figure in it: there were trophies enough, prisoners of exalted rank, without him. He was fascinated by a young man, who looked to be his own age, but was as tall and slim as James was ruddy and stocky: a most dainty young man, but no weakling, who rode with an air of disdain that verged on indifference, his milk-white palfrey sadly muddied about the hocks by the filthy London streets. He looked about him disdainfully, as though aware of every bad smell, of every tawdry sight, yet with an absolutely complete detachment, almost a world-weariness. "I've never seen such a spiritual face," James thought. But Charles, Duke of Orléans, three years James's senior, was not spiritual at all, only tremendously intellectual. James met him some two months later, for when he was returned to the Tower on January 28th, 1416, he found the duke had settled down there. James was, in fact, a trifle nettled at his reception. "Make yourself comfortable, my lord King," the young duke had said, languidly, "I've taken the best rooms, but then, you see, I got here first, and I'm three years older than Your Majesty, and a great deal more unfortunate."

"I've been here far longer than you ever will," James had replied somewhat testily; "as for age, I never heard that it went before honour, and as for misfortune, we shall see. Shall I challenge you to prove yours with your sword, tomorrow, in the tilting court beyond the moat?"

"No, no," said Charles, "my sweet boy, I've just been in one war, I certainly don't want another, real or make-believe. You tell me the story of your life, and I'll tell you mine—in fact, let's write them down: I'm a poet, and I hear Your Majesty is also a disciple of the Muses. We can make ourselves a cosy and civilised life together here, if we take a little trouble; let's share our quarters; it will give us twice the more space than if we are just two crusty bachelors hiding each in his hole."

It was astonishing how quickly the grim rooms in the Tower that James thought he knew better than he would ever know any others, could change under the touch of the young Frenchman. As though by magic, carpets were laid on the floors; lovely hangings appeared, rich tapestries, comfortable chairs, couches; statues, too, little ivory Madonnas, "That one's Flemish, she over there is Basque," said Charles. And the food, too, improved out of recognition. Charles sent for a French cook. "I'll die if I have to eat what they give us here," he said, and by means of continual complaints, and of always assuming everyone existed for the special purpose of making him comfortable, Charles d'Orléans succeeded in getting everything for which he asked. He was intensely musical, and for James, it was sheer delight to have someone who always wanted to practise, was always ready to go over a new tune, to transpose a song into another key, to sight-read a difficult passage; to transcribe some primitive air that James would whistle or hum: at last, James had a friend, and, though Charles was less ardent or impetuous, it was evident that for him, too, James made all the difference between a bearable and an unbearable captivity. Charles told him all about his youth. "I had the gentlest, happiest, most splendid and most monotonous childhood you can imagine," he said. "My father was the lover of the Queen of France—one of the lovers—my mother was Valentine Visconti of Milan."

"What relation to Louise Visconti, who was Henry IV of England's flirt when he was Earl of Derby?" James asked.

"Oh, you Scots, with your passion for genealogy and the cousinage," said Charles; "I don't know—yes, I do, perfectly well, but I don't care. Not now. I'm telling you about my youth, not my forbears."

James smiled. "Go ahead," he said.

"My father Louis was murdered, as you know," Charles went on, "by the Duke of Burgundy, who succeeded him as Queen Isabeau's chief lover. I was married when I was ten to the daughter of my father's

137

mistress, to little Isabella of France, who was not much older than I, though she was already a widow—the widow of King Richard II."

"I know that, too," said James, "and your people were angry because Henry IV wouldn't return her dowry and so she had none."

"Yes, my people did very badly out of Charles VI. He gave me a widowed virgin without a penny for a wife, and he refused to bring my father's murderer to justice. He was raving mad, and so did not do anything about him. Indeed, instead of punishing the murderer, he let him sleep with his wife. My mother died in 1408, and the next year my wife died in childbirth, leaving me a daughter. A year later I married Bonne d'Armagnac, whose father promised to avenge my father's death on John the Fearless, Duke of Burgundy, who had hired the assassins to kill my father. I like Bonne very much, and I miss her here—d'you suppose I could bring her to share my captivity? I suppose not, it would look as if I were too acquiescent, were settling down here completely: and anyway, there is my duchy to manage."

James looked enviously at Charles. "You've loved and you've fought—you're a lot ahead of me," he said.

But Charles said, "Love is all right; it is my chief indoor amusement. But 'fought'—you can have all the fighting I did. That awful mess on Crispin's day! Heavens, it was horrible! I was wounded, and I must have fainted from loss of blood, for when I came to, I was under a heap of dead, I couldn't move, being still in full armour. I was practically suffocated, when Sir Charles Waller, who was systematically going through the pile and stripping the dead of any valuables they might have, got my vizor open, and saw I was still breathing, and carried me off to your king. Then that long, long march to Calais—victors and vanquished, captors and captured, all arrived worn out. And the burghers of Calais had shut the gates of their town and manned the walls, and would only let in a few English lords. Some of the English archers, who had taken noble prisoners, sold them in

138

exchange for food. We were all desperately hungry, footsore, and worn out. I only had one real meal in six days; that was when your King Henry gave a banquet, and gave each of us a damask robe (I'd rather have had a velvet one for this damp English weather) and scolded us for our sins: what a self-righteous young prig he is! He really thinks because he's good at fighting, God has chosen him to be the scourge of the French! Then, hardly had we digested our one dinner, when we had to go on board ship and we lost it again—and fast. I was on King Henry's vessel, luckily, for there was the most tremendous storm on the crossing—we made straight for Dover but two ships belonging to one English lord were lost, and several, full of prisoners, grounded on the Dutch coast. I must say your King Henry kept marvellously calm. You felt you would never drown with him around, he was so sure the winds and the waves existed for his especial benefit."

"How did you begin writing verse?" asked James.

And Charles replied, "My mother was a friend of the poet Petrarch's so I wrote poetry almost before prose. Mother used to make me copy sonnets when she was teaching me to write; first, she made me write the names of the gods and goddesses, to teach me the alphabet: A, for Apollo; B, for Bacchus, and so forth, and then I graduated to sonnets," and he began quoting some of his own lines:

> My heart, my thought and I went out
> Upon one summer's day

and

> Time has put off his muddy cloak
> Of wind and cold and rain.

Then James, not to be outdone, sang him some of his songs: a ballad for Beltane, and *Waly, Waly up the Bank,* which made Charles laugh, because of the funny

139

primitive tongue in which it was written. "Like what our peasants speak," he said, and James said, "It *is* what *our* peasants speak. I want to write so that all my people can understand me, and most of my people are peasants—but a very few are nobles."

Three hundred and eighteen days on end at 13 shillings fourpence a day James stayed in the Tower that year. Each day new schemes, new hopes arose, or were minted, to reconcile two bored young men with life; but every one of them faded or failed. In September the Emperor Sigismund (then German king) and Henry V entered into a formal alliance. Henry also made an agreement with the Duke of Burgundy: but as soon as Burgundy had marched on Paris with a cavalry force, Henry landed again in France with 1,000 gunners and 17,000 armed cavalry and as many archers, and began the systematic conquest of Normandy by taking Caen. He scorched the earth, leaving starvation and desolation behind him. He met with no resistance except that after Agincourt Charles VI had all the bridges to Paris broken. But Henry's men quickly made temporary ones, or rafts.

James was allowed to go north in March, 1417, with the Bishop of Durham and the Earls of Westmoreland and of Northumberland. They rode together, as far as Pontefract, through the pale slow northern spring; the wild daffodils were flooding the banks and the sides of the hedgerows, and each oak tree they passed stood in a pool of wild, scented blue hyacinths. James was in the highest spirits. At last, he thought, I am on my way home. And it was so good to see Henry Percy again, now they were both grown up; Henry had just married the Earl of Westmoreland's daughter, and the three splendid young men galloped and laughed and travelled happily together, with the portly bishop, delighted to be rid of his colleagues for once, and to be in secular and aristocratic company, keeping a worldly and a watchful eye upon them. They had an immense retinue, and for the first time in years, James felt that life held something for him. This spring journey through the enchanted countryside gave promise that, perhaps, being a king might mean some happiness after all. Charles d'Orléans was with them, and though the cynical, embittered Frenchman hardly fitted in with the three gay burly northerners, they were all very polite to him—"Far too polite," he grumbled, "I wish you could bring yourselves to be as rude to me as you are to each other; I shouldn't feel such an outsider, such a foreigner if you could." The others enjoyed his sarcastic comments on the land: "A good country for white and red cattle, and for wheat," he said, "venison, deer, roedeer, partridges, quail, and a marvellous quantity of hares. Few castles," he added, "few fortified towns, but many people, all of whom are, alas, good archers, even when they don't know it themselves. No wine, except that which comes by sea, and, since wine is dear, only the likes of us drink it—and we get gout, because it's so sour."

But when they got to Pontefract, there was no sign of the eleven chief nobles and prelates of Scotland who were to meet James and his party to negotiate his release. James sent messages to King Henry telling him his "great desire" to go further north, and Henry proved "more gracious than James could say or write" and allowed him to go on to Raby—a tremendous pile, straddling the high road, where James, like Sister Anne in the tale of Bluebeard, looked daily northwards to see if anyone was coming. But absolutely no one came. James was bitterly mortified: the English could not be blamed, for it was his own people did not require him; he was unwanted, bypassed, mocked by his unfaithful subjects. Yet it was not they, he cried to his sore heart, who were at fault: they had been given no choice; they owed him no allegiance who had sworn him none: it was his wicked uncle who was sole villain, and there was nothing to be done except to try and engineer a rising against Albany. But Douglas in the South, and Mar in the North, were practically independent; friends of his though they were, James could hardly expect them to roll King Log off the throne when they knew he, James, would prove King

141

Stork. So he rode back to Pontefract, his head and his heart low. But kindly Northumberland, who was sorry for him, cheered and tended him; he had grown fond of James. So Charles d'Orléans and James lived that whole summer a normal country life, as paying guests of the Northumberlands.

When James came South, in the late summer, he was sent to Windsor, whilst Charles was conveyed back to the Tower. "I shall be lonely," Charles said, "without you to beat at chess. And there'll be no one to whom I can teach French."

James grunted, but he was pleased: this civilised creature, for all his mannerisms, was more European, more part of the great world outside, and counted for more than lightweights such as Griffith Glendower, or boors like Murdoch.

Now James was at Windsor, he was, as king, allowed to exercise many of his functions. Although he still was guarded with extreme vigilance, he had a full and an active life. It was to him that all Scotsmen came, whether arriving in England for tournaments, or en route to join the wars on the continent, armed with safe-conducts. For war was still the only means of livelihood for most gentlefolk, and wherever there was a war, the knighthood of Europe flocked to it. And when there was no war, they had to make do with tilts and tourneys.

From Murdoch, James had heard nothing, and certainly his cousin was far from keeping his word to try and bring James back to his rightful throne. On the contrary, he had taken his place as Albany's heir, and was busily deputising for his now ageing father. From Griffith, James heard, however. *His* magician father, who had once played quite a considerable role on the world's stage, had refused to avail himself of King Henry's offer of pardon, made before Agincourt, and repeated again on his return. The English king, now so secure in the hearts of his people, found the old Welsh agitator no menace now. He could afford to be generous, and thought that were Owen tamed and restored to his

142

savage semi-royal palace of Sycharth, he might well be a feather, even if a slightly bedraggled one, in his conqueror's cap. But Owen Glendower would not play. Lurking in the woods, this elderly man, now nearing seventy, who had defied the Lancastrians ever since 1399, was starving. "Being now driven to such misery, that he in a manner despaired of all comfort, he fled into desert places and solitary caves, where, being destitute of all relief and succour, dreading to shew his face to any creature, and finally lacking enough to sustain nature, for pure hunger he miserably pined away and died," so Griffith wrote to James, asking him to have some Masses said for his father's soul.

At the same time James learned from John Lyon, his representative, of the results of the Council of Constance, which still was sitting, but whose main purposes had already been completed. St. Bridget of Sweden had been canonised in a lovely ceremony, her silver image held high over the colourful crowds, who shouted, "We have another intercessor with God for us." And, on November 11th, 1417, all three popes having been disposed of, Oddo Colonna was unanimously elected pope, and was anointed as Martin V. So the Great Schism of the West was healed.

As soon as James made his formal obedience to Martin V he was authorised to keep a portable altar, and to have Mass said daily, even "before daybreak and in places under interdict."

James had begun to buy books. Not, of course, on the scale his friend Humphrey, Duke of Gloucester, bought them, nor even on the scale of King Henry's other brother, John, Duke of Bedford, who later bought the whole library of Charles VI in Paris, some 700 volumes. James bought books singly, and, whenever he could, he bought them on credit, to be paid for "when I shall come into mine own."

He was also permitted now to roam about the countryside, to ride where he would, and to amuse himself on the River Thames, so long as he was never alone, but always had a guard with him. One July day when he was amusing himself on the water in a small boat, with only one Thomas Haseley, clerk of the crown, for company and keeper, he saw a well-dressed gentleman walking in an adjoining meadow, and beckoning to him. James rowed to land and moored; jumping out, with Thomas Haseley following at a respectful distance, he approached the stranger, who introduced himself as Sir John Mortimer of Hatfield. At the name of Mortimer, James winced and his escort visibly started, for Edmund Mortimer was the legitimate pretender to the throne of England, far nearer in blood to the crown than King Henry. And it was but two years since when, only a few months before Agincourt, Richard Mortimer, Earl of Cambridge, Sir Thomas Gray, and Lord Scrope of Marsham had been apprehended for their share in a mysterious plot to assassinate King Henry on the eve of his departure overseas. Thus to be seen in the company of a Mortimer was in itself highly suspicious, and James felt very uncomfortable. Getting out of Haseley's earshot, Mortimer explained he had a plan for carrying James up to Scotland, if James would but trust him: he had a list of all the places where safe lodgings and fresh horses could be had between Windsor and Edinburgh. It was but an eight days' journey, and King James would find himself well taken care of en route. "What do you want of me instead?" James asked.

Mortimer replied, "Only an understanding that when you are come to your own, you will do all in your power to bring King Richard back onto the English throne—if it can, indeed, be proven that the Scots mammet is he. If he is dead, then you shall work for the restoration of my cousin Edmund, who in that event is the rightful kind."

James looked doubtfully at Sir John: he was a ferrety, thin, sharp-nosed little man, with mad, burning eyes, and a low, soft conspiratorial voice: tiny flecks of saliva frothed from his mouth as he talked, and his lips were crusted with old spume. They walked back to James's boat, and James said to Haseley, who had caught up with them: "Sir John needs to go down to Windsor, and begs a lift of us—will you sit in the stern, and I'll put him in the bow, whilst I row?"

When they got to town, James set down Sir John, and asked him, "Is there anyone around me through whom I may send you an answer?"

"Tom Payn, the ostler, is one of us."

"Lollards?" questioned James, and Sir John first shook his head violently, and then said, "Yes. Yet, I pray you, never, never use that word—it's death."

James climbed the castle stairs slowly to his own room. He knew already he would not go, and wondered why not. What kept him? No loyalty to Henry, certainly, though perhaps a certain kingly comradeship. Or was it just accidie, that world weariness, which was a besetting sin of the age, making him anxious to avoid making decisions? But James discounted such spurious humility, for had he not, in this case at least, already made a decision, and one which, like all his good actions, he regretted? Pride kept him from treachery, as pride kept him from cowardice. The greatest of all sins had one advantage, it cast out the lesser crew, Beelzebub defeating Satan. James's device was a branch of thistles with a spring of rue, with the motto *Pour ma défense.* But the tragedy was that the King of Scots could do nothing for his own defence. He could not slink home to his kingdom, he could not cheat his captor, nor be beholden to a traitor.

So James walked to the stables, and found Tom Payn, a slip of a lad, currycombing a strawberry roan gelding. James patted the horse, and as the boy pulled his own forelock, James told him: "The answer is, no."

"Very good, Sire," said Tom Payn, bowing low, and James sauntered out of the cobbled yard, the pleasant smell of dung and saddle leather in his nostrils.

About a fortnight later, King Henry came to Windsor, and sent for James, giving him to read a letter concerning Tom Payn written by Thomas Haseley. "At midnight beside your castle of Windsor where is the King of Scots kept a prisoner," James read, "this said traitor should have gone with the said king toward Scotland, in proof whereof I found in the traitor's purse a schedule written of all places of lodgings appointed for him from Windsor to Edinburgh in Scotland." Thomas Haseley had added that he had lain in wait for five days and six nights for poor Tom Payn before apprehending the rascal. And he also embroidered upon the story of Sir John Mortimer's trip in the boat with James. Henry V watched James as he read. "Is this true, James? Does the King of Scotland connive with grooms?" he asked.

James turned scarlet. "You may believe what you will," he said, staring defiantly at Henry. "The truth is that I refused to be a party to the Lollard intrigues. Not that I care who is king in England, but because to cheat you by flight would be to bring myself down to your level, who captured me in time of truce."

Henry looked amused. "Well scratched, young cub," he said. "I'll hang young Payn and give Haseley a present for his pains. As for you, my lord King, you shall return to the Tower; there are no more Lollards there, nor elsewhere now. Since my victories, their talk of peace and their dislike for fighting have brought them into disfavour. They are scarecrows; when my war goes ill, out they come, but fair weather and fortune's favour drive them where they belong, underground."

Charles d'Orléans was delighted to see James again. "Serves you right for funking," he told him, "he who won't run away, lives to rue the day. But now we can settle down to versifying again."

"You may swell yourself into a poet, or even a versifier," said James, "I regard myself only as a maker—a maker of rhymes, of tunes and tales, making up in enthusiasm what I lack in inspiration."

"We'll both endure as writers," said Charles smugly, "and perhaps that's why we're shut up here together. Providence never makes mistakes, and our destiny may be not as kings or rulers, but as national bards and poets. Here we have time, time to mourn and to mend our bad

146

luck and our bad verses. It's your turn now to read me what you've been mulling."

So the two young men settled down to a good meal of goose stuffed with herbs and garlic, served with apple fool and sour cream; it was washed down by plenty of the sour imported claret that Charles complained gave him the bellyache.

PART TWO

1419-1424

JOAN BEAUFORT

CHAPTER ONE

☐ Two years had passed. Sir John Oldcastle, the Lollard leader, had been caught and roasted; his widow had cheerfully remarried—her fifth husband. Albany had instigated an unsuccessful breaking of the truce whilst Henry V's back was turned, so shameful and so disastrous that it was nicknamed "The Foul Raid." He had, also, offered 30,000 livres to the Duke of Burgundy—he, who had no money with which to ransom James! But already some Scots had gone to seek service with Charles, the French dauphin, now all of fifteen years old. His mother queen, Isabeau, declared him ill-gotten, and bastardised her own son. On September 10th, 1419, at the Pont de Montereau, this son watched his men cut the old Duke of Burgundy, John the Fearless, to pieces with axes and swords before his eyes. Thus was revenged the death of Charles d'Orléans' father at Burgundy's hands. Though Charles d'Orléans was delighted, it was a dastardly deed, and Charles, the dauphin, forever after trembled if he walked on a plank, and was terrified to cross a bridge. Mingy and pasty-faced, he would stop eating, shiver and shrink if any stranger so much as looked at him. Yet it was to this man's service that now rallied a force of seven thousand Scotsmen under Albany's second son, John, Earl of Buchan and Constable of Scotland, and under Archibald, Earl of Wigtown, son and heir of James's brother-in-law, the Earl of Douglas. And it was to this wretched youngster, who, for all his poor showing, stood for a free France, that a decade or so later was sent Joan the Maid.

James was penniless, or at least exceedingly hard up. Albany would not send him any money either from the crown revenues, or from James's Earldom of Carrick, and James was at his wit's end to find the wherewithal to pay his servants their wages, or his tailor; the English, it is true, paid his board and lodging—such as it was—and occasionally gave him 20 pounds for having his apparel mended, or 60 pounds to pay divers merchants. He wrote appealing directly to the cities whose customs he had been granted as a boy—Edinburgh, Stirling, and Perth—but failed to get any money from them. In Flanders, however, the new Duke of Burgundy, Philip the Good, authorised James to levy customs on all Scottish merchandise coming into the country. James, in exchange, granted Burgundy the right to take a tenth on the same merchandise. Sir John Pelham had been more than kind: he lent James money and books, and often sent him food and wine—a haunch of venison, a brace of partridges, a dozen or two plovers' eggs, or some fresh pike. James preferred staying at Pevensey in the summer, but moved back to the Tower in the winters—for Lady Joan, Sir John's valiant wife, and their children returned to town, and the loneliness of the soggy Sussex flats without them was more than James could face.

Early in May, 1420, James was expecting Sir John, who was bringing an important message from King Henry. James was twenty-six now—the age Henry had been when he came to the throne. He had around him almost a small court, and on many matters—such as ecclesiastical policy—he had very different ideas from Albany and had managed to get quite a lot done, by dealing directly with the papacy. As he waited in the castle grounds that evening, for Sir John to arrive, he talked with his favourite chaplain, Thomas Myrton. John Lyon had proved more of a diplomat than a priest, and James kept him busy, sending him to and from the Council of Constance, which still dragged on, and to and from Scotland, on many errands to do with James's everlastingly delayed ransom and release.

"I fear I shall be sadly removed from my people when I do get home," said James. "I've grown very English in my exile."

But Thomas Myrton told him not to worry. "People are so alike the world over; there is much more likeness between them than difference. All men like to eat, to sleep, to fight, to make love," he told James. "You'll find your Scots no different from yourself. Judge everyone as you do yourself, only less harshly: you cannot be sure anyone else is as nasty as you know you are within yourself."

James smiled, "Do you, also, suffer from that—that almost nausea of yourself? I feel so often, if only I didn't have to live with this frightful person James Stewart—if I didn't have to see his face, and think his thoughts, maybe everything would be all right."

"It wouldn't be," said Thomas Myrton, grimly, "because were you Henry of Agincourt, you would find the same difficulties exactly. It's hard to get upsides with oneself, whoever one is. The best way is not to bother: one's disadvantages are like a horse's harness: one must needs try to see they don't chafe and fret the horse so it goes badly, or becomes unmanageable. But the great thing is that the horse should keep going."

"Yes," James said, and added, "my mother would have had me a priest, and I think I have had better schooling for priest than for prince."

"No," Thomas Myrton said, "the best education for the one is the best for the other; and you've been tremendously lucky."

"Lucky!" said James. "You mean unlucky?"

"Far from it. Reflect. You've grown up at court, a king, knowing from childhood what your job was to be, so you could prepare yourself for it. And you've been free of all intrigues, free from hate and from misdirected love; from parents who would hold you back, from a father who might have been jealous of you, or a mother who might have feared for you. All that is negative and gnawing and clutching about human relationships you have escaped. And you've been able to watch: to observe, detached, impartial, curious, and interested, the machinery of government, the working of the state, the life of a court, and the folly of mankind. In all history, few kings have had your chances."

James shielded his eyes against the sun. "Here comes Sir John," he said, "my apprenticeship is over, I fancy; I hope I have learnt my part, for I am now setting out to play it in the world."

"How do you know?" asked Myrton.

"Last time Sir John was down he told me the king had graciously given ear to my request to serve under him: he promised he would bring next time my orders, when, where," said James.

"I hope I may continue to serve under *you*," said Thomas Myrton, and King James smiled and slipped his arm into his chaplain's.

A week later, James was at Southampton. He was in a delighted bustle, spending a sum big for him—over 150 pounds—for the purchase of armour, horses, tents, and banners. He bought clothes, too, for though in France in the field armour only was worn, in the evenings, or when living in the cities between campaigns, he understood that Henry and his entourage were richly dressed. So he bought two embroidered doublets, and a surcote with tight sleeves, gathered and bunched at the shoulder and a vair-trimmed houppelande and jerkins of sheepskin for his men; they wore kilts and plaids for the most part, so did not require the long hose affected by the English.

The sea delighted James—he had forgotten his early anguish, and the day he sailed was calm and blue; he had the sensation of going off on holiday, of glad release. At last he was going about a man's business; he was a king, going to serve under the greatest commander of the age; for Henry V was most certainly that—there was no one could hold a candle to him. The ship was beautiful, with many white sails, and James could not stare enough at all the strange manoeuvres, the hoisting, the lowering, the tacking and luffing; the whole art and craft of navigation entranced him. He sat on a coil of rope and scribbled a few lines: "The waves are wilting to and fro," he began.

Calais was on the surface English enough—yet, definitely, James felt it was already a foreign city. Though only English was spoken within the walls, yet the bread was differently baked, the loaves crustier than in London, the butter stamped with delightful shapes; there was wine in plenty, too, in the taverns, instead of beer, and James borrowed one of his men's clothes, and for the first time in his life, went out incognito, and mouched about the dirty streets on foot, hung about outside a chandler's shop, and visited the market where he bought himself some wonderfully stinking goat's cheese which he ate for his breakfast next morning with great relish.

But later that day, riding through the devastated country, he began to perceive the effects of war—of this war, in which he was so anxious to engage. The villages, fairly frequent, were hardly populated except by old, old men and women—the rest of their inhabitants had fled. Like madmen the French had all run from the country into the walled towns and with them had taken their wives and children and their bags and baggage. Many houses had been broken into, many wantonly burnt by departing soldiery, who, as they left, had often thrown, by the roadside, sometimes miles away, objects that must have been treasured by their owners, but had proved too heavy and burdensome a booty to be worth their weight. About noon, just as James was wondering where they should eat their midday meal, and had sighted a clump of willows near a brook as providing agreeable shade and water for horses and men, a girl, in torn and ragged clothes, indeed, half naked, ran out from some bushes.

She carried a small baby, and held it, puling and bawling, up to James. "My lord," she sobbed, tears pouring down her dirty face, "take it—kill it if you will, but I have no milk for it, and I can't bear to see it starve, and I can't bring myself to leave it or strangle it, take it out of my sight, I want to die first, not to watch it die."

When James offered her money, she laughed, weakly, but still derisively: "Your English money," she said, "won't buy dust here, or dung: *no* money will buy food —there isn't gold enough in all France to buy a pint of milk for my baby, or some groats."

James did not know what he should do next, but Thomas Myrton said he would put woman and child before him on his horse. "I'll come on slowly, after you," he told James. "I'm in no hurry, no one's going to hurt me, and maybe we can beg a mouthful to eat, the three of us." James gave the woman a wrap; she rejected one of his new surcotes but accepted an old plaid, and rode on.

On the third evening they reached Troyes, and James was astonished at the lightness and delicacy of the roofs and spires: it looked as though every building were craning up, standing on the very tips of its toes in order to try and reach the sky and hang on to heaven by its eyelashes.

"How I've wasted my life," James said to William Giffard, "this country is where I should have been these past fourteen years."

They went straight to the bishop's palace, where Henry V was staying with Charles VI and Isabeau of Bavaria, his queen, and young Catherine, who was to marry Henry. It was evening, and dusk had fallen when they halted in the great courtyard, and James replied to the challenge of the guard. They were expected, and lackeys helped James from his horse, and led it away. He bade William Giffard see what became of it, for it was his new, and best-loved beast. As they walked, interminably, it seemed to James, through room after room, hung with cramoisy wrought in gold or silver thread, or with verdure tapestries, he was glad, after all, that he had been brought up at the simple English court. There was a tremendous falseness about all this grandeur, and, when he at last was ushered into the huge room where Henry V was sitting with the Queen of France, the new Duke of Burgundy, and the whole French court, he could sense the corruption—he felt it as a dog feels a cat or a ghost—by a physical reaction. The queen looked a very Jezebel, and she stared impudently at James whilst he bowed over her hand, as though appraising his worth as a stallion simply; slightly raising her finely arched eyebrows, with a tiny, ironic smile, she dismissed him as chaste. Though she said nothing but words of conventional and courteous greeting, "We are happy to welcome our cousin of Scotland, we trust he made a good journey," James felt her quizzical contempt, her casual indifference. Whilst he resented, with the clear fervour of the pure, the whole miasma of this stagnant, fetid atmosphere, yet, king and grown man as he was, he bridled at her assumption of the possession of an ancient wisdom, at her too sweet flesh mocking his callow virtue. He turned with relief and almost with affection to Henry, who welcomed him with ostentatious warmth, as though to prove to himself by thus hugging close this obviously simple and sincere young king, that he, too, was on the side of the angels; that he was for life and for goodness and for health, in spite of all appearances, in spite of keeping this decaying, slimy, verdegreen company.

Soon they moved, to the playing of many hidden and most skilful musicians, into another room, where a splendid supper awaited them; James, remembering the desolation through which he had travelled all the days since he landed in France, was sick at heart at sight of so much food, so much waste, so much extravagance. He sat on young Catherine's left, Henry V on her right. The young princess flirted kittenishly, gaily, with them both.

"Have you come to find and to conquer both a bride and a kingdom here, as Henry did?" she asked James, coyly, looking up at him through thick, curly eyelashes. Before James could answer, Queen Isabeau said, loudly:

"We shall lose all our girls if so many Scots and English gentlemen come to take them so far from home." Catherine modestly, bashfully, cast down her eyes. James felt she was sly; there was something in the mincing clipped speech, in the affected droop of the sleepy eyelids, in the posed, heraldic innocence, that he mistrusted.

"I'm glad it's Henry she's marrying, and not me," he thought, and wondered what manner of girl her sister, Charles d'Orléans' sad bride, had been.

After supper he held the wool that one of Princess Catherine's maids-of-honour was winding. She was a young girl who told him she came, like the queen, from Bavaria. Though unmarried, she was quite obviously pregnant.

"Yes," she told James delightedly, without a trace of shame, "I'm with child by the emperor, by Sigismund. It was not nearly as difficult as I feared, to lie with an emperor! I did my best, and I certainly am fortunate to be in my happy condition. You know," she told James gravely, "royal blood makes a man far more agreeable, and far more appetising, not to speak of the nice presents one gets on the side. That's why I can't understand Her Majesty of France condescending to mere dukes, as she does."

James concealed his disgusted surprise at the girl's talk (she could not have been more than fifteen) and she went on to tell him how the Elector of Saxony had ordered his chancellor to make a list of courtesans in the city of Constance during the council, and he did as well as he could, but the elector still complained that the list was not complete.

"'If you want it complete, I must put in first, the first lady of her profession,' said the chancellor; and everyone knew who she was—the Empress Barbara of course." James looked surprised, and the girl laughed.

"Did you not know she was mad for men?" she added, and in a whisper said, "Worse even than our own dearest first lady."

James said aloud, slowly, "Poor lack-of-love."

"Light-of-love, you mean," said the girl, gaily, opening her eyes, but James shook his head. "She loved too little, not too much," he said. "There's all the difference in the world between the love which gives and the love which takes."

The girl yawned. "How learned you are," she scoffed. "I don't care which love it is, or whose, so long as—" And she went on speaking filthily until James chided her with:

"I fear here is one king whose potency you will never learn," then left her, pleading fatigue from his long journey.

He had never imagined such a crapulous court. Even the faces were animal muzzles—lascivious goats, leering monkeys, bitches, cats—it was hard to find any resemblance to a human being amongst any of the courtiers. Henry himself seemed coarsened by this company; he looked dark, malevolent, almost sinister. As James passed in one corner a quartet of pretty girls were talking about the clap one of them had caught; in another, a group of men were discussing ways of swindling the natives; elsewhere a soldier boasted to his companions how he had stolen an old man's ox, and made the owner drive it ten miles to where he wanted to roast it for supper.

As James bowed before the high table, he saw the poor mad French king was still eating; he could not find his way to his mouth with his spoon, but slopped wolfishly, in desperate hunger, missing his lips, and spilling, whilst the courtiers laughed and pointed at him as at a motley fool. He stank so that James, bowing to him, retched from the foul stench of excrement and fetid sweat that rose. James's erstwhile informant was standing behind him, giggling. As he turned to go, she told him loudly, "When His Majesty's linen is to be changed, or he is to be washed or undressed, twelve men with blackened faces, fully armed, overpower him, and strip him, and scrub him with cold water and strong brushes."

"Shame on you, Madame," James said under his

159

breath, "for mocking an afflicted fellow creature who is your king."

James rose early next morning, and went to Mass in the cathedral. As he walked there from his hostelry, he saw a Jew slink by, and a few minutes after, a crowd of men pursuing him. One asked James which way the pest carrier went. James pretended he had seen no man. "Why think you the Jews carry plague more than other men?" he asked. "Know you not that the pope long ago forbade the slaughter or the plunder of Jews under pain of excommunication?"

"The pope does not know what the Jews do to us: they slip plague into our wells, and will not drink from them themselves," said a man. "They cut up Christian babes and eat them, to keep the plague from themselves," said another.

"They bring leprosy with their kisses," said another, and another agreed, "That they do. 'Twas for that Philip the Fair burnt all the lepers in France a hundred years ago—would our king would burn all the Jews today. So might we be freed from the plague."

"We can help the king get started by burning this one," said another man, "we're wasting our time talking to this good stranger, and mayhap our quarry is escaping whilst we chatter—go to it, friends, let's get going."

James found Henry already in the cathedral, following the Ordinary from a huge, gold-embossed missal. James knelt down beside him. If he were going to fight under him, he could not begin better than by praying with him, he thought. And James earnestly commended himself, and his companion, to Him from Whom is all rule, from Whom derives all sovereignty; to the King, unto Whom all live.

Henry took James with him to the siege of Rouen, then at its last gasp. The defenders had driven out 60,000 old men, women, and children, hoping Henry would allow them to pass through the lines back to the countryside from which they originally had fled into the city. But Henry would not let them pass, and they died miser-

watch the English stuffing on capons and butter and eggs and fruits and milk, stolen from their countrymen and cousins, perhaps even from their own gardens.

Sometimes Henry would throw a roll that he had bitten—a crusty, white, fragrant still warm roll, as far as he could toward the beleaguered walls, and some sentry would see it, and perhaps slip down and race towards them to snatch it. Then Henry would take a bow from one of his archers, and shoot the man as though he were a hind. And hardly ever miss, for he was a superb marksman.

And the worst for the French was that their own king, in his madness, had been taken over and delivered to the enemy by his strumpet whore of a wife, and was being lugged around as an exhibit in Henry's train. "Citizens of Rouen—or Beaugé—or Melun—see, here is your monarch: if you resist the English, you are fighting also against him, against your lawful liege; you are then rebels, and outside the pale of Christian society, outside the proper order of the world, outside of human decency, so that when you are taken, we can deal with you accordingly—as beasts not as men." So announced King Henry's herald, parading the mad King Charles.

And then, one July morning, James learned why Henry had sent to England for him to come. He had thought, in his idiotic innocence, that it was in order that he might learn warfare under a gallant general; in order that his education as king might include the craft of war, the management of soldiers. He was to discover it was quite otherwise. Henry and Catherine were staying at Corbeil; the Hôtel de Ville there, though not quite as splendidly spacious as the bishop's palace in Troyes, was still comfortable. James and his suite were staying outside of Rouen with a local nobleman, the Sieur de Beaurepas, who was on the Burgundian side—"because my aunt is the duke's niece," he explained to James. "Your Scots," he went on, "are nothing but winebags and mutton munchers, and as for your Douglas, our women around here bogey their children with his name: 'Douglas will get you if you're not quiet, Douglas will come and eat you.'"

James froze, and de Beaurepas realised he had made a gaffe: "I'm sorry, Sire: I thought it would not irk you if I spoke ill of your rebellious subjects—after all, since they are fighting against you, you cannot think too well of them," he whined, embarrassed. James opened his mouth to begin explaining that he was held prisoner by the English king; that his people, in his absence, could not be expected to do otherwise than obey Albany, his Regent; and that, in this instance, he wholeheartedly approved Albany's assistance of the old ally, France, though he naturally abhorred the reason for such assistance—to keep himself, James, out of the way, by deflecting money meant for his ransom, and people interested in ransoming him. But then he thought, what's the use? And bowing, he rode off to his day's work. When he got to the English king's lodging, Henry greeted him with a cat-who-has-eaten-the-canary expression: "Catherine thinks she is with child," he said, and James offered his congratulations. Then Henry said, "I've got a surprise for you," and called to a knight who brought out two standards beaten with James's arms, two tunics similarly beaten, and two pennons beaten with his badges. Henry handed them to James. "I had these made for you by my own armourer," he said. "Like them?" James's eyes sparkled. "Of course, I do, Sire: many thanks. I pray I may make good use of them."

"I thought you needed to identify yourself a bit more," said Henry. "Amongst the defenders of Melun there are quite a few Scots. I want you to issue a proclamation, ordering the Scots in the army of the Dauphin to lay down their arms, as they have taken them up against you, their lawful suzerain."

James replied, instantly, gazing steadfastly into Henry's eyes: "As a prisoner and in your hands, I have no power over my subjects, nor are they under any allegiance to obey my command. If I had any power over

164

them, I would tell them not to desert France, our ancient ally, in her sad extremity: I would bid them fight on."

Henry looked as though he might literally explode: a great vein throbbed on his forehead; his eyes popped; James expected to be knocked down. But after a few instants Henry V managed, somehow, to get hold of himself, and said, in an unctuously smooth voice: "Happy shall be the subjects of a king who shews himself endowed with such wisdom." Then he added, with a smile, quite calmed now: "James, your language does you credit. But, alas, I fear your words will bring cold comfort to your rebellious subjects. *I* will issue the proclamation for you, and I will have my heralds trumpet a warning before the walls of Melun that every Scot who is found within when the city falls, will be hanged as a traitor to his king—and that also included your distinguished cousinage, if any member of it should be so foolish as to bide by a besieged garrison. But I do not think we will find any but the lowest rank of soldier inside the walls."

"You can't mean what you say," said James.

Henry V smiled again, "I always do. Have you forgotten how the French prisoners in our camp were killed during the fighting on the day of Agincourt, owing to a falsely spread rumour?"

James gasped, but Henry stared at him, coolly. "Do you remember the first beast you ever killed? I caught a tiny rabbit when I was a small boy, and it died in my hands of sheer fright. I sorrowed for that little animal more than I've sorrowed since. You must grow up, James." And Henry, still smiling, dismissed him: "Take your standards and pennons—even if you sulk in your tent like Achilles or hide them, they and you will serve my purposes, willy-nilly. I'm glad you answered me as you did—good boy; now let's get on with the day's work. Take two dozen men over to Rozières—you know the village across the river, and see if you can't buy some scaling ladders—or get some made—they have an excellent master carpenter there, I'm told. . . ."

James saw it was hopeless. He turned to William Giffard. "Let's be gone," he said.

On September 17th, Archibald Douglas, the Earl of Wigtown, shouted loudly in the cobbled courtyard outside James's rooms in de Beaurepas' snug little castle, and James ran down to greet his nephew—taller than he, and older, a superb figure of a man, dwarfing the surrounding Frenchmen, and his own retainers. "I've just come from Corbeil, from Henry," Douglas said, "and I got from him another safe-conduct to come on to you. Henry told me, what I knew already, that you have protested against the use of your name. Buchan has announced at once his refusal even to acknowledge any orders given by you under these circumstances and in view of this compulsion, so don't fret yourself unduly nor overmuch about that bad business. I've come to bring you some good news for a change. Albany's dead."

"Then I can go home?" questioned James eagerly, but his nephew replied:

"Not so fast. Murdoch has succeeded to the governorship."

"He hasn't had himself proclaimed king, by any chance?" enquired James sarcastically, "King Murdoch the Great?"

"Oh, no; he has acted with great circumspection. He has merely announced that, pending your release, he is prepared to continue performing his father's functions. He has had a new Great Seal made, with Murdoch, Regent and Governor, upon it."

James drew Archibald Douglas with him up the stairs. "Come up," he begged, "and have a good square meal. Her ladyship here keeps a fine kitchen, and I must say I'm greedy; years of prison fare have made me fond of goodies." James could not bear to speak more of Scotland then.

Melun fell on All Saints' Day. Fierce battles had been fought for it daily by the fall sun and by dim torch and candlelight; Henry had dug trenches and mines in which he had laid fires. He let fireballs and burning pitch down also, into the town, and when the inhabitants complained, he announced, "Fire is only a custom of war, and war without fire is no better than are sausages without mustard." In the deep trenches dug under the city walls Henry fought himself, hand-to-hand battles with the defenders: he even met Barberan, the leader of the beleaguered, there, and they went at it fiercely until some of Henry's men came along and insisted he withdraw. The siege had taken a year, the cords for drawing water from the wells were worn out, and the besieged fought with kitchen spits for spearheads. Henry promised to spare the lives of all that surrendered. But after victory, he put the leaders of the citizens, including Barberan who had headed the citizens' defence, into prison at Chastelet, and left them there to die of hunger. When they pleaded for food, he sent them hay, saying he understood they had eaten so much horse meat that they were become nags.

James, riding into Melun behind Henry, had very mixed feelings. He had enjoyed the military part of the siege; even after his words with Henry he had gone right on, working for him, and fighting with him. For it was such sheer joy to be fully employed, to feel he was in action, instead of in undesired repose. But seeing the tired, hopeless, hungry faces that apathetically watched the triumphal entry of Henry V and of his victorious troops into the conquered city, with only the emaciated children raising a feeble cheer, made James realise that war is fun only for the rich and the great; that for the people, any people, all people, it is as unsought and unwelcome as dogs and hunter are to their defenceless quarry.

The two kings together heard a Te Deum and a Mass of Thanksgiving, and then all the English amongst the besieged (there were only a dozen or so antique followers of King Richard II who had been in France since the beginning of King Henry IV's reign, and had been unlucky enough to get themselves caught now) and the twenty-two Scots who were amongst the garrison, were hanged on a gallows put up by Henry's friend, the master carpenter of Rozières. The twenty-two Scots, lean and haggard and unshaven, appealed personally to James to save their lives, using language he hadn't heard since his childhood, his own Scots tongue. He wept to hear them, but, fighting back his tears, told them that he was a prisoner no less than they, and that if King Henry spared his life, it was only his clemency; nothing he, James, could say or do would influence the English monarch. But still he did his utmost, and sought out Henry immediately, and begged for the Scotsmen's lives, even offering to ransom them out of his own pockets. "Add their ransom to the sum you are charging my country for me," he begged Henry, "and I will gladly pay it, and will take them into my service, or will pay for their return to Scotland."

But Henry refused even to discuss the matter with James. So then James stood beside Thomas Myrton at the gallows. It took some hours on a hot dappled July morning, with fat cumulus clouds piled into cool castellated shapes backstage on a blue sky. First the men were all forced to dig their own graves; no coffins, Henry had said, but they could be wrapped in their plaids. James got a big tankard of wine, and laced it well with brandy; he gave each man a good drink as soon as the chaplain had finished with him; the men, their hands bound, drank in turn from the big wooden ladle James held. His hand was shaking so that at first he spilt quite a lot. One of the older men comforted him, saying, "Dinna fash yersel, laddie," quietly and kindly, and looked up to see James biting back his tears.

They hung so quietly, with hardly a struggle or a twitch; they were so weak from hunger that Henry's executioner had almost to lift them up on to the gallows platform. James watched it all, helping to cut down each body as it stopped jerking, and helping the physician who certified each man dead, digging a sharp pin into their wrists to make sure. James felt that he must share all he could of his subjects' shame and agony. But also, in order that he might savour his own humiliation to the full, he tried to be as completely aware as possible of exactly what was happening. When it was all over, the executioner broke down, became utterly hysterical, and besought Henry to let him depart "out of this unlusty soldier's life into the life of England."

James, though he had never felt so utterly nauseated, yet was glad he had to suffer to the uttermost dregs of this dire experience. As a child, aged about five, he had once realised that the meat he was eating at supper was a calf he had seen that morning, tied to the scullery table before the cook slit its throat. He had petted it, and the little creature had licked his fingers. "That is for the salt in them," his nurse had told him, "cupboard love." As he chewed each mouthful, he had then and there attempted to face and to accept the whole reality, of the calf's death and of his eating its flesh. Now, a grown man, he was conscious of himself repeating again his childish gesture. "These are my people; I am a prisoner; I am their king. This is what happens to the vanquished."

As the seventeenth man was being noosed, and even the horror had become almost automatic, numbing, Henry came up to James. "Are you not afraid that this insistence of yours may be misconstrued? That your own folk may say that since these men were rebels, and disobeyed you, you came personally to twit each man with his failure, and to jeer as he died?"

James was too angry to speak, but the eighteenth prisoner, waiting his turn, his mouth still unstopped, a little runt of a fellow, thin, weedy, and unshaven, said to King Henry, "I think Your Majesty is wrong. There's nary a Scot alive who'll doubt King James." And James said, "Thank you," and put his arms around the man and kissed him. The fellow, though a cold sweat of fear was pouring down his face, and he was shivering with fright, managed to bare his black stumps in a ghastly grin, and to smile back at his king. And, as he died, number nineteen, stepping up to be noosed and gagged and bound, tossed his blue bonnet into the air, and yelled—a croaky, quavering yell, but still loud enough—"Long live King James!"

A month later, James rode into Paris in Henry's train; Charles VI rode too, and the ladies, Catherine and her mother, followed next day in their litters. All the Parisians were dressed in red, and when the two kings arrived on the place outside Notre Dame, a passion was acted before them, and when it was done, the two kings went into the cathedral, and a Te Deum was sung.

A tiny pig cost more than a man could earn in a month; there were no Brie cheeses, no eggs, no peas nor beans in the city, no white bread, no figs nor grapes, nor almonds, no wood for the stoves, so that men climbed by night into the gardens of the king's palace and cut down the trees and flowering shrubs, for firewood.

When the new Queen of England arrived, two coats of ermine were carried before her litter, and men thought this must signify that she was Queen both of England and of France. And indeed, by the Treaty of Troyes that was how it was to be: Charles VI was to be succeeded as King of France by his son-in-law, and his son (who had been carried out of Paris before the English could catch him there, by Tannequy du Castel) was disinherited.

James went as soon as he could to the Scots College, and whilst he was in the city, for the space of some two months, he spent most of his time attending lectures at the university. James had never been to Oxford, where Henry V had studied, and he took gladly and gratefully to university life. The faculty seemed unperturbed by the war. They made thin, donnish jokes about the discomforts. "Roger ate roast rat fifteen times in one week," one of Roger of Edinburgh's colleagues told James, "and for wine, Rhibault's servant boiled up the old lees from some castaway empty bottles he had found and served it at a great charge."

James did not care for the manners of the French court any more now that it was safely returned to its home; though Henry insisted that James must keep

Christmas with them, and there was much feasting, yet James was as surly and as grouchy as he could be. Catherine, however, had taken a fancy to him, called him "my thistle, my little thistle," and insisted he squire her whenever Henry was otherwise engaged—which was often, for there was a tremendous amount of organisational work. Catherine, in front of her ladies, and James's entourage, would stroke and pet him: he disliked it intensely, until once during a rare moment whilst they were alone together—the attendants had gone to fetch torches and tapers—she took his hand, quite gently, and said, "I only tease you because I'm glad to find someone unluckier than I—you are a measure I use, James, and that's why I use you so ill."

James stooped gently and kissed the tiny, finicky fingers, birdlike and bony: "Courage, Catherine," he said, "nothing lasts; this too will pass away."

Her laughter rang out as the procession of lightbearers returned. "But you are of wonderful comfort, I must say, to a lonely girl!" she whispered, as James drew his hand away. It was nice to know she meant him no ill, and as he set off with Henry and Catherine for England, he wondered if she realised what the provisions of the Treaty of Troyes meant—of the treaty in which the giving of her body to Henry was an integral part? The King of England was at once to take the name of Regent; he was to succeed to the thrones of both England and France, although by a special provision he must restore to France all his conquests.

"Poor little Catherine," James thought, quite tenderly, "who means so much, and who is so little," and he rode up to her litter and asked her through the curtains if she felt all right. She poked her mischievous small head out, and looked laughingly at James, her bright eyes shiny like polished pebbles as she said, "I would be perfectly all right were it not for my sickness from my pregnancy," and she made a monkey face at James before drawing her head back.

They reached London in mid-February. Catherine was

171

met at Blackheath by numbers of the London craftsmen clad in white, with red hoods and caps: each guild wore its distinctive badge. She found it hard to understand this new bleak bourgeois country, where burghers and merchants played such a large part.

At the coronation banquet at Westminster James sat on her left, wearing a doublet of cloth of scarlet, with a cape of ermine. Henry Beaufort, resplendent in new robes, sat on her right. As it was Lent, all the dishes were of fish: there were whale and porpoise, and there were Whitstable oysters; there were herring and mackerel and perch and eggs stewed in broth; there were fifteen courses and all of fish, and James whispered to Catherine, "You must take care you don't turn into a mermaid—it's in your husband's family, you know, and maybe it's catching."

"Oh, Melusine, you mean?" Catherine said, and laughed. "I'm sure she never saw so many fish in all the sea, let alone ate them. Was she really Henry's ancestress?"

"Of course," said James, "and she's some relation of yours, too, isn't she, the Angevine girl who was a sea-spirit?"

Catherine shook her head. "If she is, she was kept dark in my nursery," she said; then asked: "James, who is that Sir Richard Whittington, and why does a mere knight wear such splendid clothes?"

"He is Lord Mayor of London, and your husband owes him 21,000 pounds, which is quite a lot of money—he was one of the main backers of Agincourt."

"What a funny way you talk, as though war were commerce," complained Catherine.

"It is a commercial transaction all right," said James. "Look, here is Whittington coming toward you."

With a great trumpeting from the heralds, Sir Richard, a dignified, greying man dressed in the magnificent robes of the city of London, came across to Catherine, and in bad French offered her a great wad of crackling parchments. "It is our custom for the ladies after a banquet to throw aromatic herbs upon the fire; they make a pretty blaze and a pleasant smell. Would Your Majesty deign tonight to cast in instead these old papers?"

Catherine frowned, not understanding, and looked apprehensively at the dusty leaves. "What can this commoner want with me?" she asked James, but he whispered, "Throw them on the fire and be very gracious —they are Henry's bonds, with his signature, that he will repay Sir Richard. This is the hugest wedding present ever made to a king by a commoner, I'll wager."

Catherine did as she was bid, clapping her frail childish hands at the blaze, and making herself most agreeable to Sir Richard. After the banquet there was dancing, and James, who should have opened the ball with Catherine, walked across to Sir Richard, and asked if he would replace him. "You have done so much more for England than I ever have or shall: it is only fitting that you should be the first man to dance with England's queen," he said.

Amid the applause, James took his leave, and went back to the Tower. He found Charles d'Orléans already in bed, a French nightcap absurdly covering the luxuriant chestnut hair. James gave him what details he could about Burgundy's murder, and Charles gave him in return the gossip of the court.

"Have you been writing?" Charles asked, and James replied:

"Not a thing. But campaigning, if you remember, is hardly the atmosphere."

"I don't know," said Charles, "I can imagine very romantic moments around the watch fires. How about romance, by the way—have you given Scotland a queen?"

"Not yet," said James.

CHAPTER TWO

☐ Easter was early that year—two days before Lady Day, and James was cold as he rode down to Leicester to join Henry and Catherine there. The longer willow stems were already green-tipped. James, stopping to eat at a hostelry, watched a small five-year-old, with a sandy kitten in her arms, solemnly hold one fat foot over a daisy. "Why do you do that?" he asked, and she, shy but courteous, answered:

"If I don't grow over the first I see, ere the year be out, 'twill grow over me."

James hated the spring, now; especially this year. His malaise was increased by Henry's uxoriousness, especially as Catherine tried to make him feel she and he were laughing at Henry together. She had a miscarriage just after the coronation—the junketings had been too much for her. Since her recovery, James had been with her a great deal, whilst Henry progressed through the kingdom. He had become intimate with her, casual and easy, and knew himself also very attracted to her. Although every girl in the court set her cap at him, he had evaded them all, and had the reputation of being invulnerable. His devotion to the queen was, for Henry as for the rest of the court, an accepted conceit, a part of

James's role as a pattern of chivalry. No one—except Catherine—took it seriously. Most thought it was a deliberate escape—when ladies waxed too amorous, became insistent, James took refuge in his devotion to Henry's queen. It also made life much more comfortable: since James amused his wife, Henry was only too glad to have him around; he was so completely certain of himself as husband and as lover, that it never entered his head to suspect Catherine, in spite of her more than shady upbringing. But James felt his role acutely; although hallowed by the customs of the time, and although, traditionally, such dancing attendance on the queen was part of court etiquette, he felt himself a rudderless ship. Yet Catherine was kind: she listened to his verses, and he would complain to her how he was wasting so much ink and paper to no purpose:

> O empty sail, where is the wind shall blow
> Me to the port?

he asked her, or himself.

James was absorbed in his scribbling that Easter, for when Henry was home, Catherine had to be entirely attentive to him and James could control the defects of his loneliness only with his writing. He had perfected his ballad on *Trust in God* and that Easter Sunday evening, he sang it in his cool, steady, serious voice, accompanying himself on a lute and sitting at Catherine's feet on a stool, whilst Henry sat up beside her on a carved oak throne, and played with her fingers.

> Be not o'er proud of thy prosperity
> For as it comes, so it will pass away
> Thy time to count is short, thou soon wilt see
> For of green grass soon comes the following hay.
> Labour in truth, while light is of the day
> Trust most in God, for He best help thee can
> And for each inch He will thee give a span
> Since word is thrall and thought is only free
> Daunt thou thy tongue that power has o'er thee.

"I have done a good job training you, James, have I not?" Henry said and James smiled up at him, and said, "That is for others to say, Sire, not for me."

Henry looked at Catherine. "Her Majesty would agree, I think? In all athletic and manly exercises, in the use of weapons, in his skill in horsemanship, his speed in running, his dexterity as a wrestler, his firm and fair aim as a jouster and tourneyer, is not our friend James a magnificent specimen of a king?"

"Stop," laughed James, "are you burying me? or selling?"

Catherine, laughing too, but lasciviously, took up Henry's itemization: "Chest broad and full, arms somewhat long and muscular, flanks thin and spare, limbs beautifully formed."

"A poet who makes his songs not by art, but finds them in the profound depths of his own nature," Henry went on.

"Clear blue piercing eyes," said Catherine.

"What mean you by this catalogue?" James asked, now blushing hotly.

And Henry said, "Catherine and I think marriage so happy an estate that we want to see you married, too, and we are just discussing you as a prospect—so we can talk about you to the ladies we know who seek husbands."

James shrugged his shoulders good-naturedly, and went on strumming on the brass strings of his lute. "I've grown into a confirmed bachelor," he said.

"I'm going to knight you on St. George's day, in St. George's chapel at Windsor," said Henry. "I want you to have the Garter."

James looked pleased. "I haven't earned my spurs," he said, blushing again.

"Oh, yes, you have—and I'm taking you with me when I go abroad again."

Though James knew that the knighthood and the projected marriage, and the carrying him off to France, were all political manoeuvres, yet he did not feel resentful. He realised it was imperative for Henry to detach the Scots from the Dauphin; issuing proclamations in James's name had been of no avail; producing James had been of even less. Buchan had just taken four thousand men as reinforcements, out from Leith, and had reached Poitiers safely as James learnt from Catherine; he knew from Douglas, who was actively working to get him back again, that Douglas and Mar were in Scotland collecting as many more again. James knew that his best hope now of getting home was to connive with Burgundy and Henry in stopping Scottish help to France. He was getting money from Burgundy, too, and a certain amount from Henry. So he played politics with the best, and both ends against the middle, played Douglas, played Burgundy, even played Henry now.

Henry, Catherine, and James went on a stately progress through the North, for Catherine must be shewn to the English people: captured France and Scotland must ride together in their conqueror's triumph. They went first to Leicester, then through Nottingham and Pontefract to York. The great nobles were always ready to welcome the king at the end of the winter, to eat up the salt meat, and finish up the winter supplies, and they were most cordial in their proffered hospitality then; whereas they cursed the king if he should happen to descend upon them in the summer, when they were busy harvesting, or in the autumn, when they had everything stored and put away ready for the winter, and were not at all anxious to dig into their reserves.

James had never before seen York minster, and exclaimed with delight at the "glass wall held together by slender columns" and told Catherine that not even the Sainte Chapelle in her Paris had moved him so much.

Then the wind changed again for him. For Henry suddenly ordered him back to Windsor, and sent him there with an escort of three knights, giving him no explanation, but telling him curtly that he would see him again on the twenty-third of April. It was several days before James learnt of the battle of Beaugé. There the Scots had been attacked during a truce, whilst they were playing football, having laid down their arms. The Duke of Clarence (Henry's brother Thomas), who had been left in France as commander in chief, had tried to defile at the head of his troops over a narrow bridge. Wearing splendid armour, with a coronet of jewels on his helmet, he had been recognised at once, and attacked by a Scottish squire who shivered a lance on him; then he was wounded in the face by Sir William Swinton, and finally had been dispatched by the Earl of Buchan himself. There had followed a great slaughter of English, no less than three earls had been killed and two taken prisoner, these latter being John, Earl of Somerset, and Edmund Beaufort, both nephews of Henry Beaufort, Bishop of Winchester. The bridge had been literally jammed with English dead, and it was a great come-back for the Scots, and had broken in an instant the spell of Agincourt. The Dauphin had made Buchan Constable of France, and his mad father, King Charles VI, coming out of his habitual stupor on hearing the news, had bravely asked the English with whom he was surrounded: "What think you *now* of the Scottish tugmuttons?"

James was sad for the death of the Duke of Clarence, whom he had liked and admired, and he was sorry for Henry, remembering his own childish grief for his brother David. And he knew that in his heart he had rather Clarence had killed his cousin Buchan, than Buchan Clarence, even though he was delighted that so many of his people had fought so well, and was especially pleased that so many Stewarts had distinguished themselves—Stewart of Darnley and Stewart of Railston in particular. On the whole, he thought he had best keep his own counsel about the battle, and say nothing.

He arrived at Windsor late one April afternoon. He felt sick and sorry. It was all to do again, he foresaw: this wretched victory had made it unlikely that Henry would be able to detach the Scots from the Dauphin. James must now coax Henry into negotiation with Douglas and Mar, and into plotting against Murdoch to send him home. His release seemed further than ever, and he felt life sad and more than half sour.

He slept badly. Partly from indigestion, for on arrival at the castle he had been exceedingly hungry, and as they were late and he was unexpected, toasted cheese on rather new bread was all he could get to eat. And afterward he and Charles d'Orléans had talked and drunken late, and later still in his own room, James had read the *Consolations* of Boethius by candlelight far into the night.

The nightingales had kept him awake, too, shouting in the waning moonlight: they were still singing when he woke a few hours later and it was already dawn. He leaned on his elbows on the window ledge and bewailed his deathly life.

> Saying right thus, what have I done to fail
> full of pain and penance
> My freedom in this world and my plesaunce?

He heard the bells ring for matins, and, looking down, saw below him in the April gay garden, a little arbour of hawthorn, and noticed "on the small green twistis sitting, the little nightingale that sung, so loud and clear."

Although he was very sleepy, he took in and remembered all his life long every detail of that morning. It seemed to him as though the earth had taken a deep breath, and was waiting. There was no smoke yet from the chimneys of the little town, and there was heavy dew, or a light frost, on the lawns. The air was full of shouting birds—the nightingale was gradually drowned by awakening blackbird and thrush, chaffinch and starling, with alternating cuckoos answering each other in the neighbouring woods.

To James, as he leaned on his elbows, watching the world wake, it was like the moment before the music begins, when the fiddlers hold their bows poised; it was as it must have been on that first morning, in the still in-

180

stant before the sons of God broke their astonished, delighted silence, and shouted for joy. And then, as James himself has described:

> therewith cast I down my eye again
> Where I saw walking neath my prison tower
> Full secretly, new coming here to prayer
> The fairest and the freshest young flower
> That ever I beheld before that hour.
> Entranced I gazed, and with the sudden start
> Rushed instant all my blood into my heart
> My heart, my will, my nature and my mind
> Were changed clean into another kind
> Only through letting of mine eyen fall
> My heart became her thrall
> For ever of free will; for naught was seen
> But gentleness in her soft look serene
> Yet still above all she had this I note
> Beauty enough to make a world to dote
>   . . . for of menace
> There nothing was in her sweet face
> Ah, sweet, are you a worldly créature
> Or heavenly thing in likeness of nature
> Or are you God Cupid's own princess?

Could she be real? This richly dressed girl with long golden hair, wearing a blood-red balas ruby heart on a long chain around her neck was perhaps some apparition: saint to console him, or spirit to warn? But her slippered feet made a warm shuffling sound on the garden path, and she cast a serviceable shadow on the silvery lawn. She was carrying a nice fat prayer book, too: neither ghosts nor ghouls carried them, he felt sure. James was only about fifteen feet now directly above her, and he could see that she was reading matins for the dead, as she walked. He watched her go, very slowly, remaining himself unseen, and when she passed out of sight it was as though the sun had set, and a cold wind had risen. James had never felt anything to compare

181

with the emptiness he felt when she was gone. He waited a long time, hoping she might return again the way she came, but when she did not, he assumed she had gone on into the chapel. After a while he dozed off, until the coldness of the stone roused him, and he woke to weep that he had ever seen her, since now he no longer saw. And to realise poignantly her departure. Yet he comforted himself that he and she were both in this very real world, and for the first time, James realised how marvellous it was to exist at that particular moment in time, at just that moment, and no other; to be alive now, in the same world at exactly the same instant in history, and in the same country, as the only girl that mattered or could ever matter to him, was such unbelievable good fortune!

She, and only she, would be his queen. Of that he was quite certain, yet a minute later was as sure that it could never be, that she was obviously intended for one of the king's brothers, or for some local English noble. "Perhaps she is already wed," James gloomed, and vowed if that were so, he would remain unwed.

When his servant brought his breakfast, James asked him if he knew who the lady might be. And then regretted his question. The man was so stupid, how could he possibly know? Luckily he didn't. When Charles d'Orléans came in, a little later, James very coherently described what he had seen, and was so utterly changed, so completely radiant that Charles, dropping his cynicism for once, rejoiced with him. "There's nothing like it as an experience, is there?" he said. "It's the only magic: everything and everyone is transformed. You've never seen what a good fellow I am until now, have you? You've never realised how heavenly the noise is that the thrushes make, or the smell of the air. And you're going to be knighted in two days, and you're sure to meet her then, if not before. I'll find out who she is before evening, I promise."

But, when Charles had gone, James was quite sure he didn't want anyone else to find out but himself, and he set about it with delight. It was almost too easy—James would have wished innumerable obstacles even to discovering her name; he wanted to prove to himself, to her, that nothing could be hard that was on the way to her. But, actually, all that was necessary was to ask the old captain downstairs in the castle guardroom: "Who was the girl walking through the gardens early today?"

And the captain said, "Girl? Gardens? Oh, I expect that was Lady Joan—Lady Joan Beaufort, my lord Somerset's sister—the bishop's niece. Her stepfather, the Duke of Clarence, was killed at Beaugé but lately, and they are bringing his body back from France for burial, here, on St. George's day. Her mother was Lady Margaret Holland, you know, descended from Edward I, she was."

"And Lady Joan stems then from Edward III through her father, too, does she not?" asked James, knowing the captain's weakness for heraldry.

"That's right. She's a pretty child," said the old captain, "a good girl, too."

James wondered how he was going to live through the next two days, until his investiture brought him his chance of meeting her. He'd met Somerset often in France, and his brother Edmund, too, and he had always liked every Beaufort he met; they were a pushing family, always eager to do well for themselves, but very clannish. James, entirely without kin, and feeling his uncle and Murdoch's behaviour very strongly, clung to any one with a warm family life and with strong ties. He had liked the bishop and trusted him; he wondered now why he had kept this niece so long up his sleeve. "It's strange I did not meet her last year at Pontefract," thought James, "seeing her aunt is Countess of Westmoreland, and her young cousin has just married Henry Percy." But there were many, many girls about the court—and to meet every one of them, James would have had to have lived there continuously—and he was there so little, in snatches only between bouts of prison. Well, now he knew who she was, and she was eminently suitable: if

Henry wanted him to marry an English girl, he would certainly be willing to take this one: but would she marry him? James started at once to write her a long poem: it was all about himself, his childhood, his sea voyage, his dreary imprisonment. And it was all about his quest for Joan, full of appeals to Venus:

> . . . queen of life, Star of benevolence
> Piteous princess, and planet merciable.

He described himself dreaming that Venus sent him to Minerva, blaming his "feminine and woeful tender heart." Minerva sent him on to Fortune. And Fortune, who lived in an ugly pit, "deep as any hell," told him that

> Half of his life was here away . . .
> Spend well therefore the remnant of the day.

The poem kept him very busy for the next two days: that, and polishing his new armour. He had been given a doublet of blue cloth for the occasion of his knighthood, at the exchequer's expense. On St. George's Eve, he ate an early supper and then, accompanied by William Giffard and Thomas Myrton, he went to St. George's chapel to spend the whole night in prayer and vigil. His mind, which should have been on holy things, hovered continually, unreasonably, around Joan; yet there seemed no irreverence: for was she not part of the good for which he was grateful, as she was part of the good for which he prayed? Now it was as if, after the long wasted pointless years, suddenly everything had meaning: everything focussed into place and the jumbled, haphazard, disjointed kaleidoscope of life became an orderly, patterned mosaic. The focus of whose pattern was Joan, and only Joan.

He heard whispering behind him, and women's voices, but did not turn his head, yet guessed it might be Joan, for the Duke of Clarence's catafalque stood in front of the high altar. James was kneeling in the Lady Chapel, his arms before him; as the two women walked up to the communion rail, he could see their faces: one was Joan and the older woman he recognised instantly as her mother whom he recalled having met several times. They were in mourning now, with black veils. Joan's fairness seemed the more startling; her hair almost burnt the crepe, curls escaping from under her hennin like tiny yellow flames. They knelt some time, and Joan began to look about her; James could see her without turning his head, and stared with such hungry yet devout admiration that she smiled—a friendly, amused smile, as though to say, "My friend, I'm no goddess, no statue, I'm just a girl."

James loved the smile. "There's no cunning in it—it's so clear," he thought, and added to himself, "it's so different from Catherine's. But then my queen and my court *should* be different from Henry's in every way."

And he said a brief prayer for the Duke of Clarence, but couldn't help thinking how lucky the man had been to have had Joan for a stepdaughter, and still was, to have her kneeling there praying for him now; but thought, too, "Perhaps I shall be even more lucky, for I can pray she will be my wife and that she shall pray for me as her husband." For he thought of her immediately, completely, as his wife: he had always felt he was not called to a celibate life, and now he was sure that, God willing, here was the girl he was destined to marry.

"I'll never marry anyone else if I can't get her," he vowed again and prayed hard that she was not already betrothed. He feared very much lest she might be—those Beauforts were so tremendously ambitious that such an attractive girl would certainly have been earmarked for one of the king's brothers. But perhaps that's why she hadn't been in town much, or at court, because she was being saved for someone? James decided it was no good worrying; it was enough to be here, on the eve of his accolade, with Joan near him. God was indeed giving him more than he desired or deserved.

As the women left, Joan looked very kindly in his direction, and moved her lips as though saying a prayer for him: he hoped so much she was.

Next day at his knighting he looked magnificent. His hair, that was auburn, in color between white and red, fell to his shoulders, glossy and well-groomed; he made his responses clearly: "What is the function of knighthood?" his sponsor asked him, and he replied:

"To protect the Church, to fight against treachery, to reverence the priesthood, to fend off injustice from the poor, to make peace in my own province, to shed my blood for my brethren, and, if need be, to lay down my life."

An enormous crowd witnessed the ceremony, packing the chapel, and hundreds more waited outside to see the new-made knights march processionally through the little town. Women threw bunches of primroses at them, and daffodils; country girls in their kerchiefs cheered and sighed, for it was the first time since Agincourt that Henry V had held an investiture. Charles d'Orléans, murmuring the very bourgeois names of some of the other candidates, whispered to James, as he sat next him at breakfast in the castle after the long Mass and the longer walk was over, a line from Langland:

Soapsellers and their sons for silver are made knights.

But James hissed him for his unchristian arrogance.

The Emperor Sigismund was at the table, and Charles, pointing him out to James, was full of gossip about him.

"When he got to Dover, Humphrey, Duke of Gloucester, rode out to meet him into the sea until the water was above his horse's shanks, and holding the bow of his boat, asked him if he claimed suzerainty over England, and only permitted the emperor to land after the latter had promised he claimed none."

Henry Beaufort, the bishop, who had said Mass for the new knights and was sitting on the other side of James, added maliciously: "When the emperor gave a supper party at Constance, he gave his guests spiced dishes and wine, which seemed to all to shew a want of good breeding."

"He gave nothing in the offertory at Mass this morning," said Charles, and Henry Beaufort added: "He was so drunk at the council that he could only do business early; the King of France, being mad, was at his best after he had dined, late in the day, so they hardly ever met."

"He looks a mild, rather messy sort of man, doesn't he?" the bishop said. "He is actually brutish and cruel. After he defeated the Venetians at Motta, he made their captain hack off the right hands of one hundred and eight of his own men: and when his own Hungarian nobles revolted, he called thirty of them into his tent, and beheaded them with his own hands, there and then, one at a time. He would have decapitated the whole lot, and only was stopped because the rest refused to enter when they saw the blood trickling out of the fringes of the tent. I'm telling you all this," the bishop added, with mock sternness, "and I hope you are paying proper attention to my words, because I've been told that the Emperor Sigismund is here looking for a nobly-born bride for . . ." He was not able to finish before James had sprung up from the table, and was forcing his way past the squires carrying the dishes, and the seneschals bearing the beakers of wine, to where the king sat.

"I must ask Henry at once, now," he had decided. But Henry, when thus brusquely approached, was more than slightly noncommittal.

"Your first cousin kills Joan's stepfather, who was my brother, and you choose the day of his funeral to ask me for her hand," he said.

James winced.

Henry said, "You shall accompany me on my new campaign, and then we'll see. I've just had emissaries from your brother-in-law, the Earl of Douglas; he is most anxious to get you home; mayhap we can arrive at some agreement."

187

Whilst King Henry spoke James thought only, "I must meet her today, I must speak to her, I must, I must."

Just then Humphrey, Duke of Gloucester, crossed the room toward the two kings and said, "Come and meet my niece by marriage, who is also my cousin: Joan Beaufort. She was telling me just now she would like to salute the new knights."

It was to be as easy as that. She actually *wanted* to meet him! James walked the length of the room, following Humphrey, to where Catherine was sitting; close by stood Joan, her face still and quiet as a lake. Her eyes were big and grey, with lots of dark gold eyelashes she had cut short. Joan went down on one knee to James; but he raised her and kissed her hand. He did not say anything, but thought how good her fingers smelt—like fresh bread.

After some moments more of silence: "This must be a great day for Your Majesty," Joan said, and James replied, "The happiest of my life, since I met your ladyship upon it."

He stood in front of her now, feeling self-conscious in his new armour, like a schoolboy. "Your stepfather was a true friend of mine—I'm sorry for your loss," he stammered, and Joan said, "He was a very noble, gentle man."

James didn't know what to say next, but ventured: "You are Geoffrey Chaucer's great-niece?"

Joan looked delighted, "Yes, by marriage. He married my grandmother's sister."

"Did you know him?" asked James.

"Oh, yes," said Joan.

She looked ardent, James thought, despite her mourning. She was dressed all in black velvet trimmed with ermine, so she appeared most regal. They talked a little while longer. Neither remembered after exactly what either of them had said, but each noticed everything about the other: he, the great ruby rising and falling on her bosom as she breathed, and the charming way she seemed to seek confirmation of everything she said, looking at him as though she were speaking in a foreign language and he were her teacher; she, the way this man who she knew "excelled in all science practical or speculative," was an "expert mediciner, cunning in theology and right crafty with the lute," was tongue-tied and awkward with her as if he had been a country bumpkin of sixteen, instead of a king of twenty-six.

Both were much amused when the Emperor Sigismund pompously presented the new knights each with a little knife and ring not worth more than a silver coin. But James gave his to Joan, placing it on her finger, "I make you my queen with an emperor's ring," he said, smiling, and she accepted it.

James saw Joan again next morning: she walked once more under his tower, and he looked out. But this time she looked up, and smiled at him. She picked some red wallflowers—gillyflowers, James called them—and tried to throw them up to him: she succeeded after the third try, and both were out of breath and laughing. When she went away, James wrote in his poem for her how when he woke from his dream of Venus and Minerva and Fortune, a white dove had fluttered through the bars of his window and had alighted on his hand, with her red gillyflowers in its mouth, and he slept with them under his pillow. He saw her again, briefly a few more times, at court, but then very early in June, James and Henry were at Dover, waiting for a wind to sail again for France. They left on June 5th, and Humphrey of Gloucester went with them; he and James were jointly charged with the siege of Dreux, which surrendered on August 20th. James was very well pleased, for this was his first big assignment: he and Humphrey worked admirably together, James planning the mechanics of the siege, and Humphrey the ballistics—he arranged the formations of archers, saw to the making of catapults and other engines, arranged for the single cannon to be dragged into place. Both were punctiliously chivalrous: James solemnly paid a generous sum to a poor milkmaid for the pails his greyhounds had riotously spilt, whilst

Humphrey treated the garrison to a tun of Gascony wine the evening the town surrendered. Humphrey had disciplinary trouble with the Irish who would steal babies and hold them to ransom for ridiculously low sums, which were yet more than the parents could pay; they also would steal cows and ride them back to camp. The Scots were not much more disciplined; James insisted on paying out of his own pocket for a barn full of corn, wine and fodder, which his unruly folk had burnt.

Both James and Humphrey went on to join Henry at Meaux; but there the siege dragged on: the garrison of 1,100 picked men held out for more than seven months. James lived at Rouen, inside the city this time, as did also Henry's secretariat. James had four esquires, two valets, and ten archers with him, commanded by a knight, Sir William Meryng, who was his keeper and who was responsible to King Henry that his prisoner should not escape. James was now, for the first time, in no hurry to go home. He had been most successful at Dreux, yet was very anxious to win still more laurels; he enjoyed France, enjoyed campaigning, and loved to think he was doing it all for Joan. He had sent her a message; though he had not written how he felt, he had to tell her of the little Norman city that he had taken in her name and for her sake: so he wrote from Rouen: it was a stiff letter, after the manner of the time, but James could not help his love shining through it; he hoped Joan reading it would remember how comfortably together they both had felt at their first meeting. He had requested Henry to tell Joan he had asked for her hand, and Henry had promised he would, but had not kept his word.

James joined Henry and Catherine in Paris for Whitsun. The whole court lived together as one family. They met at morning Mass, had breakfast together, and then would ride, hunt, hawk, play bowls, tennis, stoolball, or tilt; in the evenings in the great hall, they would dance or make music—both James and Henry being proficient on the lute, the harp and the organ—play chess or throw dice or knucklebones, sing, or read romances. They sat through many solemn banquets and feastings, lasting sometimes all day, in which there would be interludes of pageant or pantomime. Giants or knights—errant would ride on horseback into the hall and would challenge all comers; ships and forests would be wheeled in, incredibly elaborate machines, whilst nymphs and sprites, often wrinkled and raddled old men in female dress, would make fulsome speeches from aloft on these very precarious properties.

To James, starved as he had been of family or of normal life, such surroundings should have been most healing. Indeed, he often wondered at the feeling he had of malaise, of incongruity. For all the splendour and the loveliness, the colours, the lights, the perfumes, the jewels, the beautiful women, and the heroic men, there was to him inevitably a slightly out-of-key quality about every festivity. The captive kings, the cruelty and misery on which all the pomp rested and depended, so that its girders sank down through the glittering surface to primeval, squelching slime, made him continually aware that somewhere, either within earshot, or just out of hearing, some human being was starving, or beaten, or bleeding, or tortured. And the sticky, artificial and meretricious quality of every emotion sickened him. The virginity of girls was a counter with which they gambled, and each man had his price, whether prince or pauper. It was these intangible things which sapped the vitality and spotted the characters of all but the most outstandingly virtuous individuals, and James had to admit that the Lancasters, Henry V and Humphrey and Bedford, stood up remarkably well under the manifold temptations and kept themselves singularly pure in the rotten, corrupt world in which they lived, and which revolved around and depended upon them.

Spring had come early that year, and in February there had been already more blue and yellow violets than in most years in April, and by the beginning of May good ripe cherries were being sold in the streets. But later in May, a frost blighted the vines, and James was shivering as he followed Henry through the ruined streets of Meaux after it had finally been taken. A slight snow was falling, and James thought, "How misfortune anonymises people and cities! Only glory or great fortune distinguishes them. Indeed even individuals rarely benefit by misery. It brutalises and animalises all except the saints. Ordinary folk are nicer and better when they are happy, contented, fortunate."

No Scots were to be executed this time, and for this small mercy James was heartily thankful. Amongst the ruins he and Henry suddenly came upon a gaunt monk standing amongst a group of men and women, some clerical, some in lay attire: they all were swaying, praying aloud, with eyes set on the monk as he led them, or closed in ecstasy. Some were lashing themselves with iron-tipped leather thongs—from their bony bodies flecks of blood flew. Henry, whose weather eye was always cocked towards a possible heresy, went up to their leader, and asked of him who he might be, and what he and his followers thought to do thus in the devastated city.

"I am Vincent Ferrer," he replied, "and we do penance for the sins of those who died defending this city." He was dark, semitic, with a high, hooked nose. His burning eyes took in the two kings. Then, to Henry he said, "And who are you that thus oppress the people of Christ?"

"I am the scourge of God, sent to punish the people of God for their sins," said Henry. James shuddered at the blasphemy, but Vincent accepted the statement, and he and Henry walked off apace together and remained in lonely, secret communication for the space of upwards of three hours. When they returned, Vincent Ferrer said aloud to his followers, who were waiting for him, as he left them, still praying and still swaying, still flaying themselves, and still standing, only colder and hungrier, and paler than before, that Henry's quarrel was so just that undoubtedly God was and would be on his side. But in farewell to Henry he said, privately:

"Your time is short." Henry nodded; he hardly even

looked startled; it was as though the monk were telling him something he already knew. When they had gone on to their lodging, Henry told James:

"On the barren moor where he met his death, Archbishop Scrope told my father, as he cursed him, that he would die in the flower of his age, and warned him that we should all do likewise, and that in the fourth generation our name would be cut clean off, and that Henry of Windsor would lose all Henry of Monmouth had won."

"Who is Henry of Windsor?" James asked, but Henry said he knew him not.

James carried Joan's image in his mind and heart all that long winter. He thought of her constantly, yet only with delight, never with impatience. For him time present was keeping her warm and cared for in his thoughts; time future would be, if God lent life, keeping her warm and cared for in his arms. He had little fear she would marry whilst he was away, for he had told both Henry and the Bishop of Winchester that he wanted to marry Joan, and he thought it was worth both their whiles to keep her for him: Beaufort would like a king for nephew; Henry was anxious for James to take back to Scotland an English queen. And Joan was too near the throne to be married except by royal command.

On December 6th all the bells in England and France had pealed: Henry V had a son, born at Windsor. Rumours crept out to France; the soothsayers warned and James remembered Henry's saying that Henry of Windsor would lose all Henry of Monmouth had gained. But James knew these croaks did not touch Henry of Agincourt, who was more completely happy than James had ever seen him. "Never was such a May," Henry said, as he and James rode out of Rouen to the north, to meet Catherine. She had left the baby and was coming to Henry, who under the flowering, scented lime trees was so above himself that James thought: "Such happiness, such success, could not be safe here below: fallen man isn't meant to enjoy such content; Henry will become intoxicated, and surfeit; or his luck will leave him, and he will stumble. France, Catherine, a son—Henry has every-thing he ever wanted." Riding with him that morning, James had a feeling that Henry's life was motionless, at the top of the swing. When he saw Catherine, he knew the down-drop had begun. She was more beautiful than ever, more imperious; but James, as he watched Henry jump from his horse, run to hers, and lift her off it, into his arms, saw the theatrical quality of her welcome, and guessed from her secret, subtle face that she had a lover. "I hope Henry finds her out," was his first thought, and his second, "I hope he does not."

"How fares our bachelor king?" Catherine's voice broke in on his thoughts.

James knelt; she was standing beside Henry now, her green silk houppelande all embroidered with yellow and pink and blue flowers, a coronet of enamelled flowers keeping her white veil in place. "I fear our place as your slave has been taken during our long absence," he said. She blushed; but Henry noticed nothing.

"Kate," he said, "aren't you hungry? Let's eat." And trestle-tables were brought for the court which picnicked under the lindens, with Rouen in the distance, veiled in a blue mist.

"What light, what colour," James said, "does it not dazzle you after the English greys and fogs?"

Catherine said, "I'm so glad to be home. For France is ever truly my home, and now it is my lord's, since he has brought me here, as I first brought him." That evening Henry distributed lavish rewards to his nobles in honour of his new son: a castle to one, to be held for one red rose a year: a barony to another with a bunch of pinks for dues; fair lands for a clutch of wild ducks' eggs and a fine manor for a thimbleful of black peppercorns.

For all that last, enchanted summer, Henry and James and Bedford rode around northern France besieging here, driving off cattle and stealing food there, every-where bringing death and discomfort. James was aware of the strange contrast: God had given them this deli-cious country to enjoy, and the best they could do for it was to impoverish and destroy. Soon, although Henry still turned his troops on to the country to pillage, they came back, day after day, empty handed. There was even no more bread. And the English soldiers, or the French or Scots or Irish or Welsh or Burgundians, had already stolen all the cattle. Often the rival French armies had skirmished and engaged each other, doing incalculable damage to the countryside, but none to the English. At last, after several wet days, came a sudden conversion of cloud into clear air, and in a sodden field, sheltering behind a little shrine, Henry's men found six steers. It was early morning, and the famished soldiers were driving the beasts down the field, when a priest came out of the little oratory, in surplice and stole, and cursed them roundly. The men made off, driving the thin beasts at a gallop before them as they ran. When they got back to camp, they had a great roasting of the meat. As they sat at dinner the king was served also some of the meat, and James was with him, and after eating, James went amongst the men to see that the wine the king had sent them was properly distributed. Under a pine tree he found a soldier shewing his companions a pair of beautifully wrought tiny silver gilt slippers, studded all over with precious stones.

"Whence had you those?" James asked. At first the man hid them, disclaimed them, then gruffly:

"I took them off the saint in the shrine where we found the steers today," he said. "What saint? Whose shrine?" James asked to learn it was St. Fiacre to whom the little oratory was dedicated. James looked shocked, and there was a silence: evidently the fellow's companions were not too happy either about his sacrilegious theft. Soon afterward the priest came storming into the camp, a fat man in a stained cassock, asking to see the king, to claim redress, payment for his stolen cattle and the restoration of the saint's footwear. But King Henry was firm: an invading army obviously lived off the land, so long as one Frenchman resisted his lawful lord (Henry), so long would Henry's righteous armies take their food where they found it. For the shoes, Henry knew nothing of them—the priest was welcome to find the culprit and bring him to Henry for justice, and Henry would see then that he was properly punished.

The priest went at last, still slipperless and still cursing: he had hunted the saint's jewelled relics in vain. And Henry went off to relieve Cosne, for such a force of French and Scots were besieging it, that the sorely tried garrison could not hold out and had sent desperately to Henry for his help and for immediate reinforcements.

On his way there, Henry fell sick, of a nasty, quick-spreading skin ailment, that made him stink whilst still in the field, even whilst he was actually riding his charger. It looked to Henry very like the sickness of which his father had died. But the doctor, summoned, had declared it to be *fy*, or St. Fiacre's evil. Henry jogged uncomfortably back to Vincennes; though no man might speak of the king's illness, by the time they reached the city, Henry could ride no longer, and had to be borne in a litter. He sent James on to Bedford, and bade both swear to carry on the relief of Cosne. But James had no relish for the task, and no wish to confront his subjects again in person. So, the third day out, when already they could see the walls of beleaguered Cosne, James spread chalk and water on his face, and feigned to stagger as he found his way to Bedford's tent.

"I feel uncommonly sick," he told John Bedford, "I pray I am not stricken with St. Fiacre's evil, for I too ate the stolen meat." Bedford, alarmed by his looks and his symptoms, urged him to go back to Vincennes. "Go there quickly—in a litter if needs be. We cannot have both our kings ill and stricken. Henry's physicians who are assembled there can tend you also." Safely out of Bedford's sight, James washed the chalk off his face, and rode happily back. But when he got near Vincennes anxious messengers, on their way to take the sad news to Bedford, told him that the king's life was despaired of. James reached the king's bedside on the last day of Henry's life, ironically enough St. Fiacre's day, August 30th. Henry

196

recognised James, and whispered to him, "Yours is, indeed, a cursed nation. Wherever I go, I am bearded by Scots, dead or alive. No wonder they are so savage and resentful in life, when they wreak such cruel vengeance after death." James feared he sympathised with the dead Scottish sainted king, St. Fiacre of the stolen slippers, more than with this now most precariously alive English one. But he made no reply, only knelt down beside Henry's pallet, and made the responses to the seven penitential psalms, which were being mumbled around the young king by two priests. When they reached the verse "Ut aedificentur muri Jerusalem" Henry cried out with a loud voice, "Good Lord, Thou knowest that my mind was to re-edify the walls of Jerusalem," and swiftly died. James, watching the physicians test the body for life, and find none, thought, "And instead, you tore down the walls of Rouen, Paris, Melun . . . will God take account of the intention or the action? We are told it is the intention which counts."

When he returned next morning Henry's servants were busy cutting up his body and boiling it to extract the bones. The stench was awful: Henry's physician was assisting, trying to discover what was the real nature of the illness that had carried the king off so swiftly. "Whatever it was, reached his bones too—see how the muscles about them are swollen and puffy?" he told James, but James fled, and was horribly sick to his stomach on the grass outside the death chamber. He went to the chamberlain to protest the boiling of Henry's body, already dismembered.

"It was forbidden by Pope Boniface VIII," he said, angrily. But Henry's chamberlain, furious with the Scots king for butting in, insisted, "It's always allowed in such cases—we brought the Earl of Suffolk home after Agincourt in just this manner, and the Duke of Clarence after Beaugé. And we'll bring our Henry home."

Henry's bones were placed on a car covered with black hangings, above a bed on which the full-sized figure of the dead king lay with a crown of gold on his head, in his right hand a sceptre of gold, in his left hand a golden ball. Six horses richly draped and each bearing a different coat of arms dragged the hearse: the first horse bore the arms of St. George, the second, the arms of Normandy, the third, the arms of King Arthur, the fourth, those of St. Edward, the fifth, those of France only, and the sixth, those of England and France. James followed first, alone, on horseback; he carried his shield reversed, his lance butt end upward. After him rode the Duke of Exeter, and then the earls of March, Warwick, and Stafford. Catherine travelled alone in her litter, surrounded by her ladies on horseback; she and her escorts kept seven miles behind the main procession.

Twelve captains, five hundred men at arms all in black harness, their horses barbed in black mail also carrying long torches, accompanied the coffin over which was carried a rich canopy. Rows of priests ceaselessly swinging censers of incense and chanting incessantly, walked alongside the hearse; in every town through which the cortege passed, Abbéville, Montreuil, Boulogne and Calais, Masses were said continuously from daybreak to noon for the repose of the soul of Henry Lancaster, king once of England and heir to France.

The evening they reached Calais, whilst James sat in his hostelry playing cards with the earls, a messenger came from the queen that she would speak with him, instantly. James looked at the inquisitive faces of the other men: he had no doubt they were wondering what his relations were, what they had been, what they would be, with the lovely widow. Aloud he said to the messenger, a pretty, beardless boy:

"Pray tell Her Majesty I cannot come tonight. I am kept here by state matters of great urgency. But I shall be most honoured and happy to attend her tomorrow morning, after Mass."

And when he spoke with Catherine next day, for all her gentle, feline melancholy, her plaintive miauling, he was distant, remote, correct; and thereafter he was most careful never to be with the queen alone.

They arrived in London on November 5th, and were met by a thousand torches. In Westminster Abbey four hundred candles burnt, each made from six pounds of the purest beeswax. Ten mitred abbots buried Henry V beside Edward the Confessor.

CHAPTER THREE

☐ James spent the next fifteen months wooing Joan and preparing to go home. He was in the keeping still of Sir William Meryng, but as Humphrey, Duke of Gloucester, was Protector of the realm, John, Duke of Bedford, was Regent of France, and Henry Beaufort, Cardinal Bishop of Winchester, was chancellor (it was the latter, in effect, who ruled all), James had absolutely nothing of which he could, or did, complain. He lived with the court most of the time; neither Queen Catherine nor he, though they saw each other daily, ever referred to her summons at Calais. She and her baby, now Henry VI, kept even greater style than when Henry V was alive. James acted in effect as Scottish charge d'affaires in London: there was a constant coming and going of ambassadors from Scotland to discuss the truce (which had to be renewed after the death of Henry V) and James's release, his return and, above all, his ransom. Archibald, Earl of Douglas, James's nephew (James's brother-in-law was now styled Duke of Touraine), William Hay, Constable of the Realm, and many others came from Scotland with safe-conducts to London, and were severally entertained by King James, and by so many friends as either his alliance or his virtues had acquired. James did his visitors proud: his accounts show they were served mutton, turbot, crab, plaice, sole, mackerel, cod, merling, capons, pullets, pigeons, rabbits, and herons!

James's nephew, the new Earl of Douglas, had a good story to tell him. "Murdoch's sons are completely out of hand," he said. "They had not seen their father for eighteen years; their grandfather, Albany, had always let them do exactly what they liked. Now they very much resent Murdoch's return, and his attempts to discipline them. No man lacks property in Scotland today if he has strength to take it; nor holds it longer than he has power to keep it. Murdoch had brought back with him from England one of the best-trained and most beautiful falcons I ever saw."

"I know," interrupted James, "King Henry gave it him. I fear I coveted it greatly."

"So did Murdoch's sons. The two eldest were setting off for a day's hawking one morning lately, and came in before leaving, to see their father. The falcon was sitting on its perch—its hood was off, as Murdoch had just given it a piece of raw meat and was holding a slice of apple for it. The younger men both asked Murdoch to let them fly the bird that day; Murdoch refused with an oath, and they began to wrangle. Walter said the most unpardonable things, but it was Alexander who snatched the peregrine from off her perch and wrung her neck. 'If I cannot have her, neither shall you,' he told his father. Murdoch was completely silent. Then he said, quietly, 'It's time I sent for him who shall bring you and this kingdom to order, who is my lord and yours.' And men say he has written to you asking that you come back."

"I have received no letter," said James.

But he sent his chaplain posthaste to Bishop Wardlaw, and the old man replied that he could guarantee that Murdoch would make no move against James should he come, and that all the nobles were prepared for his return, and would give him a royal welcome.

James was walking home from Monastic Compline with Joan. They had gone together to Westminster Ab-

202

bey: it was the second anniversary of their first meeting, and James, fretting from the continual delays, was begging Joan to let him come to her room after supper.

"Why should you not let me come now, let me make love to you now, since I'm going to for the rest of both our lives?" James asked Joan. She was always warm and friendly and loving to him, but, though she welcomed him and wanted to be with him from morning until night, she was very chary of intimacy. He would not let her out of his sight at the court, and everyone accepted the fact that they never seemed to wish to talk to anyone except each other, to be with anyone except each other. But it was as though she knew the long delay would try them both, and rationed her favours: she but rarely let James kiss her, though they walked hand in hand. Now she replied, squeezing his fingers:

"You'll not think me a prude if I tell you?"

James pressed her arm against his side, and said, "How can I tell what I shall think until I know what you will tell me?" And then, before she could speak, he went on, passionately:

"I promise I'll not bother you at all, but we live in such a crowd though we see each other every day and all day, we are never alone together for a moment. Even now, though I am carrying your vesperal, and we are side by side, my keeper walks behind us at a polite distance, and behind him my two squires and your two ladies are flirting tactfully, so that we may be able to say a few pretty nothings to each other. But I don't want to say pretty nothings, Joan; I don't want to say any more, anything to you that the streets can hear. I promise I will be good; but I want to be near you, and to have you to myself, so you aren't always half listening to the bells, or the gulls, or the clip-clop of the horses' hoofs."

Joan put her hand on his. "James, until I met you," she told him, "I wasn't sure whether I would be a nun. Maybe, in part, because I was over twenty and unmarried; but, at least also in part, because I love my Lord Christ. Now, if I let you come to me—well, St. Augustine has put it far better than I can. He says if a man should take to himself anyone for a time until he find another worthy either of his means or of his honour to marry, in his soul he is an adulterer, not with her whom he is desirous of finding, but with her with whom he so lies as not to have with her the partnership of a husband. I don't want, just because I am both the girl you want now and the one you will want hereafter, for our married life to start with an adultery."

James looked down at her admiringly, "You are wonderfully subtle—you talk like one of the old schoolmen. But I wouldn't rape you, Joan—I'd just talk to you."

"You would want to rape me," Joan said, "and I would certainly want you to. And marriage is a sacrament, whose species are the very bodies of the married—we are the bread and wine, we are the water and the oil, James—you and I. It would be playing with holy things —it would be more, far more, than using a palm to switch the flies away, that was to be blessed on Palm Sunday—to make too free with our bodies before God's blessing gave us leave to use them for our delight and His glory."

James said nothing for a moment. Then he said, "But the sacramental grace of marriage comes directly to us— it's only ratified by the priest, it's not given us by him. It's we who are the means of grace for each other."

"Yes," Joan interrupted quickly, "that's why we mustn't be the means of sin before we are the means of grace— the joy must be part of the grace and must flow from it, only simultaneously."

They had reached the palace now, and James put his arm around Joan. "You are my queen," he said, "and I am entirely at your orders. With my body I thee worship —whether I do it as I do now, with only my heart and in anticipation, or, when I shall be your husband, with the whole of me. Let it be as you will; so long as you love me and will marry me, that's all my care. I've waited almost thirty years to love with my flesh—I can wait a few more months."

Joan's grey eyes filled with tears. "It seems to you now that I don't love you enough—to let you come, doesn't it?" she said. "Actually, and I think this is true—I certainly pray it is—that I love you so much I cannot allow you to love me less," and giving him her hand to kiss, she led the way into the palace.

The Treaty with Scotland for the liberation of James was finally signed on December 4th, 1423, in London. The arrangements were most complicated, and the Scots proved themselves strangely bad at driving a bargain. The English asked 40,000 pounds for James; tacitly they admitted he had been taken in time of truce by agreeing to call the sum, not ransom money, but expenses. It was to be paid within six years of his release. They only expected to get 36,000 pounds, which worked out at 2,000 pounds for every year of his captivity, but they would have taken actually far less. The terms of the treaty included the delivery of twenty-one Scottish hostages to England, before James would be permitted to cross the Border. The cessation of Scottish aid to France was suggested, indeed urged, and even the withdrawal of the Scottish troops already there, but these high matters were to be incorporated in the truce James would make between England and Scotland once he was crowned king. As to James's marriage, the treaty expressed itself in very coy language: "The King of Scots knew several noble ladies, even of royal stock, and if he were pleased to declare his will, they could discuss further, but if he did not open the subject, the English ambassadors could not begin, since ladies of the realm of England, at least noble ladies, were not wont to offer themselves to men unasked."

As the date of James's marriage approached, the Scottish council shewed itself more generous with money. At Christmas he got two hundred marks in money from them, and cloth of gold worth nearly as much again. Also, 10,000 marks of James's ransom were remitted as Joan's dowry: a financial transaction of dubious morality. Indeed, years later, Humphrey of Gloucester, in his bitter quarrel with Henry Beaufort, wrote to Henry VI that James's marriage "was a great defraudation of your highness, for the said Cardinal Beaufort caused you to pardon him 10,000 marks."

James and Joan were married on Sunday, February 13th, at St. Mary Overy, in Southwark. Henry Beaufort officiated; Thomas Beaufort, now Duke of Exeter, gave away his niece. The wedding feast was tremendous. The bishop gave it at his palace hard by the church, and paid for it, also, out of public funds.

But of course it was to the English crown's interest to detach the Scots from their French alliance, and James's marriage with Joan promised to do just this more concretely than by any other means, so England owed the Beauforts the wherewithal to furnish them with the wedding meats. James, throughout the long ceremony, bore himself with quiet dignity, sedately, almost solemnly. When Thomas Beaufort twitted him with being o'er long in the face, James replied: "I'm too old mutton to dress lamb." But when Joan, gay and jubilant, asked him if he were pleased, he said, "Not pleased, no, I'm happy. Now that we belong to each other, nothing else matters."

Catherine sat on James's left, and pretended to be a wise old dowager, though actually she was not yet as old as Joan. "I do hope that Joan is able to have children. You English—" she began to James, but he interrupted her, bringing his fist down with a bang. "We English," he said, "I ask you! I like that! You forget I haven't any English blood nearer than St. Margaret, and she was three centuries ago. . . ."

Catherine looked very put out. "You always interrupt," she said, "yet you seem to want for your children the English blood that you refuse for yourselves. I was trying to tell you that it is the usage in France that any lady, daughter to any great lord, if the king should wish to marry her, first that she should be seen and viewed all naked by certain ladies properly chosen for their knowledge, to know if she were meet to bring forth children."

James smiled. " 'Tis more often the man's fault than

206

the girl's if she is barren," he said. "I'll take my chances. Stewarts and Beauforts are not customarily fruitless singly, and I think I can vouch for the combination."

The bishop was talking to his newly married niece. "Did you know, Joan, that the marriage blessing, which I gave you this morning in the Mass, is the same primeval blessing that God gave to Adam and Eve, and is the only one not lost either by original sin or by the sentence of the deluge, 'quae sola nec per originalis peccati poenam, nec per diluvi est ablata sententiam'?"

For the young people the formalities seemed endless. After waiting so many years, these few hours were the last straw, and the more entirely unnecessary that now there was nothing but the social obligations of their rank to keep them from their happiness.

But the population of London, which had grown very fond of the handsome young monarch during his eighteen years long stay amongst them, had to see the pair drive right through the city in the splendid coach, the glass coach it was called, drawn by six white horses, in which usually only kings paraded after their coronation.

And then there were all the various ceremonies to perform: bride and groom each had to endow so many beggars, to bless so many children, to play host to such a multitude of guests.

At last, at long last, it was time for Joan to go upstairs and to change her dress, of heavy cloth-of-gold embroidered with forget-me-nots in blue turquoises, for the traditional white silk night robe. Since she was not yet crowned, she wore a crown only of rubies and pearls: a tiara, rather, for she could not wear the plain gold circlet until she was in her husband's country, crowned as his queen.

When she was ready, she was piped up the great staircase to their room with Scots music. Sixty-one Scotsmen had come from James's country to London as their king's guests, and James had found twelve excellent pipers amongst them, and wanted both olltraidheacht, or martial music, and suaintraidheacht, or peaceful music. The bishop gave the customary blessing to the marriage bed and Joan was kissed and bidden Godspeed by her mother and sister, and after, the whole gay company left, with the torches, and the music. Then, with only candles lit and the heavy curtains spread, James came "to bliss with her that is my sovereign."

In the morning the men dragged a big silver bath into the royal chamber, and filled it with warmed water. James still slept whilst Joan, shivering in the February air, was bathed by two maids, who cried aloud at her beauty, as they poured water over her from their silver ewers, and rubbed her with ground ivy and thyme leaves. James, waking, gazed unobserved through the bed curtains at his wife's loveliness, and praised Him who had made so glorious a creature. The maids dressed Joan now in riding clothes, for today the Queen of Scots and her king were to begin their voyage home. They stripped the fine silk sheets off the bed and carried them down to the ambassadors and visitors from Scotland, that these might witness that their king had married a virgin, fair and honourable amongst women. When the newly married bride came down with her husband, Joan's mother was busy amongst the wedding presents, packing the many gold and silver vessels and the sundry rich and curious hangings—the most marvellous being those into which the history of Hercules had most curiously been woven—but she rose from her knees and curtsied full deeply to the queen, her daughter.

When James and Joan rode out, it was already afternoon, and they were a tremendous gathering of people. They seemed almost an army for numbers, but without banners; instead, there were many, many baggage cars, many laden pack horses. The English muttered sullenly that the King of Scots was taking away a hundred times more than that with which he came; certainly, besides the wedding presents, there were horses loaded with musical instruments—James was taking an organ, besides many lutes and harps; there were several suits of armour; there were Joan's trunks; and there were the sixty-one Scotsmen who had come for the festivities and who were all determined to ride home on their king's band waggon. James and Joan rode together, right in the middle of the vast caravanserai in which they were travelling; now neither cared how much they were surrounded by day nor by how many people they were cluttered, for theirs alone was the night, where in darkness and in silence, they could be together and alone.

"It is like dancing to invisible, unheard music," Joan said, when they were out of earshot. "Were you disappointed?" James asked her. "In you, of course not," said Joan, "nor in myself. In love—yes; but only as one is always disappointed when one crosses any frontier. All the fuss about safe-conducts, about differences of language, about the journey, and then, one crosses, and the grass is the same the other side, the sky is as blue, the shapes of the trees are the same. So this is all, one thinks, one need not really have gone to all that trouble and expense, one might just as well have stayed quietly at home. And then, gradually, one begins to notice the differences, the strangeness. And the further one travels, the more one realises that this country is quite unlike the one left behind, is quite unlike any other. And that there is no turning back, no possible return."

"I suppose everyone has the same experience," James said. "One is led to expect so much."

Joan replied: "A girl is taught to think of little else from childhood. Her whole life is one-pointed toward her wedding night, toward love and the lover. So when everything is over, and one lies still, and a little sore, one thinks, Is that all? Is that everything? And then one begins to realise that it is all, and is everything, and to want it again, and again, and to wonder how one ever lived without, before."

James thought for a moment, and then said, "Yes, you are right. I think the sequence is that first, it's imaginatively too important, so that for an instant, one is let down, right down, like dropping into a deep, cold well, and then one begins to realise how tremendous it is. And by that time one of the most important moments in one's life has come and gone, and one is wonderfully sleepy, and that is all."

Their horses spattered brown mud behind them whilst around them everywhere lay the faint green of early spring. The going was heavy; in the ditches young watercress leaves and celandines were just shewing. "I think in everything one must begin by getting used to the simplicity and to the silence," Joan said. "Everything is given to one so unexpectedly." She pointed with her jewelled riding whip to the horizon, to the gently rounded hills, some wooded, some pasture, with scudding white clouds racing above them in a wind that was turning furiously the wings of a white windmill. "When He who made and who minds all this beauty, came on earth, He came as just another Jewish baby, in no wise especially remarkable. And when He comes to you and to me now He comes as a small piece of bread. And you, in the daytime, you give orders, or pass laws, or sign statutes, or do whatever it is that a king does, and you are dressed for your part. But at night you are all bare—there is nothing in my arms except what your mother gave, and what the earth will receive. I've married a king, I keep saying with my mind; but in my heart and in my arms there is only a naked man."

In each village, even in the tiniest hamlets, the church bells pealed as they passed through, and all the villagers crowded round the young king and his bride to do them honour. Joan and James rode hand-in-hand: they were so delighted with each other, that they included in their delight all the people amongst whom they passed, everyone whom they saw, each person to whom they spoke. Though fine and clear, it was cold, and there were many floods out, so their progress was much delayed by having often to march many miles out of their way before reaching a bridge. But they took the delays in very good part, though many of their escort grumbled loudly enough at each enforced detour. James said he wished the journey would go on forever: "You and I riding home through

210

spring country—Paradise can be no more perfect." "Paradise it will be when we can do this forever," Joan said, "here it must so soon end."

They crossed the Trent between Lincoln and Retford, paying five shillings to Thomas, the bargeman. They rode on to Brancepeth, arriving on March 1st. Here they spent the whole of a month waiting for the hostages, who were in no hurry. Richard Nevile was in attendance on James and his queen, with a staff of a hundred and sixty knights and men-at-arms. Twenty-seven hostages finally assembled, whose wealth amounted to 17,400 marks, and James gave his personal obligation under his privy seal "binding himself and his heirs to pay 40,000 pounds to Henry and his heirs in annual instalments of 10,000 marks." Now, also, James signed alone for Scotland a truce with England to last for seven years. The Scots serving Charles VII in France were exempted from its provisions, although it was stipulated that reinforcements were not to be sent. But James knew that his brother-in-law, the new Duke of Touraine, had sailed early in March from Scotland with a force of 6,500 men, so that James's truce could not interfere with the Douglas' plans.

Bride and groom left Durham on March 29th, accompanied by Henry Percy and his wife. Henry Percy had been himself so long in exile that he was most sympathetic to his old schoolfellow, and, since Henry's wife and Joan were cousins, James felt he was leaving the Border in good hands. The two young men talked earnestly of how they might keep peace during their reigns —for Henry was practically independent politically, and was entirely so administratively, having, of course, the right of punishing by death, after trial by jury. "How to prevent lawless subjects from ruining the lives of the poor shepherds and crofters and farmers" was James's query. "The trouble is," Henry replied, "that no person here has a single avocation. You are a farmer *and* a sheep stealer; a carpenter *and* a horse thief. Everyone raids, poaches, and lifts in their spare time. Every landowner is also a fighter, a freebooter: every castle has a pen for the sheep its lords steal. Scott of Harden lives quietly at home, for example, until his cupbearer puts a single spur on his plate. That is a sign the larder is empty, and off he goes on a raid."

James had been getting imploring messages from Murdoch, whose eldest son, Sir Alexander Stewart, since the falcon incident, had been living in absolute defiance of any authority that Murdoch might pretend to have. Now, just as he was going to enter his kingdom, Murdoch sent James word that Alexander, in defiance of the treaty James had just signed with England, had signed an agreement with France promising that he would prevent his subjects from helping the old enemy England, and on coming to the kingdom or governorship of the realm, would as far as lay in his power, continue the war.

"That is simply open rebellion," said Henry Percy; "if he comes here I'll hand him over to you as a traitor."

James sighed and looked at the landscape. The Roman Wall marched away to right and to left; "but no wall could keep either England or Scotland safe from each other—especially when neither were safe from themselves," James thought. Aloud he said, "I fear I shall have a busy homecoming, Joan. What am I bringing you to? What kind of life, after your sheltered London?"

"I'd rather be in the worst place in the world with you, James, than anywhere else without you, however safe or pleasant."

"That's right," said Henry Percy to James, "don't you worry about Joan. Beauforts manage to survive quite nicely. She is a queen now and you can trust her to behave like one."

"Of course I know that," James said impatiently, "but I want her happiness."

At Percy's Cross the English contingent left James amongst his own people; the lords and gentlemen who had accompanied him and Joan since they left Durham, went south to their homes. Here, on the high fells, was a skiey no man's land along the Roman road they travelled daylong. So lonely was it that a curlew was company, a plover was greeted as a friend, and even the lovers' hearts quailed. Past Camo they rode, and Otterburn, over land where there were few living, and many dead; the air was more peopled with ghosts than the earth with living men. Their caravan crept between Girdle Fell, just on two thousand feet high, and Reid Swire, to their right, some fifteen hundred bleak feet above a remote sea; then just beyond Carter Fell they came to the frontier: a simple stone, a block of granite with a double-headed arrow scratched on it; southwards marked England, northwards Scotland. James jumped off his horse, and lifted Joan down from hers, and carried her across his threshold. Then he knelt and very reverently kissed the soil he had left eighteen years before. "I have been a long while gone," he said. Standing up, he drew his sword, and, kissing first the blade, he held it up so the hilt made a cross and prayed: "O God, spare me but a little, and I shall bring in changes such as men dream not of, though I should toil like a slave to achieve them." And then, loudly, and with great solemnity, he swore: "If God grant me but the life of a dog, I will make the key keep the castle and the bracken bush the cow, throughout my unhappy country."

On April 5th the royal cavalcade reached Melrose. There James's uncle, the Earl of Athol, met them: a suavely venerable patriarch, who greeted his nephew and new niece most warmly. "I don't like him," Joan said when the monks had shewn the bridal couple to the guest chamber, "he's too cordial; he's too anxious to please you—why should an old man so fawn upon a younger one? He has some ulterior motive. And he gives away nothing. After all, the first duty in talking is to give oneself away with both hands: if you don't the person you're talking to has perfect right to wonder why."

James yawned and pulled on his nightshirt. "I'm sorry you don't like the first of my family you have met," he said, "but all in-laws are, I'm told, better absent than present, so let's not take your impressions too tragically, my sweet. He's a poor old body, not worth your wasting one of your lovely thoughts upon."

Joan reflected. "Your uncles have not brought you good fortune to date," she said in a very unconvinced and stubborn voice.

In the morning James and Joan heard a solemn Mass of thanksgiving at the high altar of Melrose Abbey under the splendid east window, with its five lights divided by the cross transom. They knelt above the body of Robert the Bruce; and James renewed, silently, and from his very full heart, his vow to Scotland over the body of the greatest Scotsman of all, the hero-king.

Here too at Melrose, James confirmed the treaties he had made with England on her alien soil. Here came, falling over each other to greet the new ruler and to curry favour with him, the nobility and gentry of the kingdom. They had been given so much rope by the too affable Albany, that they had difficulty even in putting on court manners: Joan thought she had never seen a more savage and unprepossessing looking lot of ruffians. They came into James's presence unshaven, and though their clothes were generally rich and splendid, in a barbaric way, they were rarely clean: after the day's audiences, the great hall smelt like a brock's earth, and Joan insisted the doors be fastened open, and new rushes laid daily on the floor. This immediately gave her a reputation for pernicketiness which grew with the years. The way the great lords would come in, helter-skelter like a crowd of farmers on market day, to talk over the affairs of the realm as though they were the prices of mutton and geese, shocked her profoundly. Almost the first to appear was James's cousin, the Earl of Mar, now a completely reformed character, and a very able man. James took the line with him—and later with his own nephew Douglas, his brother-in-law's heir and the new earl—that Scotland was more to them all three than was any of their particular stakes in it: James was indeed king, but that was just his job, as Mar's was to hold the northern Lowlands against the constantly irrupting Highlands, and Douglas' to keep the South and the Border against the naturally warlike temperament of its inhabitants as well as against the English.

Four great boroughs—St. Andrews, Perth, Edinburgh and Aberdeen—sent messages passionately desiring the coming of the king, for the good government of the realm and added that his arrival within their walls, for many days expected, would be most pleasing to them.

James had brought north with him David and Nicholas Dunbar—David was the Earl of March's legitimate son: Nicholas one of his bastards—and John Heryng, a cousin of theirs, all three of whom he had redeemed from the Tower, where they had been since 1421, having been taken prisoners in some Border fighting. Now he found these three were very useful men upon whom he could rely. For he saw already, in those first few days at Melrose, that one of his greatest problems was going to be the building up of any kind of a civil service, of a secretariat. David and Nicholas were devoted and charming young men; they and John Heryng and Joan constituted themselves a quartet to sift James's visitors, to comment freely on them, and to see to it, as far as they could, that his orders were carried out.

"A very important-looking messenger," announced David, the fifth morning after their arrival, "has just stopped at the abbey gates. I must tell the monks to put someone more efficient on duty than poor Brother Aethelred—he's so shortsighted he takes ages to puzzle over everyone's credentials, and then by the time he lets them in, our sentries think they have been properly investigated, whereas in fact, Brother Aethelred is so pleased at being able to see the passes or letters or safe-conducts at all, that he never tries to decipher them."

Joan looked down. The courtyard was in a bustle: two monks were struggling with a handcart of dirty washing, pulling it across to the laundry; a farmer was unloading a cartload of lambs for the Easter feasts; Murdoch's messenger shivered in the April chill, whilst his horse fidgeted. John Heryng slipped out of the room and came back with a sealed packet. "I told the messenger to go to the kitchen and have a good hot meal and some beer," he said.

James read the letter in which Murdoch complained again of his son Walter Stewart's contempt for all authority, and in which Murdoch begged James to take over the control of the unruly young man. James threw the letter over to David Dunbar, and said nothing.

"Sir Walter will be here tonight," said David, "he's never missed a free meal in hall since he arrived here on Friday. He's out all day, and up to no good, I'll wager."

"What are you going to do?" Joan asked James. She was scared by the way his mouth had snapped shut like a trap whilst reading the missive.

"You'll see soon enough, darling," said James. "It's a queer kind of irony of historic justice that whilst Albany killed my brother when my father handed him over because he was unmanageable, now Albany's son hands me *his* son to kill."

"To kill?" Joan asked, and James replied:

"I'm afraid so. He's a rebel and a murderer."

> John the Miller had ground small, small, small
> The king's son of heaven shall pay for all, for all,

quoted Joan.

"Who wrote that?" asked James.

"John Wycliffe," said Joan.

And James looked up, shocked: "You quote me a heretic!"

Joan smiled, "The Church never condemns a man—only his doctrine. That's not a heretical doctrine—the only things of John Wycliffe's one shouldn't read or quote are books or propositions actually condemned."

James smiled. "You may be John of Gaunt's granddaughter, but you have imbibed the Lancastrian orthodoxy for all that," he said.

Joan waited until they were quite alone. Then she said, "I do wish you wouldn't kill Walter Stewart."

"My own sweet love," James replied, "I've got to get this country into proper shape—and I fear bloodletting will be part of the process."

"But they're all of your own blood—these family feuds will never end, if you start now killing the people who first killed you."

"There is not any wickedness which beareth not its punishment and repentance at the last," said James. "We must have but patience to attend the last act of these tragedies played on this theatre of the world."

"I'm scared for you—and a trifle scared *of* you, too," Joan said. "I did not know of this side of you; I was unaware of the statesman and the schemer. I saw only the poet and the lover."

James smiled, "Clemency becomes a woman, and a queen; I shall look to you always to have mercy and to ask it. But I must strike down the tallest heads; I must reduce this miserable kingdom to order—even if, and perhaps the more because my own kith and kin are among the worst offenders against the peace. But any man whom I apprehend, will have trial by a jury of his peers. That I promise."

And with that Joan had to be content.

They were at dinner, all the court and the guests, including Sir Walter, when James made a sudden, slight signal with his hand. At once the hall doors were shut and barred, and at the same time, two armed men slipped behind Sir Walter Stewart, and pinioned his arms. His two squires, Malcolm Fleming of Cumernauld and Thomas Boyd of Kilmarnock, were about to jump up and go to their lord's assistance, but found that they, too, sat now between two standing soldiers. James said in ringing tones, "I accuse Sir Walter Stewart of treason against this realm and against my person, and I command that he be held on the Bass Rock until his trial by his peers. John Heryng, you and Sir Robert Lauder will act jointly as his guard."

"My lord King," began Sir Walter, but the rest of his speech was lost as he was pushed unceremoniously out

217

of the hall. Joan and the other ladies present sat silent during the scuffle and the commotion; but as soon as the three men had been taken out, a babel of talk burst forth.

Two days later James made his solemn entry into Edinburgh. Murdoch was there to meet him, and outwardly the two men greeted each other with a great show of feeling. Joan could not help regretting James's lack of height; he was dwarfed, for all the real royalness of his presence, by the burly Murdoch's actual size. But in all other respects James looked the better man. "Murdoch's grown very stout," Joan whispered to David Dunbar, who was acting as her squire. "He looks bloated, too, and sleepy; I shouldn't say he was in very good health," David whispered back.

In spite of Joan's dislike of him, the Earl of Athol was always with the king. "Perhaps it is because James knew his own father for such a short while," suggested David, to combat her. "He maybe looks to his last remaining uncle as to his father."

"He finds him quite useful, and picks his brains—that I know," said Joan. "But what I don't know is whether the advice Athol gives James is as good as James's own judgement—that's what I'm afraid of—that James should be persuaded by Athol's age and experience to a course of action disapproved by his own native perspicacity."

The son of James's old nurse came to the castle in Edinburgh to pay his homage. He brought a bucket of ewe's milk, "for your lady queen—they tell me ladies like to use it for their toilet," he said, and Joan, after thanking him, did indeed use it for her bath, and felt most refreshed.

Joan found it a great strain to be forever meeting new people—and an endless series of new relatives, and to have to remember what James told her of each one. Athol, sensing her dislike of him, would purposely try to muddle her, giving her the information she asked of him in such a rambling and confused fashion, pretending to be more in his dotage than he was, that Joan was misled to believe it was the husband who was James's cousin, when it really was the wife, or that it was the brother who had been taken prisoner or killed, when it was in truth the father. And when she blundered, Athol would make excuses for her loudly, as a stranger and an Englishwoman.

On May 20th, they were back at Melrose, and Joan was delighted to be in the rose-coloured buildings in their fertile valley again, after the savage splendour and more than savage discomfort of the castle on the rock that was Edinburgh. In the evening Bishop Wardlaw arrived, and James frankly sobbed as he knelt to kiss his ring, with Joan beside him. The bishop was gay and a trifle embarrassed by James's emotion. "Son, son, this is no day upon which to weep," he said. "I shall die happy after I have crowned you. And now you are grown from a pretty pleasant child into a fair image of the true king. And you have brought Scotland a lovely lass for queen." But the old man, for all his delight in James's return, which was for him the political culmination of his whole life's work, could really talk or think of nothing but his newly founded university of St. Andrews.

"To hear him blather on," James told Joan, "you'd think Paris and Padua were but branches of it."

The crowning took place the very next day, May 21st, at Scone, holy city of Scotland, the land of sounding shields, hallowed by solemn oaths and coronations since 906 when on the Hill of Belief, King Constantine II held assembly and swore to his people upon the Gospels. James could not be crowned upon Jacob's stone, the pillow the prophet had used at Bethel, which was the traditional coronation stone of the Scottish kings, for King Edward I of England had stolen it, and carried it to Westminster. But all other of the ancient Scottish rites were fulfilled "maxima cum solemnitate," with the greatest possible solemnity. In the morning, before the king came publicly forth, there came to him two bishops, two abbots, with twenty-four other of the clergy, four noblemen, the constable and the marshal, having their batons of office in their hands, six commissioners of the barons, and as many of the boroughs. They brought forth the king, the constable holding his right hand and the marshal his left. He was set under a cloth of state, a gold canopy. Then the churchmen, nobles, barons, and burgesses present, asked the king if he were the lawful sovereign, and if he were willing to accept the dignity of the crown, which they did now offer to His Majesty. Then the herald that stood on the king's right recited his genealogy. After the same questions had been asked of the queen (except that for lawful sovereign, she was instead asked whether she were the lawful wife of the lawful sovereign), the herald that stood on her left recited her genealogy. Then, when the king had signified, he would accept the crown, all present cried loudly, "God bless you, Sir."

The Lyon King of Arms was then called by the Lord Marshal, and the other lesser heralds went to the stage prepared for them. The Lyon took the king by the hand, and led him outside where stood all the people assembled, and called aloud, "that the king is willing to accept the crown." And the king took the queen's hand and shewed her after to the people, who with cries and shouts all with one voice said, "God bless him who is to be our king! God bless her who is to be our queen!"

When they had gone back to where the canopy was, and the king and queen had sat down once more upon their thrones there, Bishop Wardlaw made a sermon, at the end of which the Lyon brought two vials of sacred oil, delivering one to the constable and one to the marshal; then he delivered them in turn to the bishop, who therewith anointed the king on the crown of the head, the palms of the hands, his elbows, and shoulder blades.

The bishop proceeded to the royal robing: first taking each garment in turn from the marshal and the constable, and at every piece he put on him, he said "Indue, Rex, tunicam justitiae." Then Murdoch handed the crown to the bishop, who set it on the king's head, and after took from Murdoch the queen's crown, and set that upon her head whilst the heralds repeated the six generations of their descent.

Then the Lyon brought the Gospels to the king, and knelt on one knee before him, and, laying his hand on the holy book, James swore to be a father to the people, to do justice, to maintain the religion he professed, to rout out all heretics in his realm, to procure peace to the Church to the uttermost of his power, to preserve the rights, rents, and privileges of his crown, and not to transfer nor alienate the same, to quash all oppressions, and to defend the fatherless and the widow.

On a parchment was written the obligatory oath of the people, and this now the marshal held and standing beside the king, read it aloud, all holding up their hands and repeating after him:

"I become your man, as my liege king, in Land, Life, and Worldly Honour against all men living. So help me God." The constable took the crown off the king's head, and laid it down before the king, and all the noblemen came up, one by one, and touched the crown, saying "God help me as I shall support thee." Which done, all again holding up their hands declared: "I swear and hold up my hand to maintain, defend, and support thee, and if any harm or dishonour shall come near thee, I shall prevent it with all my goodly power, and warn you thereof, as I wish the Lord in my need to help me."

Came then the Mass, and the incensing, and throughout the daylong ceremony, Joan and James sat hand-in-hand. All the bishops, nobles, and prelates of the kingdom, except those fighting overseas, and the twenty-one serving as hostages for James in England, were present. At the day's end, James conferred knighthood on twenty-five noblemen—the first knighting since the death of James's father, Robert III, now nearly twenty years before. The new knights included Alexander, Walter Stewart's rascally brother, and Murdoch looked smug and inscrutable as he congratulated both his own rebellious son and his former fellow prisoner. He permitted himself a familiar "this is rather different from the circumstances of our London meeting, eh, Jamie?" at the feast, but James could not trust himself to reply, and so remained silent.

Joan thought she would be crushed to death in her heavy robes as the hot, sunny day dragged on, and the room grew stuffier and more fetid from the crowd. These robes were of the heaviest cloth of gold, plentifully decorated with ermine and ermine tails, and Joan's crown, though it looked slender enough, was wonderfully heavy too, and pressed like a chafing harness on her temples. But she bore herself with tremendous dignity, her aching head held so high that many muttered "yon English lass looks proud enough."

It was not until evening that James and Joan, who had both received communion at the High Mass, were able to break their fast at the feasting that followed upon Compline. When at last, long past midnight, they could withdraw to their own rooms, and their attendants disrobed them, James, lying at last in his own palace by his own queen, murmured again to her the words he had written for her:

> So I am come again
> To bliss with her that is my sovereign.

Next morning, before she woke, he scribbled sleepily, propping himself on the pillow beside her in the great bed, these other lines which he read to her when she woke:

> As you have been the succour and sweet well
> The remedy of careful heart's cure
> And in the huge weltering waves' fell
> Of love's rage, blissful haven and sure
> O anchor and truce of our good adventure
> You have of your man with good will made conquest
> Mercy, therefore, and bring his heart to rest.

CHAPTER FOUR

☐ "Certain discreet persons of the three estates shall sit three times in the year where the king likes to command," Bishop Wardlaw was reading aloud to the Earl of Athol.

"Three times is many times," Athol said, "I always thinks myself to summon parliament once a year is sufficient."

"Noster legifer rex, our law-making king," smiled the bishop. "It's his long sojourn in England. They think a lot of parliament there. The king uses it against the nobles, and the burghers use it against the nobles—" "—and the nobles use it against each other and everybody else," Athol finished for him.

The two men were sitting in a tavern at Perth—a very overcrowded town, since James's first parliament had been meeting there for a month past. It was to end its first session the next day, and whilst waiting for the winding up, Athol and the bishop were reviewing the situation. "It seems nonsense to me to set eighteen men to mend the laws that need mending—as though the laws could be cobbled, like boots," said Athol.

A messenger, dressed gorgeously in a green doublet laced with red, with red and green striped hose, bunched shoulders and bishopy sleeves, appeared at the tavern door. "His Majesty desires you both to honour him with your company at dinner presently," he said, bowing low and sweeping the floor with his hat. Both men returned the bow, rising from their seats, and the bishop said, "We are delighted; pray inform His Majesty we will be with him very shortly."

To Athol, Wardlaw said, "Our James has acquired in England a corruption of manners falsely called politeness."

Athol said nothing; from behind his little pig eyes, narrowed by thought, he was wondering how single-mindedly for James the bishop was, now he had got his king safe home.

When they arrived in the great hall James was waiting at the high table for the bishop to say grace. It was a tremendous banquet, such food as had not been seen in Scotland for many a day, for Joan had brought French cooks with her from England, and tonight was the first opportunity they had been given to shew their skill before so large an audience. As soon as James and Joan had retired—which they did early, for Joan was pregnant and felt queasy at long feasting and late hours—the talk turned to the statutes which had been enacted that day and the previous days. Though all men there had shared in the making or the reaffirming of the laws, not all felt their proprietorship of them. "A narrow sleeve and little pockets urged in dress," snorted the old Duchess of Albany, Isabella, a mannish, implacable woman, "you would think that Scotland's king had other fish to fry than fussing upon the details of women's fashions."

"He should start his fashion-ruling with his own messengers," said Athol. "Those youths are dressed in enough cloth to clothe a courtesan."

"If you'll consider the statutes of the parliaments of Richard II and Henry V of England, you'll find a curious similarity between them and the laws we have just made —or in whose making we have just acquiesced," said Athol's grandson, Sir Robert Graham, shaking his red head disgustedly. "That's what I can't stomach," he added, "that our king should ape the English; that they should lead and we follow; 'tis a pretty pass we've come to when we are beholden to England for our laws."

"Twelvepence in the pound on all rent and goods," sighed Adam Hepburn of Hailes, just knighted and rather officious. "This heavy taxation is all very well for one year—we can put up with it for the once, since, after all, it was worth something to us to get us out of that undignified position we were in with our king in captivity in England. But to have to produce so much money, every year, the people are certainly going to resent that."

"Before you know it there will be riots here as they had in King Richard's reign in England."

"Two shillings on the boll of wheat, sixpence on rye and peas and oats—it's going to be harder on the crofters than on us," said Sir James Swinton.

"Don't forget that drawing oxen and riding horses are exempt," the Earl of Mar broke in.

Murdoch drawled, "The punishments seem pretty stiff to me; for failure to pay in fifteen days in gold and silver, both fine and imprisonment!"

"Well, the king has got to find his ransom money somehow," put in Sir William Ogilvie, the new treasurer, a spare, sallow man.

"I like that one about no man travelling with more men than he could sustain," said Sir John Stewart of Corstorphine, the chamberlain. "Travellers have been moving in packs like wolves lately, and upsetting the domestic economy of the towns and villages through which they passed."

"Since no man dare travel singly how would you have them move?" asked Bishop Wardlaw.

"Our King James may find himself in trouble with our Holy Father by his ruling that no clerks pass over the sea except by the king's leave and that no clerks purchase pensions or benefices within the realm," said Ingram Lindsay, an illegitimate son of the Earl of Crawford, who had himself purchased a pension out of the deanery of Aberdeen. "After all, Henry II of England was excommunicated for less."

"For more, you mean," said Bishop Wardlaw, tartly. "James has got to murder me before he matches Henry II's record."

"I'm delighted that we've got football forbidden, and that instead all men must busk themselves to be archers," said William Lauder, the warlike Bishop of Glasgow. "I don't know what the young men are coming to, playing silly games instead of preparing themselves to defend their country."

Murdoch roared again, in his slow, massive voice, "I'm indeed glad I got my father's game and salmon laws confirmed, for the closed season is a very necessary thing if we are to keep a plentiful supply of salmon. And the herring net law is an old and a sound one, that's another I'm glad to see repeated. And so is the one about the pulling down of rooks' nests from the trees."

"Most of James's fancy new laws are just old ones writ large," said Sir Alexander Seton of Gordon, another of the new knights. "That rule about no muir burning, and the one against the burning of the heather in March—they're both as old as I am."

"At least," agreed Murdoch, "it was the parliament of 1401 that brought them in, and also the one that imposes a fine on all who slay hares in time of snow."

"Some of the punishments are savage—forfeit of the trees if any rooks' nests are to be found in them at Beltane—that's hard," said Sir Alexander Seton.

"Some of the punishments are not near savage enough," countered Murdoch's son Alexander. "For slayers of the king's deer, James imposes a fine only. I should certainly have imposed death."

"A forty-shilling fine for stealers of green wood and for fellers of trees is all very well in theory, but who is going to catch the offenders?" asked young Sir Thomas Stewart, the Earl of Mar's son.

"We must all help to catch offenders, and do anything

else we can to keep the peace, or see that it is kept," said Bishop Wardlaw. "That's the meaning of the first statute of all: 'that all men should assist the king to punish rebels.'"

The good old bishop was tired; sleepy too, for the long days of dozing in the council chamber were telling on him. Often now, he would take a cat nap and not know just what anyone had said. But, when the occasion roused him, he could speak out his mind, and now, for example, fairly let himself go.

"If we are to have firm and sure peace throughout the realm, we've got to work for it. If any man excite or come amuff against another, then his lands and his goods are forfeit. That's how the king is to be helped; firstly, by your attendance at parliament; then, by your support of the laws *you* have made," he said. An awkward silence fell—as though everyone thought such remarks belonged inside a church, not at a banqueting table. Then, into the spilt puddle of silence, Mar threw a few bathetic words, to mop it up, and the talk began again, piano, crescendo, fortissimo.

As James left Perth for Edinburgh the next morning with Joan beside him in a litter, the royal procession met another: of women only, many old and bedraggled, many young and bedizened, and some hardly more than chirruping children; one particularly lovely little girl, surely only about twelve years old, curtsied deeply as the queen's litter went by, and then again to James, who gallantly took off his cap and waved it at her.

"Who may those ladies be?" asked Joan, and James said, "They are the common women—the whores—who by one of the new statutes are to be put at the utmost ends of the town, where is least peril of fire."

"Where will they live? Must they go to hostelries?" Joan asked.

And James said, "Gracious, no. No decent hostelry would accept them."

Joan looked at the sorry company processing back the

way she and James had come. "Poor souls," she said, "I've had so much from a man, that I wish I could share with them, who have so little."

James was thinking about hostelries. "They must be built in all boroughs and towns of the realm," he said aloud, "and in all thoroughfares where right of passage is, with stables and chamberings and bread and ale and fodder at reasonable prices."

Joan asked, "Is it true that poor travellers may no longer stay with friends, but must put up at the inn or pay a penalty of fifty shillings?"

"Well," said James, "nobles may stay with their friends, but their attendants and their horses must go to hostelries, and all ordinary folk who voyage whether on foot or on horseback must go to the inn."

"That's hard—you penalise the ones who can afford it least," said Joan. "In England no one I ever met had ever stayed in a hostelry in all their lives. You always stayed with relations, or with the relations of relations, and if they were full up, or had the plague, then you went to the nearest monastery or convent and paid them a little something for the holy souls when you left. Much nicer. I think hostelries are awful. Can you imagine our staying in a hostelry with me in my present condition?"

James laughed. "I'm only trying to prevent people living above their means," he said. "So many people spend all their substance on entertaining their friends, or keeping showy hospitality for chance travellers they don't even know. It's become a matter of honour, that each lord or knight along any of the great roads shall offer travellers more varied and better hospitality than the last one. Then, because they spend all their money on this sort of rivalry, they come to me and refuse to pay taxes, pleading they cannot because they have so many mouths to feed. And when the assessor comes, they shew a clutter of relatives encamped, with all their servants and attendants, who might just as well be paying their own way at the hostelry."

"James, how are you going to enforce all these laws

you have just made?" Joan broke in to ask, and James sighed deeply:

"Ah, that is, indeed, the problem here. We have no incorruptible judiciary—do you remember poor Henry V and the stern justice who imprisoned him? We have no justices of the peace in the country districts, nor any watch and ward."

"What will happen—if you make laws and no one carries them out and many laugh at them?"

"Some will be carried out, and, indeed, in some places all will be carried out," James replied. "It depends how remote the places are from the reach of my servants, and it depends, too, on whether the local nobles are or are not my friends."

"You've laid your plans on an immense, all-embracing scale, political, ecclesiastical, and even economic," said Joan.

"Yes, I want to govern the country through the medium of the parliament—and I want it to be really representative—to be, not just the king's council of great lords but to include delegates from the smaller landed gentry and from the commercial classes too. And to make them come I shall do as in the Gospel parable of the great feast—I shall compel them to come in. I shall make their tenure of their own lands conditional on service in parliament, as it used to be on feudal service in the old days."

Joan found it hard to attend to what James was saying; her litter swayed so, and he had almost to shout to make her hear.

"Let's eat," he said, "I'm hungry for food—and to talk to you—you are so right-minded about everything; I want you to be associated with me from the start in everything." James called a halt; they were amongst the Pentland Hills, and he wanted Joan to be as glad to see them as he was. "Aren't they lovely, the way they are folded into the distance, hill over hill, like a child's game, hand over hand?"

And Joan agreed, "There's a sort of hush today; as

though the midsummer knew it carried the seed of winter in its womb, and didn't want it yet to quicken."

"Is our child stirring?" James put his hand on her belly. "You're so slight, I can't feel any change."

She smiled. "We sat down here to eat, and to talk," she said, "and not to make love. You were telling me about parliament." But she let his hand stay, putting hers upon it.

"I want to insist that all the great spiritual and temporal lords attend parliament—I want to fine them if they don't come, and if they go on not coming, I would like to take away from them the right or the power to come. There's no sense in having representative government if you don't pay attention to it—you might as well have an absolute sovereign."

"But you can't have an absolute sovereign in a Christian country, can you?" Joan asked, naïvely. "Surely the individual person always has *some* rights no one can take away."

"The right to live, and the right to love whomever they will—that's very important, isn't it, my Joan?"

Joan was gnawing a grouse wing. James poured her some wine. Suddenly he said, "Let's play truant, Joan. Let's not go on to Edinburgh tonight—let's disappear."

"What do you mean?" Joan put her bone down and looked anxiously at James.

"Just what I say," James said. "There's a fair at Peebles, and I'd like to go and to go alone, with you. It would be excellent policy, too, so don't look at me as if I'd suddenly become stark staring mad. I would be enabled to see, and to feel, the tempo of the country better than by weeks of legislating. And this is the time to do it —when everyone is discussing the new laws."

Joan thought for a moment. "But how, physically, can we disappear? Or rumour would have it we had been murdered—or there would be a hue and cry for us."

James thought for a long moment. "You shall be threatened with a miscarriage, so we must stop here. We'll go down to the castle there." He pointed to the valley beyond. "It is Traquair, and you shall see what we can contrive."

Joan was delighted. "The lord of that castle is Sir William Younger," said James. "I think he will understand."

They rode gently down to the castle, the lacy hemlock embroidering the road's edges once they got out of the bracken and the heather. "I'm so glad whenever we leave the high, empty barren places," said Joan, "and that everlasting bracken and heather."

But James chided her, "Bracken is the best friend we have—the roof over us, the bed under, thatch for man, and litter for beast. And heather! Heather is the stuffing of our mattresses and pillows, the plaster of our walls. Joan! you can never be truly Queen of Scots until you appreciate both heather and bracken."

Sir William Younger was most obliging, and James had the news spread about next day that Her Majesty was a trifle indisposed, and would rest for a day or so at Traquair Castle.

No one recognised the young people who strolled into the Peebles fair the next day. The fair grounds were set up in the churchyard, and James said: "I hope the poor dead have some share in our fun," to which Joan replied:

"Surely they must—there's no reason the communion of saints should not include the gay, as well as the glorious."

"Look, the glove is up," James said, and pointed to a giant cloth painted glove, stuck high on a flag pole, that was sign the fair was open to all.

Few people in Scotland had any idea of what their new king or queen looked like. No new coins had yet been struck, and the few seals affixed by James had been seen only by a few courtiers. So he and Joan talked with everyone whom they would, and shared in all the fun of the fair, accepted as just another pair of lovers. "I wish you had seen the fair at Troyes," James said, as they watched a strong man challenge all comers, and throw them (James had lasted one minute longer than anyone else yet, and was getting back his wind before trying again, watching how the others fared). "One lasted two months in the summer; that was the Warm Fair, and then all the merchants went on to the Autumn Fair at Provins, and came back to Troyes for the Cold Fair there, which lasted another two months."

"Did the peace of the fair hold so long?" asked Joan.

"Yes; during four months of the year there was a town peace and a family peace, because of the fair. And all the merchants and other men coming or going to the fair, were protected by the peace of the fair for the whole of their journey, from whencever it might be. I met some men, Genoese, who brought there to sell dates from Algeria, and dried figs—the sweetest fruit of the bitterest tree in all the world, they told me. They had come by sea to Marseilles and across France."

"There is a whole town, here," Joan said, after they had walked along rows of booths and stalls, and had not come yet to an end; "there are whole streets."

"We're lucky in our weather," said James, "if it rained, your 'streets' would be impassable."

"Do you always have such lovely blue skies for Beltane?" Joan asked, and James replied:

"I do not well remember. But they say Bel, or Baal, was a powerful god or ghost, and watches over his fair, even over the weather, so long as men have first lit the Beltane fires, and driven the cattle between them before setting them out to grass."

"Look, there at the giants," Joan half shouted, almost scared, as a group of men on immensely high stilts began to dance. They had clowns' masks, and flowing garments, painted with zodiacal signs and stars.

"Let's to the marriage mart—it is said many hundred boys and girls are betrothed here each year," said James.

They found a crowded booth—some eight feet by eight feet, so jammed they could not get in, but learnt that inside parents were affiancing their children, so much dowry being specified, so much money put up, with a fee to the merchant, in each case. "That's one easy way to get rich," James said. "My nobles certainly don't pay *me* to marry off their daughters, though my father always had to do it, and take the grumbles if the marriage didn't work, too, and I'm sure I will in my turn."

They were now in a small open space, where a little dark dirty man was shaking a staff in the face of two sleepy bears to make them dance.

James almost gave himself away by his skill at archery.

"Where learnt ye to shoot sae straight?" a disgruntled competitor asked him, after he had won two skins of ale and a pig at the shooting butts.

"He must have been away at the wars in England, and mayhap have even been a prisoner there, else he'd never have had time to practise as he needs, to shoot so," hazarded a spectator. James admitted the charge.

"That's a good guess of yours. I was some years in England. That's where I found my girl here."

"She's a pretty wench; but we have nice-looking girls at home," said a yokel. "Come here, Margaret," and a plump fifteen-year-old turned squealing as he poked her back, and giggled: "What ails you, Angus, to be so fresh with me?"

"Since you're wed with my brother I can ask you to turn around to meet my friend here, and his wife—he's the best bowman we've seen in many a long day." Margaret and Joan curtsied prettily to each other, and a new man joined their group, Margaret's husband.

"Come away, Margaret," he said, "I've just bought me two ells of scarlet cloth, and a sack of lentils, and they seem woeful light to me; I'm away to find the fair guard with the public scales so I can know whether I'm cheated before I go to the office and have the deal registered and sealed with the great seal of Peebles."

"May I not stay?" Margaret asked. "The marionette show is to begin in an hour, and I want to see Harlequin and Columbine; they say they're new come from France."

"I must go now, for the cloth fair will end at noon: they will cry 'Hare, Hare,' and begin the leather fair, and I must have made end to my affair before that," said

Margaret's husband, "but I'll come back for you, if you'll but tell me whereabouts you'll be."

"I think 'tis a shame so many of our young lords should have to go to England to languish there as hostages for King James," a girl, obviously of the rich burgher class, told Joan.

"It will do them no harm to travel a bit," James said; "no harm will come if they kick spurs into their horses instead of using them to spur on a rebellion."

"Who speaks here of rebellion?" an old gaffer said anxiously. "There's never a chance of that, now the king's home. That yon Murdoch and his sons be muttony men, ready enough to bleat but no hand at blows."

James led Joan to the menagerie of strange beasts, and James said, "These remind me of my long days in London—look, there's a mangy lion, nearly as fatuous as the Tower lions."

"That doesn't look to me a very wild cat," Joan said, pointing to a sleeping, contented tabby, in a cage. James laughed.

"But see there, the wily fox," he said, "the chalk-white ermine, the camel full of hair, the little squirrel full of business, the nice ape, the luface unicorn."

"The unicorn looks to me like a cow whose two horns have been grafted together by some operation when she was a small calf," Joan said sceptically.

"His enormous horn voids venom," James said, keeping a very straight face, "and look now at that dromedary, and the warlike porcupine, and that piercing lynx."

"They smell foul," Joan said; "think you we smell so to them?"

James tossed the caber with the best, and danced a fine sword dance, taking off his shoes and insisting on dancing it barefoot, the brave way, so that one mistake or misjudged step meant a nasty cut. At last even he was weary, and when he asked someone in the crowd where he and Joan could get a reasonable night's lodging, several voices offered them hospitality. But, thanking them all, James said he'd rather just rent a room and pay what was fair.

A last farmer going late home carried him and Joan in his creaking cart up into some hills, to a starvecrow mountainy croft, well named "Labour in Vain." He gave his guests the cow byre in which to sleep, and as the cattle were at grass, James and Joan lay close in great comfort.

"I like you more and more," Joan murmured when King James had settled down. "I always thought I'd get tired or bored with the bodily part of love, but I find I want it more, not less."

"How could one want a good thing less?" James said. "Silly child! You don't get tired of eating, or even of sleeping."

"But it seems to me I lived perfectly well without you for many years, and now I couldn't. I might live, don't let me lie, but I would be far from perfectly happy."

After a while, Joan asked, "Can't we creep out and sleep under the stars? I'm so horridly eaten up by fleas and the harvesters and by all the other insects. It's not very romantic to fret for so little but nor is it to scratch, and I can't stop myself."

They crept out, and stood shivering, their bared feet soaked in the heavy dew, and then found their way by wriggling into the heart of a haycock for warmth, where they snuggled down. When both had stopped trembling, James looked down at Joan mistily visible in the moonlight, and said:

"Only your face between me and the earth," and Joan replied:

"Only your face between me and the stars." Then James asked:

"Don't you now envy Tristan and Iseult?"

"Why?" Joan asked, and James reminded her of their long sojourn in the Cornish woods, far from any other human creatures, where they drank spring water and ate berries, and were all in all to each other whilst they were in hiding from King Mark.

"I don't envy any woman, either in history or in legend," said Joan firmly, "who wasn't or who is not yours. And how could I envy anyone who isn't us?"

235

James ruffled her hair, and kissed her and improvised:

> Yellow, yellow was her head
> But she of love was happy
> He would have loved but she would not
> For all his yellow locks

"Your locks look red to me, and I will love as often as you wish, and your lines don't rhyme, but otherwise that's a nice poem," said Joan, and added, plaintively, "I'm nearly as sore bitten in this new-mown hay as I was in the old."

They woke in the dawn to the delightful squealing of the farmer's pigs: small pigs, big pigs, a whole orchestra of pigs. After a hearty breakfast of new milk and bannocks, they went into the town to hear Mass, and after went back to the fair, where James seriously observed the prices asked, and the duties and taxes, noted what money was used, and what forms of barter, and then they walked to a hostelry a little way out of town, arriving about noon. James gave his orders:

"Let the board be served and the napery white, for we will dine and dance."

Whilst waiting for their food, James scribbled for Joan:

> All the wenches of the west
> Were up at the cockcrow
> Then came they to the town's end
> Without more of delay
> He behind and she before
> To see what was most gay.
> And all who lookéd them upon
> Laughed much at their array
> Some said that they were market folk
> And some the Queen of May
> Was come
> To Peebles at the play.

"Don't you like hostelries, now?" James asked Joan, and she admitted this was a pleasant place. As dinner was being served, a nice gigot of lamb, with rowanberry jelly and new peas, a parcel of girls came in, hot and laughing from the fair. One cried her curch was not enough starched, another complained loudly: "I'm that evil sunburnt, I'm gipsy looking, and not fit to be seen!" All had clean-washed kirtles of grey, well pressed with many pleats, and almost all wore doeskin gloves and morocco shoes.

The landlord appeared now, thumbing a lute, and very soon James had borrrowed it from him, and began playing.

"Give us a song," he asked the girls, and they sang some ballad and he improvised the accompaniment. *Hardiknute* one gave, and another, *Hero and Leander* and *The Banks of Helicon*. The landlord himself asked for *The Cherry and the Slae.* And when it came to *Waly, Waly up the Bank* even Joan joined in, for she had Scots enough to sing that since it was James's own.

James hired a horse from their host when the gay meal was over, and Joan got up behind him and all cried good luck to them, and the host's wife said:

"We're right sorry to see you go—none of us ever heard anyone make music as you did. God bless you."

They rode soberly back, and were sad to change into their own clothes and characters once more, in Sir William's friendly castle.

"I never believed I'd be happier as one of the people," Joan said, "but those boys and girls had such a good life, I wish we were simple folk like them. And yet, this country as a whole seems very fearful."

James sighed. "Yes, except for a few folk living on the edge of a free borough, most folk are still plagued by English raids, or highlandmen, or cruel overlords, or local feuds. It's going to be hard to coax my people back into normal ways of life. They're too well acquainted with theft and rape and kidnappings and murder."

"Not since the Bruce has Scotland had a really strong

king," Joan reflected. "That Murdoch's own son should have carried off the customs men of Linlithgow and held them prisoners in Dumbarton until they paid him ever more and more is a sorry tale," she added.

"He wasn't the only one," James said glumly, "nor even the worst."

Back in Edinburgh James worked hard. Joan, living out at the douce Palace of Holyrood oft-times did not see him between Mass and supper. He had set up a kingdom-wide enquiry into the rights of possession by the nobles of what had once been crown lands, for during the two regencies, the king's demesne had shrunk until the only certain source of royal income was the borough dues. Since the whole running of the country was financed out of the royal pocket, this was patently a parlous state of affairs; James was hamstrung in all his reforms simply from lack of cash to carry them out; their implementation must wait upon his tax-collectors' success. He investigated, too, with great thoroughness, all the various claims to pensions from customs and burgh ferms. Many times his men were resisted; often it was as in the Gospel story, that the king's servants were seized and maltreated as they came to make their queries. The old Earl of Lennox, Murdoch's father-in-law, actually had James's auditor publicly beaten, before all his own retainers. As soon as the news of this outrage trickled back to James, he sent soldiers and had the aged earl arrested and brought to Edinburgh Castle. "I've as much right to the crown lands as yourself, Jamie," was all the old man would say, unrepentantly. "They're my daughter's dowry, and I'll be minding them for her."

"But why should your daughter have a dowry from the crown lands? Why should she have any lien on them at all?"

The old man growled, "Well, she married your cousin, didn't she? Him that was regent for you."

James was too angry to argue. "Take him away," he said, and had the old man secured in the castle dungeon.

Sir Robert Graham, Athol's grandson, was another who treated James's messengers with contumely.

"Must this Englishman put his nose into my private affairs?" he asked. "This pint-sized busybody has no right to ask impertinent questions of good Scotsmen," he fumed.

James had him confined in Dunbar Castle from which he quickly escaped, and hid himself, sulking in the Highlands.

Always the Earl of Athol was close to the king, and James seemed to find both his company and his counsel excellent. He was the only person, the only subject upon whom or which James and Joan disagreed. "I think he's insincere and untrustworthy," she said.

"But why should he be?" James argued. "He's my own uncle—he's everything to gain by loyalty to me, by helping me. And he does help me greatly."

In August, James and Joan were at Melrose. James had grown very fond of the Abbot John Fogo, and with his old tutor's (Bishop Wardlaw's) firm approval, chose him as his confessor. "He has looked deep into God's heart," Bishop Wardlaw told James.

"It seems strange to me," James confided to the abbot, "that I find it less hard to lead an interior life now, in the midst of my very active exterior existence, and in all the turmoil of a court, than when I was living as a peaceful prisoner."

John Fogo smiled. "That's only natural," he said. "When you were your own master, as you were when a prisoner, you had to discipline and mortify yourself; you had to impose your own order and tempo on yourself. It was up to you how much time and energy you gave to conversation with God. Now you have no choice: you do not make the pattern any more of even your spiritual life. The mortifications, the duties and delights, the shapes of each day and hour are given you; you need only adapt yourself, and snatch for your quiet what moments you can. You are harnessed, and, of course, you find it easier to run in harness. Everyone does. That's why monasteries exist. You have much for which to be grateful."

James worried that he had so little time for actual prayer. "After morning Mass, until Compline, there is no moment when I can withdraw," he said.

"Why withdraw?" said the abbot. "God is closer to you than your jugular vein or than your breathing; there is no distance between Him and you: the whole journey is from yourself to Him. And that voyage is made by growing, not by withdrawal. St. Austin makes Him say, 'Grow and you shall feed upon me; but not I into you, but you in Me shall be changed.'"

"But I so rarely feel near Him," said James.

"Why should you feel?" retorted the abbot. "If you are, what does it matter what you feel? Remember, the circumstances of your life are given you as the raw material from which you must carve your steps to heaven." And with that he dismissed his royal penitent.

At last, when the exchequer was almost empty the tax money began to come in. "We shall have near 15,000 marks," Sir William Ogilvie jubilantly told James, "but there is much grumbling."

Of this sum James sent 9,500 marks to England, as the first instalment of his ransom. His own bitterness, and the country's, at sending so much good money out of the land, when there was such crying need for so many things that might be done with it, and that fearfully needed doing, was aggravated by the news, which trickled back to Scotland during the last weeks of August, of the battle of Verneuil.

It was the Scots' pride was the chief cause of this, their most complete defeat at the hands of the English. "They are ardent and steady in battle, but presumptuous and conceited to excess," Joan's brother had long ago told James. Sir John Swinton, one of the heroes of Beaugé, now confirmed this view to James. Sir John had been badly wounded at Verneuil himself; he dragged his right leg, stiff and almost useless, behind him, and gratefully sat down as soon as James had motioned him to do so. He described the battle formation: "On August 17th, we were very well placed, on a slight hill, with two rows of Frenchmen before us," he said. "But after the English archers attacked, they quickly routed the two lanes of French, who fell back upon us; we rushed down to relieve them and entered the mêlée and were mown down. There was terrible slaughter. Your brother-in-law, the Duke of Touraine, is dead, and his second son, James, and the Earl of Buchan, Murdoch's son that was married to Douglas' daughter, and Messire Karados, his nephew, and Sir Walter Lindsay. Truly a holocaust of our leaders, and our army is cut to pieces."

James asked where the Douglases and Buchan had been interred, and Swinton replied: "In Tours Cathedral; Douglas had been made Lieutenant General of France. France has given him a royal funeral."

James ordered court mourning. His heart was heavy. His brother-in-law had not only been always staunchly loyal, but had given promise that he would be the very able ruler of a large part of Scotland. James felt as though one of the few solid props he had now was taken from him. "I am most selfish about his death," he said to Joan, "I should be sad for him, and am truly sorry only for myself."

Athol had suggested James make a tour of all the Stewart estates, a visitation, to see in what shape they were after the regency. James had agreed and he and his uncle set off, leaving Joan at Melrose. It was the first time the lovers had been parted since their marriage, and Joan grieved to see James go. "Am I publicly pregnant enough for you now?" she asked him, smiling to hide her tears. Athol seemed to savour her sorrow, and she determined not to let him see how much James's departure hurt her.

"I fear our sovereign lady will be lonely," Athol said, slowly, staring at her as they were mounting. Joan lifted her face to James. "Lonely for one man, however great

241

the crowds," she said, loudly, "lonely for myself—of course not—how could I be, James, since I am carrying our child?"

When they were gone, Joan sank into the somnolent, comatose life of any pregnant woman nearing her term. She felt as though everything were blurred; she, who had been so quick at the uptake, her keen mind reaching forward like an arrow ahead of the winging quarry, now huddled, slow and soggy, dragging along after other people's conversation.

"I am become as ungainly in my mind as in my body," she complained to the faithful William Giffard, now installed as her chamberlain, "you'd think pregnancy were infectious, and my brain had caught it from my body."

But William Giffard said, scratching his head with long nails so the white scurf poured down, "No, I think you are like the earth, sleeping with the seed within it, as it does in winter. The building that goes on, underground and hidden, in the flesh as in the soil, the battle that goes on, of life taking to itself a human shape; the unknown process of the soul's creation, these need all windows fastened, all shutters down."

William acted as Joan's interpreter, for still her Scots was, at best, unhandy, and spoken with a strong English accent. She had now, however, a sweet group of girls to serve her, including a young Douglas, James's niece, and another, a Kennedy, whose brother was taking Holy Orders. James's relatives crowded the court this summer, and were glad to enjoy the luxuries Joan had introduced. She insisted on the etiquette she had learnt in England: both men and women must walk backwards out of her presence or James's, and no one might sit down until she or James gave permission. Meals were formal, too: the cupbearer and the steward were not empty names, and even for breakfast Joan insisted on grace being said.

Soon the elaboration grew beyond what either James or Joan had intended, and Bishop Wardlaw persuaded James to pass sumptuary laws, forbidding the wearing of furs or jewels except by nobles with a rent roll of over 200 pounds a year, and baked meat was to be served only thrice a week.

Joan worried much about James whilst he was gone, and felt lonely, alien, and remote. There was no one who came to her except to ask favours, and she wondered sometimes if they were the only people who existed.

James, meanwhile, was seeing anew his country, and learning to love and to be intimate with it. He enjoyed the life, riding all day, over the jewel-bright hills, or through deep, romantic glens. He had never seen such landscapes: after the prettiness of England and the dull, war-ravaged monotony of northern France, the magnificence, the variety, and the scale of Scotland awed and thrilled him, filling him with deep wonder. At night, he would put up in some town, Ayr, or Glasgow, or maybe Troon, and meet the chief folk. Next morning, after Mass, he would hold court, and administer justice. He sent heralds about the streets before, bidding all come who had a suit against their neighbour, or any unsettled claim, and confide in the king's justice. As much as it was possible, he had messengers ride ahead of him, and prepare the people for his coming, and urge the country folk to come to plead their cases before the king in town.

At Galashiels a poor, weather-beaten old woman was supported, almost carried, into the room where the king sat. She pointed to her feet. She could no longer walk, she explained, for she had been shod with iron horseshoes, the nails driven deep into her flesh. "I had told the ungracious person MacDonald that I would carry my complaint against him all the way to King James, and that way I should get justice done," said the old woman, her dewlap quivering with indignation. "And he told me he would give me a pair of shoes for walking to the king's court. Then two of his men took my arms, and drew me to the fire, where they had me shod with the molten metal. I was sick many months, but now I am somewhat healed, and came to you—my two good grandsons carried my litter, and"—her voice sank to a very confidential whisper—"Your Majesty, Huthcart told me to tell you that your time is short."

"Who may Huthcart be?" asked the king, but the old woman would not tell him, becoming stubborn and secretive, and the two grandsons whispered to the king: "Dinna reason with her, she's not herself since her troubles; she's a bit saft in the head, but she's been wonderful good to us, brought us up since we were kids, as our mother died in childbed."

James turned to the crowded roomful of assembled men, watching, silent and suspicious, the working of this strange new thing, the king's justice. Then he said, very loudly and clearly, "I swear by Scotland that I will do to this ungracious person, MacDonald, as he has done to this poor woman here."

And he did.

Joan's daughter, Margaret, was born on Christmas Eve. "St. Adam and St. Eve's day," said James, "*tristes* patrons." Joan lay in bed in Holyrood watching the snow drive against her window panes—she had her windows glazed a little while before so that she might look out on to the green gardens and parks surrounding the gentle palace. James came in with a tiny necklace of well-matching pearls. "Scottish pearls from the Tay," he said, "for our Margaret, our pearl." He fastened the string round the baby's neck whilst Joan held her up. "Pearls are for tears," she said sadly. "I hope your gift will not bring sorrow to our little girl." As she kissed the soft head, she said, "God is very good to turn our selfish personal delight in each other into something so perfectly impersonal—you or I couldn't have invented those fingers if we spent all of our lives trying—and yet He let us help Him in their making and He only makes them through us."

Amongst the crowd that poured in to offer both Christmas and birthday greetings to the little new princess, was the Earl of Athol. "You love her well, methinks," he told Joan, "though she be but a lass," and Joan said gently that she prayed Queen Margaret, the child's ancestress, might look down kindly upon her.

"Ay, you must be very close to that other English wench," said Athol. Marjory Norton, Joan's old nurse, whom she had brought with her from England, was holding the baby whilst Athol spoke: though she did not understand his Scots, she sensed his remarks were disparaging and whisked the precious baby indignantly away.

At the christening my Lord Home bore the towel, my Lord Livingston the basin, my Lord Sempill the ewer. There served His Majesty at dinner that day, the Earl of Montrose, the carver, the Earl of Orkney, the cupbearer, Earl Cassilis, the server. The queen was served by Lord Seton, carver, Lord Home, cupbearer, Lord Sempill, server. There sat solemnly at supper the Earl of Athol, the Earl of Argyll, the Earl of Mar, the Earl of Caithness, the Earl of Strathmore, Lord Urquhart and nineteen other lords. Bishop Wardlaw, the Bishop of St. Andrews, performed the ceremony.

PART THREE

1425-1437

HUTHCART

CHAPTER ONE

☐ Joan wished she could escape from the sound of knocking. If she looked up, she could not help seeing out of the window the workmen busy building the scaffold, and even if she forced herself not to look, she could not help hearing the hammering; and sometimes fragments of the men's talk came up to her, though as they spoke Scots she could not catch all it was that they said. James had insisted she appear with him that morning, crowned and in full state, when he pronounced sentence on his cousin Murdoch and on Murdoch's sons, Walter and Alexander, and on Murdoch's father-in-law, the aged Earl of Lennox. Only one of Murdoch's sons, James Stewart, had escaped. In open rebellion, he had attacked and burnt the borough of Dumbarton, killing the king's uncle, Sir John Stewart of Dundonald, and now had fled to Ireland, with his wife, and the warlike Bishop Finlay of Argyll, who had deserted his flock to make common cause with James Stewart against King James.

The Albanies had fair trial by their peers, and the finding of the assize of twenty-one nobles, of all the earls then in Scotland except one, had been unanimous. Now in a few hours Walter Stewart, that splendid, arrogant, handsome young ruffian, who even at his trial dwarfed

249

her James, and looked more of a chieftain than he, would be headless. And tomorrow Alexander, Murdoch, and old Lennox were to die, all convicted by their peers, and all condemned by their king.

Nurse Marjory came in with the baby; it was time to feed her, and Joan was glad to forget her worries, to bury her doubts in her delicious feeling of physical closeness to her little golden-headed daughter. Yet her thoughts would not stay with tiny Margaret, but circles about big, hulking Murdoch, and Murdoch's judge. She remembered Murdoch as she knew him when she was a child. The clumsy, uncouth Scot, good at games, unexpectedly good on a horse, had been rather a friend of Henry IV. They had, she imagined, in common a certain deliberate obtuseness, and almost wilful refusal to see below the surfaces of people; they saw only what they willed to see, and they willed to see only the obvious, only what was presented to them on a salver. King Henry was by far the cleverer man; a sincere and painstaking musician, he would spend on practising his notes the time and energy he should, as king, have given to discovering the true inwardness of his people. Murdoch had much of this same fault, this denying of his own finer vision. He was not, Joan thought, half as green as he was cabbage-looking. But perhaps this self-blinding came naturally to men in power? Could one remain a king without it? And perhaps our free will was only God's disregard for our struggles and our disobedience? Perhaps He, too, the All-Seeing, cared not to look too close.

Joan's thoughts had been hovering about James, her James, all the while; but she had denied them. "I don't want to think about him just now," she told herself, and then realised that even if Henry IV and Murdoch and even James and God could blind themselves, she could not. She must beat about the bush no longer, must not cheat nor pretend. She must try and reconcile in her mind the irreconcilables in James's character. Her husband, the prince of lovers, the paragon of chivalry, the gentlest of men, had said he would "hew down the tall-

250

est heads in his kingdom" and he had kept his word. It was impossible to avoid seeing that he had been watching and biding his time ever since he came to the throne, waiting for Murdoch to betray himself, to open his mouth and put his foot into it, to dig a pit and fall down therein. Murdoch had seized crown lands and had used them and their revenues for himself throughout his regency; his father had held back monies given by the pope for the release of James, and applied them to his, Murdoch's, release; their regencies, both of Albany and of Murdoch, were of their own making, for either could, and both unquestionably should, have ransomed James at any moment; yet the fact that James should almost joyfully indulge in this wholesale obliteration of a part of his own family, seemed horrible to Joan. And it was the more horrible because she loved James with her whole being, with every part of her. Nothing he did or was could ever alter that for an instant: their relationship was a true cleaving of each to each, in the flesh that was closer than any other human contact. Even to Margaret, her child, she felt less close. There are people for whom the umbilical cord is never cut: who all their lives remain closest to their mother, but Joan had not been of these, and she did not feel Margaret would be, either. For herself, she was wholly given, wholly dedicated, to James: whatever share of her she might lend to others or they might borrow, depended on their relationship to James, for in and through him she loved, and judged, and saw. But, though finding unexpected sides to him could not alter her love or her affection, the very steadiness and fixity of her focus made her see clearly, inexorably: she saw him steadily and saw him whole. And she hated, not anything that she saw, but the things that caused what she saw. She hated the years of frustration and imprisonment, of bitterness and farness, which had warped his stem-straight nature, and frozen the warm currents of his heart. More and more, as she watched, kingship iced in him the fountains, halted the fresh springs; more and more it was only in her that his songs,

251

his music, his delight in life, began and ended. Joan thought that perhaps, as a woman, she should be pleased by this and flattered: it should give her a sense of almost absolute power. She knew herself to be his rest, his peace, his haven, his air, his sky. But she was neither pleased nor flattered, for she cared not at all what she was to him but only what he was to his God, his people, and to himself. She was glad to comfort him, pleased to provide whatever he might require of her, whatever he might need from her. But she thought him lamed who had only her for wings; he should reach heaven with his own; though they must soar together, it should be side by side. That he could, and did, use her, every part of her, was wonderful and right, but whilst opening doors for her, in her and through her, she hated it that he must slam those same doors in himself. Neither gained if he blew out a candle in himself for every one he lighted in her, and, to quote his own poem to her, the blood of all his body must not cease to flow to and from his own heart because of the channels it had found in hers.

She was hardly aware that Margaret had ceased suckling, and that Marjory was speaking to her. "It's not nice for Your Majesty to have these cruel happenings take place right here under your own window," the nurse murmured, and sucked the air in between her teeth with a disapproving hiss, which Joan remembered used to awe her when she herself was still in the nursery. She went on: "'Twould seem as though in this savage country death alone is such a small thing that it is necessary to add to it torture or public dishonour, else no one would even notice it or give it another thought."

Joan smiled, handing the old woman the baby. "Marjory, my dear," she said most gently, "my husband's cousins have plotted against him. They kept him from his throne for eighteen years. They raised a rebellion against him—just as my lord of Northumberland did: you remember the battle of Shrewsbury, don't you? King Henry had to kill my lord of Northumberland; King

James has to kill his cousins. And he has done more for them than King Henry did for his English rebels—he has granted them trial by their peers. Upon my soul," Joan concluded, "I believe this is the first time in history that traitors caught red-handed were allowed such a favour."

Nurse Marjory grunted. "Seems to me the peers had to find them guilty, or it might have gone badly for them to; it might have looked as if they sympathised with the rebels, or had thoughts themselves of rebellion." Nurse Marjory had always regarded Joan's present eminence with a certain disapproval. "That a chit like her should come to be queen," she had been known to confide to some of her cronies, "not but what I'm glad that my little girl's got a good husband and a nice home. Every woman should have that. But queen now. That's a different kettle of fish, and mark my words, no good will come of it, mind you." And she would go on: "Who'd have thought it now, my little Lady Joan a queen." But since she saw that Joan was really put out, and in trouble, she tactfully changed the subject. " 'Tis wonderful how His Majesty doats on the baby," she said, cuddling little Margaret. "He makes as much fuss over her as though she were a boy," and then she bit her lip and could have kicked herself, for what was the good of saying a thing like that? When everyone knew the queen was crazy to have a boy, and one was needed so badly for the succession? Before she could gather her wits together again James came in, and Marjory curtsied deeply and gladly slipped away with the baby in her arms.

"My love, I hate you to have all this tragedy so close," James said, going to the window and looking down at the scaffold with a professional and interested eye. Then he added, seeing Joan look downcast, "Can you bear to be present at the executions? I know you hate the whole business, and I promise you I would not ask you unless I thought it was necessary and politic."

"James," Joan exclaimed, "must I? Need I? I was there for the pronouncing of the doom, when you were wearing the regalia, and I my crown: what further good would my presence serve at the end? I have shewn all Scotland that I associate myself completely with you."

James hesitated. Then said, "My cousin, James Stewart, has escaped to Ireland—you know that?"

"Yes," Joan replied, "and Bishop Finlay of Argyll with him."

"I am naturally going to ask your uncle, Henry Winchester, and the Council of Regency in England to extradite him, and hand him over to me. He killed thirty-two of my innocent subjects besides my poor aged uncle. But I have my doubts whether even your pro-Scots Uncle Beaufort will agree to hand over so useful a hostage. I rather fancy my cousin James will follow my sad example and will occupy sundry English prisons for some time to come."

Joan asked, "Do you want me to try and persuade Uncle Henry? I've never tried to get anything serious out of him, but he was wonderful about birthdays, and he was very good about reducing your ransom as our wedding present, and footing the bill for all the wedding expenses. I'd much rather work on Uncle Henry to hand James Stewart over, then have to appear at these executions, or later at his."

James kissed the back of Joan's neck and stroked her high coif, "It's not what I want you to do, it's what I don't want your countrymen to think, that makes it necessary to ask you to witness these executions by my side. I want the English to realise that I regard you as my equal partner. My partner in all the duties and burdens, as well as in the pleasures, of kingship. That's why you were crowned the same day as I, not, as my mother and all Scottish queens before you, the day after. You and I are not only one flesh, but one sceptre. That's why I closed this recent session of parliament with the request that every bishop hold processions and offer up special prayers for us both in our bairntime."

"But since you are here," pleaded Joan, "may I not hide in your shadow? If you were away, I'd gladly deputise, but that we should have to share this horror, to watch this together, seems too much."

"I know all you suffer, my sweet," James said, "but you must see that I need you. Otherwise James Stewart can tell the English, 'See the queen is secretly one of ours. She refrained from appearing at the judicial murder of my father and brothers because she knows that is the only way she can express her disapproval of her husband's actions.' If you stay away, he will be able to tell your English cousins—even though he knows it is not true: 'I think there is no doubt but that the queen is sympathetic. She dislikes bloodshed, and finds such sanguinary tactics uncouth and displeasing.'"

"So I do," Joan said, her eyes flashing, "but is that any reason for not trusting me?"

"How can there be any question of my not trusting you absolutely, my heart?" James said gently, putting his arms right around her. "It's simply that I know exactly what James Stewart will tell your people. And it will make things that much more difficult for me if he can."

"I've seen men die before," Joan was speaking slowly now, her hand in James's, "killed in tournaments; and I watched with Mother when her brother died. But I've never seen a man killed coldly, for a crime. Yet," and here the loveliest smile came over her face and danced on her lips, as mockingly remote from her cruel words as were her cool eyes, "I'd gladly see everyone else in the whole world cut into little pieces slowly, if they had hurt you, James."

James kissed her several times. "O my queen, my queen," he murmured. They clung closely together for a while. Then he broke the silence, saying, in his most everyday voice, "I prorogued parliament, as you know, before arranging for it to meet again today here. That was to give the accused time to prepare for their defence. But next time, would you have us meet here, or once more in Perth?"

Joan answered quickly, "Oh, Perth, please. I shall never want to be in Stirling again, after this happening.

And Perth is much safer for you, for us all, I am sure. This is much too near England," and she shivered slightly.

"But, my darling," objected James, "we have a seven-year truce with your country."

"I know, I know," said Joan, "but I'd make sicher and take your parliament back to Perth, anyway."

"Now we must go," James said, as a herald appeared. Joan clung to James's hand, as a scared child might, and, holding on to it tightly, she went down the winding grey stair after James and followed him out into the splendid May morning. A huge crowd had gathered, and James almost had to push a way past for himself and Joan, though the herald was preceding them with the customary, "Make way! Make way! for Their Majesties, James, by the Grace of God King of Scotland, and the Lady Joan, his Queen."

The crowd parted, fell back, as they came to the grassy sward that had been a platform for country dancing, a tiltyard, but had never before been a setting for a scaffold. Joan looked at the white hawthorn bushes, dotted upon the green hill, and could smell their queer, semen-salt smell, blowing toward her. There was a pleasant breeze, that blew her veil over her face, and she had to take her hand out of James's to move it back. Then she saw, only too clearly, the scaffold, clumsy, ugly, almost lonely, because the crowd kept so well back from it. Beside it stood the black-vizored headsman, leaning his weight slightly on his axe. Then Walter Stewart was led out from the castle dungeon, between two guards, his arms tied behind him, his head and neck bare, his hair cropped short. He gave a low, ironical bow as he passed Joan; she did not start nor shrink, keeping her eyes steadily fixed on him. A priest followed close behind him, and as he passed her, Joan could hear that he was reading the prayers for the dying: "Go, Christian soul, go, in the name of God who created thee, of Christ who redeemed thee. . . ." It was all so quickly over, and so neatly done, almost as though it were not really happening at all: she could hardly believe that a man had just died; it was rather that it was a dress rehearsal of some play, or a scene from some pageant. Joan thought of the long, dark, hidden growth, bit by little bit, of this body in the womb, from a drop emitted in desire, to this absurdly swift and messy end, and so back to the dust from which came not only this sweet flesh, but all that had shared its pilgrimage to Persephone: the bread, the water, and the wine, the soft silks and warm furs, and prayed that for God it might make sense, though to her it did not.

Joan looked sideways at James, but did not dare even whisper to him, for his face was grim, and the crowd's pity for Walter Stewart, and their open admiration of his manly bearing, was loud and articulate.

"Wish they'd given him to me instead of to the gallows; I'd have made better use of him," a rouged tart said saucily, and a younger girl beside her said, "You'd have kept him out of mischief the day, so long as he kept you busy the night, eh?" " 'Tis a fine manner of man he was, whatever his actions," an older woman said, a bright kerchief tied around her fair hair. "Scotland should not have only death to give a man the like of that," said a countryman, shaking his homespun blue bonnet, disapprovingly.

Back in her room, Joan was suddenly sick, retching into her washbasin, her crown precariously balancing on her head. When she came to feed Margaret again, she found she hadn't a drop of milk, and although her breasts were swollen and sore for days, she had to find a wet nurse that very evening, for she could no longer feed the child. And as she lay beside James that night, after all their passion was spent and a deep peace bought with it, she wondered whether, by the very fact of lying with a man and loving him, one did not really move further away from the reality of the man himself. "All we share," she thought, "even the little death that every orgasm is, yet is nothing compared with what divides us. For between us is our image of the beloved, and though at first

257

that may be small as a man's hand, it grows and grows. For between us and every reality is the cloud of our imaginings, a thick curtain of imagination through which we can hardly see and barely feel. And sometimes we recognise the reality only through the passing of our love. And sometimes the recognition is itself the end. "Already between me and James," she thought, "there is my own image of James, my lover and my lord, of James, the begetter of Margaret, of James, my king; and all these Jameses are what-James-is-to-me, they are a graven image I have made of James, before which I fall down and worship. Whereas before I knew him in the flesh I could watch James-in-himself, or James-to-the-world, and that was the real James. But was it?" she wondered, and before she could answer her own questions, James woke, and his slight movement aroused them both, and, whilst their passion did with them what it would, Joan wondered no more that night.

But the next morning, when Murdoch, Alexander, and the aged Lennox were led out, Joan wrenched her mind away from the horrible scene she had to watch, and tried to recapture the detached, objective view she had taken for those few moments in last night's dark. But try as she would she could not shut out entirely her apprehension of Murdoch's boorish dignity, the sullen splendour of Alexander Stewart, groomed as though for a wedding, or the pathos of old Lennox who in his squeaky old man's falsetto told the crowd, "Gentlemen, if I appear to you to be unsteady and shaky, I assure you it is neither from drink nor fear; it is simply that I am an old man and tired," at which a gust of pity shook the crowd and touched Joan herself, so that tears ran down her cheeks, unchecked. It was horrible, she found afterwards, remembering the things she could not forget: the bump, almost bounce, of the heads as they rolled on to the new pine planks, and the quantities of blood—she had not realised people had so much—which went on spurting out of the headless necks for ages, messing up everything around, and, worst of all, the strange smell, like the taste of ink, that the blood and sawdust gave off in the hot sun.

Only gradually did she realise that, had James not killed Murdoch and his family, they would have killed him. It was not the horror of Dumbarton, nor the siege of Inchmurrin, old Lennox's castle on Loch Lomond, which held out against the king's forces for two weeks after his death, which convinced her, but strangely enough, old Athol, who would bleat on endlessly about the enormities of the Albany family. It was Athol, she later learnt, who had persuaded not only James, but most of the other lords, that all four of the Albanies must be executed for the security of the throne. He had insisted they were too near the throne to play stoolball with it; the day of the kingmaker was over, and if James wanted his laws to be obeyed, he must make a proper example of open lawlessness. "You condemn open and manifest rebels in a statute, and forbid leagues or bands which may engender discord between yourself and your people," said Athol, "therefore, you cannot be soft when it comes to enforcing your own statutes—or you'll be open to punishment for their infraction, yourself. If the statutes are broken do you recall what the damages are? I'll refresh your memory: 'To be punished after the form and ordinance of the said parliament,'" Athol concluded forcefully.

Joan was not sure she approved of Athol taking this line, though she had to admit the reasonableness of his arguments. "After all," she said to James, "he is just Lennox's age—and it looks as though he had some old, long-pent-up grievance against him that he now has finally settled."

"Why won't you credit the poor man simply with loyalty to me and a modicum of family affection, my love?" James asked.

And Joan said, "Don't forget that you and Murdoch were in exactly the same relationship to Athol—so much for family affection."

James had to concede that there she had made a point.

259

"As for loyalty," she added, "if he's so loyal, why did I myself hear him telling your nephew, the Earl of Douglas, just how much money you were getting from the forfeited estates of the whole Albany family—he had every penny reckoned from the lands of Fife and Monteith and the revenues of Lennox?"

James looked up quickly, as if this point, too, had made its mark, but he made no reply to Joan except to stroke her hair gently and murmur a couplet he had written for her:

<blockquote>
this flower
So heartily has to my help acceded
That from the death her man she has defended.
</blockquote>

"Oh, may that never be true—and yet, may it be true if it must," Joan exclaimed.

CHAPTER TWO

☐ "What's the modern version of that old, old problem: Can an archdeacon be saved?" James threw the question to a group of young students with whom he was spending a somewhat riotous evening at St. Andrews University. He was staying with Bishop Wardlaw, of course, and he was a temporary bachelor, for his young daughter Elizabeth, "a sister for Margaret," had recently been born, and the two babies and their mother were only to join him for Christmas. The young men looked politely at their knuckles as all young men look at all times, who think their elders facetious fools to try and make a bridge of banter across the generations. One of the more friendly thought he would try and help out the poor old king. "We're more interested in politics than in theology here, Sire," he said, with a pleasantly informative smile, and the slightly raised voice of one speaking to the deaf (and perhaps deficient). James, whose mind and hearing were excellent, winced at the patronage, but decided he must continue to unbend.

"And what are your primers—Plato? Or the *Politics* of Aristotle themselves?"

"Neither, Sire," said another long-leggitty youth, still,

for all the down on his lip, smelling of sweet milk, like a calf, "we're completely contemporary."

"Marsiglio of Padua, Sire," said a third boy, and a fourth broke in, "Dante—the *De Monarchia*."

James smiled at their sudden animation—the names were like puffs from a bellows on dying embers; suddenly a little flame had sprung up, and was catching, taking. They talked on into the night, arguing, laughing, remaking the world, and James listened purposefully. He did not really care that they only tolerated him; for he was as unable as they to separate himself from his time. They were boys, building new *Argos* to reaffirm their faith in an untarnished fleece; he, already past his meridian, was desperately trying to redeem the time.

He was glad, as he crossed the iron-hard grass of the quadrangle under the icy stars, that he was his age. "I'd not have any of my life to do again," he thought. "The best is now, or is before. And I am glad I did not have too perfect a childhood, like poor Charles d'Orléans, or too glorious a youth, like Alexander of Macedon. For like I'd be always moving with backward steps, having a standard the present could not catch up." But then as the thought of Joan came into his mind, it leapt to meet her, and he became warm all over; whenever he thought of her it was the same; it was as though he were actually warming his cold hands at a tiny, secret brasier. "But for her," he thought, "there is nothing behind me that is not better so," and once again the bitterness of his mother's and his brother's deaths, of his capture, of his father's death, of the dank despair of his long adolescent years soured his memory. "If the month of March comes in like a lion, they say 'twill go out like a lamb," he mused, and hoped that maybe it might be so with his life, and that he and Joan might now have come to quiet waters. And as he thanked God for bringing him safely through the past, to his present content, a dark figure slipped out to meet him from the royal quarters.

"Who goes?" James called, his hand instantly on his sword, but he did not need the familiar voice to tell him it was his old tutor. "Why did you desert me just now, and leave me to the mercy of that gang of young know-alls?" James chided him, slipping his arm into his.

"I thought they would be less intimidated by you alone than by the pair of us," said the bishop. "Our combination must have been overpowering, and I was moved to pity of the hapless young."

"And had none left for me?" James scolded, but the old bishop patted his shoulder, and, as they reached his pleasant, well-lighted college room, asked, "They're a nice group of boys?"

James agreed heartily, but then said, "All the same, I'm going to ask the Holy Father to let me move you all to Perth."

"Indeed," the old bishop sounded both surprised and annoyed, "that would break my heart, Jamie," he said. "We're well enough off here and it seems to me only right and proper that the senior see in Scotland should have the first university. I've spent all my life here, and this university means everything to me. Don't move it until I am dead, don't take away my best toy."

"You'd be far safer at Perth," James said. "You're on the edge of rich country there, and you would not have the victualling problem you have here. The St. Andrews folk, town and gown both, are often really hard put to it to find food enough to live and work upon. And the surrounding country is so often stripped by English marauders that it can do you very little good. Also I'd like to have you with me, close to me, handy, so I could consult you all the time, not merely by messenger."

Bishop Wardlaw gave a deep sigh. "You must have your will," he said, "but I'm an old dog, and would hate to have to learn new tricks. And I'm no courtier. I want to spend what little life God lends me further, in preparing my soul to meet Him and the minds of the young to cope with life."

"Don't forget I was sent from here because it wasn't safe," James reminded him and then, suddenly asked: "Where are my moleskins?"

"I had to throw them away, Jamie, please forgive me," the bishop said. "First they stank and then they shrivelled. And," he went on, "don't forget it was from your uncle you were unsafe; amongst my present students I have no king's son with a predatory uncle. But I'm too old to argue, and you always were my favourite pupil, and now have so far outdistanced your old master that 'tis you today should be teaching me."

James put a footstool under the old man's feet, and settled a cushion in his back. "You are always my master, and I your grateful and delighted pupil," he said. "Do you remember my astonishment when you read us Cardinal Peter of Ailly's *Imago Mundi*, which described how in the East people believe the world is round, and that it is but one of the planets, and not the other way about, as St. Thomas and all our masters taught?"

Bishop Wardlaw smiled. "Yes, and now all the best philosophers amongst the Italians are coming to accept the cardinal's theories, and even some of the newer men in Paris. But I was always interested in what came from the East to us. Do you remember my making you read the *Thrie Tales of the Thrie Priests of Peebles* that was by one of the English poet Gower's pupils?"

"Of course I do," James said, "and the third tale was the most exciting. . . ."

"The story of Barlaam and Josaphat," interrupted the bishop.

"Whose feast day is November 27th," began James.

"Apud Indos, Persis finitimos, in India, on the confines of Persia," went on the bishop, "and their acts were written by St. John Damascene; but the third priest's tale, that you and I liked the best, is from Vincent de Beauvais, though he makes proper acknowledgement to John of Damascus. Barlaam is an eastern prince, and he leaves his throne, and his wife and child, because of a story Josaphat tells him, about the man with three friends. Do you remember, James?"

James thought a moment, then said, slowly, "The first friend was Great Possessions, and for his sake he fell into many perils, but on his last day all this first friend had to offer was some useless rags for his funeral. The second friend was Kith-and-Kin—is that right?"

"Yes," replied the bishop, "and his only service was to bear his body to the grave; after which, returning home, he gives heed to his bodily cares, leaving the man's memory as surely buried as he left his body. But the third friend is Good Works, and that friend stays with him in the grave, and after."

"It's a pious enough tale," said James, "but why do you find it so enthralling? Why used I?"

"Because it comes from India, and because of its effect on Barlaam. He was a great prince, and the son of a great prince, yet when he heard it, he left his sleeping wife and son, and became a recluse."

"Would you have me leave Scotland and Joan and my children, then?" James asked, and the bishop, horrified, said, "You are not so called, Jamie. You were born to be king. Yet, you know, they have discovered strange things in the East: did you know they use the city of Ujjain as the meridian, and can compute the whole earth's distances therefrom?"

James yawned. "You are ever the same," he said, stooping to kiss the old bishop's ring. "You will always be happy so long as you are learning or teaching. But for me I am tired, and growing middle-aged, and must to my bed."

"Have one more glass?" pleaded the bishop. "This is your first visit to me since you left me as a child of twelve."

James accepted. "By the way," he said, "I fear I shall be taking some of your boys from you to exchange them for the present hostages that are biding their time in England until my ransom is paid. The ones who are there now have already done nearly two years, and I hate every day any Scot has to spend in exile, especially since it is for my sake. So I want to change the young men as often as I can, and bring back home the ones there and send new ones to England."

"How do you reckon the money part of the transaction —who is worth how much, and why?" the bishop asked.

"That's my chief difficulty," James said, "it's so hard to find replacements of the same value as the original hostages. The Master of Athol, for example, is my own first cousin, and my heir until I have a son, and he is worth more than anyone I can find to send in his stead. So I must just leave him in London," James concluded.

"Won't that upset his father? The old earl's woeful elderly."

"I've made it up to him financially as much as I can— releasing him from taxes, granting him customs—and I think he has quite a high regard for his duty both to his king and his nephew," said James, pompously.

"How's the money coming in for your ransom, by the way?" asked the bishop, and James replied: "I got 14,000 marks the first year, but so much less this year that I daren't tell you."

"How much?"

"Only just over half last year's total."

"What are you going to do?" asked the bishop.

James looked sheepish, a small boy caught helping a lame duck. "The tax was so unpopular I've stopped asking for it."

"James," exclaimed the surprised bishop, "how then are you going to raise the ransom money?"

"I don't know," said James in a small voice. "Mayhap if I don't ask for it I will not be able to pay it."

"But the hostages then?" queried Bishop Wardlaw.

James looked miserable, "I know. There must be a way out."

There were a few moments' silence, whilst James sipped his mead appreciatively. "Such a pleasant hot drink this—much nicer then mulled claret or spiced beer —I can't think why we never have it at court," he said.

"You know," the bishop said thoughtfully, "it wouldn't be such a bad thing if all the nobility and gentry took their turns at living in England as hostages—so long as they didn't have to stay there too long."

A mischievous gleam came into James's eye. "That thought occurred to me, also," he confessed. "It would educate and civilise them—look what it's done for me—and at the same time remove them from too obviously powerful positions here."

"Jamie," the bishop sounded quite excited, "it's not such a foolish plan at all—this remitting the tax of twelvepence in the pound and continuing the hostage system."

"That latter part I can't avoid, remember," James said. "It irks me tremendously, as a matter of fact, to have to give the English anything for nothing."

"You alter the whole composition of your parliament, though," the bishop went on, as if James had not interrupted, "with so many nobles, Sire, but you get something much nearer what you wanted, more like the English two-chambered house, with representatives from the shires, and even from the towns, elected, responsible for seeing the laws they made carried out in their own part of the world."

James yawned, "Yes, that is exactly what I do want. But I don't know whether anyone else in Scotland does—or ever will—and I don't know yet if the hostages remaining in England will help in the long run." He knelt down and kissed Wardlaw's ring again, "Good night, my lord—I am right sleepy after all this fine talk," and so, still teasing the old man, James left the room and went to his bed.

For Joan, that Christmas at St. Andrews was the loveliest she could remember. It was a bitterly cold winter, with much snow, and the little steep town, with the collegiate buildings snowcapped, their Gothic outlines muffled to a strange cosiness by their white coverlets, enchanted her. An immense ship of the Lombards was wrecked in the storms at Leith, and pedlars surreptitiously brought to the court stolen loot from it for sale—the strangest toys, gilded birds that flapped their wings and sang, and a furred mouse that ran squeaking along the ground; and statuettes of saints, gold-leafed and studded with gems. Joan bought one of St. Margaret for her little daughter's first birthday, though James scolded her for it. But she countered with, "All treasure trove belongs to the king—I'm merely buying in what is yours anyway."

"It is that to which I was objecting," James laughed. "Why buy a dog and bark yourself?"

Christmas was made the more splendid by the presence at court of the Earls of Douglas, Mar, Angus, and Moray—the last back from his year in England as a hostage. Joan questioned him eagerly on his life there.

"We lived at our own expense, in the Tower," said Moray. "We had all our own servants and retainers, and they could come back and forth to Scotland as often as we wished, to fetch gold and silver, or armour, or clothes, or eating vessels, or horses—though I bought English horses myself, they are much bigger than ours, and are properly currycombed every day, and are broken young to wear bits and bridles."

"Were you kept in confinement?" Joan asked, and Moray replied: "No, no; no one of us was pinned or barred or even shut up in a house."

Joan was amazed. "You mean you went daily at large in the town on your own assurance?" she asked.

"Yes, indeed; did not the king when he was in England?" Moray asked, surprised in his turn.

Joan replied, "No, he had a guard at all times."

"We saw to our own purveying and to everything that was needful," said Moray.

"So you enjoyed your time in England?" Joan asked, and was touchingly pleased when Moray warmly assured her he did; indeed, his only grievance was that he had been rather bored. Court life was fun, and he liked Humphrey, Duke of Gloucester, and his Dutch wife Jacoba, but there were not enough tournaments; his liver grew sluggish and he got fat.

The Scottish court amused itself vastly until Twelfth Night. James and Joan, partly unconsciously, partly deliberately, made the celebrations as like a Westminster

Christmas as possible. James was afraid Joan might be homesick for London; he was so himself, a trifle, though he did not realise it, and would never have admitted it. Only the old bishop disapproved; by long preaching he assayed to discourage "the riotous custom of banqueting brought into Scotland from England by King James at his homecoming." Joan stealthily watched the company for signs of disaffection, for some brooding over the Albany executions, but could find nothing to disquiet her. In fact, Douglas told her that before his death, Walter Stewart had himself admitted the king had done "justly and according to law."

At the New Year the snow melted, and after the court returned to Edinburgh, a strange duel took place—between a knight called Henry Knox and a certain plebeian tailor. James himself presided, and the tilting was held before the gates of Edinburgh Castle. The tailor accused his gently-born opponent of making treasonable speeches against the king, and was so fervent in the king's cause that he had persuaded James to let him challenge Henry Knox. The whole scene was faintly farcical, for James was very careless of treasonable speeches, and would have men free of their tongues; but the zealous citizen was more loyal to the king than the king was to himself, and Henry Knox felt very much mortified at such a thing having to happen to him—and was ashamed to go down to history as the first Scottish gentleman to be challenged by a tradesman. His position was indeed ridiculous. For a great crowd gathered, despite the howling gale-paced wind, and Joan wondered whether it was wholly wise to make such specious mockery of the usages of chivalry. The general atmosphere was far from knightly; it was more like that at a wrestling match or a fair, although many nobles were present, in their plumed and coroneted caps, and many great ladies, in their best clothes; yet these cared nothing for the occasion, and came only to see their friends or to be seen by them. King James separated the opponents after a short scrimmage—poor Henry Knox was obviously failing, and the time was not yet when a gentleman could have accepted defeat at the hands of a mere artisan. So the king pardoned Knox, and gave hearty thanks and a purseful of golden money to the tailor for having so gallantly defended him.

CHAPTER THREE

☐ "The ambassador from France is come," announced the herald, and a shiver of excited anticipation went through the court—for the one to step forward was Messire Alain Chartier, poet and secretary to King Charles VII.

"He's not very attractive," commented one lady, looking at the plump-figured, smooth-faced little man, who now settled himself on somewhat experimental legs, and pompously, humourlessly, delivered a very long speech which he read from a parchment in his hand.

"Is his love as long as are his lines?" loudly whispered a pretty girl. "If so, I'm afraid I'd have fallen asleep before he got to the . . . to the point," she finished.

He had come, Alain Chartier explained, in the hour of France's most terrible need—most supreme need. The English were besieging Orléans—the French king was in a desperate plight; his situation was serious. The ambassador continued: "My master made every effort to get ready to go to Scotland, to seek shelter with your king. He is surrounded by deadly enemies; the Duke of Brittany on the west; on the north, the Duke of Burgundy and the English; the Duke of Savoy on the east; the Prince of Orange and the King of Aragon on the south."

When Alain Chartier had finished his speech (he was so proud of it he ever kept a copy of it amongst his most private papers) he relaxed amongst the courtiers. To Queen Joan he described the King of France in moving terms, for he knew she was the most likely person to resist his schemes, and the sole reason for Scotland's unprecedented English alliance. "A young man, my king," he sighed, "with so little money. And without money, no effective good can be done in war." As Joan made no reply, Chartier then turned to James, "And so, Sire, without hope of aid, despairing of any help, counsel or sympathy, penniless, without servants, without fighting men, grieving in his heart, left desolate and in great straits, my lord, the king, would lift up his voice and weep."

"Would that be all he does?" James asked rather unsympathetically.

Chartier coloured. "Ah, Sire, you are pleased to make merry at our plight," he said. "My lord the king is a most pious man—he confesses daily to the Bishop of Chartres, his confessor, and on great feast days he hears Mass thrice."

James considered. "What does your king ask of us, and what does he offer?"

Chartier listed: "He asks the hand of the most noble princess, Margaret, your daughter, for his son, the most noble Dauphin, Louis. And he further asks 6,000 men to accompany her, to bring succour to the sweet land of France. If your daughter in the course of time become queen, she shall have the jointure customarily bestowed upon the king's wife by the law and customs of France; if Louis should die before succeeding his father, she shall have 12,000 French pounds a year."

James promised to think deeply about the question; the shocked look on Joan's face made him realise that even to talk of sending their beloved little girl overseas horrified her.

A few days later, two more ambassadors came: Regnault of Chartres, who brought pretty presents for Queen Joan, was one. He offered her a mule, three barrels of sweet chestnuts, and many apples and pears. With him came Sir John Stewart of Darnley, made Comte d'Evreux for his share in the victory of Beaugé. ("I traded the title for 50,000 gold écus," he told James in a loud aside, "so I really am no longer count: but I still retain the right to quarter the lilies of France upon my shield.") The mule, a dainty, pearl-grey little creature, created quite a stir because Regnault insisted upon bringing her into the banqueting hall, where she comported herself very well, submitting to everyone's admiration and caresses, but relieving herself when she felt nature's call, without a thought for the wonderful brocades and silks she was splashing.

The ambassadors argued intelligently for the treaty they wanted. "The English are angry because you do not pay the ransom, no?" Chartier asked and James had to agree that this seemed to be the case. "Your nobles are not pleased because they can no longer go abroad and fight—so they stay home and fight, no?" And again James had to concede that this was true. "You need very badly money, no?" Chartier questioned again, and again an affirmative answer was the only truth. So James gave a great party, a betrothal party for Margaret, and the little golden-headed three-year-old, with her briar-rose skin and grey shining eyes like starlight, charmed everyone with her sweet manners and her baby talk. Chartier enjoyed the party, too; he read aloud a long poem of his, called *The Battle of the Four Ladies*. These were four rivals, who argued as to which was the most unfortunate; the one whose lover had been killed at Agincourt, the one whose lover had there been taken prisoner, the one whose lover had just disappeared, or the one whose lover had run away from the battle. He described the horrid condition of his war-torn country very graphically; how Paris was under martial law, and the peasants did not even dare go into the vineyards to pick the grapes. But the ladies did not care for such painful realities, and hurried him back into talk of his romances; they revelled in another of his poems that described how everyone sees well the deep lakes of love before them, but no one even tries to avoid falling in. On the contrary, they step willingly down into them.

The ladies agreed with him that love had two chief enemies, tepidity and melancholy. So he returned to France soothed and petted.

But no Scots went to France for many a year, though some Scots had stayed there—Sir Hugh Kennedy, for example, who was fighting with four thousand infantry under the Frenchman La Hire. He was at Chinon when an eighteen-year-old peasant girl appeared, and although the Dauphin disguised himself, she found him instantly. It was Scottish archers led the march to the coronation of Charles at Rheims and many Scots watched his anointing; John Carmichael was there, as well as Sir Hugh Kennedy, and also Michael Norwill, a squire to whom the King of France gave 150 écus, and a portrait of Joan, the Maid, armed, presenting a letter to her king and kneeling upon one knee. "These bear to your King James," King Charles had said, "and tell him France is well succoured by a girl, not his but our own." At Lagny the Scots fought loyally beside Joan, and at Arras it was a Scots archer who gave her a file to help her escape.

Meanwhile, the English were very concerned by the rumour of a new Scots alliance with France. Henry Beaufort, the queen's uncle, new-made a cardinal, determined to make the long journey to Scotland himself, to discover from James just what was going on—why the ransom was not being paid, why there was always so much stickiness about the exchange of hostages, why there were so many breaches of the truce. James agreed to come to meet him on the Border—"but wild horses will not force me across it again," he said. The cardinal was received at Berwick by Henry Percy, with one hundred horses; he arrived at Coldingham in a very well-sprung carriage and charged King James nineteen shillings for a feather bed to use inside the carriage from Haddington to Dunbar and back. Yet the cardinal did not accomplish much; indeed, his meeting with James

274

had one deplorable result in that the forces the cardinal had raised for a crusade against the Hussites in Bohemia, were, as a result of his meeting with James, used by him instead to assist Bedford against the Maid. And so, though he never realised it, and it was the very last thing he would have wished, in actual fact, James contributed not a little to Joan of Arc's defeat.

Now, after only four years of his reign, James's kingdom was beginning to take shape from his laws. "No man's greatness shall appal me in doing right, nor the meanness of any make him so contemptible that I shall not give ear to his grievance," James had declared, and in parliament after parliament he had destroyed the actual, but increased the pictorial, powers of the great nobles. He originated the system by which every judge must appoint counsel for the poor, and by which all judges, chosen in any future parliament, must "swear to judge faithfully and lawfully according to their knowledge all causes and complaints laid before them without favour or hatred, fraud or colour." He insisted, almost savagely, that all able men must work, they must yoke their oxen and plough; it was only the unemployable might beg, and then must have a license to do so or must themselves dig so much land daily. Yet the estates were firmly for the king, and the solidarity of the nation behind him was felt as an almost tangible bulwark of approval in the case of the condemnation of the Albanies. Treachery there was, and in plenty, but it was local, individual; as a whole the temper of the country was surprisingly (since his was a stern rule) on James's side. His relationships with foreign powers continued friendly—although in some cases, as that of his meeting with Beaufort, for instance, both sides felt they were biding their time.

That his subjects might have occasion to avoid sloth and idleness, James imported from Europe and England the best artisans and manufacturers whom either large privileges or money could obtain. Organs he brought, too, from the continent for the Scottish churches, and choristers, and from Hungary mares and stallions, to improve the indigenous breed of little Scottish horses, furry like foxes.

James was his own foreign minister, and by treaties with Holland and with Flanders, with Eric the Red of Denmark, who came himself to Scotland to pay tribute, for the Western Isles, and with the Dukes of Burgundy, he increased Scottish commerce, and enriched his country with much trade. For all his dislike of sailing, he was an enthusiast about his navy; instead of the single ship he had owned whilst a prisoner, now he built, and also bought, from near-by Zealand, many ships; and even Joan had at least one new little ship of her very own.

In all these activities, in this slow building up of his nation, James had on his side the whole power of the Church, and the loyalty of all the people, and of the burghers, of all who laboured, as of all who bought and sold, who kept shop or who made things, who were artisans and merchants. In his hammering of Scotland into a unity, where the king's word was law, and that law was justice for all, from lowest to highest, James, always reserved, always self-controlled, grew more and more to resemble his own image of himself as king. Only with Joan would he allow the identification to become less absolute; she still could thaw him: for her, with her, he was still James the man, James the human being; else he grew more and more to fit his profession as if it were a mould into which he deliberately cast and held himself, until, even for his intimates—for William Giffard or Bishop Wardlaw, for the Earls of Mar and Douglas— even in their thoughts of him, he was not "James" but "the King." With Joan only could he escape this tight armature, this kingship he had put on, had built up around himself. But only with Joan, and through his art— his music and his poetry. When he was setting a song of his own to music, the cuirass, the thick armour-plating of his kingship melted or slipped from him, and he escaped, was free, and could frolic or frivol, wrapped in his poet element again, the judge, the ruler, the lawgiver, the fighter, and the monarch laid aside.

It was as if he knew that he needed Joan for his own sanity and suppleness, knew that without her he would rust up entirely, or change into some stiff effigy of a king. He made his council-general enact a rule that all lords, spiritual and temporal, must take an oath of fealty to Joan without which they would not be admitted to their fiefs or seas. He insisted Joan reign with him; jointly they dealt with affairs of state; she witnessed all the documents concerning Margaret's betrothal; she shared with James all his building projects: together they rebuilt the church and the lovely palace of Linlithgow after it had been burnt; and together builded the great monastery at Edinburgh for the Franciscans of the Observantine reform of St. Bernardine of Siena. This was so magnificent a building that the Minimi, the least, as the brethren liked to call themselves, refused to live in so palatial an establishment, until the king persuaded their superior, whom he had sent for to Cologne as being a holy and wise man, that to refuse was less humble than to accept; and finally, James and Joan founded together the Charterhouse on the South Inch of Perth.

This was the only establishment of Carthusians in Scotland; James had learnt to love the order in England. He had there often gone to Sheen, where the Carthusians had a monastery well endowed by the Beauforts. The people, English or Scottish, did not care for them, although "it must be admitted, they are honourably distinguished for not working miracles," the notoriously anticlerical young Earl of Moray told James.

"But they withdraw into cities and there chant their idle songs in a magical manner," grumbled Thomas Berry, one of the queen's squires.

The three of them were riding down to see how the building was progressing; the great, new Charterhouse that rose like the upturned keel of an immense ship and already towered above all the surrounding dwellings, although there was still a cobweb of scaffolding about it.

"They are contemplatives," James said, "and I grew to love them during my long years of exile."

He remembered now, almost with the same tangible sense that he remembered the smell of the muddy English fields, and the soft southern air so scented in spring with all the green things growing, the sandalled prior, Oswald da Corda, who had been his director, and the technique he had begun to learn from him of imageless prayer. And he remembered well, too, the sensation of pushing distractions away, almost as physically as he would push aside the cloud of gnats when he was riding on a summer's day through Windsor forest, or push back the bare, cold twigs as he galloped through a thicket after the Berkshire hounds on a brisk autumn morning.

He had real need now of what he had learnt, he thought, for in the bustling glare of kingship the daily, hourly swarm of phantasms cluttered and smeared the windows of his mind and heart, and he constantly needed to wipe them away, so that each time he did so he could anew "begin to live with God only for Him alone."

He had sent for Oswald da Corda, who had, after Sheen, been vicar of the Grande Chartreuse, the mother house near Grenoble, in the remote fastnesses of the Dauphiné Alps. Later, James was to send for Adam of Hanglaid, a Scotsman who had long lived at the Grande Chartreuse, and who succeeded Oswald as prior. In contrast to his love for the Carthusians, James was stern with the Benedictines and the Augustinians, bidding them set their houses in order, "lest the royal munificence, which built and nobly endowed your monasteries, repent that it erected marble dwellings when it observes how impudently you have abandoned religious conduct." Nor was he soft-hearted with the clergy when it came to the revenues of the crown. He had even dubbed his own ancestor, David I, a "sore saint for the crown" because he had overspent himself, and had impoverished the royal heritage in the endowment of religious houses, leaving the very kingdom thereby weakened and in debt.

Throughout his reign James was engaged in a long and complicated tussle with the papacy, during which, even through which, he was working towards a concordat. But he was just as much working away from papal interference in internal Scottish affairs, in local questions of politics and finance. The great problem was whether the king, or the local hierarchy, could choose a bishop or abbot, and then apply for his confirmation from Rome, or whether they must accept men nominated by Rome and imposed on the locality, often with no knowledge of the regional problems, sometimes even a complete foreigner. Even when a Scotsman was appointed from Rome to a Scottish benefice, he would almost inevitably be a Curia man, a man who had spent most of his adult life in Rome, or at all events outside of Scotland, and was unaware of its particular needs and difficulties. In James's case, his troubles with the papacy were crystallised, as it were, in the cases of Croyser and Cameron. Croyser was a papal nominee, but parliament was strongly against him, and though the pope, himself, wrote to ask James to restore him to his favour and to the benefices parliament had taken from him (for treason, because all clerics had been forbidden to accept benefices from the pope without first asking the king's permission), James would not budge. On the other hand, James's own man, John Cameron, went over to the papal side at the Council of Basle, under threat of excommunication. James's answer had been to forbid him to come home or to land in Scotland.

James was constantly moving, and whenever possible, he took Joan with him. He had to be everywhere, for the country had been left in such a disordered and disorganised state that the only hope of getting it into some sort of working order again, was to visit every corner of it, and himself, with his own hands, to get the elements of justice, and the rudiments of civil service, and of a civic order, functioning again. James had learnt from the Lancastrian progresses through England, how essential it was for the sovereign to be in close and constant touch in every part of his kingdom, with the people. And as soon as there was brought to him any rumour of disaffection, any story of some noble getting above himself, at once James would set off to investigate, and would take with him writers and lawyers, so as to have the whole affair properly thrashed out, and a complete record made.

On such occasions, though Joan accompanied him, the children were left at Perth or at Holyrood with a household of their own, besides the trusty Nurse Marjory. In August, 1428, Joan went with James as far north as Aberdeen. She was alarmed for her husband, for he was out on the trail of wild caterans, wild clansmen, led by such semi-independent lords as Alexander, Lord of the Isles, who had not been present at James's coronation, but who had been almost constantly heard of since, as raiding here, looting there, burning crofts and castles indiscriminately, and generally behaving like an outlaw and a hooligan. She had insisted on going with the king, but he categorically refused to take her further than Aberdeen. "I must go quicker than you can keep up with me now," he told her. "You would hinder, not help me, by coming," and she had to accept that. James reached Inverness in two days' hard riding; he was glad now he had insisted the castle there be repaired and set in order in the first year of his reign.

He had sent summonses out warily and singly to the Highland chiefs; when he had collected some fifty of these together under his roof, he chose a jury of twelve from among them, to try the others: then, of those found guilty only of minor offences, he chose another twelve to try the twelve members of the jury. It was a brilliantly successful plan; only three men were found guilty of crimes meriting death. Of these, the chiefs MacGowrie and MacArthur were beheaded, and the third, a Campbell, was hanged. The rest of the fifty, including young Alexander, Lord of the Isles, and his mother, were given short terms of imprisonment. James was grimly pleased: he even broke into Latin verse, improvising a couplet which Joan at a later date roughly translated:

> Let us wile the gang to a castle strong
> For by Christ's wrong, they deserve to hang.

But James made merry too soon.

For, after a very brief spell of prison, Alexander was released, and James attached him to the queen's service, as one of her squires. It was the custom then that young nobles should serve at court, and James hoped to tame the young lord, whom he thought not vicious, but badly brought up, and who might improve if removed from the influence of his mother, the savage old countess. Her James imprisoned in the fortified abbey of Incholm, under the guard of the chronicler Bower, who, as he himself relates, was a great deal more frightened by her than she by him.

But Alexander did not take kindly to court life. The courtiers laughed at this brash cub, who gave himself the most tremendous airs, kicking up a great stour, or dust, of self-importance wherever he was. So he slunk off, and suddenly appeared again in the Highlands, at the head of a tribal army, with which he took and burnt Inverness. This time James was swift in his wrath. He had enforced the old "weapon-shewings," by which able-bodied men must produce their weapons twice a year in peacetime, and must also instantly answer the king's summons and be ready to fight, with their gear. Thus with real speed he was able to collect an army and dash north. The Highlands were alerted; war was everywhere, and James arrived with his army at Strathnave, to find a wide plain strewn with dead; the Mackays and Murrays to the tune of 1,200 a side had fought each other and killed each other; of both clans, only a total of nine souls survived. James pushed on, leaving the dead to the hungry eagles, and at Lochaber, on June 23rd, met Alexander's rebel army, some ten thousand strong. It was marshy ground, and for a while the two forces faced each other. Then James unfurled the royal standard, the lonely lion, and Clan Chattan and Clan Cameron left their formations: first in a trickle, then a great running of them, all coming to James, and, laying their arms at his feet, they surrendered without a blow.

Alexander was left on the field with a very thin, diminished following, and soon they, too, started coming over to James. Alexander looked silly standing in the mud waving a sword all by himself and shouting rallying cries to his men as they dashed past him earnestly toward the king, and James and his friends broke into loud laughter, which Alexander must have heard, from the beet-root colour of his face when he, at the tail end of his deserting men, had perforce also to surrender unconditionally. This time James was "making sicher," and turned north after the battle, dragging Alexander along as an inducement to the various remaining rebels—some were Alexander's own followers but many of the chiefs were as independent of him as they were of James—to give themselves up. James crossed to Skye, and went on by boat to the Outer Isles, to the Hebrides; the inhabitants crawled half-naked out of smoke-filled stone huts to stare at the strangers. But no one anywhere, any more opposed James; he yanked his siege engines across the oddly-named seas such as the Minch, yet still nowhere could he find an enemy; only purple heather and blue hills and peewits and sandpipers crying, and the white wings of cormorant and gull over all.

A month later, whilst James and Joan were sitting at their orisons, at Mass in the chapel of Holyrood, Joan heard a curious dragging sound. She glanced around, and saw young Alexander, naked but for the cords about his neck, and a loincloth, carrying his sword by the point, and crawling on his hands and knees up the aisle. All around arose guffaws of smothered laughter; the officiating priest, turning for the *orate fratres*, started at the strange sight, but turned back to the altar to continue with his Mass. Joan rose horrified from her *prie-dieu*, and throwing her rich cloak over the young man's nakedness and shame, she knelt to ask his life of the king. James was not very willing to grant her request, but just then the sacring bell rang, and, when they lifted up their faces again after the Elevation, Joan's was wet with tears. "No man's death is worth your sorrow," whispered the king, and with no further words, turned again to his devotions. But from that time, Alexander, beholden for his life to the queen's pity, hated her as all men do a woman to whom they needs must be grateful.

CHAPTER FOUR

☐ Sir Hugh Kennedy was back in Scotland, after more years than he liked to remember. Already he ached for Lorraine, for the soft pussy-willow-coloured fields, and the smooth, velvety air, here in Scotland where the air smelt nuttily of gorse, and was *pétillant* like cowslip wine. He was walking in the gardens at Linlithgow, amongst formal beds of tulips and forget-me-nots set in box beds, and lozenged around a sundial. The jackdaws and rooks were building busily in the elms, and a pale egg-yolk-coloured sun did its best to avoid the crowds of scudding small clouds, like a woman struggling to free herself from a billow of pretty, but obstructing, veils. With Sir Hugh walked Queen Joan, and on her arm hung Princess Margaret, as tall as her mother, a slim child nearly twelve, her oval face ending tidily in the neatest, slightly pointed little chin, her eyes blue as the space between stars, and her gold hair dancing out under her coif. She was questioning Sir Hugh eagerly:

"What happened to Joan? Were you with her when—when the English burnt her? She wasn't a witch, was she?" Margaret's words tumbled over each other, as she looked passionately up at tall Sir Hugh. With her free hand she was dragging along little Jamie, her five-year-old brother, heir to Scotland. The poor child had a great birthmark over half his face—his whole forehead, one cheek and part of his nose were scarlet, the skin thick as though someone had hit him hard, or as though it were some other stuff than skin. Everything had been done to try and get rid of the unsightly defect: ten pounds of almonds weekly had been pounded and crushed to make pastes and compresses, brews and stews of hemp agrimony and hawthorn, of dandelion milk and the juice of Solomon's-seal, were constantly essayed, but to no avail.

"Joan was a girl worthy remembrance," said Sir Hugh slowly, "I knew her well and was with her on her journeys, and I assisted at her victories and I was with her at her end."

"Died she well?" It was Joan asking.

"As died the saints," said Sir Hugh. "They would not let her have a cross, so I brake two sticks and tied them, and held them high, at the end of my lance, that she might see the rood."

"God bless you, Sir Hugh, for that! You did right well," cried little Margaret, "that is an immortal glory for Scotland—that it was you who helped her so."

"Will you trust your daughter to me to carry over to France, Your Majesty?" Sir Hugh asked Joan.

Joan stopped, and a look of frightened pain came over her face. Margaret's little hand tightened on her mother's arm, and she dug in her nails. "Don't, please, talk of that," Joan said, pleading, "there is no need she go for some years. She is too young, and the Dauphin does not yet need a wife; she can bide by me until she is fourteen, surely! It's such a long way, and she's but a bairn still." And Margaret said, fiercely, "I don't want to marry any man; I don't want to leave my father and my mother and Jamie here, and Elizabeth." Sir Hugh said, "But, my lady, if you will come with me, I will bring you to a fair prince who will make you queen, and he will be King of France, and your husband, as your father is King of Scotland and your mother's husband."

"I had rather be plain Meg at home than Your Majesty in any other land," said poor Margaret.

"Would you not grow to be as your mother is?" Sir Hugh asked. "In all other ways, yes," Margaret took Joan's hand and kissed it, her eyes moist and shining with love, "for she and the king my father are the best people in the whole world, I know; but that they are king and queen has nothing to do with it."

"I left my country and my parents and all my people for your father's sake," Joan said, playing devil's advocate.

"And you must do and be what God has intended you shall," said Sir Hugh, softly.

But again Margaret shook her head. "No," she said, "I asked Abbot Fogo about that, and he said God wants me to love Him and to live to His glory, and to be happy because He is happy, but how I live, not where I live, is the matter of importance."

"You are a very important person, my sweet princess," said Sir Hugh. "His Lordship of Mortain, your own uncle, and Lord Scrope are even now come here from England to ask your hand for King Henry VI and now here's myself, come to ask your hand for the Dauphin of France."

"Could I not marry King Henry, Mother?" Margaret asked. "Then I could sometimes see you, and there would be cousins for me to play with—King Henry himself is a cousin, and he is King of France too, so if you want me queen, I would be doubly queen there and of both countries, without so far to go."

Sir Hugh got very red. "You are too young, or I would be sorry I had heard a Scots lass tell me that Henry of England is King of France. More Scots blood has been shed to disprove that nonsensical claim in the last thirty years than has been shed since Wallace died to prove the King of England was not King of Scotland also! And you asked me about Joan the Maid: for what, think you, fought she and died?"

Margaret was silent. Then: "I'm sorry," she began, "if I said anything my country or any one of my brave countrymen alive or dead would take amiss. But King Henry is still my cousin and my neighbour, and still King of England, you will grant him that? May I not marry him, Mother?"

Sir Hugh looked shocked. "But you were betrothed to the Dauphin when you were three; only the pope can undo those solemn vows," he said.

Joan intervened. "Don't make a betrothal seem more serious than it is," she said, quickly. "After all, Lord Scrope has offered the town of Berwick-upon-Tweed for Joan, and bade James learn to forget his French, or as he said: 'If ye be so enamoured of France, love her after our manner. Come, take a share, be partakers of our victories.' And a betrothal is only a political, not a religious ceremony." She went on, "My husband's grandmother, King Robert I's wife, was betrothed to another before she married him, and the pope granted a dispensation."

"Yes," Sir Hugh said, hotly, "and that is why the Earl of Athol thinks he has a better claim to the crown than King James."

Joan and Margaret both looked tremendously startled. "Uncle Athol thinks he should be king!" said Margaret, and Joan gasped: "The Earl of Athol more right to the throne than James!"

Sir Hugh realised he had said too much. "Forgive me," he said to Joan, "I thought I said only what all men knew. Don't let me suggest that the earl is disloyal; he no doubt will abide most faithfully by the king his nephew, and by the decision of parliament and the act of succession by which James succeeded to the throne. But, actually, Athol is the eldest son of the second marriage of Robert II, born after wedlock, not before, as was His Majesty's father, and born without impediment of betrothal, or consanguinity—you remember King Robert II's queen was also within the prohibited degrees, and a dispensation had to be obtained on that score, too?"

Joan looked grave. "Yes, I knew all these thing, but I

never thought they could affect James's position. He succeeded by the will and choice of the people, freely expressed."

"Of course, of course," said Sir Hugh, "no one ever has questioned, and I am sure no one ever will question, either of those indubitable facts. It was only hearing Your Majesty lightly suggest that Princess Margaret could put aside her betrothal to the Dauphin, upon which, and upon her ancient alliance with Scotland, France has pinned so many hopes, that made me speak out of turn. Do not give my words, spoken I fear in heat and even with some anger, another thought. I most humbly ask Your Majesty's pardon for my indiscretion, as for my annoyance."

"Do you know what answer my father made to my Lord Scrope?" said Margaret, anxious to smooth Sir Hugh down. "He said, 'If England would conquer France, then it would very soon conquer Scotland also.'"

They spoke no more then of such weighty matters, for Joan knew as well as Sir Hugh, that Alain Chartier and the other French ambassadors were even now in Perth with the king, discussing the terms of the marriage settlement. There was really no hope left; the negotiations had gone too far, and Margaret must be wed. But Joan's heart was very heavy, and she and Margaret and the court and the royal nursery journeyed to Perth in deep dejection, as though going to an interment rather than a wedding.

Meanwhile Alain Chartier, at Perth with King James, had been discussing the marriage all day. The king had taken the French poet down to see his new Charterhouse, now finished and the most magnificent building in the city. It was raining, and they rode back up slippery streets, swaying coldly on their wet saddles, discussing the details: James was to send two thousand men as Margaret's escort, not the six thousand France had asked at the time of the betrothal, for now the King of France could neither pay for nor feed so many Scotsmen. Indeed, if he found when the two thousand of the escort arrived, that he did not need them after all, the King of France was to be at liberty to send them home, paying their passages, of course. Such a difference in France's need of men had the victories of one girl made: the French were desperate suppliants no longer, but were become hagglers, bargainers.

When Joan reached Perth, she besought James to think of some way of at least postponing Margaret's departure. She had become desperate, single-minded, almost hysterical, caring for nothing except to keep her child with her. James tried to reason with her:

"We've made every excuse; first, she must not go, because she was the heir until a son was born; then, when the twins came, she must stay awhile to get to know her baby brothers; then there was poor little Alexander's death; even Jamie's fiery face has helped us keep her awhile longer, for we said since one twin died, and the other was deformed, we could not spare her. But now that Jamie is such a fine lad of five, there is really nothing more we can say. And maybe it is selfishness in us that would keep her; the greatest gift we can give those whom we love is to set them free from us."

They were in the nursery, the gayest room in the house. Little James was riding his rocking horse whilst his parents played with baby Joanna; now it was his turn to come on to his father's knee for a story.

"What sort of a story would you like?" James asked, and young James said, "A true story."

"Oh, no," Margaret said, "untrue stories are much better. I only like untrue stories."

"And I true ones," said Elizabeth.

James thought. "I'm not sure there are any really untrue ones; somewhere, sometime, they must be true, or must become true, else they'd not be worth the telling," he said. "I'll tell you one about your great-great-great ever so many times great-grandfather."

"Is it true?" Jamie asked, and his father said:

"Quite true. Once upon a time King David was out hunting with his nobles on a lovely summer morning, and by-and-by they reached a great wood girdling a wide plain. King David had outdistanced all his followers, all his courtiers, and there was none with him but one man, and the king knew well that this man was a traitor."

"Oh, Father," Elizabeth asked, "why did he not kill him, quickly?"

"Don't interrupt," said Jamie, and Joan said, "Hush, children," and James went on:

"When he saw there was no one else in sight, the king stopped, looked straight at this man and said, 'Lo, here am I now, and there is none with me, and we are equally armed, and equally mounted. There is nobody who can see or hear either of us, nor bring assistance; therefore, if courage be in thee, if thou be stout enough and bold enough, perform that thou hadst purposed to do. For, if it be in thy mind to slay me, when canst thou do it more fairly, when more privately, when more manfully? Hast thou prepared poison? Leave that to a woman. Dost purpose to lie in wait for me in my bed? Leave that to an adulteress. Dost think to lie in ambush and attack me with a sword? No man doubts that this is more the office of an assassin than of a soldier. Come on, then, body to body; act the part of a man and a warrior, so that thy treason may at least be without baseness, though it cannot be attempted with perfidy.' When the knight heard these words he leapt off his horse, threw aside his weapons and fell at the royal feet. 'Fear nothing,' said the king, 'for no evil will I do unto thee.' Then having required of him only a promise of future fealty, he returned him in good time to his companions, and related to no man what had been said or done between them. Isn't that a good tale, Elizabeth?"

Elizabeth said, "Good indeed," and James smiled. "If the king were alone with the knight, from whom think you that we have the tale?" he asked.

"From the repentant knight," Elizabeth said, stoutly, after but a moment's hesitation. But James smiled.

"You don't think, just possibly that though the story is

true, it also might be untrue? In the sense I explained?"

And, grudgingly, Elizabeth admitted the possibility, whilst Margaret clapped her hands to see her father win.

At the great banquet that night, the final details of the marriage arrangements were discussed. Charles VII was to send the ships to carry Margaret and her escort and to provide the drink, the bread, and the salt; James was to send the meat, fish, butter, cheese, and wood for the voyage. All through the long feasting it seemed to Joan as though the French were gloating over having put through a good deal. It was as though Margaret had been skewered and trussed and packaged for them like a roasting fowl, or honeyed, like a well-baked ham. When she and James were at long last alone again together, Joan was silent, too near tears to trust herself to speak, and it was he who said: "It is shame indeed that our beloved child has been used as a pawn in our political wrangles, withheld from France, as a gambit, as a talking point in my negotiations with England, and that now she is finally delivered to France, that she may make Scotland more secure to the south; that she may renew the ancient covenant and alliance in her person. And yet, though it is true we have delayed sending her through policy, we also have delayed because I could not bear to part with her. We have at least gained some years of her sweet company." And he sighed.

Joan's tears now flowed unchecked, and James went on, "And the worse is that we know nothing of him to whom we are sending her. His parents are most horrible: I hated and despised all I saw of the French court, and yet it is to France we send her. We have pleaded the inclemency of the weather, the danger of pirates at sea, and the holy season of Lent. But we have not spoken of our hearts, nor our love, and no delays will ease them: they will but make the final separation harder. There is nothing more for it. She is growing up, we have made a good marriage for her, as parents should, and now go she must."

For weeks thereafter was much feasting; for a great

king must keep great state, entertain in high style, and give splendid gifts. "Distinctions exist to be shewn": a king must flaunt his majesty, as a beggar his misery. Joan said good-bye to Margaret at Perth, and God knows what great weeping there was on both sides; James rode with her to Dumbarton, and on March 27th bade her a farewell "which his overmastering emotion obliged him to bring to an abrupt close." She sailed convoyed by eleven ships, with an escort finally of only one thousand lords, knights, and other gentlemen, headed by the Earl of Orkney, whose father had sailed for France with hers.

The English had spies even about the Scottish court, and one of these, seeing three men going into church one spring afternoon, tied his horse to a tree and followed them in to hear them discussing the bringing up of the ships. When the spy went out, he found his horse stolen; and the poor foolish man was in a terrible plight. How explain his ridiculous presence, in full armour, on foot, knowing no Scots? There was nowhere to hide. When the three conspirators came out of the church hard on the Englishman's heels, they questioned him, and he grudgingly admitted who he was; he was, of course, instantly carried off to jail, but managed to talk on the way, giving a simple message—the number of vessels, and the date of sailing—which figures he asked an unsuspecting young knight, going to England on a safe-conduct for some tournaments, to convey to a friend of his.

So the English, forewarned, sent out 180 ships to capture Margaret, but whilst they waited off the coast of Brittany, they amused themselves pursuing and capturing some Flemish boats which were carrying wine from La Rochelle to Flanders. Having got much of the wine on board, and not a little of it safely inside them, the English were then themselves attacked and disposed of their prey by a Spanish fleet. During these various sea battles, Margaret's ship, whose good captain, Perys Percipey, seemed able to make his vessel fly rather than sail, reached La Rochelle, and Margaret landed, and was able to spend a few peaceful nights in the priory of Nioul, before going on to Tours for the solemnization of her marriage.

Joan and James were doing accounts, trying to reckon together how much Margaret's marriage and her journey had cost. "I can't see why you remitted the tax you ordered towards the wedding, when we are so short of money," Joan said.

But James refused to go back on his word: "When I heard the complaints of the poor at the sum I proposed to levy to defray the expenses, I promised only to ask gifts of money for this purpose from those as rich or richer than I; that is, from the great nobles and the great churchmen. It seems horrible to me that I should ask the poor to give up their little luxuries—perhaps a silk kerchief bought once in a lifetime, or a joint of lamb at Easter, in order that Margaret might have more jewels. That is why I decided to approach, courteously and singly, only the peers."

"And they, singly or severally, gave you, grudgingly, the least they could—am I right?" asked Joan.

"I'm afraid so," conceded James.

The truce with England, which had lasted the twelve years which had passed since James brought Joan home to Scotland, was now at an end, and James, advised by Athol, plotted to besiege Roxburgh or Berwick, the two great Scots Border castles still in the hands of the English. Things were going ill for the English in France: the Duke of Burgundy had joined with the King of France, and now it was the English who were besieged there and their key castle of Calais was in grave danger. Humphrey of Gloucester was on the way to its relief, with a large force. "Now is the time," said the Earl of Athol, "to attack behind his back." James was against the idea, and Joan thought it mean and nasty, but James always bowed to Athol's advice and did so again on this occasion.

Roxburgh was chosen, rather than Berwick, in spite of

the fact that quite recently the English had been busy both reinforcing and repairing it. But Athol declared it would be more logical to defeat first that English garrison deepest set on Scottish soil, whilst James was rather inclined to try for Berwick, leaving the English in Roxburgh encircled. "But let's do what Uncle Walter says," said James, giving way. "We're going to take both castles, aren't we? So let us surround and storm them in his order."

James set out, therefore, with Athol as his mentor, and a perfectly enormous army—if the collection of every able-bodied man in the country, between sixteen and sixty, who turned up, some say to the tune of 200,000 strong, could be called an army. But from the beginning of the campaign everything went terribly wrong. It was nearing harvest time, and the men resented being taken from the fields—shepherds and neatherds had been exempted from the ordinance, but farmers had not, and the empty lowland fields lay spoiling in the August sun, whilst James and his hordes encamped about Roxburgh. For a fortnight nothing was done because of a detestable split and most unworthy difference arising from jealousies—the king's support hardly saving Athol from the anger of the younger captains. Then, after losing all their fine guns, both cannon and mortars and gunpowder and carriages and waggons and many other things indispensable for a siege, suddenly one evening, in the midst of a bitter orgy of recrimination, which was being indulged in by Sir Robert Stewart, Athol's grandson, who thought he knew better than the king, the queen arrived. She had come from Perth in a light carriage, alone but for a couple of squires. Even James gave her a poor welcome. "This is no place for a lass," he told her, but she assured him she must talk with him privately, and he dismissed the council of war that was meeting in his tent, and, taking her arm, led her across some pasture to a stone barn.

"Here we can speak," he said, ordering two of his men to keep guard. Inside were a few bales of last year's clover and they sat down on these. Both must have remembered a night long ago at Peebles, but neither referred to it.

"James, Sir Robert Graham is planning rebellion against you," Joan said breathlessly, "I've got the proofs, and you must believe me. And Sir Robert Stewart is in it, too, and your Uncle Athol is behind them."

"Joan," said James, slowly, "being alone has unsteadied your mind, my darling." But she met his smile steadily and replied, "Being without me has unhinged *you*, my heart. Don't you realise—it is perfectly logical. Athol is angry because his son is still a hostage in England after twelve years. His grandson plays on the old man, and because his father is away, leads the earl by the nose. Sir Robert Graham on his side is angry, because of your English wife and ways, because you imprisoned him unlawfully, as he thought, and because you have sent his nephew Malise to England as a hostage, and given Malise's earldom of Strathearn to Athol."

"Then, Sir Robert should be cross with Athol, and they would cancel out," said James, still smiling.

"You find it hard to believe that men hate you," said Joan. "You want so desperately to be loved that you pretend to yourself that you are popular! The people love you—because you bring them gifts—justice, good government. But many of the nobles hate you—mostly your own cousinage. Remember that if anything should . . . . should happen to you and to Jamie, it is Athol would inherit, and it is his grandson Sir Robert Stewart who would eventually be king."

"Athol has a claim, certainly," James said thoughtfully.

"He thinks he has a better claim than yours," countered Joan, "because your grandfather only married your grandmother after your father was born. Whereas *his* mother and your grandfather were legally married before either David Strathearn or Walter Athol was born."

James stirred the dried leaves that had blown into the barn with his sword. "For an Englishwoman, Joan," he smiled, "you are grown quite good at genealogy."

"Oh, James, cease treating me as though I were a child —and an idiot child at that! I came here because I know that Athol and Graham are leagued together against you. And they are your nearest relatives, now that you have killed the Albanies."

"Would you have me kill them, too, now?" James asked. "What a bloodthirsty wench you are become suddenly, my Joan."

"You've imprisoned both your nephews—the Earl of Douglas and young Kennedy, and James Stewart is paid by the English, and is living in Ireland with his sister-in-law in comfortable exiled sin, and . . ." Joan paused for breath whilst James interrupted:

"And George March and his son Patrick Dunbar are up to no good, being rebels who have taken refuge in England, and . . ."

"And you must drop this siege and come home, James," Joan concluded for him.

"You haven't given me a reason yet, my sweetest lady," James said, and she replied, "Because you will never take Roxburgh with the divisions there are amongst you all. Sir Robert Graham is spreading the story, even to Perth and Edinburgh, that you have gathered this big army here, in order to invade England, and the soldiers, who have no wish to start a war, nor to go to foreign parts, are very dissatisfied. They say that since Margaret has been married to the French king's son, you are bound by treaty to make this new war, and that since the truce with England is ended, this is the beginning of a long campaign."

"They say. What do they say? Let them say," replied James. "Since when have you been listening to servants' gossip? And since when was a siege raised because of rumours? But certainly this army is not like the English army with which I served against Drux or Melun. These men are made of lambs' wool; they have no idea of discipline or of co-ordination; fighting with them is like serving a tennis ball against a mattress. Maybe I should take

297

them out on a long campaign, and make soldiers of them."

"Please, please," Joan said, "you can't take castles with woolly soldiers. Do as I ask."

But James was not convinced. "Treachery is nothing," he mused aloud. "I've lived with it all my life. And always from my nearest relations. In fact, I should be very surprised to hear of a traitor who was not an uncle or a cousin, for then I should think perhaps there was something wrong with me as king, after all. Or if an uncle or cousin were not a traitor, then I should wonder if something was not amiss with them; I should wonder what was ailing them."

"There's another reason why you must come home," said Joan, with the air of one checkmating at long last; "if you don't, you'll surely be excommunicated and Scotland will be laid under an interdict."

"And why?" James asked, then added, quickly, "Oh, because I won't forgive Croyser, and Cameron won't forgive me? Oh, Joan," he added, clasping his arms round her suddenly, and kissing her for the first time since her arrival. "My dear, it is so wonderful you are come. You cannot imagine how horrible men are without women, left alone together. It must be that only through women are we ever nice at all."

"Are you ever?" Joan whispered. "Sometimes I wonder, when you treat me as you did today. But I am very glad to be a woman, for if, as you say, it is only because of women men are ever nice, it is certainly also only because of *a* woman, any of us are saved, and the only perfect human being created since Eve was a woman."

"Hm," said James, "you are doubting the hypostatic union?"

"James, you are impossible—either we talk of matters of state, or you may make love to me, but I refuse to discuss the finer points of theology just now," grumbled Joan, "it's not the moment."

"You began!" said James, and then went on, "but do explain why I'm to be excommunicated."

"The pope himself has written asking you to restore Croyser to his benefices."

"Talk of simony," interrupted James.

"And he is sending Cardinal Albergati's own secretary, Aeneas Sylvius Piccolomini, to you to ask for his reinstatement," continued Joan. "If you will not do as you are so politely asked, well then, there will be certain consequences, amongst which are an interdict on Scotland and a personal excommunication on yourself. You simply must come home, or you will find that in your absence the whole country has fallen into something far more crippling than any paralysis: Mass will not be said."

James, stroking Joan's hair—he had loosened her coif and they were half lying back against a stout bale of dried clover—interrupted her:

"I do not feel that I am really in such bad odour in Rome as you fear, my sweet. I am fairly certain His Holiness Eugenius IV knows how passionately I stand here in Scotland for everything he represents, and how steadfastly I have fought and fight against all traces of Wycliffe and of Huss. We do have our continual troubles over barratry, but the whole point of the Council of Constance was the reform of the Church from within, in the head and in the members, and I know His Holiness is on my side fundamentally also on this point. But if Aeneas Sylvius is really on his way, and may be arriving any day . . ."

"He has arrived," Joan interpolated.

"Then I had better get back to Perth," said James. "After all, the spiritual welfare of this whole nation matters more than whether we take Roxburgh back from the English this week or next."

In the casual manner of mediaeval warfare, which still prevailed in such local forays, James explained the position to Randolph Grey, the Archbishop of York, and to the Bishop of Durham and to Henry Percy, all of whom were opposing him, and having arranged a truce, he called off the siege and travelled back to Perth with Joan. But the Earl of Athol, riding in his wake, said to

Sir Robert Graham, quite loudly, so loudly indeed that perhaps James himself heard, and certainly there were others who did: "A strange resolution, methinks, to disband an army for a tale of treason, for where could there be greater safety for a king than in an army?"

Many, even of the infantrymen, also grumbled that the king should turn aside from so important a business as a siege, as real warfare, for a woman, and thought it the more strange since that woman was but his wife.

When the royal party, with such hangers-on as had not gone home to help with the belated harvests, arrived at Perth, they found the streets full of papal flags flying, and a general air of bustle and excitement. James learned that Aeneas was well lodged—he had taken one of the best inns, and James hastened to send enquiries as to whether the papal envoy was comfortable and to invite him to dinner. Aeneas sent word he would gladly come. When he arrived, splendidly dressed in red samite, with such quantities of ermine edging all over him that he looked positively stoaty and only partly human, James was surprised to discover he was not a priest—he was not even in minor orders.

"I fear I agree with St. Austin," Aeneas observed, after bowing low to James and seating himself comfortably at the king's right, as if they had known each other all their lives, "when he said, 'Make me chaste, O Lord, but not yet.'" He sighed. "I am very susceptible to female charm," he added. And then, indicating the queen, he sighed again, and whispered to James: "You are a most fortunate man—to go through life attended by such beauty."

"Ah, there I entirely agree with you," said James. Then asked, "Did you have a good journey? You had a long way to come—from Rome here."

"A horrible journey," said the envoy cheerfully. "I had not imagined I should survive such detestable adventures."

"If it does not awaken discomfort too poignantly," said

James, with a twinkle, "would you share them with us by relating them?"

"Gladly," said Aeneas. "The nastiest happenings become agreeable when one looks back on them, and especially when one tells them to a sympathetic audience. Even if it be so only because one is puffed up at the success of one's own survival."

"You are a philosopher," said James.

Aeneas inclined his head in acknowledgement of the compliment. "When I got to Calais I was arrested by the English and most maliciously thrown into prison," he said, "and there I would be until this day, were it not for the goodness of Your Majesty's uncle"—he bowed to Joan—"Cardinal Beaufort, who ordered my release. Then, when I got to London, I waited about a great while, having been promised a safe-conduct, and finally was refused it, so I had to go back to Bruges." He took a long drink of wine. "What abominable claret," he sighed. "It is monstrous the French should sell you such vinegar." He whispered now to James, "Alas, for my feeble flesh—I had dawdled so long in London I left there a pignus amoris—a tiny token of love—a very Cupid of a boy." He took a large mouthful of goose. "I am most impressed by the amount of meat and fish you have to eat here—even the poor seem to gorge themselves on salmon and venison."

At the mention of venison Athol caught James's eye with a barely perceptible wink, and James, himself, laughed out loud. "You put me to shame," he said to Aeneas, "for by your mention of venison you prove to me how little my laws are observed."

Aeneas went on, as if he had not heard, "But bread— that seems to be a luxury."

"Please tell us more about your terrible voyage," Joan said politely, and Aeneas went on:

"Ah, yes—well, I finally got a boat at Sluys, but there was a great storm at sea, in my terror I vowed I would walk the first ten miles on Scottish soil. We landed in

301

Northumberland, practically cast ashore, and I managed to get to a farmhouse on the English side of the river Tweed—no boatman would take me, so I had to risk spending the night on English soil. We ate well—much chicken and pork, but no bread or wine. I had a little of both I had taken from the boat, not knowing when I would eat again, and the pregnant women—and many of the farm women seemed in that happy condition—came and sniffed at the bread, so I had to offer it to them. Then, about midnight, all the men ran away—there was a rumour the Scots were coming and the men all took refuge in a tower. I was left with my guide, and my two servants, and one hundred women, who sat all around me cleaning hemp or spinning. I became very sleepy, and two young women shewed me a loft covered with straw, and offered to sleep with me, but I pretexted I was too scared of the Scots to be of any use to them—actually, I *was* too afraid of having my throat cut to be found in mortal sin. The heifers and the nanny goats prevented my sleeping a wink by pulling the straw out of my pallet. Sometime in the night there was a terrible commotion and all the women rushed out of the house, but I was too tired and lay still. I learned next morning that the newcomers were friends. I regarded my safety as the reward of my continence!"

"What happened next morning?" asked James.

"I managed to cross the Tweed in a small boat. But when I got on to Scottish soil and had to keep my vow, my feet got so frost-bitten that I was laid up for several days, and then had to be carried with them bound and bandaged. But I had performed my vow."

Joan said she hoped he was finding Scotland more agreeable now he had arrived at court, and Aeneas said, "Yes, indeed, Your Majesty. Such fair women and such freedom between the sexes; a kiss here means less than a hand-squeeze in Italy." To James, he added, whispering: "Scottish ladies are most amorously disposed. I dread more than ever now the responsibility of continence—a virtue which it is so much easier to talk about than to observe, and one much better suited to philosophers than to poets—for you erred in calling me a philosopher, Sire, I am much more naturally of a poet."

"So am I," smiled James. "We must give each other the pleasure of hearing each other's compositions."

"I would not bore you with mine," said Aeneas, "but if you insist—*The Two Lovers*, my tale of Euryalus and Lucretia—a true story, by the way, is my favourite among my works."

James said, "Perhaps we may have the pleasure of hearing Your Excellency read it us?"

So, after supper had been cleared, Aeneas settled down in great content. When he had finished, James and Joan were enthusiastic. "A most beautiful story—you have made the woman so wonderfully loving," commended Joan.

"Ah, yes," said Aeneas, "men are credited always with the stronger passion, but almost all women are of such a nature that they most desire whatever they are most strictly forbidden."

"We get that from Eve," smiled Joan.

"Hence, it is about as easy," Aeneas went on, "to guard an unwilling woman as to watch a flock of fleas in the burning sun."

"That's how Lucretia managed to enjoy her lover right under her husband's nose," said James.

James was determined that Aeneas should have a good impression of Scotland. He gave him a fine horse, and a charming necklace of pearls and paid his fare both ways, and gave him money for casual expenses besides. But still Aeneas found Scotland strange and savage; only three hours of daylight, he complained, and the beggars asking at the church doors for black stones, and taking them gratefully back to their houses to burn, puzzled him, and he thought an oxhide hung before the entrance for a door was a barbaric custom.

His opinion of Scottish civilisation was hardly raised by two men quarrelling so loudly one evening at the royal dinner table—the whole court ate together—that

303

the entire assembly stopped to listen to them. One of the men jumped and drew his sword, and instantly, James, who had been observing the scene in the same silence as the rest, sprang to his feet. In a voice of thunder he declared.

"Put up your sword, and come here, both of you."

When the men reached the high table, at which Aeneas was sitting next James, the king turned to Sir Robert Stewart, then the chamberlain, and asked him, in a deadly quiet voice, "Cut off his hand that drew the sword."

Sir Robert started back in horror, and before he could comply with the king's order, Queen Joan had risen, and threw herself on her knees, clasping her hands together, and implored James, "Don't, James, please don't, please spare him. I will myself be warranty for his good behaviour hereafter. Please, I beseech you."

James said angrily: "I'll pardon him since you ask it, but I declare his estates forfeit to the crown, and he must do public penance."

Mingled with the sigh of relief that went up from the whole assembly, Aeneas felt, and knew James felt too, the contempt of males for one giving way to a female.

James invited Aeneas to assist at his parliament. It had been such a cold winter, that the spring meeting had been delayed until the roads were unfrozen; they had, indeed, in many places been impassable. Edinburgh now looked magnificent in its mantle of snow. One of the first acts of this parliament—James's twelfth—was to acknowledge, with proper thanks, that the king's peace had not been broken in the Highlands. Then statutes were made for the increase of precious metals; the laws against taking specie or jewels out of Scotland were reiterated and emphasised. Aeneas was sitting with Queen Joan:

"Will that apply to the pearls your husband gave me?" he asked, laughingly, and Joan whispered she thought not. "There seems to be nothing the Scots like so well as abusing the English or listening to abuse of them," Aeneas said, after listening awhile. "The Highlanders and Lowlanders speak different languages, is that not so? Yet they understand one another?"

Joan said yes, that was the case, as far as she knew. "But my Scots is hardly better than yours, I'm ashamed to say. James spoils me and speaks always French or English with me."

"You are happy together, are you not?" the envoy asked.

Looking down at James, seated amongst the rude nobles, spitting on the floor, blowing their noses on their fingers or sleeves, stamping their feet, talking, Joan said, "We are completely happy together. I am often frightened, for I wonder if two people should be so happy—here."

Aeneas put his hand over hers. "Ah, Majesty, there is no here if one is happy. One is already there. St. Bernard says love flows ever back to its source and there draws anew whence it may flow again. Only by love can the creature answer to the creator, and repay like with like."

"But it is James I love, not God," she whispered, and Aeneas replied: "But the love wherewith you love him comes from God, is given you by God for the purpose of loving and flows back to Him through your husband. You are most fortunate, Your Majesty."

Before Joan could answer, there was a great commotion, and Sir Robert Graham marched between the sitting lords, right up to the king.

"What can he be doing—has he some message for James?" Joan murmured, but Sir Robert laid his right hand—his hands and head were bare, else he was in full armour—on the king's shoulder, and stared down at him:

"I declare thee, James Stewart, to be relieved of thy office of king by the will and good pleasure of the three estates of this realm, and I hereby put thee under the ban of these three estates," he shouted very loudly but very slowly.

He could hardly finish for the sighs of astonishment, of wonder and surprise that went up from all present.

There was a half move on the part of several to jump up
—Sir Robert Lauder was on his feet the first. But most
were watching what the king would do, and he sat perfectly still. He had not raised his hand to ward off Sir
Robert's, nor gestured in any way. Since James was silent
no man stirred. And the silence spread like a puff of incense borne down a church, from the king to the whole
assembly. Sir Robert felt it, and straightened himself,
and turned to the assembled parliament.

"Is it not as I say?" he asked, still arrogantly, but the
pride crumbled on his lips and spilled on to the floor, as
he saw and heard and understood the whole company's
denial of his treason, their complete affirmation of loyalty, in that extraordinary, contagious silence. Suddenly
it was broken, and by Sir Robert, stumbling—almost
running—down the length of the chamber. The whole
room listened, heard him slam the door, heard his horse's
quick hoofbeats as he rode off. Then the king spoke.

"Go after and arrest him," he said. And then turned to
Thomas Somervill of Carnwath, and asking him: "Pray
go on with what you were saying about the closing time
for taverns, before we were so rudely interrupted."

Aeneas was almost dancing about in the gallery, and
Joan had to lay a restraining hand on his arm.

"Splendid, your husband was splendid, magnificent,"
he said, the tears pouring down his cheeks in his excitement. "But how cold you people are! How we should
have applauded him in Italy! We should have carried
him shoulder high and given him a triumph, strewn roses
in his path. . . ."

Joan laughed. "We order our lives—and our excite-
ments—differently here," she said, her face shining with
love and pride.

CHAPTER FIVE

☐ That summer there was the Black Hour. On a sunny day, June 17th, at 3:00 P.M., it was as though night had fallen; and what a night: the light was absolutely blotted out. Every minute seemed like an age, for no man had any idea whether the light would ever return, or whether, for their sins, or for some catastrophic, universal reason, the whole firmament would remain so, returned to primeval night once more. But the light came again, after what seemed eternity (it was only a few hours), but other portents followed. At harvest time a blazing star was seen, trailing across the sky. Dolphins swam up the Tweed and were taken; a sow had a litter of pigs with heads like dogs.

Joan had been much comforted by the behaviour of the three estates, but she was anxious and worried that Sir Robert Graham was not taken. All the answer she could get from James, or from any man, as to his whereabouts, was that "he had fled to the country of the wild Scots." But James kept receiving strange, anonymous defiances, notes scrawled on tree bark, or once on a linen kerchief; these were handed him surreptitiously when he was waiting for his horse, or when his horse was halted in the press of the crowd. These notes informed him that since he had been deposed by the will of the three estates, he was king no longer, and that it was no treason to plot against him, nor to murder him, nor to kill. Each missive shrieked louder, shriller defiance, and all were in patently the same hand.

Joan had a new baby, another girl, little Annabella. She had no boys after the twins, and fiery-faced James remained the only son. James had insisted that his heir should have a Scottish nurse, and Janet, the wife of Adam of Liddale, took care of him, and he stayed in his own chambers in Edinburgh, wherever the court or his parents might be. Nothing would remove his huge birthmark, and after the grinding of forty-eight pounds of almonds had been in vain, attempts to blanch the mark were abandoned. It faded as he grew, so that it only appeared noticeably unsightly when he was angry, but it never lessened in extent. King James made his son, in spite of Joan's fear of the unlucky title, Duke of Rothesay, and the boy had his own establishment separate from his sisters, from his sixth year, with a chamberlain, Michael Ramsay, who kept itemized accounts, how much milk, how many coals, how many rushes, the small duke and his household used; and he had also a tutor, who had written authorisation to chastise the person of the most noble duke should occasion arise. . . .

Joan decided that they should spend that Christmas at Perth, and the court moved down in mid-December. As the outriders of the royal party came to the waters of Leith, just as they reached the ford, an old woman rose up, who had been crouching out of the wind, amongst some dead bracken. "I would speak with the king," she said, and the outriders tried to push her away. But then, as the king came up, she risked being trampled to death to rush in amongst the horses and to clutch at his bridle. He stopped instantly. "My lord king," she said, "an' ye pass this water, ye shall never return again alive! My lord king, this night I saw you with a shroud about your feet."

James leant down to her. "Was it not your feet that were shod?" he asked, and she replied, "The same, and you comforted me, and revenged me on mine enemy. For this I am warning you. Turn again, turn ye again, my lord king." But James said, kindly: "The King of Scotland turns not back," and rode on.

Next day, as they came to the next ford, when the king's horse had already stepped down into the water, somehow, the old woman was there again, her hand on his bridle. "Lord king," she wailed, "turn ye again! An' ye pass this water, ye shall never return again alive! I dreamed I saw you this night, and your shroud was about your waist!" But again, courteously, with a sweet smile, James made her the same reply.

On the third morning, the royal cavalcade reached the walls of Perth, and there was a third stream, hardly more than a little brook. This time, as the party drew near, they saw the old crone waiting for them. The king rode first, and as he came up, greeted her most civilly, but she shook her head, and wept, and moaned aloud, "Lord king, lord king, turn ye again! I dreamed I saw you this night, and your shroud was over your head and upon your eyes."

But still the king answered her gently, and said, "God bless us both, Mother, now and in the hour of our son, Sir Robert Stewart, the old woman sprang out of him, causing his horse to shy. "God damn your eyes," he said, taking his whip and preparing to use it on her. But she stopped him.

"My lord of Athol, I dreamed I saw you this night," she said, fixing him with her stare, and leaning close to him she whispered, "and there was a crown upon your head."

Athol put his whip down, fumbled in his wallet and found a coin, which he gave her. She waited until he was across the stream, and then threw the money after him and spat: "And you shall sink lower than that coin before you rise higher," she said, and hobbled back the way she had come.

The new papal nuncio joined the court for Christmas. They were staying at the Blackfriars, outside the city walls, for such a numerous company was hard to house. The new nuncio was the Bishop of Urbino, Anthony Altani, and he found his reception and welcome "most gratifying," as he wrote to Eugenius IV. Christmas Day, in spite of the wise woman's gloomy prognostications, had been very gay: amongst the many presents, had been unexpected and magnificent ones from Henry VI of England to James: twelve ells of scarlet cloth, twenty ells of worsted of a red colour, eight dozen pewter mugs, a bale of English broadcloth, and twenty butts of wine. But in the evening, as they were sitting down to play chess, after James had put a big pine log on the fire with the tongs, he said, "I had such a strange dream last night."

The Earl of Orkney asked, "What was it?"

James rubbed his forehead as though trying to remember, then he said, "I dreamed I was attacked by a snake and a toad. And I had no weapons—I was completely unarmed, so I fought them with these fire tongs." He looked down at his hands. "That was what reminded me of my dream—putting that log on the fire just now."

No one paid much attention to this conversation except the queen. She told Marjory Norton, the nurse, when she went up to feed Annabella. "Dreaming of snakes never did anyone any good," said Marjory, ominously.

When, however, on the next day, and the next day, nothing happened, the queen began to relax; perhaps, she hoped, there had just been a bad patch in their stars, and now it was over? But on New Year's Eve, the servants came secretly to Joan, and told her the old wise woman was below. When Joan came into the servants' quarters, she found the haggard, shrivelled creature drinking a glass of ale with the cooks. "Tell my lord king," she said, standing and bowing low to the queen, "tell him what thing that belongeth to a person, be it late, be it soon, at the end ever it cometh."

"You know more than you will say, don't you, Mother?" Joan said as she sat down on a none-too-clean tressle and motioned the old crone to sit opposite.

"I know nothing of myself. I am called a soothsayer because I say truly that which Huthcart tells me," replied the old woman.

"Does Huthcart tell you from whom danger threatens my husband?"

The old woman hesitated a second. Then she said: "Robert Graham is a man that dares give attempt upon those things which no honest man dare even think." But more than that she would not utter.

It was a mild winter, and between discussing ecclesiastical affairs with the Bishop of Urbino, and attending to the affairs of State, King James was able to play quite a lot of tennis. He played in the moat, which was sheltered from the winds; it was an admirable place, for the green background was most restful to the eyes. There was one slight drawback—a little square hole, which was the exit of the drains from the privy under Joan's sitting room. James kept meaning to have the hole stopped and kept forgetting—each morning he would curse his bad memory as his tennis balls got stuck and fouled in this hole.

Parliament met on February 4th, and busied itself, to its own edification and to the great satisfaction of the nuncio, with ecclesiastical matters. There were the usual Lollards to be scolded: Marjery Buchan and her husband had been caught with a great brass pot standing over the fire with a piece of bacon and oatmeal seething in it on a Friday; when remonstrated with, Marjery said, "Every faithful woman is not bound to fast on Fridays: it were better to eat the fragments left on Thursday night than to go to market to bring themselves in debt to buy fish." She was fined, but not much, and the council turned to discussing if there were not some way to stop the constant lawsuits which occurred over papal appointments to Scottish benefices.

On the evening of the 20th of February, there had been much music—"and other honest solaces of great pleasure and disport." James sat down rather late to play a game of chess, with a certain knight who, for reasons that may be guessed, was known as the "King of Love."

"Let's play, Sir King," said James, "for one of us two must fall. It is said a king shall die in Scotland this year, and you and I are the only kings here." James won the game, and laughingly asked, "What means that, think you, Sir King?"—to be given no reply except an embarrassed smirk.

At last everyone left. Walter, Earl of Athol, and his grandson, Sir Robert Stewart, the chamberlain, stayed on to drink the voidecup, as it was Fastern's eve (Shrove Tuesday) and there would be no more wine drinking until Easter. They were the last to leave. When there were only the women left, James started to undress in front of the fire; he had already his armour off, and was standing in his shirt, cape, coverchief and furred slippers, and was leaning against the chimney by the queen; some of her ladies were warming themselves beside Joan. James bade Walter Straton, the youngest of the queen's squires, "Go down to the cellar and get us a stoup more wine." He turned to Joan. "I had that hole stopped at last, two days ago, with stone," he told her, "the one wherein I always lost my tennis balls, and today I did not lose a single one."

Mary Seton, one of the queen's ladies, said, "A little squire—you know, young John Archibald—told me he dreamed Robert Graham should have slain Your Majesty. But my lord of Athol would not let him tell you the tale."

Another girl broke in, "Christopher Chambers wanted to see Your Majesty, but he never managed to reach you, did he?"

James said, "No, but I know what he wanted—his
312

money back, or the interest upon it. I fear I owe both him and his brother not a little."

Kate Douglas said, "The old soothsayer woman was here again, too—she wanted to see you very urgently, but Sir Robert Stewart, the chamberlain, was rough with her and would not let her in."

The king now put on his nightgown which Joan had been warming. "Well, since we must early to Mass in the morning, I'll to bed," he said.

"Shall you take communion," asked the queen, "or will you break your fast before we go?"

"I hope to communicate," said James. "I was shriven but last week by the nuncio."

"Will he be saying Mass?" asked Kate Douglas, but James said, "No, he has gone to St. Andrews for a few days' retreat."

Just then there was a noise outside, loud challenges by the sentries, cries and shouts and clashing of arms. Everyone froze into listening silence; then Joan rushed to the door, to find the bolts gone. She turned back to James, as there was a horrible sound of men coming up the stairs, and the yells of the little squire, on his way up from the cellar; those listening in the room clearly heard his beaker fall, and then his death scream.

"You must hide, James, 'tis you they are after," said Joan, and James looked up the chimney, but there was too much fire and smoke for him to be able to climb up. He picked up the tongs of iron and under his feet he mightily yanked up a plank of the chamber floor and entered down beneath amongst the ordure of the privy. He was putting out all his strength, and, to work the more freely, he had cast off his night clothes, and was naked but for his drawers. Joan stood in front of him, and, once he was down, righted the plank over his head, and stood on it, her long robes concealing any signs of disturbance.

Kate Douglas meanwhile had stuck her slender arm in the place of the bolt, just as the intruders reached the door. They knocked, but when there was no reply, they broke in, breaking Kate's arm with a horrid scrunch and knocking her right over. They poured in, to find only the queen and her ladies. Sir Robert Graham, his red head bared, was leading the group; next after came Sir Robert Stewart, then Christopher and Thomas Chambers, Sir John and Sir Thomas Hall, two men named Barclay, and last the Earl of Athol, followed by a rabble of rough Highlandmen—eight or ten of them. "Where's the lass?" they asked the earl and would have carried off the queen, who resisted, shrieking.

"It's no lass we're seeking—you were told we were kidnapping a lass but for safety. Let the queen be—it is the king we're after," said Athol.

They went on past the ladies into the bedrooms, tore down the hangings, poked under the bed with their swords. They went on and on, until they were out of hearing and all was quiet again. Joan thought they had gone on out the other way, for now all was absolutely still again, as it had been in the tense awful moment when they first heard the men below challenging the guard. Joan moved, stooped, lifted the board, and called softly down, "Come up, come up quickly, you must be suffocated down there, James; come up and flee out the front; they've gone round to the back. I'll send Mary Seton for Sir David Dunbar—his lodging is hard by."

Mary slipped out, and James came close, and put his hands on the sides of the hole; he was half out, and Joan was pulling him, when the traitors came trooping back the same way, and seeing the king, rushed at him. James dropped back down, and Joan flung herself over all the hole, and, as she lay there, Sir Robert wounded her with his sword, and would have run her through and killed her, but his son Robin, that was close behind him, pulled his arm back, and bade his father leave the woman be. Meanwhile, they had pulled Joan from off the hole, and Sir John Hall jumped down into the dark, his brother following him.

The women could hear James cry, "Send for a priest, let me but have a priest, give me time to be shriven," but

314

the brothers' only answer was to attack him more fiercely. With his bare hands James nearly throttled Sir John: he had the advantage that his eyes were now used to the dark, whilst the brothers were blinded for the first few moments. James got Sir John's sword from him, and cut at Sir Thomas, and badly wounded him. But then Sir Robert Graham jumped down too, and drove James back to the end of the privy to where his tennis balls had rolled down. There, where he might have found safety, might have scrambled out of the square hole, James fell dead, after about six minutes' hard fighting; he had sixteen wounds. Sir Thomas would have spared him, but Robert Graham went on thrusting his sword into the fallen figure of his king even after it lay still.

Meanwhile Sir David Dunbar had arrived, coming up the same stairway that the rebels had used. He was followed by two men at arms, the only ones left alive, as the sentries had all been killed. Sir David made straight for Graham, who was just straightening himself as he came out of the hole, but lost the fingers of his left hand from one stroke of Graham's sword, before the latter fled. All the murderers escaped, and Sir David went after them, cutting at Athol, who, unhurt, ran squealing down the stairs, and was protected by the rear-guard swordplay of Sir Thomas Hall. The queen, bleeding profusely from her three flesh wounds, Kate Douglas, who was only half-conscious from the pain of her twisted, broken arm, and could not get up, and the three other girls, unwounded, were left alone in the firelight in the smashed-up room; the dead king was still in the drain below. As soon as the girls got the queen up, she insisted on scrambling down into the drain; Mary Seton followed her, and they felt their way to the body of James: one of the girls lighting them with a smouldering torch caught up from the almost dead fire. Somehow the two women dragged the king back to the hole, and the four of them got him out: two lifting from below, two pulling from above. Joan would not yet accept, aloud, the fact that he was dead, and kept begging the others to be gentle, to

315

mind they did not bang or bruise him. Interiorly, she was saying to herself, over and over, "I must try and realise, must try and realise, James is dead, James is dead," but the words meant nothing, they were simply something she was saying to dull her own bodily pain.

The women laid James down, in front of the fire, of which only the barest embers still burned. It was practically dark, for the murderers had overset the lamps, and had taken their torches with them. Joan began to shiver and to shake: she found she could not speak from her teeth chattering. "It is the loss of blood," Mary Seton said. Now Sir David Dunbar came back with a surgeon, and lights, and servants. Joan's wounds were dressed, and she was carried to her bed. Kate Douglas was laid beside her in the same bed, for they did not want to move her more than was needful.

Two days later the nuncio arrived, having ridden hard. James's body, wrapt in a velvet pall, but in no coffin, was carried in procession to the Charterhouse he had built. On seeing the body the Bishop of Urbino had uttered a great cry, and many tearful sighs, and, reverently lifting the pall, he kissed the piteous wounds. "I will stake my soul that the king died in a state of grace, like a martyr, for his defence of the common cause and the administration of justice against certain wicked men," he said, and then, at Joan's request, he climbed into the pulpit and announced the same remark pontifically.

Joan watched daylong by the high catafalque on which James lay in front of the high altar. His heart had been removed, and was taken, in a silver casket, to Jerusalem, by a good young knight of Rhodes, who afterwards brought it back, and interred it with the king's body. Joan hardly left her vigil; as the weeks went by, James's face fell in a little, the dead hair grew longer; the bruised nails on the waxy hands also. Otherwise, he looked very much as he had done in life, perhaps a little younger than latterly, a little less than his forty-three years. All the murderers were caught within forty days, except the two Barclays, who had fled to Brittany. There they were caught and executed by the duke, whose son later married James's daughter Isabella (she who was so simple some said she was wanting). All the other murderers were caught in Scotland and were condemned to the same death.

The false Earl of Athol was led before his dead nephew, crowned with an iron crown; on his breast was pinned a sign with the one word "Traitor." He and his grandson, Sir Robert Graham, and Graham's son Robin, the two Chambers and the two Halls (both the latter still wearing the marks of James's fingers on their throats) were brought face to face with their dead victim before they were led out to the torture. After torture they were beheaded, and then torn limb from limb and quartered by the hangman. The butchered bits were hung at the gates of towns and burghs as a warning, whilst their heads were set on iron spikes and displayed, high on the most conspicuous places in villages and cities.

After each one had died, Joan, stirring the living hair around James's dead ears with her warm breath, whispered to him: "He suffered more than you, Jamie."

James was buried on a sunny April day, under the high altar in his Charterhouse. Joan found in the anonymity of the funeral Mass comfort for her desolation. One more man had gone to meet his Maker, and him, too, the Church included in her compassion, as she included also his murderers, and she would include also, one day, his widow, and one day, his son. The same words were used over and over again, words rinsed by the whole world's weeping, and used and rinsed again, and they would endlessly be so used and so rinsed. Eternal rest give unto him, O Lord, and let light perpetual shine upon him.

James had not cried out, nor for the water on his head, nor for Joan's salt tears on his lips. The priests swung high their censers over the King of Scots, over him to whom Joan had brought bliss, over him whose prophecy she had so tragically and in vain fulfilled, defending her

man with her own body from the death. For her farewell
to James, Joan murmured his own words:

> O, busy ghost, aye flickering to and fro
> That never art in quiet nor in rest
> Till thou comest to the place thou camest fro
> Which is thine own and very proper nest.

ACKNOWLEDGMENTS

I have used all available sources, and especially wish to thank E. W. M. Balfour-Melville, to whom every student of James I owes more than it is possible to say.

A. F.

TOP SELLING
HISTORICAL NOVELS
FROM CURTIS BOOKS

CURTIS
BOOKS

☐ ADAM AND HIS WOMEN, Sarah Clifford　　　(09120—95¢)
Here is a truly moving novel that recreates, in an entirely
fresh fashion, the Old Testament story of Adam and Eve . . .
and Lillith, the beautiful and dangerous intruder in the
Garden of Eden.

☐ THE AMAZING MRS. BONAPARTE, Harnett T. Kane
　　　　　　　　　　　　　　　　　　　　(09124—95¢)
The turbulent romantic saga of the American girl who pitted
her beauty against Napoleon's power and moves toward the
strangest destiny a woman has ever known.

☐ THE WHITE PLUME, Samuel Edwards　　　(09114—95¢)
Swordsman, artist and lover, Prince Rupert blazoned his name
across Renaissance Europe and England. His stormy love for
two women made him the talk of the Continent and gave
power to the men plotting against him.

☐ MASTER OF CASTILE, Samuel Edwards　　　(09113—95¢)
"That rare thing, a solid historical novel with swordplay,
beautiful girls and big fat chunks of history."—Stephen
Longstreet